TRANSLATION

The Beloved Disciple

Gregory Klass

Ms Krisse
Thanks so much!

[signature]

Printed in the United States of America. No part of this book may be used or reproduced in any manner whatsoever without written permission except in the case of brief quotation embodied in critical articles or reviews. For more information, address Klass Property Management LLC, 2835 Accomac Street, Saint Louis, MO 63104

"A Nicolas Legacy Book"

ISBN: 9798857111857

Cover Painting: An Arab Caravan, by John Frederick Herring, Snr

Cover Design:

First Published in the United States by: Klass Property Management, LLC

First US Edition March, 2022

Contents

Dedication   V

Prologue   VIII

1. Azofra, La Riojas, Kingdom of Leon 1214 AD   1

2. Jura Mountains, France April 2004   10

3. Saint Louis, Missouri Early December 2019   17

4. The Book of Hessulah Ephesus, Asia Minor 6 BC   25

5. Azofra, Spain Late December 2019   43

6. The First Day of the Festival of Artemis, Ephesus 6 BC   47

7. Pandemic, Saint Louis, Missouri, 2020 AD   63

8. Missouri Baptist Hospital, St Louis, MO 2020 AD   75

9. Port of Ephesus, 6 BC   78

10. Compton Heights, St Louis, MO, 2020 AD   85

11. Old God, New Religion, Mediterranean Sea, 6 BC   100

12. Azofra, May 2020   120

13. Translation, St Louis, MO, 2020 AD   124

14. Elaia, River-port of Pergamum, 6 BC   137

15. Cardinal O'Rourke Residence, Rome, 2020 AD   144

16. The Boy in the Phrygian Cap, 4 BC   153

17. Quarantine, St Louis, MO 2020 AD   169

18. The Call of the Magi, Halicarnassus, 3 BC   176

19. Return of Emmanuelle, Saint Louis, MO, 2020 AD   202

20. Love and Marriage, Myra, Asia Minor, 2 BC   209

21. Frere Jacques, Dorme-vous, 2020 AD   222

22. The Caravan, Caesarea to Babylon, 2 BC   233

23. European Vacation, Paris, France 2020 AD   250

24. Winter Solstice, Silk Road, East of Jerusalem, BC   262

25. Town of Bethlehem, Anno Domini   270

26. Mouse and Papa, Alsace-Lorraine, 2020 AD   277

27. The Black Madonna, Sinai, 1 AD   295

28. The Camino, Azofra, La Rioja, Spain, December 2020 AD   300

29. Caesarea, 1 AD   318

30. Summer Solstice, Andes Mountains, December   331

About the Author   336

This book is for my dear wife, Marge,
Now and forever called Mouse,
The reason apparent as the story unfolds.

Ancient Greece and Anatolian Peninsula
Source: Wikipedia commons

*I have set eyes on the wall of lofty Babylon on which is a road for
chariots, and the Statue of Zeus by the Alpheus, and the hanging
gardens, and the colossus of the Sun, and the huge labour of the
pyramids and the vast tomb of Mausolus, but when I saw the house
of Artemis mounted to the clouds, those other marvels lost their
brilliancy and I said, "Lo. Apart from Olympus never looked on
aught so grand."*

— Antipater of Sidon, 140 BC

TURN YOURSELF NOT
AWAY FROM THESE THREE
BEST THINGS:
GOOD THOUGHT,
GOOD WORD,
AND GOOD DEED

- ZOROASTER (1760 BC)

Prologue

Birth, Enlightenment, Prophecy

Winter Solstice

Kopet Dagh Mountains – 1793 BC

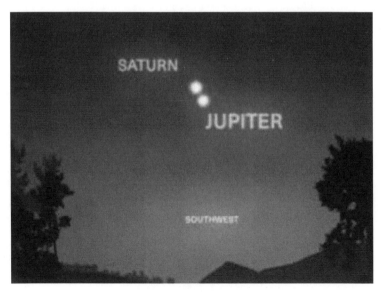

Credits: NASA/JPL-Caltech

FOR THE LAST SEVEN evenings, he stood outside his hut and watched the two wandering stars perform a cosmic dance in the winter sky. Its celestial sight etched into Pourushaspa's memory; the stars aligned to herald his son's birth. Pourushaspa, the chief priest of the Medes, interprets its meaning for the tribes — the heavenly display foretells that his son will follow in his footsteps, just as he followed the footsteps of his father and grandfather.

Each night Pourushaspa kept vigil as the two stars grew closer to each other. The stars' performance took up one-tenth of the long night, then the stars settled beneath the horizon and were eclipsed from view. But tonight, before dipping out of sight, the two Wanderers ended their cosmic chase perfectly aligned, with the elliptical star atop the other larger, closer star. Their alignment gave Pourushaspa the sense that a curtain had opened, revealing the stars as if the cosmos was their stage. What appeared to be a tiny dot flickered in front of the closest star, but Pourushaspa's vision could not discern the import of that dot or determine if he had seen it. His mind had difficulty deciding if the flicker was natural or an illusion.

The night was clear and cold, with a crispness to the air. It was the winter solstice, the shortest day before the long road to spring began. Blackness enveloped the western view, and glimmering stars above the horizon replaced the setting sun. The blackness in the east lessened as a cold deep purple silently spread into the night sky, revealing the mountaintops, early auspices of a new dawn.

The bitter cold and yesterday's snowfall enhanced the stillness of the village. Only the occasional lowing of the few cows that the village owned disturbed the peace. The midwives' footprints left impressions on the fallen snow and scurried tracks leading to and from Pourushaspa's hut's entrance. Thin white smoke rose from its roof, a small fire providing warmth for the mother and newborn.

Pourushaspa Spitāma, son of Haecadaspa Spitāma, stood before the entrance offering prayers of thanks to Mithras, the chief god of the Medes. His wife, Dughdova, rested on the makeshift bed, exhausted but triumphant from her birth-giving ordeal.

The mountain village is due east of the southern end of the vast sea that, in 1500 years, the Romans named for the Kaspi tribes that live on its southwestern shores. Over time, the nomadic Medes tribes moved from these mountains further west into an area known as Persia.

The closest star was the largest of the five stars that the Medes stargazers called The Wanderers. These wandering stars had no set position in the sky, while millions of stars stayed in the same place eternally. Their paths are their own. The Medes astrologers studied the fixed stars and the Wanderers for centuries. The furthest star had an elliptical shape with rings surrounding its center. Pourushaspa knew they performed solely to honor his son. Silently, the large star slipped below the horizon, and the cosmic dance ended. Tomorrow Pourushaspa will task the stargazers of the Medi to calculate when the Wanderer's dance will return. It was a question that would take decades for them to answer.

As he finished his prayers, with the night becoming morning, a crescent moon hovered in the predawn sky, accompanied by a single nearby star. Pourushaspa named his son after the morning star that began the first day of the new season. Pourushaspa ordered the slaughter of a bull as a sacrifice to Mithras to celebrate the birth of his son, Dawn Star.

Summer

Kopet Dagh Mountains – 1763 BC

Credits: Faravahar Wikipedia Commons

Flocks of blackbirds descended on the wooden burial tower collecting their meal before ascending into the skies that overlooked the valley. Dawn Star sat alone under Pourushaspa's Dakhma (burial tower) for five days. His solitary vigil will end when only bones remain after his father's flesh is picked clean. A flask of wine and a bowl of food that Dughdova brought on the third day sat undisturbed to his right. Particles of flesh and foul occasionally fell upon him as the scavenger birds carried off the skin and sinew that had once been Pourushaspa. Screeches, caws, and the rhythmic flapping of hundreds of wings break the silence on the mountainside. Pecks and screams settle minor conflicts over the carcass.

Dawn Star looks neither up nor down as the light and dark shadows cross his vision and are only disturbed by the sound and shadow of flapping wings. Dawn Star's thoughts reflected neither on Pourushaspa's past as a father and chief priest nor on Dawn Star's future as his successor. His unwavering eyes peer through this scene, concentrating on his prayer to the Creator. Suddenly, an infinite field of shimmering diamond patterns of bright silver outlined in onyx replaced the fluttering shadows of his vision and the presence of God consumed Dawn Star's mind.

Knowledge and understanding fill his consciousness. New thoughts emerged as memories. Ahura Mazda, the one true God, revealed the path to heaven to Dawn Star and anointed him as his Prophet. Dawn Star's mind understood the ageless struggle of good versus evil, ancient battles of angels and devils. The creator, Ahura Mazda, bestowed on Dawn Star the sentience that their soul's immortality is the reward for those who follow the path of goodness. Those that reject this path will suffer the penalty of hell. Dawn Star's mind achieved enlightenment, realizing that we must choose a life path of Good Deeds to attain glory for our immortal soul.

Enlightenment instantly imprinted understanding on his brain, a new reason he had been too blind to see. This ingrained knowledge melded into thought, thought forged into belief. The bright diamond pattern sharpened into a vision of the Cosmos. The Milky Way and all the stars in heaven were within his view. In his vision, the five Wanderers followed their paths while the remaining stars sat stationary. The Wanderers raced, continuously cycling through their orbits. The larger wanderer completed 150 orbits around the sun, while the elliptical planet completed 60 orbits. The vision transported him to a distant future. The two Wanderers that announced his birth — aligned again to announce another birth. This vision left an indelible impression on his brain, the birth of a Messiah, a babe born of a virgin, and that Dawn Star must prepare those that follow to welcome Him.

Ahura Mazda chose Dawn Star as his messenger, teacher, and prophet. Once the vision passed, Dawn Star rose and collected Pourushaspa's bones from atop the burial tower. He proceeded to the village, where he tossed the bones into a lime pit with the other dead. As Dawn Star walked among the huts, the villagers greeted him by his Medes name, Zoroaster.

Spring

Kashmar, Land of Iran – 1750 BC

Persepolis relief depicting an Immortal Guard soldier and the Cypress Tree[1]

"Always practice Good Words, Good Thoughts, and Good Deeds. By following these tenets, your soul shall attain everlasting life in heaven. Your soul will flourish like this Cypress seedling I plant here today." With those words, Zoroaster concluded his sermon by planting the Cypress branch.

As the crowd dispersed, Zoroaster's acolytes gathered around him. He had chosen the brightest among the Medes to follow him. His followers must pass on the knowledge of the Messiah to future generations. "We must continue to teach the Medes through our example. We have ended the senseless animal sacrifice to

---

1. Credits: The Circle of Ancient Iranian Studies (CAIS)

the old gods. The worship of Mithras and the other ancient gods is declining within the tribes. We have instilled a new relationship between the Medes and the one true God, Ahura Mazda. You, the high priests of the Magus, will spread the word of Ahura Mazda through Good Thoughts, Good Words, and Good Deeds."

Fravarti, one of the younger acolytes, asked, "Master, when will this Messiah come. How should we prepare for Him?"

Zoroaster replied, "Guamata, the most esteemed astrologer of the Medes, studied the paths of the two Wanderers that appeared at my birth. His calculus says the stars will re-align more than 1,000 years from now, but before 2,000 years are over. It is a very long time from now. The Magi who follow us must study the stars and look for the signs in the cosmos that will precede their merger. The heavens will provide a guide that will enter the night sky from the distant northeast quadrant. This guide will cross the heavens for many months before leaving the night sky. The Wanderers' re-alignment will signal the Messiah's imminent arrival as the cosmic guide fades from view.'

"All of us must do our part, and all who follow us must do theirs. The Magi must recruit only the best and the brightest. Once the guide arrives, the Magi must make haste to convene in Babylon and follow the guide. The Magi must welcome the newborn Messiah with gifts of gold, frankincense, and myrrh."

Zoroaster reinforced his teachings with constant proclamations.

"There are simple rules that men and women must follow.

First, Ahura Mazda gave each soul everlasting life. For one's soul to achieve heaven, one must lead a life of Good Thoughts, Good Words, and Good Deeds.

Second, Those who help others will achieve health and happiness.

Third, Ahura Mazda made the heavens and earth and everything in it. He is in everything he created. We must strive to protect this world and all its creatures.

Fourth, men and women each have duties that they must perform, but men and women are equal in the eyes of Ahura Mazda."

Author's note: Zoroastrianism spread by the example set by the Magi and other Zoroastrians. The Magus recruited the brightest to join their elite caste. Zoroastrian fire temples rose slowly among the Medes and then to neighboring kingdoms. The religion was not spread by evangelism or by conquest. Zoroastrians led devout lives, and others chose to follow.

Zoroastrianism began to flourish during the first Millenia BC and became the dominant religion of the Persian Empire in the 6th century BC. In 539 BC, Cyrus the Great, a devout Zoroastrian, conquered Babylon. Cyrus allowed Zoroastrianism to spread, but at the same time, he was tolerant of all religions. Cyrus freed the people conquered by Babylon, including the Jews who had spent nearly 70 years in captivity. He allowed the Jews to return to Jerusalem and rebuild Solomon's Temple. The Hebrew Bible refers to Cyrus as Cyrus the Messiah.

The rule of Cyrus led to 1200 years of Zoroastrianism acceptance as it became the dominant religion of Persia and the eastern Mediterranean world. For over a thousand years, Mithras worship waned until a secret society rekindled worship. Throughout the centuries, the elite priests of the Magus became counselors to kings, emperors, and pharaohs. Magi taught the Greek philosophers, including Socrates, Aristotle, and Pluto.

Zoroaster used Cypress Trees — coniferous (fir) trees that can grow for thousands of years — as the symbol of everlasting life. Zoroaster planted a Cypress Tree in Kashmar that grew for over two thousand years until its destruction in the 8th century AD during an era of religious persecution. By the ninth century, Christians and Muslims had persecuted, converted, or killed most Zoroastrians. Only a few thousand escaped and found refuge in India.

Zoroaster's caste of elite priests, Magus, were astrologers, scholars, thinkers, doctors, statesmen, warriors, philosophers, and teachers. Zoroaster was the first Magi. By the time of Augustus Caesar, the Magi, and other Zoroastrian astrologers were searching the cosmos for signs that fulfilled Zoroaster's Messianic prophecy.

1

Azofra, La Riojas, Kingdom of Leon 1214 AD

Gospel of John 21:20-25

The Beloved Disciple.

Peter turned around at that and noticed that the disciple whom Jesus loved was following (the one who had leaned against Jesus' chest during the supper) and said, "Lord, which one will betray you?"

Seeing him (the beloved disciple), Peter was prompted to ask Jesus. "But Lord, what about him?"

"Suppose I wanted him to stay until I come," Jesus replied, "how does that concern you? Your business is to follow Me."

This is how the report spread among the brothers that this disciple was not going to die. Jesus never told him, as a matter of fact, that the disciple was not going to die; all He said was, "Suppose I wanted him to stay until I come (how does that concern you?"

Conclusion. It is this same disciple who is the witness to these things; it is he who wrote them down and his testimony, we know, is true. There are still many other things that Jesus did, yet if they were written about in detail, I doubt there would be room enough in the entire world to hold the books to record them.

———— ◦•◦ ————

I lead a congregation of townsfolk and farmers in a village of twenty families in northern Spain. When I arrived, I taught the farmers to cultivate a crocus, a purple flower with red and yellow stigmas. The crocus is laborious to harvest, but it serves the village well. The townsfolk named the town, Azofra, after the spice from this flower you may know as saffron. Saffron harvested in Azofra is a crucial ingredient in the local rice, chicken, and seafood stew called paella. Romans used it in their wine to prevent hangovers. Today is warm, and most of the families are inside their modest homes for their noonday meal and afternoon rest.

Azofra never bustles. It is and always has been a sleepy village. The villagers attend the predawn Mass that I say each day. The town is in the La Riojas region of north-central Spain. Azofra sits on the Camino de Santiago, about two hundred kilometers south of Saint-Jean-Pied-de-Port, France. It is a ten-day walk from Saint-Jean to Azofra through the Pyrenees and Basque Country. Local French routes coalesce in Saint-Jean before they begin the famous Way of Saint James, a 700-kilometer (550-mile) trail to Santiago de Compostela. It takes thirty-five days to walk from Saint-Jean to de Compostela.

Pilgrims have flocked to Santiago de Compostela since the Spanish kingdoms reclaimed the northern part of the Iberian Peninsula from the Moors. The Reconquista (re-conquest) of the peninsula has already lasted over 250 years. More than half of the peninsula is now under the control of the Spanish kings. There are many routes to Santiago de Compostela, but the path from France is the most popular and an easy choice for Frank, Germanic, Norman, Dutch, and British pilgrims. Now and then, a pilgrim will stop and ask a villager for food or water. But Azofra is nondescript, and Azofra, and I, go about unnoticed.

I have never taken the vows of a religious order, but the parishioners look to me as the leader of their congregation. They call me Fray Juan (Brother John).

The parishioners are intent on building a small church — someday. Until then, I preach as my Master did, by a stream, on a hillside, or in a pasture — His message is essential.

Santiago, or Saint James, is my brother. Mary, the mother of our Master, and our mother, Salome, are sisters. Because they are sisters, our Master is our first cousin. James and I were His two most fervent disciples. When James and I argued, which was often and sometimes vehemently, Jesus would call us the "sons of thunder." Ultimately, my older brother James and I had very different fates. Herod Agrippa beheaded James in 44 A.D. Herod Agrippa killed James to appease the Pharisees. I am, or was, the youngest of all the disciples. Over the centuries, I have tried valiantly to become a martyr like most of the disciples, but I have been unsuccessful — thus far.

Shortly after our Master returned to His Father, James spread His Word in Spain. He loved the country and especially the Galician people of northwest Spain. In 42 A.D., Peter summoned James to Jerusalem to lead the Christian congregation of Jews that worshiped at the Second Temple of Solomon. It was a time of great turmoil, and the Pharisees and Sadducees were at odds over the spread of Hellenization in Judaea. Hellenization supplanted Jewish culture with Greek culture, language, laws, philosophy, and religion. At the same time, the disciples were spreading His Word, adding to the religious and political tensions. Meanwhile, the populace had grown desperately poor as excessive taxation sucked the resources from the four kingdoms to pay for the Herod family's massive building projects. By this time, Herod and his family had ruled Judaea for almost 100 years.

James longed to continue his ministry in Galicia. James had confided in me that he had met a fair-skinned, redheaded woman, and his love for her was calling him to return. But Peter needed James' passion in Jerusalem to combat the Pharisees and Sadducees. I think James' longing for the girl stoked his rhetoric and thus put James' life in danger.

James and the other disciples travelled in all directions to perform their ministries, but I was not free to choose my path. As Jesus was dying on the cross,

He commanded that I become Mary's son and Mary become my mother. "Son, behold thy Mother; Mother, behold thy Son." That was His final command to me as He was actively dying on the cross. I must treat Mary as my mother and provide for the rest of her days. Later, after He had risen, but before He joined His Father in heaven, His last statement about me was that I would remain on Earth until he came again. "Suppose I wanted him to stay until I come?" Oh, how I have grown tired of life and pray anxiously for that day when I will see Him again. Mary and Salome were growing old when we sailed to Finis Terra (the end of the world) in Spain to bury James.

After James's execution and burial, Judaea was a dangerous place for Mary to live, so Mary, Salome, and I moved to Ephesus, the bustling Greco-Roman capital of Asia Minor. Mary and Salome sailed from Finis Terra to Caesarea Maritima in Samaria to collect their meager belongings while I walked to Rome from Compostela to visit Peter. From there, I took passage on a ship to Ephesus and rejoined my mother and aunt. Scallop shells were in abundance on the shore in Finis Terra. I set a trail of shells from Finis Terra to Compostela and then to Rome, so I could always find my way back.

Hessulah, the captain of the ship who took us to Finis Terra, and the most remarkable woman I ever met, transported Mary and Salome to Samaria and accompanied them to Nazareth to collect their belongings, afterward she brought them to Ephesus. Mary and Salome lived their last ten years quietly on the side of Mount Koressus, a twenty-five-kilometer walk from the center of Ephesus.

While in Ephesus, I wrote my Gospel story and a few letters called Epistles, which was how I earned the name the Evangelist. I lived openly in Ephesus until 120 A.D., about twenty years beyond when I should have realistically died from old age. My presence was drawing suspicion as my time on Earth continued. I slowly comprehended that the Lord meant what He said when He last spoke to Peter. I aged but did not die, and naturally, people grew suspicious, so I collected a few belongings and began to travel.

I left Ephesus and obscured my identity; I traveled south along the Anatolian coastal villages. I kept to myself and remained inconspicuous wherever I went.

I was living in Myra on the southwest coast of Anatolia by the end of the third century. In Myra, I watched over Nicolas and his sister Alina. Nicolas and Alina are descendants of Hessulah and her husband, Melchior, the Zoroastrian Magi. At the beginning of the fourth century, around 303 A.D., the Roman Emperor Diocletian began another campaign of persecuting Christians. I was duty-bound to protect Nicolas and Alina; I owed that and much more to Hessulah.

In 312 A.D., Emperor Constantine legalized Christianity throughout the Empire. Almost immediately, the tables turned as Christians now persecuted Greek, Egyptian, and Roman pagans. Christians also persecuted the Zoroastrians although both sects believed in a single god.

I left the city of Myra after Nicolas' death and helped Alina, her family, and some friends move to a safe place. Afterward, I wandered around the coast of the Mediterranean for a few centuries. Finally, after the Reconquista reclaimed half of the Iberian Peninsula from the Moors, I settled in northern Spain. I felt compelled to be close to my brother's grave in Santiago de Compostela. I do not know why the Lord chose me to stay on this Earth, but I sensed that I was best serving Him by living near Santiago. is thirty miles east of Finis Terra, the westernmost point of Europe. Finis Terra is Latin and means "The End of the World."

Occasionally, I would marry, but mostly I lived in solitude, as I was cautious about growing close to someone. In the year of our Lord, 1214, word reached Azofra that Francis, the revered holy man from Assisi, was walking from Italy to pay homage at my brother's grave. Francis crossed the Alps from Italy, following the reverse path of Hannibal and his elephants. He entered northeast Spain, but instead of heading due west to join the French route that runs by Azofra, he turned south and west toward the Templar Chapel at the Ermita de San Bartolome in the Rio Lobos Canyon.

When word of Francis' pilgrimage reached me, I took it as a sign that I should seek him out. I set out to meet him at the Hermitage. The Knights Templar constructed the chapel at the Hermitage to house the Hebrew Arc of the Covenant — the Holiest of Holies — that housed the Ten Commandments Moses carried down from Mount Sinai. The chapel was built in anticipation that the Knights Templar would find the Arc in Ethiopia. Symbolism is an essential Templar trait. I have used the chapel to house my writings in the secret room the Templars built to hold the Arc. The chapel sits in the geographic center of the Iberian Peninsula below a once-sacred, now-ancient, necropolis whose long-forgotten gods still watch over its dead.

By the faint light of early morning, I approached the chapel from a distance. I watched as a group of half-starved, barefoot men in old brown robes stood around in prayer, some standing, some moving in slow circles. One man pretended he was praying but chased a hen trotting in circles. I knew these men must be the Companions of Francis, a collection of odd and circumspect men. The Companions constantly traveled with Francis and five years earlier, they were instrumental in helping Francis establish the Franciscan Order within the Church.

Thirty feet to their right stood a thin, solitary figure whose mouth was moving. The man seemed to be conversing with the local wildlife and flora. Immediately I knew that it was Francis. People said that Francis saw God in all living things. He also felt the presence of God in the rocks, water, air, and Earth. God is everywhere, and in everything He created.

Francis is very slight and of average height; his frame is a testament to the stories of his fasting. As I moved toward Francis, I could not help but notice his eyes. The emaciated often have pronounced, almost bulging eyes that pop out through the deep dark sockets of his face. Francis's eyes were like that; they were his most prominent physical feature. His eyes evoked intelligence and humility and his face exuded a sincerity that welcomed everyone he met, including the animals.

As I approached, Francis began to speak without turning to face me, as he still faced his local audience, he said, "Now that you have found me. How can I help you?"

"Do you know me?" I asked.

"You are the Evangelist, are you not?"

"How did you know?"

Francis explained, "I noticed you when you approached the chapel yard a few moments ago. Your aura is different from anyone I have ever met. I believe the hand of Jesus has been upon you, and He left His mark." Francis continued, "I knew you were alive when I read your Gospel. The Lord speaks with purpose. He would not jest about wanting you to stay until He returns."

I exclaimed, "You remind me of Him in some ways." I paused, "Will you walk with me?".

I quietly led Francis further from his Companions and introduced myself, "Yes, I am John, the Beloved Disciple." Francis of Assisi and Nicolas of Myra, the Catholic Church's two greatest saints, are the only men in whom I have confided my identity.

I joined Francis and his companions the next day as their Camino continued westward. Leaving the chapel at the Hermitage, we took the western road out of the canyon turning north toward Burgos to join the Camino's popular French route. We spoke at length on many subjects on this ambulatory excursion. Several weeks later as we reached Santiago de Compostela, Francis steered our discussion to me, and Francis asked, "What mission has the Lord set out for you?"

I sighed, "The Lord never told me why he wanted me to stay. It is challenging when one does not know their purpose. Initially, I tried to help guide the early church to keep it on a righteous path; but my influence diminished as the Church evolved; leaders emerged, leaders, with more earthly ambitions. These leaders did not comprehend His message or possess genuine faith. Instead, they diverted from His path and concentrated on what they could understand — building power structures, implementing rules and regulations, and developing an organization. The Church became more important to them than the Word of the Lord.

"I broke off contact with the Church after the Council of Nicaea. I sent Nicolas to the Council on a mission, but that mission failed. There have been many Popes since Nicaea. Some popes are good men, holy men, but all Popes are men with ambition, and ambitious men are not men of God. I don't understand why He has kept me alive, but I know that I cannot trust my mission to men who are not 'of God'."

Francis asked, "Why do you reveal yourself to me?"

"I realize that in time I will need help. I can sense the true faith within you. I know that I can trust you."

Francis agreed. "Of course, I will keep your confidence, but I will no longer be here at some point." Francis paused momentarily before continuing, "We can use the Hermitage of Saint Bartholomew as a place where you can return if you need to contact me or, in the future, the leader of my Order. We will entrust your existence and location to each new leader and establish a process in the Brotherhood to protect your identity. We will call the leader the Minister General. He will, in theory, keep each Pope informed of your existence and activities — or not, as you both see fit."

After I nodded my understanding, Francis asked, "John, do you mind a personal question? Do you consider it a blessing or a curse that our Lord has yet to call you to Him?"

I thought for a bit before I answered Francis, "For a long time, I was angry that He called others to heaven, especially some that did not love Him as much. Still, they offered up their lives in martyrdom as the ultimate praise for Him. I envied their glory; the Jews beheaded my brother James; the Romans tortured and hung Peter upside down; Saul of Tarsus stoned Stephen the protomartyr to death, and poor Bartholomew was skinned alive. I was 300 years old when I met Nicolas of Myra. I confessed my envy of the martyrs to him when we had a similar conversation.

"Nicolas said, "It is far easier to be a martyr than to wait in solitude forever. The Lord chose you, above all others, for the most difficult mission." Since then, I have considered it a blessing and thank the Lord daily for this honor. I think He sent Nicolas to give me hope in my time of doubt."

"Tell me more about Nicolas," asked Francis.

I thought for a moment and replied, "About Nicolas? Yes, there is much to tell. But to understand the story of Nicolas, you must go back further. You must know the story of Hessulah of Myra."

"Hessulah? I have never heard of Hessulah of Myra. Who is she?"

"Hessulah is Nicolas' ancestor. She was a most remarkable woman. She was present at our Lord's birth. Hessulah knew my Master when He was a young man. She cared for Mary after His crucifixion. She helped us bury James. Yes, to know Nicolas, you must know the story of Hessulah. I will tell you her story on the walk back."

Francis then asked, "You mentioned another person whose name is unfamiliar. I think you called her Alina."

"Yes, Alina is Nicolas's sister. Alina did all the work, while Nicolas, being a man, received all the credit."

———◦○◦———

Our journey ended when we reached Azofra. Before we parted, Francis asked, "Have you written down Hessulah's story? Nicolas's or Alina's story?"

"No, I have not. Why?"

"You are John the Evangelist; John the Gospel-Writer. Perhaps the reason Our Lord kept you here is to write?"

I looked intently at Francis, realizing he may have uncovered one of the reasons the Lord chose me to stay.

I replied, "Perhaps, perhaps."

2

JURΛ MOUNTΛINS, FRΛNCE ΛPRIL 2004

Alsace Lorraine, Present Day[1]

◄◆►

---

1. Credit:
   http://anthonyfassio.blogspot.com/2010/04/le-cordon-bleu-instruction-1
   3.html

EMMANUELLE CHASTETÉ LEFT HER apartment in Nancy at 5 a.m. and drove three hours to the small town of Ornans to begin a weekend hike in the French Jura Mountains near the Swiss border. Emmanuelle hoped to collect dinosaur fossils during her hike as Jura is the root name of the Jurassic Period.

She tied a small nylon tent to the bottom of her backpack. The rucksack included healthy snacks, fruit and survival essentials, a knife, hatchet, compass, sunscreen, fire starter, lighter, and matches. Two large water thermoses stretched the nylon netting on each side of the sack. She kept a tightly rolled sleeping bag securely tied atop the backpack.

The morning temperature at the base of the mountain was cold. The air would warm during the day, but the cooler air in the higher elevations would moderate any additional warmth. A perpetual cloud of mist hung over the peaks of this section of the range, and Emmanuelle usually hiked to about 1,000 meters below the bottom of the cloud. The temperature of two or three degrees above freezing Celsius (~38 degrees F) would stay consistent as the day warmed, as she moved to the cooler elevations. Several layers of light clothing and a warm spring sun provided her ample warmth and comfort. After fifteen minutes, she removed her gloves and clipped them to her backpack.

As she continued her hike up the mountain, Emmanuelle noticed remnants of late spring snow in shaded areas as she collected fallen twigs and small branches for a later fire. By early afternoon she stopped and tied them into a bundle she attached to her backpack. The fire would provide enough warmth for the evening. Scatterings of purple and yellow crocus peeked through the thin layers of the snow.

As she hiked up the mountain, the air became lighter, forcing her lungs to take deeper breaths. Pulling the fresh light air deep into her lungs burned and reinvigorated her. That sense of renewal of life helped drive her passion for mountain hiking.

By mid-afternoon, the warm sun summoned her to the higher elevations as the sun seemed to lift the curtain of mist higher up the mountainside, revealing a small alpine lake and meadows. She climbed to these new heights and set her camp by the lakeside. Emmanuelle collected dry grass and started a small fire before the sun began to set and usher in colder air.

The solitude and exercise rejuvenated her. Her thoughts were mainly on the future once she completed university. Gazing westward, looking back at her trail and further across the valley, she peered deeper into France. She camped one thousand meters below the summit; by sunset, the mist was moving down the mountainside toward her camp. She thought about challenging the mountain in the morning and hiking to its peak but resisted that invitation, even though the other side would reveal the beauty of the Jura in Switzerland.

Her mind envisioned the land that the Elsasser (Alsatian) tribes settled almost three thousand years earlier. The Alsatians were a sect of the Alemannia (All Men) tribe (whence the name Germany). Now, Alsatians live on the same land, but the invisible boundaries of France, Germany, and Switzerland separate the people. She mused that some considered America a fourth homeland, as it was the primary destination of the Alsatian exodus in the 1800s.

She stooped over the grass and sticks and lit a small fire. She drank the rest of the water in the first bottle and ate a protein bar and an apple. She left enough food in her backpack for snacks tomorrow morning and afternoon. She knew she would sleep well tonight in the solitude of the mountain. She massaged her tight calves, hoping her leg muscles would be recovered and fresh for tomorrow's hike.

The peacefulness of the setting sun and enveloping darkness announced bedtime. As the sun set behind the western peaks, she looked at the stars to see if she could identify an aphelion as the point where an object was farthest from the sun. Identifying an aphelion started as a contest with her father when she was a child. She watched the stars appear and tried to identify the five visible planets.

She left her thoughts about finding a job when she graduated from university for the walk back, and planned to sleep late tomorrow as the return down the mountain is always three times faster than the climb up.

While deep asleep during the night, Emmanuelle was unaware of the mist sliding down the mountain and enveloping her small encampment.

In the morning, she awakened to unexpected noises — many voices— outside her tent. She arose, grabbed her backpack, and stepped into the fresh morning air. A glance revealed a mist-filled cloud obstructing her view of France and the valleys and mountains to the west. She turned and looked up the mountain toward the unexpected sounds. At sundown, she had fallen asleep in complete solitude, and now, next to her tiny encampment, was a quaint mountain village bustling with people. At first, she thought the villagers were children, but a second glance confirmed that they were primarily adults, albeit short adults. She was confused and a little stunned, but unafraid as nothing was intimidating about the people or the village — other than that, it had just appeared! She thought "Am I Dorothy Gale and I've landed in Munchkin Land. Or is this Brigadoon?"

Warily, Emmanuelle approached the village. The first to confront her was an Olde English Sheepdog, a puppy by its looks as its hairy coat was a mix of white and black. The friendly puppy yipped and danced around Emmanuelle inviting her to play. Emmanuelle befriended the up until a young woman yelled in Alsatian, "Max, quiet down and come over here." Max obediently ran off.

She walked to where the majority assembled and stood among them; only they ignored her for the most part. The villagers spoke an older, more formal Alsatian dialect. Listening to the townspeople's conversations, Emmanuelle pieced together that their leader had died, and they were assembling to bury him. No one approached or questioned Emmanuelle, but she received strange and sideways glances. She thought her presence, though unusual, almost seemed expected.

The flow of the crowd pulled her along as it made its way to the village chapel. The tug from the crowd pulled her inside; the seats and aisles overflowed with the assembly. Emmanuelle stayed in the rear of the chapel, hoping to remain relatively unnoticed or as inconspicuous as the tallest person in the room could be. An old Spanish friar approached the altar and addressed the crowd. The friar was of indeterminate age, maybe in his mid-seventies, and spoke Alsatian with a Spanish accent. "Wilkommen, my friends, please make room for everyone. We will celebrate Mass, and afterward, we will walk to the gravesite where we will hold a short vigil beside his final resting place."

After the Mass, pallbearers carried the casket outside and loaded it onto a bed of evergreen and holly of the two-horse caisson, an ornate carriage, now a hearse, drawn by two spirited show-horses. The congregation spilled from the chapel and formed an escort clustered behind the caisson. The funeral director, a man formally attired with a top hat, held the reins of both horses; the red bay repeatedly lifted his right hoof and tapped the ground while the dapple-gray to its right swayed his long neck in an arc, hoping for the march to begin. A pallbearer signaled to the director the casket was loaded correctly. With a tug on the reins, the dapple-gray lifted its head, stood on his back legs, and slightly lurched forward, the red bay following its lead. The procession proceeded slowly from the chapel in a semi-organized fashion to the burial site, a small graveyard on the other side of the village's Alpen lake. Emmanuelle moved in step with the villagers wondering why she had not seen the lake, cemetery, or village on her hike yesterday.

She noticed the Spanish friar mingling with the townsfolk, offering words of kindness to everyone. The townsfolk visibly mourned their leader as they walked behind his hearse. Each took turns at the front of the procession until everyone could lead. Emmanuelle stayed in the swell of the crowd even though a few townsfolk indicated she should take a turn at the front.

The burial took place a mile from the village chapel along the side of the mountain. The grave was near a large and ancient Cypress tree that overlooked a valley to the south and east. As she stared at the valley, a villager remarked that the nearby mountains were in Switzerland. The friar and the people conversed in an Alsatian dialect that seemed very dated, a much older version of her native Alsatian.

The Spanish friar approached Emmanuelle after the ceremony at the gravesite and spoke first. "Please take a walk with me, Emmanuelle."

"How do you know my name?" she inquired.

I said conspiratorially, "There are few secrets in these villages, and" I paused and smiled, "that is the name on your backpack. The townsfolk call me Brother John. You can call me John."

"Brother John, or John, are you a Franciscan?"

I replied, "Many think so."

Emmanuelle's brow crumpled as she pondered my answer, but she relaxed and smiled. "The man that you buried today?"

"Yes?"

"Was that who I think it was?"

I replied. "It depends on who you think it was. Please follow me to the gravesite."

They stood before a small number of tombstones. The name on the tombstone by the freshly dug grave, "S. Claus" with "Died 2014" below the name. Emmanuelle gasped as she looked above the name and saw the birth year. "How can that be? He was over 200 years old."

"Indeed." Said Brother John.

Emmanuelle looked at the gravestone next to it and it said H. Claus, with a similar lifespan but one that ended 15 years earlier. She inquired, "Who is H. Claus?"

"Mrs. Claus. Her first name was Holly."

The other tombstones that Emmanuelle could read belonged to: "K. Kringle", "Born 1521", Zwarte Piet, Sinter Klaas, Fr. Christmas, Fr. Frost, the Ice Maiden, and Saint Nicolas. The age of the carving on the stone made the dates mostly unrecognizable.

She laughed nervously and asked, "Zwarte Piet? Is that Black Peter" She paused, "Where are we?"

"Yes, Black Pete was a greatly misunderstood character. I would love to tell you his story sometime. As to where are we, you were camping in the Jura Mountains and crossed through a cloud or an invisible field that protects these villages. The villages have special protection and have remained hidden from outsiders. Only special people gain entrance."

"Well, I am not special, nor did anyone invite me here. What exactly happened?"

"I am not sure, but there is always a reason."

"What reason is that? Why am I here? Who are you? Who are these people? Are you Spanish?"

I raised an eyebrow at the rash of questions and offered, "Do you hike often?"

Emmanuelle, hoping for answers to her staccato of questions, did not expect the abrupt change in subject, "Yes, I hike as often as possible. This hike is a weekend trip. I plan to hike for a month after finishing my studies in a few weeks."

The old monk replied, "I live along the Camino de Santiago, on the French Route, in a small village called Azofra. It is in the foothills of the Pyrenees in La Riojas. Please join me in Azofra after you complete your studies. We will walk the Camino, and I will explain everything then."

Unsure why she replied as she did; words flowed from her mouth, "Sure. I would love that. How do I find you?"

"I am the only friar that Azofra has ever had. I am easy to find. Just go to the church of Our Lady of the Angels. It is the only church in the village."

Emmanuelle paused at the statement, "I am the only friar the village ever had." She seemed unable to think of an appropriate way to question that statement, so she ignored its implications. "How do we coordinate, so you know when I will arrive?"

"I will be ready whenever you walk into the town, and we will be on our way. I am always near the church."

Emmanuelle turned around, and one of the townsfolk led her to a small feast of baked goods, casseroles, sausages, and plenty of beer. The sheepdog, Max, found Emmanuelle and stood guard by her side.

3

Saint Louis, Missouri Early December 2019

MARGE AND GREG HAVE the same conversation every year. The 2019 Christmas season is no different. Greg asks pleasantly, "What are we getting the kids and grandkids for Christmas this year?"

Marge was unable to hide her exasperation, "We? What do you mean by 'we'? 'We' are not getting them anything. I am getting everything, just like I do every year. It's the first Christmas since you retired; again, you did nothing to help. It has been the same each Christmas for the last forty years. Every gift they open is a surprise — for them and you! You think writing everyone a check is your great contribution."

"I love Christmas traditions." Greg quietly remarked to himself.

The next day, with that conversation fresh in her mind, Marge grew more incredulous as a new conversation unfolded when Greg said, "I surfed the web last night. I discovered that Klass is a derivative of Nicolas. I think I am related to Saint Nicolas. I think I can prove it with more research."

Marge burst out, "Have you lost your mind? You are not Santa Claus! I repeat you are not friggin' Santa Claus." Marge had lived through a lot with Greg, but this might be a new low. She could not believe her ears.

"I am not saying that I am Santa Claus, but the ancestry site says that the Klass name is a derivative of Nicholas. Saint Nicholas may have been an ancestor. And look at me, I am 66 years old, and I am finally able to grow my first beard, and it is white."

Marge sarcastically responded, "Hmm. Do you call that a beard? It is white, but so is the snow outside, and that is not a beard."

"Well, whatever it is, I am growing it until this pandemic ends."

"Good God! Please get rid of it! It is scraggly and dirty. Besides, it makes you look old! Who would ever want that mess on their face?"

Greg chuckled, "Me! And I am old—and look at this stomach."

"That is nothing to be proud of. It's because of all the beer you guzzle."

"What's the problem with that?"

"Nothing, nothing is the problem with that," was Marge's sarcastic reply.

Marge and Greg had been going on like this for years. Nothing was unique about them. Nothing was monumental about them, for sure. Life was just a continual series of bickering and bantering. They were warmhearted to each other, just an old married couple, comfortable with each other, bored with each other at times, madly in love a long time ago. At their age and after a lifetime of hard work, Marge and Greg had many ideas, memories, an adequate income, and fleeting energy.

Marge's favorite memory is how they inadvertently became 'Mouse' and, more purposefully, 'Papa.' In truth, Marge liked her given name, Margaret, but Marge's shortened name never felt right. At a family dinner several years earlier, when Charlie, the firstborn grandchild, was 18 months old, Marge and Greg had to decide what the grandkids would call them. Charlie was beginning to speak, and grandparent nicknames were a necessity. Marge needed help with her name as none of the traditional terms suited her.

Their three daughters with two spouses, a future son-in-law, Marge, Greg, and Charlie, gathered in the dining room of their turn-of-the-century Arts and Craft home. The original builders carved 1901 into the mantel of the room's fireplace. The double-oaken pocket doors opened to the front parlor. Marge prepared several delicious side dishes: twice-baked potatoes, green bean casserole, asparagus, and homemade applesauce for Charlie. Greg grilled and served a tri-tip steak, then filled everyone's glasses with an inexpensive red wine.

Charlie was in his highchair between Marge and Greg, waiting to speak. But multiple wine-infused conversations left no room for his small voice. Charlie wanted to get Marge's attention by calling her name during a lull in the discussions. His little voice tried to call out 'Marge,' but everyone distinctly heard 'Mouse.' In a fraction of a second, Marge grabbed that name and held it tight. In the blink of an eye, Marge became Mouse — once and forever. The first grandchild claimed one of the few advantages of the firstborn of the second generation, the ability to dictate a grandparent's name. And Mouse loved it. Mouse would never need to worry about the grandmother moniker of Big Marge. Greg then declared himself "Papa" because his father was "Papa George" in the Klass family and intended to make it a tradition. Of course, only the grandchildren call him Papa. Mouse has a few names for Greg due to his antics, and Papa isn't one of them. Anyway, that's how they came to be Mouse and Papa.

———————◦○◦———————

By mid-February 2020, news reports appeared concerning a virus in China. Within weeks, the news became alarming; soon, the virus spread and devastated Italy. Greg moaned to no one; "A funny thing happened on the way to retirement. This virus is going to change everything."

———————◦○◦———————

In planning their first few years of retirement, Greg and Mouse were utterly unprepared as the virus stopped everything in its tracks. On an unseasonably hot day in early April, Mouse and Greg sat outside, each in their respective deck chairs. The pandemic gripped the country and the world. People are getting very sick, and many are dying. Little is known of the virus, how it started, how it's transmitted, or who is vulnerable. It's called Covid-19 due to the fact it first affected humans in the year 2019. Early hotspots in the US emerged in New

York and Seattle. Travel is slowing down; layoffs are beginning, and rumors are rampant. Information from the government is more suspect than information on the Internet. And the Internet information was total nonsense. Greg and Mouse decided to lay low, limit their activities and wait. The grandkids stayed home and waved from the window whenever Mouse and Papa walked by. The alley behind their home is now the meeting spot for a drink with Kevin, Jenn, Ron and Allison their next-door neighbors. Each couple sat in front of their garage doors at least six feet from each other. Greg said, "These are strange days indeed. I'm finally retired with no place to go. I can't see the grandkids. I can't work, travel, eat out, or golf. Just a lot of 'cant's'."

Mouse replied, "We just must be safe. Nobody knows much yet."

Greg moaned a saying he learned at college, "Must be time to sit around and contemplate one's navel."

The next day, on the backyard deck, Mouse's chair had a new, water-repellant cushion and faced the garden. At this time, her garden was a glorious color bomb of pastel perennials, the usual spring surge of peonies, iris, columbine, and phlox. Greg's deck chair had no cushion and faced the aluminum siding on the back of the house. He disliked his view of the sunroom siding, but after 30-plus years of marriage, he had long ago learned the value of picking his battles. In his opinion, getting a cushion and a better view of flowers wasn't worth an afternoon of marital discord. Along that same thread, Greg reminded himself that he always viewed the wall in a restaurant. One of the two reasons why he insisted on eating at the bar whenever possible. Happy wife, happy life.

Mouse loved the company of her garden more than people; she felt she was giving back to the earth by puttering in the dirt. She proclaimed her Karl Rosenfield peonies the 'queen of all perennials.' Weeds could not grow in her cramped garden. Mouse preferred to think of it as an 'English cottage garden.' She was pragmatic in most aspects of her life but did allow flights of fancy where her garden was concerned. Mouse found room for both the romantic and the realistic in her backyard oasis: Mouse made space for greens and vegetables for a freshly picked salad. Everyone ate their greens daily, just one of Mouse's house rules.

German immigrants built their south-city subdivision in St. Louis. In the late 1800s and early 1900s, the established ruling class prohibited German immigrants from moving into their communities, especially into the upscale Central West End. In response, the German immigrants built their subdivision between 1890 and 1910. The builders finished their house in 1901, three years before the fantastic World's Fair left its mark on Saint Louis.

Those turn-of-the-century immigrants brought remarkable craftsmanship from the old country. The deck on the back of the 120-year-old home is the only thing they added. Mouse's flower gardens surround the backyard and its postage stamp of a lawn. Freshly potted tomato plants ringed the deck. The home's exterior brickwork and interior woodwork all withstood the march of time -- if you kept up with the maintenance. Greg, unfortunately, lacked even ordinary household maintenance skills.

Greg thought it was time for another cold beer in his deck chair. Retirement meant it was always 5 o'clock, the perfect time to splurge on a lovely craft beer. Greg loved his lagers, pale ales, IPAs, pilsners, and Belgian pints. Mouse loved whatever was on sale. Quantity over quality was a must for her every time.

Mouse began today's conversation, "I forgot to mention something you might be interested in; remember when the kids gave us those DNA kits as our gifts for Christmas? We spit in the tubes and mail them away. I know I forgot about them, so you must have too. There was an email in my inbox today about the results, but I haven't opened it yet. I thought it would be fun for us to read the results together. God only knows what secrets my ancestors have been hiding from us!"

Greg interpreted Mouse's comment as a slight against his ancestors. But he wasn't sure she was wrong, so he went inside and turned on the Macintosh. He retrieved the emails from the DNA company, clicked on the link to the DNA website, and logged on. The website displayed their names, Margaret Klass and Gregory Klass. Greg selected Mouse's ancestry composition results by clicking on her name and printing her report, then he retrieved and printed his report. He stopped at the fridge, grabbed a couple of beers, and took the papers outside.

He handed Mouse a beer and her report as the late afternoon sunlight winnowed over the red clay-topped roofs around them. Mouse was not surprised that she was of nearly 100% Northern European ancestry. The bulk of her ancestors came from Northwestern Europe. Mouse said, "This confirms everything I already knew. I am entirely German. The kids could have saved a few bucks." It matched what she had learned from family stories over the years told by grandparents on both sides and later repeated by her parents. It also represented what she saw in the mirror every day. Childhood pictures of Mouse and her sisters resembled the women in Marlene Dietrich's movies and posters. Marlene Dietrich was a German-born American movie star for over sixty years, from 1919 through 1984. Mouse quietly compared herself to Marlene, sultry and desirable at any age.

Greg's DNA composition showed a component from the Grand Est area in France. Greg understood that his father's family was German. His Nana, Papa George's mother, always mentioned her homeland as Alsace-Lorraine. After World War II, the French renamed the Alsace-Lorraine and its surrounding areas the Grand Est (Great East). Greg quickly googled 'Grand Est' on his phone. Grand Est was a newer term to describe the region due east of Paris. Google confirmed his limited understanding of Alsace-Lorraine and added a bit more. Over the centuries, Alsace was sometimes in Germany and sometimes in France. The winner of the most recent war dictated control. Alsatians also live in a large swath of northwestern Switzerland. Many people in these regions of Switzerland, France, and Germany, still speak Alsatian, a German dialect. Greg looked at a map on the Internet and found the French Province of Lorraine on the border of Germany, just below Luxembourg and Belgium and north of Switzerland. Alsace was due south of the western part of Lorraine. So, Alsatians live in France, Germany, and Switzerland. Greg thought, "'Switzerland?' Well, that's news; I never knew Alsatians were there."

Greg's complete DNA report was far more diverse than Mouse's. He found that he was not 75% German after all, but only 38%. "Mouse, look at this!" he exclaimed. "This is an accurate report of my Irish side. My grandmother on my mother's side reflects 25% of my DNA. But my other three grandparents are German, and I know that two of them are Alsatian and the other is from Frankfurt, which is very close to Alsace. And that grandfather may or may not be Alsatian, but he always said we were as German as sauerkraut. But my DNA consists of French, German, Italian, Ashkenazi Jew, Eastern European, North African, and Western Asia, probably around Turkey.

"Italian, Jewish, North African, and Western Asia," Greg's mind swirled with thoughts. "What the hell is that about; the report identifies another small percentage of my DNA as Southern European — unidentified. I always thought I was predominantly of German with a mix of Irish heritage, but in reality I'm a — a — a mutt."

Greg soaked in the meaning of the DNA report. Thoughts popped in and out of his head as he tried to unravel the reports' meaning. "Maybe this explains why my siblings have brown, blonde, or red hair. I am darker skinned and turn tan whenever the weather turns warm. Other siblings have light skin and burn to a crisp in the sun. But we all had the same parents." His thoughts rambled. He told Mouse, "I may need DNA samples from my siblings to see if we match. This report may explain how every Halloween, depending on what type of headwear I choose, I can dress as a German mountaineer, a Greek sailor, a rabbi, a Bedouin nomad, or a Turkish sultan and get away with it each time."

Mouse replied, "You have an excessive supply of hats—a fez, your beret, a Bavarian fedora, that captain's hat, the bishop's mitre, a few cowboy hats, and too many Buffalo Bills caps."

After reading her ancestry report, Mouse put the papers down, picked up her beer, and returned to her eternal quest for the perfect diet to eat and drink everything to her heart's desire and still lose weight. Mouse appreciated the DNA kit and thanked the kids again for such a thoughtful Christmas gift.

Greg, however, was intrigued by the fecundity of his ancestors. Did they all suffer from wanderlust or what the Germans called Fernweh? How did that plethora of DNA get mixed into his more recent Alsatian ancestors? Greg tried to ascertain when, why, and how his ancestors' DNA mingled to become his DNA.

Usually, such thoughts would linger in Greg's mind for a nanosecond. It could be just the boredom and sequestering due to the pandemic that Greg entertained a theory that one of his ancestors might have an epic story. Greg toyed with this theory for a moment. He tried to shake it, but the thought became immovable.

Greg spent long periods on his laptop teaching himself the basics of genealogy research. There were no sports on TV; professional sports leagues were studying how to operate safely during a pandemic. What else could he do? So, he delved deeper into the family tree.

For weeks on end, Greg plodded in solitude, searching for his ancestors, never fully conscious of the motivation for his quest. Soon he exhausted all the US-based birth, death, and marriage records he could find online. He cross-referenced ancestors' names with ship manifests from the early 1800s to subsequent US censuses until his searches dried up and stopped providing clues. Slowly, his sights turned to his ancestral homeland, Alsace. Greg realized that he would need help from Europe to continue his search.

Unknown to Greg, his ancestors were ferociously searching for him.

4

The Book of Hessulah Ephesus, Asia Minor 6 BC

Ancient Greece and Anatolian Peninsula

Source: Wikipedia commons

———◆◇◆———

I have set eyes on the wall of lofty Babylon on which is a road for chariots, and the Statue of Zeus by the Alpheus, and the hanging gardens, and the colossus of the Sun, and the huge labour of the pyramids and the vast tomb of Mausolus, but when I saw the house of Artemis mounted to the

clouds, those other marvels lost their brilliancy and I said, "Lo. Apart from Olympus never looked on aught so grand."
Antipater of Sidon, ~140 BC

———◆◇◆———

My name is John. My Lord and Master joined his Father
11 years ago. I transcribe this chronicle as told to me
by my mother Salome; by Mary the sister of Salome; and
Hessulah of Myra, who is known to Salome and Mary. The
testimony of the three women took place eleven years after
my beloved Master left to join His Father. These women
testified truthfully to me while on a ship sailing for Finis
Terra — the end of the world — on the far coast of Spain.
We are passengers on a funeral ship to bury my brother
James. These women anointed his headless body with oil and
myrrh, as according to our custom and carefully wrapped
his body in a shroud. We stored his body safely in the ship's
hold. King Herod Agrippa of Judaea ordered my brother's
death. His death occurred during the reign of Emperor
Claudius of Rome. Everyone has heard the story of the birth
of my beloved Master — that these women were witness to.
Everyone has heard of the events that followed my Master's
birth — that I attested to. The testimony of these women is
known, by me, to be true. This is how their story begins; this
is The Book of Hessulah.

Artemision, The (third)Temple of Artemis, Ephesus[1]

It's the day before Artemisia, the fourteen-day Ephesian festival dedicated to the goddess Artemis, the patron Goddess of Ephesus. Hessulah finished her early morning prayers to the revered goddess and set out on the day's hunt. The city prepared for months to host the grandest festival in the Roman Empire, and people from around the Mediterranean world arrived to celebrate her fabled Greek Goddess. Artemis, the twin sister of Apollo, adopted Ephesus as hers long before the arrival of the Greeks. However, it was the Amazons who built the first temple to Artemis in Ephesus more than twelve hundred years earlier. The Amazons inhabited Ephesus before the arrival of the Ionian Greeks from the

1. Credits: TRAVELSHOW
   https://www.travelshowtime.com/artemis-temple-in-ephesus.html

Attica region and the city of Athens. Because of its long and complicated history, the temple at which Hessulah prayed, the Artemision, was the third Temple of Artemis constructed on the site. The three-hundred-year-old temple boasts 129 columns, each over 18 meters high (60 feet), and covers almost 9,400 square meters (101,000 sq ft). She paused as a guide led visitors through the temple. Hessulah knew the guide's story well. She listened as the guide continued her lesson and rubbed the marble pillar beside her absentmindedly. Hessulah's right hand felt the smooth coldness of the all-marble structure; everything about the temple impressed her.

The guides oral history lesson began, "One hundred twenty-five years ago, the Greek poet, Antipater of Sidon, called Artemision the greatest of all man-made wonders. Greater than the pyramids and more impressive than the Gate of Ishtar or the hanging gardens of Babylon. Antipater of Sidon thought the temple was new when he wrote his ode, but it was already two hundred years old.

"After Alexander the Great conquered Persia, he absorbed Ephesus and the other Greek city-states in Anatolia. Alexander needed the Anatolian city-states to remain loyal and neutral as he continued marching east and south to conquer new lands. Alexander offered the Ephesians money to rebuild their Temple of Artemis. An arsonist had destroyed the second temple eighty years earlier. The arsonist committed the act, so his name lives forever. I will never repeat his name. The Ephesians spurned Alexander's financial support but dared not offend him for fear of military repercussions. Instead, they told Alexander that Artemis was their goddess, and only the Ephesians could build her temple.

"You see dozens of carved bas-reliefs that adorn the Temple. The reliefs show male Greek soldiers in battle with female warriors. These reliefs honor the ancient Greek victories over the Amazons. It is a Greek custom to commemorate formidable enemies, male or female. Scopas, the renowned Greek sculptor, created these reliefs.

"The Amazons built the first Artemision over a thousand years ago, but a flood destroyed it five hundred years later. The fierceness of the Amazons bore a lasting effect on the Greeks that settled here. To this day, Ephesian women claim more freedom than most Greek women. In gratitude, Ephesian women pay homage to Artemis and the Amazons. Artemisia is a testament to those freedoms and celebrates love and fertility. Over the two weeks, thousands gather and participate in games, theater, contests, and drinking. The festival culminates with a raucous wine-fueled parade when they carry the statue of Artemis through the city streets. It is the only festival where young Greek men and women can select their spouses."

The guide winked at Hessulah as she finished her lecture and stood solemnly with a hand at the ready to collect tribute from the visitors.

Daily, Hessulah would stop at the Temple to pray to Artemis. Today, she would pray to the goddess to bless her hunt. She laid her atlatl and its small spears before the goddess' statue. "Artemis. May my hunt on the sides of Mount Koressus be worthy of your praise. Please send my javelins straight and true."

Hessulah stood and tightly re-tied her waist cord around her tunic. She tucked the atlatl in the back, securing it against her tunic with her waist rope. Hessulah hoped to come across prey worthy of her skill. Her father's Egyptian manservant, Assab, made her atlatl and taught her how to use it. He told her the atlatl is an ancient weapon capable of hurling a small spear ten meters with extreme accuracy and force. Hessulah's javelins were slightly longer than she was tall. The atlatl was a flat stick, about the size of her forearm, with a handle with two holes on each side at the top of the grip for her index and middle fingers. A small, curved notch at the top of the atlatl held the dart stationary before its release. The trick was to keep the atlatl and spear raised shoulder height at the ready and then release forward. The release motion was more of a push or fling than a throw. The atlatl fired the spear with greater force than a javelin was thrown freehand. Hessulah frequently practiced improving both her accuracy and the dart's velocity.

At thirteen years of age, Hessulah earned a huntress's reputation in the local market from the vendors for her marksmanship with a bow, spear, and the atlatl. She tried to enter the hunting competitions held during the festival, but only men could participate. Even in Ephesus, Greek society forced many restrictions on women. At an early age, Hessulah pledged to herself that she would overcome all the obstacles.

Hessulah did nothing to discourage her growing reputation, as Artemis, her beloved goddess, is the goddess of the hunt.

Petrus scanned the wharves of the overcrowded Ephesian harbor. Ships from every part of the Empire filled the piers. There was an impressive collection of Numidian, Egyptian and Carthaginian ships from northern Africa; Syrian, Canaanite, and Judaean vessels from the Levant; Greek ships from Athens, Thebes, Corinth, Sparta, and Macedonia. There were more ships from Crete, Cyprus, and other Greek islands. There were flags or markings on ships from every Greek city-state along the Anatolian Peninsula (Asia Minor), including Pergamon, Miletus, Tarsus, Myra, and Halicarnassus. Many ships anchored away from where the fierce, silted Cayster River currents flowed into the harbor. Numerous ships had identifiers, either bunting identifying a family name, a favorite god, or a family symbol; the multitude of beautifully decorated ships made for an impressive sight.

The harbormaster gave Imperial Roman vessels preference by tying them to the docks. Petrus noticed Zalman's ship, his father's financier, from the prosperous desert kingdom of Nabataea. Zalman, and his wife, a daughter of Judaean king Herod, lived in Herod's new port city of Caesarea north of Jerusalem. Petrus tried to spot Herod's ship as he wished to glimpse the man who would change his life later that night. The Roman Governor is hosting a party for King Herod, and Petrus is attending as an honored guest.

Inside the port, a cacophony of languages and dialects lifted from the crowds.

In his 21st year, Petrus was interested in neither gaiety nor the festival. His dark complexion and drab olive skin set him apart from other young Greek men. Like his younger sister Hessulah, he inherited his mother's bright green eyes, but those eyes failed to find Herod's ship, and he hurried home to dress for the night he hoped would shape his destiny.

After he dressed, he presented himself to his Egyptian stepmother, Vissia, for her approval. Exotic Vissia was two years younger than Petrus; he imagined taking her to the Governor's villa and impressing the Romans with her beauty. He kept that dream and his other fantasies of Vissia in the forefront of his imagination, ready for replay. Presenting himself to her was a game he played for her attention and approval, hoping to fuel a desire within her. Tonight, he said something cryptic to Vissia. "Things will not always be like this; things will change soon."

Vissia laughed off the remark, "Things are wonderful as they are, Petrus. You look so handsome tonight. Is that a new toga? I am sure the Governor will be impressed."

Petrus heard a slight commotion in the courtyard. It was his little-bitch sister, Hessulah. She had arrived home in time to foul his mood. He heard Hessulah telling the servants a story about killing some animals and giving them to poor families. Violent thoughts toward Hessulah quickly replaced his fantasy of Vissia.

He left Vissia's chambers, called for his torchbearer, and avoided Hessulah on his way out. There will be an opportunity to set things right in the coming days. Dusk changed to dark, and Petrus instructed the torchbearer, "Slow the pace; I don't want to arrive sweating and stinking like a slave." The servant knew enough not to exchange words with Petrus. He said nothing and shortened his stride.

They walked silently through affluent Greek quarters towards the opulent Roman section renowned for its terraced homes.

The gala to honor King Herod of Judaea, who is visiting Ephesus to complete trade agreements, will bring business to Herod's newly constructed port north of Jerusalem, Caesarea Maritima. Everyone in the shipping world knew the story of the city Caesarea with its impressive artificial harbor, Caesarea Maritima. Two concrete break walls, at the north and southern end of the city, jut hundreds of yards out to the sea, framing the deep-sea harbor. Fifty of the largest freighting vessels in the Mediterranean, each capable of carrying four-hundred metric tons, transported the cement from Italy. Caesarea and Maritima were built in thirteen years and became fully operational three years ago. Within a decade, Herod had transformed a sleepy fishing village into a center of commerce with 125,000 inhabitants.

Herod built the city for business, sports, and pleasure. Herod's palace, replete with a seaside freshwater pool, held an impressive view of the deep blue Mediterranean. The city is home to public baths, theaters, and buildings of commerce and government. The Governor had told Petrus that, in a short time, Caesarea would replace Jerusalem as the capital of the province of Judaea.

Herod's palace sat on a promontory overlooking the northern end of the harbor. An amphitheater for theater and gladiator games dominated the southern break wall. A hippodrome hosting horse and chariot racing was within walking distance of the palace and amphitheater. It is a city built for pleasure, and wealthy Romans can sail to Caesarea from Rome in ten days.

Petrus planned to forge a deal with Rome's Governor of Asia Minor and Herod, the Rome-appointed Judaean king. Petrus hoped to cement his future within Roman society by negotiating an agreement that left his father with no choice but to accept. His father will be unable to refuse the deal without insulting the Governor and Herod. Insulting the Governor and Herod would come at considerable risk, as Petrus believed that the Governor and Herod would murder his father if he balked at the deal. A possibility that did not upset Petrus.

He tried to focus on the challenges of the night, but his mind ruminated about his unfulfilled life. He played out the familiar scenes to fuel his hatred of his father and sister while assuaging his guilt for the betrayal that lies ahead. The memories, never far away, flooded back. The first memory is the night he lost his mother. His memory replayed the cries emanating from her bedroom. He heard the low groans of a woman in labor and the growing pitch of the midwife's commands; the commands rose harsher in severity and urgency, followed by the squeals of a brand-new baby testing its lungs. Then his father's sobs surprised Petrus, who, before that night, would have told anyone that his father was incapable of tears, weakness, fear, or hurt. The sequence of these sounds no longer mattered to him; through the drama of that night, his impotent rage only knew that the wrong person had died in that room. His mother should have been the one to survive; his mother, who thought he was so clever, was the only person that could make him laugh, the only one ever to love him. That cursed baby should have died.

Petrus's mind kept all his memories at his beck and call. The torchbearer caught a glimpse of his tortured face as the flame reflected off the beads of sweat that had formed on Petrus's upper lip. He braced for Petrus's reprimand, but it never came.

They turned off Curetes Street and walked up the carriage path to the front of Gaius's terraced villa. As he approached the Governor's villa, he stopped and moved the memories back to their compartments, always close at hand. He will resummon his reservoir of hate when it is necessary. He quickly re-adjusted his mood and set his hopes for tonight's dinner, which would free him from his past and allow him to claim his rightful future.

The Governor's servant met them in the outer courtyard, where Petrus dismissed his torchbearer. "Find a place to wait for me. They will feed you." The Governor's servant, a beautiful red-headed foreign slave girl of a nationality Petrus could not place, led Petrus to a dining area where Gaius and Herod sat on couches before a lavish banquet.

Shortly before Petrus arrived, Gaius and Herod spoke in a private conversation. "Herod, I have recruited Petrus over the past few months. He is a sniveling Greek, but we can use him well. He will readily accept our offer. I invited him tonight to finalize his commitment, and I thought it was important for the three of us to meet as a team. We must remove the father so that he can take over the family business. Petrus will affix the family seal once we handle that detail."

Herod thought aloud, "Gaius, do me a favor and follow my lead when we speak of removing the father. We need him completely committed. I want Petrus in a position where we can manipulate him long after this transaction."

Gaius nodded. "I instructed the servants not to water down his wine. The wine will give him a sense that we are friends. Ahh, here he comes now." Gaius continued, "Petrus, my boy, welcome to my villa. Please join us; I have set this couch for you. I want to introduce you to King Herod of Judaea."

Petrus bowed and said, "Good evening, your majesty; it is my pleasure to meet you."

Herod replied, "Enough of that bowing and your majesty's business; you can call me Herod. All my business acquaintances do. And if I am to believe Gaius, I expect we will be business partners before the morning light."

"Nothing would give me greater pleasure, your, er, Herod."

It was a warm and pleasant evening; statues of the Roman goddess Diana were decorated in the festival colors, as Diana and Artemis are equivalent in Rome and Greek mythology. Gaius's most attractive female slaves were present. Two served the meal wearing very light, white tunics that revealed everything. In similar revealing outfits, two more played musical instruments in the corner, adding ambiance to the evening.

Gaius knew Petrus was young, gullible, and ripe for the plucking. His red-headed servant sat on Petrus's couch, their bodies touching. Ripples of electricity raced through him as her body, beauty, and perfume filled his senses. Petrus had difficulty concentrating on his business with Herod and Gaius while she sat beside him. He indulged in his self-importance, and the thought never occurred to him that Gaius and Herod had plotted this night.

Herod and Gaius tried to win his complete trust and set him up as a pawn if anything went awry. The seduction was simple with wine, food, flattery, and a seductive woman with the promise of status and power. They were his mentors, and Petrus would do whatever they asked.

Gaius spoke up. "My scribes have drawn up the necessary documents. Let me summarize the agreement as I have been in separate discussions with you."

"That's an excellent idea, Gaius. I'm appreciative of your efforts on our behalf." Interjected Herod.

"As do I," said Petrus rather lamely.

Gaius continued, "Very well. It is a tri-party agreement to control all the shipping in the eastern Roman Empire. Petrus will turn his family's merchant fleet into a civilian-run transport dedicated to Rome's military operations and any ventures that Herod and I, and you too, Petrus," he paused and repeated,

"Any ventures that we develop in the mutual interests of the parties. Herod shall provide preferred access to the ports under his control in Judaea and Samaria. I will deliver all the military contracts under my control. All commercial businesses under my oversight within the province of Asia Minor are required to use Petrus's transport operation. I will give Petrus a license to operate in Ostia, the port of Rome, and Petrus will contribute fifty percent of his revenue to the parties."

Petrus flinched. "Fifty percent of revenue? I thought we agreed to share the profit. Father will never agree to split half the revenue."

Herod jumped in, "It must be fifty percent of the revenue! You are the one that can control your costs. You have exclusive rights to all major shipping revenue and adjust your price accordingly. That is the only way I can proceed. I am giving up way too much to take less." Herod feigned anger at Gaius. "Gaius, I thought you said Petrus agreed to this already. You have put Petrus, and me, in a difficult spot."

"I thought we had an agreement on this point, Petrus," said Gaius. "Petrus, you do see our point, why revenue, not profit, is key to this, do you not?"

"Yes, I suppose so," Petrus replied meekly.

Herod queried, getting to the point of this assembly. "Let us speak, Petrus. If you oversaw your family business, would you become a party to this agreement?"

"Of course, but my father is healthy and will impede us until I inherit the business. What can we do if he disagrees?" Herod and Gaius nodded as witnesses to the father's betrayal by the son.

Gaius ordered Petrus's wine cup refilled. Then he commanded the servants. "All of you leave us. But don't go far; we need some privacy, even you, my dear." He dismissed the beauty whose job it was to tease Petrus. All the servants vanished inside except the red-haired beauty; she stood in Petrus' line of sight at the far end of the courtyard.

Herod interjected, "Before we go down that dark road, Petrus, tell us how you prefer to go about this."

"I hope my father accepts my advice. I will take the agreement to him, convince him that this is in the family's best interests, that he listens to reason, and affixes his seal. If he doesn't listen, what do we do?"

Herod then finished the thought, "Timo is your father's name, correct? What if Timo doesn't listen to reason? You want us to murder him and install you as the head of the business." Herod paused and said, "Why would we do that?"

Petrus was slightly confused. "Why would you kill him? Once he's dead, I will inherit the business and affix our family seal."

Herod put on a deadly face scowl, "No, Petrus, why should we murder your father and then make you the head of the business? Why wouldn't I take over the business if I were to kill Timo? I always take everything when I take the biggest risk."

"Isn't that why we are here?" asked Petrus nervously.

Herod's voice boomed, "We are here to commit to a major agreement. You are committing nothing and are asking everything of us."

Gaius, stepping in to defuse the tension, offered, "We had the scribes write down the agreement. All we need is for you to affix your family seal." Petrus saw the strutting Eagle of Herod and the Lion of Gaius's family waxen seals on the scroll. Gaius repeated as he presented the scroll to Petrus. "All we need is for you to affix your family seal, the outstretched Bow of Artemis, I believe."

Petrus lamented, "I begged my father for years to do business with Rome. When I inherit the company, I will gladly add our seal to the agreement."

Herod harrumphed and said, "This son is greater than the father. You are more astute and have better judgment than Timo. The family business will do well in your hands. The time for this opportunity is now. Are you going to take it? Delay, and it is gone."

Herod stared hard at Petrus and said, "I am sure you have heard stories of my family and what I have had to do to maintain my power. Many of those stories are true. I did whatever was necessary whenever anyone, even family, came in the way of my destiny. My favorite wife was unfaithful to me. Three of my sons planned to overthrow me. I executed all of them. If you believe this agreement is right and will secure your legacy, do not let anything or anyone, not even your father, stop you. Ambition, like prophecy, must be fulfilled. Sometimes you must act to take what is rightfully yours."

"I have never killed before; how do I do this?" Petrus looked up as he spoke. His gaze set on the alluring redhead standing beneath a torch at the far end of the inner courtyard. She slowly removed her tunic at a signal from Gaius, and the flickering light bounced off her curves. Petrus could not look weak in the eyes of this beauty. He took the bait and committed himself. He understood that once he said yes, there was no going back on his word, especially not with these two powerful men.

Petrus unleashed his frustrations as he stared at the naked girl. He could feel the heat emanating from his forehead and the back of his neck. "My father treats me like a servant. He always praises my rotten sister, even to my face. My father constantly threatens to disinherit me. He says he'd prefer to leave the business to her rather than to me, his only son. Plus, my father is healthy, and I will be old before I inherit. Good business deals like this one will evaporate. How can you help me if I cannot convince him to agree to the deal?"

Petrus felt the intensity in the room rise. Herod asked the questions that Gaius's spies had already confirmed, "Where is your father's shop, and when does he leave to go home at night?"

Petrus filled him in on his father's routine. "The shop is off Arcadiane (Harbour Street) near the docks. It is the only two-story building in the port. Our villa is in the Greek section but not far from the Roman terraced homes. It sits on a hill above the Roman Agora, close to the Artemision."

Herod continued, "How many guards does your father have? Who is the first one in the shop each day? Please give us all the details." Herod and Gaius already knew these answers, as Gaius's spies watched Timo and Petrus for weeks. It was critical that Petrus tell the truth and that Petrus committed the crime. Petrus must take the fall if anything goes wrong.

"At first light, he has breakfast, then makes his way to the shop. Each evening, he leaves the shop and returns home a half hour before sunset. His servant, an Egyptian named Assab, acts as his bodyguard. My sister is with him except when she hunts or trains with her bow or other weapons. Assab is old and not much of a fighter, to my knowledge. He meets my father at the shop every morning. Assab stays with a widow whose home is near the docks. Father walks home alone or with my sister."

"Assab? That name has a familiar ring to it," exclaimed Herod, dismissing the thought. "What would happen if your father did not come home?"

"The household would be worried. My sister will go to the shop in the morning to look for him."

"Your sister?" asked Gaius. "The one you hate?"

"Yes, her name is Hessulah. I do hate her. I have always hated her. Why do you ask?"

"We can use that to our advantage. We will need a scapegoat, someone to take the blame. I have an idea." Gaius leaned to Petrus and Herod to reveal his plan. "Listen closely; plan to meet your father at the shop tomorrow night, alone. Make sure the Egyptian has left for the day." Gaius continued speaking, saying, "Petrus, join me at the Temple of Diana tomorrow at mid-day. There is someone that I want to introduce you to; he will show you what to do."

Herod, known for his lavish gifts, commemorated the agreement by presenting Gaius and Petrus with magnificent, identical daggers. Each dagger had an ivory inset of Herod's family crest, a full-breasted strutting eagle underscored by the letters KP for Kratos Romanii, 'Roman Power.' (editor's note: Kratos is the Greek god of Strength. P is the letter rho in Latin.)

Herod handed the first dagger to Petrus and said, "May this dagger lead you to your destiny, my friend."

———— ◆ ————

Petrus confronted his demons as he walked home from the Governor's villa. He was of two minds; he yearned for his father's praise and acceptance but prayed for his father to die. His body shuddered when he thought of stabbing his father. Gaius and Herod demanded that from him, but he did not dare do it himself. Timo had made his position clear. Timo would not let him explain the benefits.

He told Timo that he, Petrus, had made the decision, and Timo must abide by it. If that did not work, he would return to Gaius and beg him to kill his father.

As the late morning sun reached its pinnacle, Petrus met Gaius at the Roman Temple of Diana. Gaius began, "Petrus, this is Quintus, the centurion in charge of the Urban Cohort." Quintus looked merciless with a stern, shaven face. In Roman fashion, he removed his helmet and clenched his forearms with Petrus. The bald, shaven Quintus clutched Petrus's arm in an iron grip. The iron grip and narrowing eyes conveyed his authority and the message he wanted Petrus to understand – "do not ever deceive me." Gaius continued, "I informed Quintus of the plan; affix the family seal to the agreement or return to the Urban Cohort with the agreement sealed and the dagger bloody. As we expect, Quintus will send a man to pick up your sister when she arrives early in the morning. Quintus will follow with a small contingent of men just after sunrise and arrest your sister. We will blame your sister for everything and execute her on the spot."

Once Petrus had left, Gaius told Quintus, "If our friend Petrus loses his nerve, I want you to kill the father. Make it look like Petrus did it and use this dagger. We want Petrus to be indebted to us." He handed Quintus the strutting-eagle dagger that Herod gave him. Remember to make it look like Petrus did it."

Quintus took the dagger and put it in his belt. "What can you tell me about Petrus?"

"He will be wealthy once his father is out of his way, and he is easy to manipulate. We will use him to transport everything for the war with the Parthians. Afterward, we can exploit him for years; he must act tomorrow night. Everyone will be at the festival, and the harbor will be quiet."

The next night Petrus sought Timo out at the docks and found him alone on the shop's second floor, about to leave for home. It was shortly before dusk.

"Hello father, where is Assab?" Petrus looked around the room.

"He left early to prepare for the festival. Do you need him for something?"

"No, I just wanted some time alone with you. I have something vital to talk to you about." Petrus handed the scroll from Gaius and Herod to his father. I want us to make a deal with Rome and the king of Judaea. We will provide all military transport between Rome and Asia Minor. We will get trading licenses for Ostia."

Timo quickly scanned the scroll. "This document says we will pay Gaius and Herod half of our revenue for them giving us Rome's business. That is illegal; further, this will ruin us. Give up half the revenue; are you insane?" Timo shouted down the remainder of Petrus's arguments. "How often have I told you that doing business with the Romans is not worth the money? They will betray you; we will have nothing in the end. I want nothing to do with Imperial Rome or its military. They only bring death and destruction."

Petrus turned red in the face at his father's rebuke. "This agreement is paramount for my future. I gave the Governor my word, and you must accept it."

Timo yelled, "It is not your word to give. I will not honor it. I will not place my seal on this scroll. You are not my son. You are your mother's son, not mine. You were never my son." Looking to wound Petrus, Timo shouted, "You are not half the man your sister is. You will leave my home now with nothing."

Drool slipped from Petrus's mouth. "Hessulah killed my mother."

Timo launched another verbal stab, "You fool. Hessulah was a baby; she did no such thing. Your mother died because she was ashamed of you."

Rage blinded Petrus while the room darkened as dusk bled into the night. His lifelong grievances welled up in him, building into a volcanic force. Petrus stepped behind Timo and pulled the dagger strapped inside his toga. With a look of fury, he repeatedly stabbed his father. Timo's arms flailed around as he tried to block the dagger's blows. Petrus's surprise attack was too much of an advantage, and Timo's energy quickly waned. With his final thrust, the blade lodged deep into Timo's back, and Petrus backed away as Timo slumped to the floor, laying crossways against his table.

Petrus surveyed the scene before him and committed its details to memory. He lusted at the gore and found he became sexually aroused. What was it his father said during the struggle? He stooped over the body and quietly spoke, "What did you say, father? You said, 'I was never your son.' Well, you are nobody's father now." He walked out as Timo's blood seeped on the dusty wood-planked floor.

Petrus never looked back. He followed the rest of Gaius and Herod's plan; first, he went to the Urban Cohort barracks about two kilometers from the shop. His rage subsided during the walk, but his self-satisfaction grew. He mentally rationalized his actions, blaming his father, but mostly he blamed his sister. When he arrived at the barracks, he was whiter than his normal olive appearance. Quintus, being a good judge of evil men, immediately knew Petrus had carried out the deed; still, he waited for Petrus to acknowledge the murder, knowing that once he admitted it, Petrus would forever be in his power. Quintus patiently stood silent, as a murderer always needed to brag about their first kill, seeking confirmation or validation of their action. Petrus spoke to Quintus, "My father is in his shop. Timo is dead. I killed him. Send your Legionnaire before first light to wait for my sister."

"First, tell me how you murdered your father."

"I presented him with the contract and demanded that he affix the family seal. But he did not listen to reason. He tried to disown me and sang praises of my sister to my face. It was insulting. He turned away, and I attacked him with the dagger Herod gave me."

"Where is the dagger?"

"Um, it's tightly wedged in his body; I left it and came here."

"You should have kept the dagger. But no matter, we will retrieve it in the morning. Did anyone see you?"

"Nobody saw me."

"Okay, my Legionnaire will grab your sister if she shows up before sunrise." Quintus continued. "I will lead a squad of eight from the Cohort later. You should join us at the shop during the first hour. We can execute her on the spot if you accuse her in front of us. We will find her if she doesn't show up. You will never see her again."

Quintus stared at Petrus when Petrus replied, "I want to be there when you arrest her. I cannot wait to see Hessulah's face when I tell her she will pay for what she did to my mother."

5

Azofra, Spain Late December 2019

Church of Our Lady of the Angels, Azofra, La Riojas, Spain[1]

I STAYED IN AZOFRA since my journey with Francis. Having traveled the Mediterranean for centuries, and with an eternity before me, I learned to make my own clothes over the centuries. Long ago, I taught myself the craft of a cobbler and fashioned my sandals after the caligae, the footwear of the typical Roman

---

1. Credit: THEFOGWATCH.COM

soldier. The Romans embedded fifty to sixty small iron hobnails into the bottom of their sandals. The exposed, rounded head of the hobnail performed two tasks. It extended the life of the leather as the nail absorbed most of the wear and tear, especially when walking upon stone or rocky ground. Secondly, the pounding sound of Roman soldiers on the march struck fear into their enemy. I preferred the hobnailed sandals because they extended the life of the leather.

A few centuries ago, I ceased to weave my cloth. Now, I buy bolts of brown fabric in the towns along the Camino. I fashion my robes in the style that Francis introduced long ago. Patches and tears sewn together in Franciscan fashion attest to the life of my oldest robe.

On this bright September day, I waited outside my small church in Azofra. I have lived here since I returned from my pilgrimage with Francis. I tend to my flock at the church of Nuestra Senora de los Angeles (Our Lady of the Angels). Emmanuelle has become a fellow pilgrim, and we frequent the Camino together. We maintain a low profile to keep the word of our travels above suspicion. Others have long had an interest in my movements. I keep to my routines in hopes of going unnoticed. I like to think that I invented the phrase, 'just because you are paranoid, doesn't mean they aren't watching you.'

I covered my old motorcycle with a heavy cloth tarp and ensured my satellite phone was out of sight. I occasionally use the phone to speak with the villages. But I told Emmanuelle that I don't trust technology and have never used a motor car or phone. It is a minor deceit of my enterprise as it allows me to maximize my time in her company. Years ago, I convinced myself it was necessary to protect Emmanuelle from those seeking to disrupt my purpose - whatever that purpose is to become. But if I were to take a moment and consider my true motives, I might admit that I am lonely and simply enjoy her companionship. Maybe that's why I never take a moment to self-analyze my motives.

Today I am very anxious about Emmanuelle's arrival. On our past Caminos, Emmanuelle would do most of the talking, but I have a hunch that something is afoot, and I must prepare Emmanuelle.

As is my way, I avoided usual courtesies, and as she approached within earshot, I announced, "There is a change coming, Emmanuelle, something meaningful. I believe that the Star of Bethlehem precipitates it. The Star will appear during the next winter solstice in 2020. It is the Star's first appearance since the birth of my Master. And it is the third appearance of the Star in the last 4,000 years."

"The actual Star of Bethlehem? How do you know?"

"2,000 years ago, Saturn and Jupiter aligned in the western sky. The planets appeared as stars to the ancients. This alignment presaged the birth of Our Lord and was visible to the Magi and Zoroastrian astrologers. The Magi belonged to a prominent sect of scholars, soldiers, politicians, physicians, teachers, mathematicians, and astrologers. Melchior, one of the three Magi present to honor our Lord's birth in Bethlehem, calculated the paths of the stars and planets; as such, he was one of the first astronomers. The Magi followed a comet from Babylon to Jerusalem; once they arrived in Jerusalem, the comet left the night sky. The Magi's plan ended with the comet, and they waited for the appearance of the next sign. They visited Herod, the local king, hoping he could tell them where to find the newborn king. They became uncomfortable and distrustful of Herod after their meeting and returned to their camp. Later that night, the two stars, or planets as we now know them, began to draw towards each other. The Magi followed the path of these two stars each night, with their movements lasting an hour or two, pulling them nearer each other. Their movement ended when they set over the horizon. This cosmic venture lasted seven nights and led the Magi about 10 kilometers south and east to Bethlehem. Next year, these two planets will align during the winter solstice, forming the Star of Bethlehem."

"What type of change are you talking about?"

"I cannot be certain, but I believe His return is near. We must prepare for His arrival."

"Is Jesus coming from heaven on a white horse with a flaming sword?"

I answered, "I sincerely doubt that. That is not His "style" if you will. I wrote something to that effect long ago when I had a fever. Truthfully, I have no idea how He will arrive. But the appearance of the Star of Bethlehem cannot be taken for granted; it is too great of a coincidence. Our job is to prepare to do our part, whatever part that may be."

Always ready with a question, Emmanuelle asked, "What is the difference between an astrologer and an astronomer?"

I answered, "Astronomy is the science of the stars and universe. Melchior was one of the first astronomers. He computed the paths of the stars, planets, and comets. Astrology uses the stars to predict behavior and the future. The Zodiac symbols are an example of astrology. The stars were the internet of ancient times; religion, travel, past history and future events predicated upon the stars."

"Time to be on our way, Emmanuelle. We have much to discuss. We must be extra cautious from now on. They are always watching."

6

The First Day of the Festival of Artemis, Ephesus 6 BC

Hessulah knelt on the floor in half-dried blood beside her father's lifeless body, his transmogrified face now ashen grey, devoid of breath. She felt the blood dampen her knees as it soaked through her tunic. The breath that provided color to his face had long since disappeared. His bloodless face was cold to the touch. Through silent tears, she reached to touch his face and feel his pained expression; she watched for his last words and listened for his final thoughts. She tried to trace that vacant death stare to see who killed him. But alas, his stare, unheard words, and last thoughts gave no clues.

Hessulah arrived at her father's shop as the rooster's morning reveille announced the morning sun's first glimmers that peaked through the eastern hills. The 'shop', as they called it, was where her father and brother conducted the family shipping business in the port of Ephesus. Ephesus, the capitol city of Roman Asia Minor, was the economic and cultural center of the eastern half of the Empire. It was unusual that her father had not come home. So Hessulah awoke early, skipped breakfast, and walked to the docks, hoping to find him asleep in the shop. She had not expected this. She was just fourteen and had led a largely idyllic life in Ephesus. She tried to comprehend the magnitude of the scene before her and forced herself to absorb all its details. "Always look at the details." Her father had taught her to remember every detail of business deals, sailing, and people.

His body slumped against the legs of his table that he used as a high desk so he could work without sitting. His feet splayed in front of him, the vacant eyes staring forward. The dagger that killed him was lodged deep in his back, just below his right shoulder blade. She saw many other wounds on the head and neck that attested to the fierceness of the struggle and the viciousness of the attack.

She noticed something out of place at first but could not name it. She could not find Timo's presence. Her father always dominated the room. Now his body lay before her, but she could not feel him; he was absent.

She stooped over the body and reached with her right arm to remove the dagger, hoping to lessen the pain. As she grabbed the dagger's handle, her stomach convulsed in a sickening rumble, but she concentrated and remained steadfast in the task before her. Whether it was her stomach's nervous sounds, or she was in shock, she failed to hear the footsteps from behind. A large arm wrapped around her as she touched the dagger's hilt. One hand covered her mouth as another arm lifted her off the floor; the blade stayed embedded in her father's torso.

"Look what we have here; my commander was right when he said I would find you. Hmm, it looks like someone just murdered their father. You stabbed him in the back, or by the looks of it, you stabbed him - everywhere." He tightened his grip on her, then said, I am going to put you down, and you are not to move."

She turned her head and looked into the black eyes of a Roman legionnaire. She slowly reached beneath her tunic for the knife she kept bound to her leg. But somehow, her captor knew where she hid her knife and that her instinct was to use it. He let go of her mouth and quickly grasped her wrist.

"Don't try that, little miss, or you will end up on the floor dead like your father. I'll take that blade, and we will sit tight and wait for everyone else to show."

Her body was stiff from the trauma of the scene and this unimaginable consequence of it. She tried to remember what her father had taught her as her thoughts raced. She reeled her thoughts in to focus on the detail, think, plan, and then act.

Thoughts flowed through her head, "How did this Legionnaire, obviously a member of the Roman Cohort that policed the city, know it was her father? He will kill me if he must, but the soldier is not prepared to kill me yet; he's saving me for something, but what? How did the Roman know to come to her father's shop? He expected to find me here! Who are the others that are coming?"

Hessulah's mind was racing; she had been there about fifteen minutes as she tried to comprehend everything. The Roman placed Hessulah down in front of her father; she faced the doorway with her back to her father. The Roman confiscated the knife he pulled from Hessulah's sheath as she stood defiantly facing the Roman, showing no fear. She noticed a quiet movement from behind the Roman and fixed her gaze on the soldier's face. The Roman stood, looked at the knife, and said, "Pretty nice knife, ugh" Suddenly, the tip of the blade from Assab's sword burst through the soldier's stomach, and blood splashed on Hessulah's face, arms, and tunic. The soldier looked pained and surprised as he slowly collapsed to the floor. She stared hard at the soldier's face; his eyes took on that vacant dead stare. Her knife slipped from his hands and fell between his body and her feet.

Assab stood before Hessulah as she shook and began to weep. He stepped around the soldier and pulled Hessulah close to him. They turned and looked down at Timo.

"I am sorry, Hessulah." Assab whispered, "Timo is gone. Did you see anyone besides this Roman?" Hessulah, unable to speak for fear of breaking down into sobs, slowly shook her head no. Assab peered through the open window to the streets below and listened for the sounds of soldiers marching. He heard the stomp of marching feet, likely the Urban Cohort, the city's Roman security force marching toward the shop. "We must get you somewhere safe and quickly; stay close to me." He held Hessulah tightly as he leaned over her father and expertly removed the blade buried deep below the shoulder blade. Hessulah winced at the suction sound as the double-edged blade released from the muscles, tendons, and other soft tissue. Assab wiped the blade and tucked it under his belt. Hessulah bent down and retrieved her knife next to the fallen soldier. Assab half carried Hessulah out of the building just as the top half of the morning sun appeared over the hills. He held her by the arm and directed her down an alley. They slipped into an open courtyard and ducked behind its wall as the Urban Cohort turned the corner and marched toward them. Assab gently put his hand over Hessulah's mouth. They listened as the Cohort marched by and went into the shop. Once the Cohort was inside the shop, Assab grabbed Hessulah's arm, and they walked quickly to the nearby home of a widow that Assab stayed with when he was in port. Hessulah kept trying to return to be with her father, but Assab pulled her along.

Hessulah stammered, "I discovered father with that dagger in his back. I, I didn't hear the soldier come up behind me. The soldier knew to meet me there. He knew it was my father. How could he have known those things? He said I did it and that others knew as well."

"It sounds like you were in a trap. Whoever killed your father wanted you to take the blame. The Romans are involved; we cannot trust the authorities. If a Roman is responsible for this murder, the Urban Cohort will arrest and convict the first Greek they find. Look at this." Assab showed Hessulah the dagger he had pulled from her father's back. It was of Roman design but had Greek lettering. The hilt had an ivory inlay of a walking, full-breasted eagle with the letters KP engraved below.

"You believe a Roman killed my father?" she asked.

"Yes, but I don't think it was the soldier we left back there. If the Urban Cohort knew to come to your father's shop early in the morning, the murderer must have told them you would be there. The letters on the dagger, KP, stand for 'Kratos Romanian' or 'Roman Power.' The markings on the dagger's hilt are Roman, but the lettering is Greek. Kratos, as you know, is the Greek god of strength. The eagle is a Roman military symbol. It belongs to a Roman, or a highly placed Greek, in Rome's employ. Things will get unpredictable here; the Urban Cohort will be angry when they find one of their men dead."

Hessulah committed the eagle insignia to memory. She added, "When we discover who owns this dagger, we will find the person that killed father." Assab, now in his late fifties, understood his mission. He nodded and accepted his new role as Hessulah's protector.

———◀◇▶———

Timo assigned Assab as her bodyguard and teacher during childhood and early adolescence. Assab taught Hessulah the histories of Anatolia, Ephesus, Greece, Rome, and Egypt. Assab also explained much of her family history, as Timo rarely spoke to Hessulah about her mother.

Timo, like Hessulah, was born and raised in Ephesus. Most Ephesians descended from the Ionian Greeks that settled Ephesus. Ionian Greeks founded Athens, while the Dorian Greeks were Spartans, and Boeotian Greeks came from Thebes. These tribes replaced the ancient Greek Mycenaean civilization that laid the foundation for much of Greece's art, religion, education, and trade. Mycenaean Greece was the setting of Homer's epic poems, The Iliad (Trojan War) and The Odyssey (The Tales of Odysseus). The Roman poet, Virgil, wrote The Aeneid, the story of Aeneas, the Trojan prince who escaped the doomed city of Troy and founded the city of Rome.

The Mycenaeans were a bronze-age society and built mighty cities and started many settlements on the Anatolian Peninsula. The newer Greek tribes rose to power as the Mycenae culture declined around 1,100 BC. Timo's family came to Ephesus with the early Ionian colonization of the northwest Anatolian coast, hundreds of years before the Greco-Persian wars and the subsequent conquests of the peninsula, Persia, and the world by Alexander the Great.

Trading was Timo's business, but sailing was his passion. He built a successful shipping business upon his love for the sea. Timo operated a fleet of vessels that traded across the eastern half of the Mediterranean Sea. His two-story shop was close to the docks in the Ephesian port off Arcadiane, the street that led to the harbor.

At 17, when he first started trading, the shop's second floor served as his home. He lived there for eight years until he married Hestia, Hessulah's mother. Hestia's father, Philos, was in the construction business and first met Timo at the Temple of Artemis, where a mutual acquaintance had introduced them. Four months later, Philos approached Timo and began to discuss his daughter, Hestia. Timo knew that such a conversation would lead to a marriage proposal and that becoming the son-in-law of Philos could offer many advantages. Nor was this the first time an acquaintance approached Timo with a discussion about their daughter. He was wary of showing an interest in such propositions and tried not to put himself in a compromising position. His first inclination was to deflect Philos' approach quickly to avoid offending him if the discussion turned serious.

Ephesus differed from most Greek states as Ephesian law allowed women and men to choose their spouses. It was a tradition that Greek historians traced to the founding of Ephesus, and some hypothesized that it came from the original settlers, the Amazons. However, the merchant class tended toward arranged marriages to preserve and expand wealth.

Timo was intent on building his business and wanted to avoid the distraction of a wife and family. He followed his usual routine for such discussions; first, he politely listened to the father, then at the mention of a daughter, Timo would acknowledge that she must be beautiful; and even nod to convince the father he was interested. Then a servant approached and interrupted the conversation on a cue from Timo. Timo would withdraw and avoid all contact with the man until Timo knew the daughter was engaged to someone else.

But this conversation began differently; Philos was a wealthy builder above Timo's station. A mutual business acquaintance had arranged the luncheon. Timo agreed to meet with Philos out of curiosity and because of his respect for the acquaintance. Philos mentioned the dowry he was offering for his daughter, which was greater than expected. Timo wondered if the girl was no longer a virgin or with child. He weighed the opportunity in his mind; although a wife and family could distract him, it was time to think of the future. Philos could be a significant customer and give Timo's emerging business a stable base, and the girl that he described indeed piqued his interest.

After a day of thought and consultation with his trusted aide Assab, Timo sent word agreeing to the proposal. During the brief engagement, Timo soon found that he was increasingly eager to wed Hestia. Timo viewed the engagement as a business transaction that could propel his business. At a minimum, he hoped the bride was tolerable. He was not overly concerned because wives and women played a thankless role in Greek life, and he could always find comfort with a slave, if necessary.

Timo was utterly unprepared when he met Hestia. Hestia was young and vibrant, exuding elegance, and charm. Her green eyes completely mesmerized him. Per Philos' wish, the courtship was brief, and they wed at the great Artemision. He prepared for the ceremony thinking only of Hestia, not the considerable dowry Philos had set aside for Hestia's wedding.

Timo could not have been happier. Hestia was more than he could have hoped for in a wife. The dowry helped Timo expand his business, while over time, he and Hestia fell in love. Soon they had a son that Hestia named Petrus, the Greek word for Rock.

Timo had a young wife and son to care for, and with Philos' backing his ventures, Timo's business prospered. Several hundred years earlier, the Greeks had built massive walls and sectioned off an area of Ephesus to build a community of homes for the wealthy. The Romans expanded this area 200 years later, and an affluent Roman community coexisted next to the Greeks. Timo moved his family into one of the older homes in the Greek section.

These wealthy sections were off Curetes Street, about two miles from the harbor. Another, smaller Temple of Artemis was on the eastern end of the community.

Each home was three stories high and built around a large central courtyard. The marble-paved yard greeted guests, while inside, a series of columns supported the structure that housed the bedrooms and kitchen. The open courtyard summoned the hot air from the adjoining rooms and bedrooms, and cooler air from the underground chambers and shaded areas adjoining the home replaced it.

Colorful mosaics and frescoes adorned the interior floors and walls. The frescoes brought vibrant colors into the home and featured scenes from Greek history. Hercules adorned the walls of their home, and one mosaic depicted

Hercules in battle with the Minoan Centaur in Crete. The floor frescoes pictured local farmers chafing wheat and bringing in the harvest. Another wall had colorful frescoes that copied the main Temple of Artemis bas-relief stonework of battles that pitted Mycenaean-Greek soldiers fighting against the Amazon female warriors. Hestia adorned their bedroom walls with frescoes of Artemis hunting with a bow and arrow. Access to and from home was through a side door to a narrow alley leading to the large avenue, Curetes Street.

A daughter, Hessulah, born eight years after Petrus, around 16 BC, would follow. The name Hessulah is the Ephesian name for Elisabet. However, childbirth was dangerous, and there were complications with Hestia's pregnancy that the midwives could not resolve. After a night fraught with panic, pain, exhaustion, and finally optimism upon the baby's birth, the midwives could not stop the internal bleeding, and Hestia died shortly after giving birth to Hessulah. The entire household was in mourning. Hestia had brought joy to the family, and her light was gone.

Timo grew despondent after Hestia's death. He withdrew from his parental responsibilities and handed off the care of his two children to Hestia's sister Hermia. He focused entirely on his business and his grief. Hermia raised the two children for four years.

Timo's shipping business grew, and he traded and transported olive oil, grain, wine, nuts, timber, marble, and building materials across the eastern Mediterranean. Timo's ships serviced ports as far north as Byzantium and into Thrace and Macedonia. His fleet served the Greek cities in Anatolia and the countries of Syria, Samaria, and Judaea on the Levantine coast. They delivered Greek goods bound for the Spice Road that traded with China and India while they acquired precious spice, silk, and tea cargo. He could supply the Mediterranean with grains from the port of Alexandria and the northern African coast between Egypt and Numidia.

For years Timo built a thriving business. His fleet traded with the eastern Mediterranean port cities, including Piraeus, Athens's ancient port. Greece was within his reach, including Corinth and the Greek islands of Cyprus, Crete, Kos, and Rhodes. He dreamed of expanding to Rome, Sicily, Spain, and Numidia and operating the largest fleet across the Mediterranean.

———◄O►———

Ten years before Hessulah's birth, Timo met Assab, who was looking to sign on to a new ship. Timo was impressed with the quick-witted Assab, who spoke several languages. Assab did not appear physically imposing, but his wiry frame masked a hidden strength that Timo felt when they grasped forearms in greeting. Sufficient power coupled with speed and agility often offsets the advantage of powerful men; Timo knew the same was true with fighting ships, as fast, agile ships often overcame a lumbering galley.

Assab loved to talk and told Timo his life story. Assab joined the Egyptian army and found himself one of Cleopatra's bodyguards. Timo hired Assab as a sailor, but soon Assab accompanied Timo as a bodyguard. Over time, they formed a bond, and Assab became Timo's trusted advisor.

When Philos had presented his marriage offer, Timo turned to Assab for advice. Assab would give fair counsel.

"So, summing up the offer," Timo recanted, "in return for marrying his daughter, who may or may not be with another's child, Philos will provide a dowry with enough funds to erase my considerable debts, then he will commit enough business to keep two of my ships busy for an entire year. I have talked to some friends who know his daughter. They say she is quite charming."

"So, what's your problem?"

"Well, suppose she is with child?"

"And what if she is? Raise the child as your own; don't listen to wagging tongues, and she can give you more children. Many men, like me, are not blessed with children; the gods know I try frequently! This offer is too good to refuse. If she grows intolerable, you can always divorce later. If that happens, you risk losing Philos' business, but I wouldn't worry about that now."

"Should I accept the proposal? I agree with you. I needed to hear it from someone. Will you take word to Philos for me? And try to get a peek at my bride, and honestly, let me know what you think of her looks."

On the walk with Assab to the widow's house, Hessulah thought long and hard about who would have the motive to kill her father. His competitors were not ruthless. Timo was strict with his captains, but again no more so than his competitors. His crews were well-fed and paid on time. Like all Greeks, Timo had run-ins with the Roman authorities. Recently, the Romans pressed him to transport their war materials; but he graciously refused and directed them to traders and vessels that might do their bidding.

His murder was no random act of violence, and that dagger belonged to a wealthy man. The now-deceased Roman Cohort was not there by accident. The room had not been disturbed, and he had his money purse; both facts gave attestation that the murder was not random, and Timo knew the murderer.

The only answer that made sense to Hessulah was difficult to fathom. "Why would my brother murder our father?"

At the widow's cottage, she and Assab discussed their next steps and weighed the risks. Assab said, "Whoever killed Timo is in league with the Roman authorities. The Romans will catch and execute us. We must get you out of Ephesus, especially if we find out that Petrus killed Timo. Petrus has the backing of powerful Romans, his Roman friends will be well paid, and they will not stop until they have you."

"So, you think this is the work of Petrus too? If this is Petrus's handiwork, we must warn Vissia as she could be in danger too."

"I doubt that Petrus would hurt Vissia. He has lusted after her since your father brought her from Egypt."

"Regardless, we must let Vissia know; everything will change for her with Papa gone."

Leaving the cottage, they ventured past the Gates of Heracles and the 24,000-seat amphitheater and up the stone Curetes Street past the Library of Celsus. They turned left toward the section of town where the affluent Greeks dwelt.

Walking up the street, they saw two armed sentries standing watch outside her father's house. Guards at her father's home were rare and only used when her father had excessive amounts of money at home. Neither Assab nor Hessulah recognized the guards.

Not leaving anything to chance, she and Assab turned into an alley before they reached the house. They watched from a distance, peering over a stone wall. They decided to wait for the household to stir to see what happened next. After an hour and a half, her brother left the house, and three armed men followed him. The guards appeared to be soldiers by their bearing and gait. But they were not in uniform, presumably, so as not to draw added attention to themselves.

Vissia had awakened at daylight and went down to the kitchen. The servant who prepared some fruits for breakfast asked, "Will the master be joining you this morning?"

"I don't think so; he did not come home last night. Is Hessulah awake?"

"Yes, but she left before sun-up. I think she was worried about the master too." Then the servant then volunteered, "Petrus arrived with bodyguards just after Hessulah went out this morning."

Vissia mainly asked herself, "Why does Petrus have bodyguards." She thought, "Timo did not mention that large amounts of money would be at the house. That was the only time they brought in guards."

Petrus awakened a short while later. He entered the kitchen wearing a clean tunic and held a bundle resembling an old tunic. The servant asked if the tunic needed cleaning. Petrus folded the tunic again and tried to hide it in his clean tunic's folds as if doing so would make the bundle invisible to all. "No! I have it."

Vissia was sitting at a table and said, "Good morning, Petrus. Have you seen your father? He did not come home from the shop last night."

Petrus did not act surprised that Timo was away. But he exclaimed, "Why are you asking me that? I don't know where Timo is."

Vissia thought Petrus's response was somewhat out of place but dismissed it as part of Petrus's normal inconsiderate personality. "Weren't you at the shop with him last night? Timo mentioned that you were going to speak with him yesterday."

Petrus replied, "I never saw him; I had business at the Temple of Diana."

Vissia asked, "Why do you have bodyguards with you? Timo never mentioned that we might have money in the house."

Petrus got up and walked behind Vissia, placing both hands on her shoulders and digging his fingers into them, at first gently, then with more force. He would never have done this if Timo were around. Vissia became visibly uncomfortable. Petrus said, "Why all these questions? There is nothing wrong. Everything is going to be just fine. Don't worry."

Something in Petrus' tone made Vissia uneasy, and she felt a strange chill from this exchange as she stiffened under his touch. "Don't do that, please."

"Where's Hessulah?" he asked as he released his grip and sat.

"I think she went to the shop looking for Timo," Vissia replied.

"Good, very good!" Instead of waiting to be served, he immediately stood and called to his bodyguard, "It's time that we are off." He turned to Vissia. "Don't worry. Everything is under control." Then he walked out of the kitchen with his guard and with the firm belief that the plan was working perfectly.

Vissia sat there perplexed. Timo did not return last night. Hessulah left early to search for Timo. Petrus is acting very strange with his demeanor and bodyguards. A shadow of foreboding overcame her countenance.

———— ❖ ————

Assab and Hessulah watched as Petrus and his entourage left. They waited behind the stone wall until they had passed a safe distance. They entered through the door in the alley and found Vissia still in the kitchen with the servant. Hessulah said to the servant, "Please leave us."

Vissia was distraught that Timo had not come home last night and asked if either knew his whereabouts. Hessulah said, "Vissia, we have terrible news. We found Timo dead at the shop; he is dead, murdered. We had to leave him there when someone from the Urban Cohort showed up and tried to arrest me." Vissia began to sob, slowly coming to grips with her new reality. Her future, once certain, was now very much in doubt. Roman law put her under the protection of Timo's family; she quickly realizes by law Petrus inherits everything that Timo owns, including me. She shuddered, thinking of the familiarity that Petrus had shown her that morning. She could not shake the feeling, were those the hands of a killer on my shoulders?

Hessulah approached Vissia and wrapped her arms around her. Vissia regained her composure and asked, "Who do you think murdered Timo?"

Hessulah said, "We don't know for sure; we took a dagger from his body." Assab pulled the dagger from his belt and showed it to Vissia.

"I don't know that dagger," she replied, "who could have done such a thing?"

"We think either a Roman or someone close to them. We must stay away from the Roman authorities for now."

"I understand. What will you do, Hessulah?"

"Assab and I must leave Ephesus. I will start over elsewhere, and we will find out who murdered father. Do you want to come with us?"

Vissia knew she could not live on the run or in exile. "I wish I could go with you; you were so kind when Timo brought me here, but I would only hinder you." Then Vissia said, "Wait a moment. I have something of yours." Vissia ran upstairs to the bedroom that she had shared with Timo. She came back down carrying a small velvet pouch. "Your father wanted you to have this. He was saving it for the day that you married. He had bought it as a wedding gift for your mother."

Hessulah opened the pouch and pulled out an emerald necklace, matching earrings, and bracelets. It was so unexpected that she did not know how to react. More tears started to run down her face.

"I know that he would want you to have it now. It meant so much to your mother. Where will you go?" Vissia asked.

"I'm not sure yet. Please come with us; we will keep you safe."

Vissia started to ask, "Do you think..." she stopped; she had seen Petrus's hate for Hessulah firsthand; finally, she just said, "You must stay away from your brother. He has always blamed you for your mother's death. He will certainly blame you for Timo's murder as well."

Hessulah drying her eyes, acknowledged the unspoken, "I understand."

The two women hugged and cried.

Finally, Assab said, "We must go, Hessulah."

Once outside the home, Hessulah turned to Assab. "Vissia will stay with Petrus even though she knows Petrus is responsible for my father's death. She has no family in Ephesus and nowhere to go. Petrus always desired Vissia, but I don't think that desire led him to kill Timo or have him killed; there must be another reason."

Outside, Assab asked, "We must focus on getting out of the city before we figure out the reason for this predicament. Is there anyone in the city that you think we can trust?"

Hessulah thought momentarily, "Yes, there is someone I must see. Do you know father's business associate, Zalman the Nabatean? His ship was in the harbor yesterday. He was father's friend, and he is the only one I know with the resources to help us."

"I know Zalman. Zalman drives a hard bargain, but he is an honest man. How can he help us?"

Hessulah's plan sprung into her head. "We must sell these jewels and buy a small trading ship."

"There are always boats for sale. Your brother may not have killed your father, but I fear he is behind it. He is not acting innocent; he must be in league with the Romans and the Urban Cohort. It's not safe for us anywhere if he sent the soldier we met at your father's shop."

"I will take care of the jewels. I will go to Zalman and make him listen to me."

"If the Romans put out the word that a fugitive young girl is wanted for murder, anyone who helped you, including Zalman, will be imprisoned or killed."

"Well then, he better not help a young girl." Hessulah did the only thing she knew to do, what her father and Assab had taught her; she took her future into her own hands. Her life was in danger, and she must get out of Ephesus as the outline of an escape plan formed in Hessulah's mind.

———◦◦◦———

Once Hessulah left, Vissia thought through her predicament. Finally, she came to the only conclusion that made sense to her. She called the servant and said, "Prepare a sumptuous dinner for this evening. Let's make Petrus's favorite roasted lamb for dinner."

"Of course, mistress. How many will there be?"

"There will be the two of us and be sure to serve the good wine."

Petrus had always been kind to her, sometimes in a lustful, unsettling way, but kind, nonetheless. She believed that she could control Petrus and welcomed the change.

———◦◦◦———

Petrus entered his father's shop. Eight soldiers from the Urban Cohort were on the first floor as they had planned. Quintus awaited Petrus on the second floor in Timo's office. Petrus quickly walked upstairs and into the room. Petrus breathlessly inquired upon entering the room, "Did you catch her? Where is that little murderer?"

Quintus said, "No. We found the body that you said would be here and the body of our man that went to pick up your sister."

Petrus looked at the fallen soldier. "Who killed him?"

"I think it was your sister."

"She's a 13-year-old girl. How is she going to kill an experienced Roman legionnaire?"

"Who else could have done it?" asked Quintus.

Petrus drew a blank. "Maybe my sister had some help?"

Petrus looked back at Timo. Something was different from when he was here last. "What did you do with the dagger?"

"There was no dagger."

"Of course, there was a dagger, or else he wouldn't be dead, would he? Did one of your men take it?"

"I left my men downstairs. No one here took anything."

Petrus's lower lip began to tremble. "Damn, Hessulah, by Zeus!"

7

Pandemic, Saint Louis, Missouri, 2020 AD

As a child, Greg learned about his Alsatian roots and a few German phrases from Nana, his grandmother Theresa. The streets Alsace and Lorraine were close to The Sisters of Mercy Convent. The boys in most Catholic elementary schools in South Buffalo thought the Mercy Nuns were a collection of malevolents. In truth, the Sisters of Mercy operated a conglomerate of local Catholic grade schools, a hospital, a cloister, an all-girl Catholic High School, and a two-year Nursing College. They were renowned for being disciplinarians of the grade school students, but they were loved by many. Parents never listened to complains from their children about their teachers as they had survived these teaching methods without any emotional harm.

Like many young women from South Buffalo, Mouse attended their high school and nursing college, while Greg and Mouse attended their local Catholic grade schools.

Of the European immigrants in the 1800s, the Germans and Irish settled in South Buffalo, the Poles on the East Side, the Italians settled the West Side, and immigrants from everywhere meshed in North Buffalo. At that time, the busy port of Buffalo, on the eastern edge of Lake Erie, was a very disreputable place.

Several of Greg's ancestors mentioned in census books listed their heritage as German but with hometowns in Lorraine, France, and not from Germany. Five out of his eight great-grandparents were from the region of Alsace and Lorraine.

Alsace was often listed as Germany in the ship manifests and census records when the migrations were full of swing.

Kaiser Wilhelm seized Alsace's territory when Prussia defeated France in the Franco-Prussian War in 1871. Germany first came to exist as a unified country after 1870, when Otto von Bismarck, the Prussian Prime Minister, masterminded Prussian expansion and the unification of all the German states.

The Alsatians that migrated to America considered themselves Germans in language and heritage, even if their former home had been in French territory. If they migrated before 1870, they left France; after 1871, they left Germany.

Jacob Klaes, Greg's great-great-grandfather, migrated to the U.S., and Buffalo, in the 1850s, listed his home country as Prussia. Greg thought Prussia was in northeast Germany near Poland and not even close to Alsace. It was a piece of the puzzle that required research. Greg thought he solved it when looking at an 1850 map of Alsace-Lorraine. The map depicted a small stand-alone Prussian state called West Prussia that bordered Alsace, while the historical Prussian land lies hundreds of miles to the east bordering Poland. Greg assumed that Jacob was an Alsatian that departed from West Prussia. Similarly, West Bavaria bordered Alsace-Lorraine while the kingdom Bavaria lay to the east.

Jacob Klaes migrated to Buffalo in 1851 with his son Michael. Michael changed his family name from Klaes to Klass by the time of the 1860 census. Greg wondered why Michael would change his last name. It was all family history forgotten in the mists of time. But through the wonders of the Internet, Greg copied pictures of Jacob's and Michael's gravestones in the United French and German Roman Catholic Cemetery in Cheektowaga, New York, a suburb of Buffalo.

Greg thought that, at least in death, the French and German Alsatians in America were united and no longer divided by political borders. Greg knew that was a weird thought as soon as he thought it.

The data showed Greg's ancestors were part of the tremendous Alsatian migration to the U.S. in the early to mid-1800s. Six to eight million German-speaking Alsatians immigrated to America in that period, with many settling around the Great Lakes and, in Greg's case, Buffalo and Western New York. Linguistically, Alsatians brought their distinctive "hard A sound," which is still commonly heard around the Great Lakes from Western New York to Cleveland, Detroit, Chicago, and Milwaukee. Something like, 'I left my keys in the kAHr.'

As for Greg's family, the men's occupations noted in census books as laborers, tradesmen, printers, farmers, mill workers, or hired hands. The women were homemakers, wives, daughters, or widows.

The more Greg learned, the more curious he became, and he was determined to know more. He was surprised by his intense need to find out where his ancestors came from, why they emigrated, what and who they left behind, and any lessons they learned; there must be parents, brothers, sisters, and cousins who stayed.

If his parallel German lineage produced characters as bat-shit crazy as the legendary great uncle Foghorn, he just had to find out about it. Greg heard stories from South Buffalo Irish families that traveled back to their family's village in the 'Old Sod.' Each story ended the same; they met long-lost relatives and drank with them all night at the village pub.

Greg believed the native Irish claimed to be related to their 'American cousins' as a ruse to get free drinks from the gullible Irish American travelers. He wondered if he would have to buy many beers for his long-lost cousins if he went to Alsace.

He'd never heard of any Germans returning to find their roots. Those thoughts and more ebbed in and out of his internet-weary brain. He spent many quiet hours sitting at the dining room table with his computer, scribbling pages of handwritten notes full of question marks and exclamation points. Arrows linked generations and possible connections, real or imagined, in every direction.

He tried to do the online family tree, but that was beyond his computer skills, so he sketched family trees in pencil. His reading glasses were put on and taken off for what seemed like hundreds of times a day due to his near-sightedness. Yet he was undaunted. Like the pandemic, days melted into weeks, and weeks ran into months.

Mouse had never seen her husband like this; he was motivated! She missed his constant, rambling chatter that she had turned a deaf ear to for so many years. Mouse walked into the dining room and announced, "Break time!" Greg looked up from his pile of papers and said, "Huh? What?" *That woman looks familiar.*

Mouse insisted, "It's past time to take a break. We need to talk. Remember our next-door neighbor, Jenn? Yesterday she brought over a freshly baked homemade loaf of her fabulous sourdough bread, and you didn't even look up from the table. It is time to get up, sit in the backyard, and have some time together."

Greg thought in disbelief, *I love that bread! How could I not have noticed or smelled it?*

Mouse was on a roll; her arms were waving around her head. "It's time for you to tell me what's going on with your research. I would like to know more about your family's background and why you care so much. You've never shown any interest in it before this year."

Greg repeated to himself, "I would like to know more about your family's background." *That can't be the woman I married. The woman I married would never utter those words. That lady must be in serious need of companionship and maybe a drink. I best get her one, and I could use a couple myself. I can't believe I missed Jenn's sourdough bread.*

Rather than his usual stony countenance, Greg shouted, "Great idea!" He was eager to share all he had learned about these dead relatives with another living person. Mouse would know the details of the Klass genealogy; the good, the bad and the ugly. He suspected that she couldn't care less; it was just an excuse to have a drink together.

They walked out to the backyard and sat in their deck chairs beneath a large red stand-alone umbrella that blocked the slowly setting sun on this hot July afternoon. At least there was a semblance of normalcy in this simple act. The garden had dried out in the intense Missouri summer heat. Only the flowers that would be comfortable in an untended prairie were now in bloom in their city garden. Only hot colors were evident in mid-summer, bright reds, gaudy oranges, and vivid yellows. The air hung heavy with humidity. Still, the beers were ice cold, and the first slug went down easy.

"Okay, Papa, let's hear it. You better have some scandalous research details, or you're in big trouble."

"Mouse, it's pretty hard to find scandalous details. One great, great someone came to America with a wife not much older than his eldest daughter. A few young children appeared to have died, as they were not in subsequent family records. Life was hard back then." Greg responded readily, "Did you know that I have identified that the Klass name was spelled as either "Klass," "Klas," "Klaas," "Klaes," "Kless" or "Klaus" "Kloss" over the last few centuries? There may be even more spellings out there that I haven't uncovered; wait till I get to the letter 'C.'"

"Fascinating," Mouse replied in an unconvincing voice.

Undeterred, Greg continued, "No, really, I'm serious. And the name, as I have mentioned before, is a derivation of Nicolas. I am trying to determine if Sinter Klaas is a relation. Sinter Klaas is the Dutch version of Santa Claus. I'm close to finding the missing link; there's no doubt about it in my mind." The more Greg talked, the more he convinced himself. "I have researched Nicolas of Myra, the first and authentic Saint Nicolas. I've researched Sinter Klaas, Santa Claus, and Father Christmas. I am close to proving my claim that I am related to Saint Nicolas."

Oh brother, thought Mouse. "Is this how the rest of my life is going to be? My husband thinks he's Jolly Old St. Nick. Nobody said marriage would be easy, but seriously, now I'm supposed to be married to Saint Nick?"

Mouse responded, "Hold your reindeer, Santa Claus. Your blood pressure is probably in the danger zone. Back up a little before we hit the E.R. What *are* you talking about?"

"Mouse, you need to pay better attention to me. I'm sharing my family history with you, and it's unbelievable. I thought it would be obvious to you."

Mouse couldn't help herself. "What's clear to me is you're spending too much time sitting in front of a computer. You've been giving me the Big Freeze. You're wasting time and getting nothing done around the house. You need to get more exercise. All that good beer has found a nice home around your middle. Are you proud of that beer belly? Or is it a "bowlful of jelly?" Mouse was on a roll. "Now that your beard is coming in and it's white, you're starting to remind me of someone. Maybe it's something along the lines of a jolly old elf? Who could that be?"

"That's what I've been trying to tell you, Mouse. I'm not just a Klass. I'm part Klaes, Happ, Schuster, Mertz, Benz, Beilmann, Kuhn, Wack, Willert, Baumgartner, Meyer, McGlynn, Barrett, Seitz, and a whole bunch of others that I've just begun to scratch the surface. With the Internet, there's too much information, so I'm focusing on my great-great-grandparent and the folks from Alsace-Lorraine. I'm ignoring the Irish branch for now."

Greg tried to explain the research that dominated his internal thought processes while searching his family factions, choosing which branches to follow, determining mysteries needing further investigation, and discovering new avenues to find more information when one resource turned into a sudden and infuriating dead end.

"Hmm. Ok, it sounds interesting. Remind me again about this Lorraine-Alsace region." Mouse responded, trying not to sound bored with Greg's mansplaining.

"Mouse, please listen carefully; it's Alsace-Lorraine, and you know it. Over the centuries, political 'ownership' of this region has shifted back and forth between France and Germany. However, until recently, the language in Alsace remained German; actually, the Alsatian dialect is a branch of High German. 'Low German' refers to dialects in the northern areas of Germany near the Netherlands and the North Sea, where the land falls to meet the sea. It seems that generations of my folks were poor—all of them; probably the reason so many emigrated to America."

"Figures," mumbled Mouse. "There's never any money coming my way."

"That's not the point." Greg decided not to go down that line of thinking, as no Klass had ever inherited anything of value. He tried valiantly to refocus Mouse back on his story. "I have found interesting tidbits in my research that I need to research. It's tough to get beyond dates of births, marriages, and deaths and what they did for a living.

You'd have to read old German newspapers to find out, and there are two issues. First, I need help finding old newspapers, and second, I can't read German if I do. There were a lot of newspapers in the early 1900s. Buffalo had about a half dozen German-language newspapers. I am sure there were quite a few in Alsace-Lorraine. Back then, newspapers were the Internet of their day. I'd like to know things, like how they lived, how they got around, and what they were worried about."

Mouse surmised, "I guess you're not coming out of the dining room soon."

"Nope, I have a lot to uncover. But your comment on inheritance didn't go unnoticed and was almost funny."

"I'm not being funny, just realistic, as usual. One of us must. Who do you think has been cooking, cleaning, shopping for groceries, watching the grandchildren, doing the laundry, and keeping this house afloat while you surf the net?"

Greg pouted, "I'm not just surfing the net; I'm finding my roots. I always wondered about my ancestors, where we came from, and what they did. If I can document their past and add stuff about our lives, our grandchildren and great-grandchildren will appreciate it.

"It's giving those that come after us their heritage, and some of the things we do will turn into their traditions. We're all immigrants or children of immigrants. You can be anything in America, but people need to pay attention to where they're from and what made them. It's privileged and critically important work. Heck, for my whole life, I thought I was second generation, and with just a little research, I've found out that I'm fourth generation and that my grandmother spent years in an orphanage."

"You are all over the place with these ideas. Were you the constantly distracted kid with his desk moved next to the teacher's desk in grade school?" Mouse knew she was on to something Greg had never shared about his childhood, one of the few stories they had not shared over their long years.

"Not answering that. Now, you're trying to distract me. Let me give you a few snippets. Remember how I said that the name Klass is a derivation of Nicolas? Well, I've been having lots of fun with Google Maps trying to find exactly where Alsace-Lorraine is these days."

Mouse snickered, "You call that fun? You are getting old! Okay, I give; what does Saint Nicolas have to do with the Alsatians?"

"That's a great question; what does Saint Nicolas have to do with the Alsatians? I am glad you asked." Greg learned how to respond to a question from watching too many political debates; one should always repeat the question and thank the questionnaire. "I googled Nicolas, Lorraine, Alsace, and various derivations of Klass. Well, as it turns out, I discovered that the capital of the Duchy of Lorraine is a city called Nancy, or Nance, and one of its suburbs is the City of Saint Nicolas-de-Port. A French Duchy is like a state here. By the way, I found you don't spell Nicolas with an 'h,' as in the original Saint Nicolas.

"In the City of Saint Nicolas-de-Port, in Lorraine, France, there is a major cathedral called the Basilica of Saint Nicolas. Google Maps drills down to the exact location of the Basilica within the city. The name Nicolas keeps popping up repeatedly in my Klass family searches."

"OK. So, Nicolas, no 'h,' was a popular name for people, places, and things. What's your point, Santa?"

"What's my point? That's another great question! Glad you're finally interested in getting to the point, Mouse."

"Move it along. I don't have all day."

"I need to change my venue for this research. When all this staying-safe-at-home business is over, let's go to Europe! What do you think of going to Paris?"

Immediately, Mouse's mood improved from zero–to–sixty in no time. "I've always wanted to see The City of Lights."

"We can go there too, right after seeing Paris, " cracked Greg in Klass-humor. "I thought you'd like that idea. While we are there, we can take a few days, hop a train, venture into Alsace-Lorraine, and see where the ancestors came from and what that's all about too."

"I'm all in! We never made it there for our honeymoon." She responded while thinking; I hope the poor bastards over there don't all look like Greg.

Greg had bought time; it could be a couple of years until it was safe to travel internationally again. Mouse started reading book after book about France and French culture. She read romance novels set in Paris in WWII. She read historical fiction about Joan of Arc, Marie Antoinette, and Josephine Bonaparte. She fantasized about visiting a French atelier and owning a couture dress. She read up on Julia Child's French cooking techniques and served coq-a-vin.

Meanwhile, Greg continued his ancestral research, usually going off on too many digressions and digging deeper and deeper into French and German history. He continued with his charts and notes and thoroughly enjoyed being an armchair traveler before going on the real thing.

Mouse and Greg enjoyed a dry hard cider in the backyard on a mild October afternoon. Both had decided that to be sophisticated European travelers, they had to expand their alcohol profile beyond beer. Today they found it a delightful lesson trying out these ciders.

"Mouse, I've been listening to the not-so-subtle hints you've been dropping. I promise you that while in France we'll be sure to see every tourist site your heart desires. We will eat so many French pastries in the morning that you will yearn for cornflakes again. We'll march around French castles and sip French wines at every chance."

"Mai, oui! Oui, oui, oui!"

"One thing is bugging me about this Saint Nicolas thing," lamented Greg.

"What's that?" an already bored Mouse asked.

Greg continued, "It's about the City of Saint Nicolas in Lorraine, France. As you may recall, I mentioned that the Duchy of Lorraine is French. Most people from Lorraine speak French, but quite a few speak German, although the French tried to stomp it out once or twice. In one respect, France is like America, trying to suppress immigrant languages, except Alsatians in France aren't immigrants; they are natives; Alsatians were there before there was a France. But what interests me is they named the City and Basilica for Saint Nicolas."

"Yes, you said all of that before," yawned Mouse.

Greg was on a roll getting to this point, "I researched the original Saint Nicolas. Saint Nicolas is neither German, French, or Alsatian, nor is he from northern Scandinavia or Lapland, where there are reindeer. He's from a city called Myra."

"So, is Myra a suburb or village in Lorraine?" Mouse replied while studying her fingernails.

"Not at all; Myra is in Turkey."

"So, Saint Nicolas is Turkish?" Mouse's attention had turned to a fly buzzing the deck.

"No, he's Greek."

"You just said he was from Turkey." Mouse was reaching for an emery board as the fly had flown away.

"I said he was from Myra, which is now in Turkey. But he's not Turkish."

"You can cut the Abbott and Costello routine, Greg."

"Sure, but this is the interesting part." Greg instructs Mouse on everything he learned of Myra, "Myra is on the southern coast of the Anatolia Peninsula. Anatolia is a large geographic region on the Asian side of Turkey; it forms present-day Turkey's western and southern coasts. But Turks won't arrive there until 800 years after Nicolas lived. The Greeks founded and settled Anatolia. These Greek cities were part of small regional kingdoms. Myra was part of a kingdom called Lycia when Nicolas was born in 280 A.D.; all the inhabitants of Myra were Greek."

Mouse had finished filing her nails and decided on a bright red fingernail polish.

To help clarify his dilemma, Greg pulled up an ancient map of the Mediterranean world on the Mac and gave Mouse a history and geography lesson, even though Mouse doesn't care for geography or ancient history.

Greg droned on and gave a comprehensive descriptive overview of the eastern Mediterranean Sea and the lands it washes.

"Greg, you need to get a life. Besides, I can read a map."

Unperturbed, Greg continued, "Yes, I know. The unfortunate city of Troy overlooked the Aegean from the northwest coast of the Anatolia Peninsula. To the south of Troy, ancient Greeks, Ionians, Boeotians, and Dorians settled on the western shores of Anatolia. The kingdoms of Lycia and Cilicia border each other on the southern shore; all these cities and kingdoms were Greek. Interestingly, Cilicia became synonymous with the word 'pirate' when the Cilician pirates dominated the Mediterranean in the second century and early in the first century B.C. Cilician pirates controlled the Mediterranean Sea and were a constant threat to the security of Rome."

Feigning interest Mouse asked, "Is Cilicia where Sicily comes from?"

"No, Sicily is in Sicily; Cilicia is in Anatolia. Stay with me."

Mouse yawned, "Oh."

Greg rambled on, "The coastline of Anatolia was rocky, sun-drenched, and strategic. It enticed conquerors throughout the ages because it was just that strategic. Anatolia is where Europe meets Asia; it's the end of the Spice Road from China. The Nile and northern Africa are a hop, skip and jump away. Back then, Egypt was Rome's Iowa. All the grain that Rome consumed was grown in Egypt. Every few hundred years, a new conqueror of Anatolia would bring in a new set of laws, customs, and religion. They'd tear down everything old and build again. The dynasty would stick around for a few hundred years, and a new conqueror would arrive. Usually, they would build new cities on top of the old because, even back then, you couldn't beat location, location, location. The interior of Anatolia was mountainous and inhabited by nomadic tribes endlessly herding their flocks to better pastures. The coastline of Anatolia became the playground of kings and emperors because of its weather, the shore, and the sea. It was the epicenter of Western Civilization as we know it. The Eastern part of the Roman Empire stretched from Libya in North Africa to Greece and the Balkans.

"The Romans called the Anatolia Peninsula and the countries to the south' Asia Minor'. Ephesus was the capital of the Eastern Roman Empire at the time of Christ. It had the second busiest port in the world, second to Ostia, the port of Rome. In the fourth century A.D., Emperor Constantine renamed Byzantium Constantinople; Constantinople is now called Istanbul. Constantinople replaced Rome as the seat of the Roman Empire in 330 A.D."

Mouse yawned again, "Is there a point to this geography lesson?"

Greg continued, his voice gaining volume and speed, "Yes, there is. By Christ's birth, the Greeks lived on the Anatolian coast for over 1,000 years. Saint Nicolas, a real person, was Greek and was born in 280 AD. He lived in Myra on the southern coast of the Peninsula; Saint Nicolas died, in Myra, in 345 AD."

Greg pointed to the map. "My question is, 'What the hell are his bones doing in Lorraine, in the middle of France, not far from Paris? He was a nice enough guy to become a saint, I guess, but why would Alsatians, who lived in France, care about a Greek saint from Asia Minor?'" Greg pointed to France and Turkey on the map.

Uninterested, Mouse replied, "When are you going to get with the times Greg, B.C., and A.D. are old school? Everything is BCE and CE"

Exasperated, Greg muttered, "Missing the forest for the trees. There's more to this story. Besides leaving gifts for some kids, Nicolas was the patron saint of sailors. That's it."

"Maybe Alsatian sailors brought him to Lorraine," Mouse solved the puzzle for him and added, "And my glass is empty."

"What Alsatian sailors? I just showed you a map. Alsace-Lorraine is landlocked. Alsatians are not maritime people; something doesn't add up." Greg's eyes started to twinkle. He loved a good mystery almost as much as his beer.

8

Missouri Baptist Hospital, St Louis, MO 2020 AD

The Imaging machine would periodically beep as Bonnie took measurements and pictures. Mouse lay on her back as the technician rolled a handheld camera across her stomach and side, trying to get the most accurate images. Greg sat in a chair, watching the procedure. Due to the Covid-19 pandemic, each wore a cloth mask, while the technician also wore a clear plastic face shield and other Personal Protective Equipment or PPE, an acronym no one knew until the pandemic.

The command 'inhale and hold' was followed by 'exhale.' Greg watched the black, grey screen as the dark cloud-like view shifted; suddenly, bright red and green colors flashed. These vivid colors greatly enhanced standard screens' black, grey, and white. Greg had no idea if that was good or bad and wanted to avoid interrupting and asking a question that he knew would not be answered anyway, nor did he want to ask a question that might cause Mouse more concern.

Like everyone who has ever taken a CT scan, Mouse asked the technician, "Did you see anything? I am a retired nurse. You can tell me, and I won't say anything to the doctor."

Mouse got the technician's standard reply, "I only take the pictures. I can't read them." No one who has ever asked that question has ever believed that answer, but you don't press further because you will never get a different response, and you don't want to compromise someone's job. But Bonnie volunteered. "Your doctor will have these pictures in less than two hours. You can call them for your results."

They left the exam room, and Greg took Marge's arm and helped walk her down the corridor to the exit by the parking valet. Mouse said despondently, "Two hours and my doctor will have the results! It's been nice knowing you. Results are never available in two hours, especially not good results."

Having arrived at the same conclusion and equally glum at the prospective news, Greg replied, "It's your positive attitude that is your most endearing quality."

They both chuckled as the scan only confirmed the previous diagnosis and the rate of progression. They knew they were in for a hard fight and a fight that would only have one outcome.

Mouse and Greg left 'MO-BAP' Hospital, located in a wealthy western suburb of Saint Louis, and began their 20-minute drive to their city home near downtown. Mouse had spent almost 40 years in nursing until forced retirement due to severe Rheumatoid Arthritis. The years of medication left Mouse with a severely impacted immune system. They had been ultra-careful to limit their exposure since the Coronavirus, or Covid-19, would probably be lethal for Mouse. Six months of carefully following the Covid-19 protocols left them both a little tired and bored.

But Mouse had dodged that bullet only to contract another foul disease. Though not fatal to all, her immune system, after years of RA treatment, had left her at a severe disadvantage, with a prognosis of a range of years but not a long range. The doctors advised rest and medications that would keep her comfortable. She could buy a little more time if she fought it aggressively, but that would be at the expense of a good quality of life.

Greg was unprepared for such a devastating diagnosis; these things always happened to others, not someone close to him. Mouse's professional life was working in oncology and being the managing RN at a local Women's Breast Clinic. She had worked with and comforted many who received terrible news like this. Death was part of her professional life.

Now she was determined to face hers with the same courage and dignity as her patients. She was determined to make the time left about quality rather than quantity. On the other hand, Greg was a mess, Mouse always called him an emotional cripple, and it clearly showed.

"Greg, I still want to take that trip to France, we promised each other when you proposed forty years ago. I want to go to Paris."

"Remember that Mouse? Our bank account could only get us a week in Jamaica, we drove to Canada and flew out of Toronto because their flights are cheaper."

"Well, I don't care what it costs now."

"Mouse, you have always cared about what something cost!"

"I think I am running out of time."

"Stop talking like that. Anyways, no one is traveling internationally right now with this pandemic roaring. But I will try to figure something out. On a more positive note, I did hear some news on that Census job. They figured out their Covid-19 safety protocols for the other enumerators, and they will contact me in about a month to start.

"Great, that will get you out of the house."

"That works for me too, Mouse."

9

Port of Ephesus, 6 BC

The Vixen[1]

---

1. Credits: Quora, Augusta Stylianou

ZALMAN SAT IN HIS ship's quarters reading bills of lading. He was due to sail back to Caesarea in two days. He was too old to attend the festival, which always brought a sad memory.

Zalman was an enigma to most that knew him. He was from the rock-hewn city of Petra, the capital of the wealthy kingdom of Nabataea, a desert kingdom east and south of Judaea. The Nabataeans were a Bedouin Arab tribe from northern Arabia. Petra has a population of 25,000, which is remarkable considering the city is in the desert. An impenetrable two-kilometer maze of rock walls separates the city from invading forces. Any attacking force had to defeat the desert elements before reaching the maze, where they became easy targets for Petra archers.

Inside the fortress, the Nabataeans engineered an elaborate system of cisterns and aqueducts, salvaging every drop of rainwater in the area. The rock walls and desert protected the Nabataean nation while the Nabataeans guarded the water. The small nation gained immense wealth from the caravan trade between China and India in the east and the Mediterranean kingdoms to the west. Nabataea thrived due to its rugged terrain, remoteness, the desert, and its strategic positioning on the spice and silk trade routes.

Decades earlier, the Nabatean wealth needed an outlet to grow. The Elders selected Zalman to bridge the divide between Nabataea and the western world. They recruited a Magi who introduced Zalman to Pharoah Cleopatra, who had recently wed her third husband, Marc Antony, the Roman Triumvirate who ruled the Eastern Roman Empire. Zalman financed several of Cleopatra's businesses, including timber harvested from Rough Cilicia in southeastern Anatolia, then delivered to the mills and shipyards along the Levantine coast.

Cleopatra introduced Zalman to Herod, the king of Judaea. Herod and Cleopatra operated several joint business ventures that began after Herod and his father, Antipater, rescued Cleopatra's second husband, Julius Caesar, in Alexandria. Cleopatra influenced Herod and enticed him to build massive projects. Consequently, Herod developed an appetite for construction, an appetite that needed funding to flourish, and Zalman had the fortune of a nation to invest.

As their business relationship flourished, Zalman denounced his desert gods, converted to Judaism, and married one of Herod's daughters, who bore him two sons: Michael and Jacob. Shortly after the marriage, Zalman and his wife decided it was safer to maintain distance from the Herodian Court in Jerusalem. They raised their sons in the Hebrew faith.

News of Timo's death swept through Ephesus and shook Zalman; he and Timo had been friends and business associates for twenty years. Zalman made discreet inquiries into the circumstances surrounding Timo's murder, but strangely, the authorities did not conduct a formal investigation. There was a rumor that Timo's young daughter was involved, but the story's details seemed circumspect. The lack of an inquiry was highly unusual, considering Timo was an influential Ephesian businessman. Timo's household turned away a servant Zalman sent to inquire after the family.

Michael came into his quarters, "Father, there's a young street urchin on the dock asking to speak to you. He is stubborn and won't leave. Shall I turn him away more forcefully?"

Curious, Zalman said, "No, let's see what he wants." They went to the dock to meet the boy. The boy was slight and not very tall but had clear green eyes, and his clothes were shabby but clean. A new Phrygian cap covered his head, giving the street urchin the appearance of a farm boy from interior Anatolia.

When he looked into those eyes, Zalman knew that the 'boy' was Timo's daughter. Zalman noticed that the boy was carrying a familiar velvet pouch. Zalman would let the charade play out; his lip curled into a half smile before he regained the swaggering disposition of a dour, wealthy trader.

The boy said, "Sir, people in the port say you are an honest merchant and a man of his word."

"Indeed? I don't know why anyone would say that." Zalman answered, "How may I be of service?"

Hessulah handed Zalman the velvet pouch. "I need to sell this, sir, but I need a fair price."

"Where did you get this pouch?" he asked, "Did you steal it?"

"No, sir. It belonged to my mother, but she died as I was born. My father left it for me. He died recently." Zalman noticed the urchin trying to gauge his reaction to this last bit of news. Zalman kept his gaze steady.

"I am sorry about your parents, but that's not my concern. May they both receive Artemis's blessing. What is in here?" Zalman asked as he examined the velvet pouch. It wasn't a question as he knew the answer; before Hessulah could answer, he barked, "What is your name, boy?"

"I am named after the great Phrygian king, Midas."

"Oh, 'Midas' is it!" Zalman chuckled.

It had been many years since Zalman had held that pouch. He turned away and stared at the sea as he briefly took a deep breath and exhaled, releasing the sadness at what the Fates allowed to pass. Zalman turned to Hessulah and opened the pouch. As he suspected, it was the jewelry he had sold to Timo 20 years earlier: an exquisite emerald necklace, matching emerald bracelets, and emerald earrings. Timo bought the jewelry from him as a gift for his new bride, Hestia. To cover up the tears that had welled in his eyes, Zalman immediately complained, "This is poor artistry; whoever cut these stones must have used a club. The stones are not very clear. Have they ever been cleaned?" He continued. "The weather is foul; it's bad luck to buy jewelry in foul weather." Zalman always complained when bargaining, and he continued, "What am I to do with these if I buy them? Who would buy these poor stones from me?" he continued his tirade. "What will you do if I give you money for these? I can't see that they are worth much. Maybe you could use the money to find a girl and get married?" He declared as if getting married solved everything.

Hessulah knew these bargaining tactics as her father was a master of them. She momentarily enjoyed the banter and thought Zalman to be kinder than he let on. This exchange helped her understand why her father had admired Zalman. The tirade was his test, and she could not let desperation show. She immediately protested, "The quality of the stones is beyond reproach. And what I intend to do with the money is my business, but it certainly does not include finding a wife and getting married." She decided to name a price well below the value of the jewels. Hessulah was anxious to complete the deal and keep her identity intact; she said, "However, I need money; I think a fair price is..."

Before she could name a sum, Zalman interrupted, not allowing her to finish, "I can't possibly pay any more than seven hundred fifty silver pieces!" he wailed, acting as if she hustled him. Hessulah was shocked; it was more than twice what she knew the jewelry to be worth and far more than she hoped to collect.

"Are you sure?" She asked incredulously. Her need to protest and counter his offer vanished. She wanted to argue for him to lower the price, but she held back and stammered, "Seven hundred fifty is more than generous."

"I only wish I could do more," he said. "Walk with me to the temple where I keep my funds, and we can talk on the way." As they walked, Zalman instructed Midas on the role of the temples regarding money. "Temples are always guarded and serve as places where money lenders can safely transact business. Ironically, some people use temples as a house of worship." He chuckled at his humor. "Wealthy people keep their funds spread around multiple temples. That lowers their risk if one temple has a fire or theft. People with extra money lend it to others who pay back the original funds with interest. Money lent is working for you. Midas, what do you intend to do with the money for the jewelry, if I may ask?"

"I want to buy a small trading vessel and become a trader."

"A boat, you say. What does a Phrygian farm boy know about sailing?"

"I know a lot about sailing. My father taught me. I'm not a farm boy. I like the hat."

"I see. Have you found a boat to buy?"

"Yes, it's an old boat, but completely seaworthy. It can carry several tons of supplies. I intend to start trading along the coast. It only needs a crew of four."

"How are you going to find a crew?"

"Well, my father's servant is an Egyptian who knows how to sail and is my first mate. I will be the captain and the pilot. He is at the docks collecting a crew now."

"I see. Here we are, then. Let me find someone to go to the vault with us, and we can make the exchange."

About twenty years earlier, Zalman had been in love with a beautiful girl with bright green eyes. But the girl was Greek, and Zalman was Nabataean. Greeks married Greeks, and Arabs married Arabs; the relationship had little chance, but they fell in love. They met at Artemisia, the great Festival of Artemis, where unmarried men and women, regardless of race or religion, interacted in various settings while looking for a future spouse. Zalman regaled Hestia with tales of caravans, desert flowers, water that flowed from rocks, and his home, a city carved out of stone. They enjoyed each other's company at the festival and played many festival events. The attraction was mutual and rapidly escalated.

After that first encounter, they met secretly for a period. Attraction turned to love, and then the Fates intervened. With a generous bridal gift in hand, Zalman went to her father and asked for her hand. The bridal gift was an exquisite necklace, bracelet, and earrings that matched Hestia's deep green eyes. But her father refused and turned him away; his daughter would marry a wealthy Ephesian or, at minimum, a rich Greek. He forbade Hestia from seeing Zalman again; the rejection dealt Zalman's dreams of his newfound love a cruel blow.

By coincidence, several weeks later, a young man sought him in the market in need of a wedding gift for his new bride. The man described his new bride, and Zalman knew that Hestia's father had arranged a marriage for her. After negotiation over the jewels, Zalman found the young groom to be both honorable and hard-nosed. Knowing that the choices for his beloved Hestia could be much worse, Zalman sold the young man the emerald necklace with matching bracelets and earrings for a fair price, slightly more than what he had paid. He wrapped the gift in a velvet pouch. The wedding gift was the first of many amicable transactions between the two, as Timo and Zalman became business acquaintances and friends.

Midas thanked Zalman, "I am going to honor my father's memory and build a vast shipping fleet."

Zalman slipped up and said something that took Hessulah aback, "Yes, I am sure you will do honor to his memory; you have so much of your mother in you." Zalman quickly changed the subject before Hessulah could question him on what that meant, "I need to return to my ship. Let's go quickly."

10

Compton Heights, St Louis, MO, 2020 AD

Definition of "Translation"
- Version in another language
- Expressing something in a different language
- Change or transference
- Process determining amino acid sequence
- Motion in a straight line
- Removal of holy objects (such as relics) from one place to another

---

Some referred to the pandemic of 2020 as a year in Purgatory. Personal isolation continued due to ongoing worries of contagion. Seasons slowly pass, as tiny family groups celebrate birthdays, weddings become small intimate affairs with only ten guests or less in attendance, and obituaries have the requisite line noting "a celebration of life to be held at a future date."

People became immune to the death count as it climbed by the hundreds and thousands per day. At first, 25,000 seemed like a considerable number of dead, but it rose steadily to 100,000—200,000—250,000—then 350,000— and climbing.

Still, life slowly opened in commerce, education, business and government offices, restaurants, and religious services, but everyone agreed that it bore little resemblance to society before 2020. It took too many months to count before Americans traveled internationally again.

In addition to all her usual household tasks and family obligations, Mouse used the intervening months to prepare for their trip to France. She practiced basic French phrases by listening to her 'How To Speak French' CD while driving in her car. She bought new clothes online for herself and Greg, hoping they would not be readily identified as Americans, although their French, or lack thereof, would completely give them away.

Greg's continuing research in the dining room was no longer a novelty. Mouse ignored him, not regularly checking to see if he needed anything to eat or drink or if he would like a few minutes of her company. Frankly, she thought he must be nodding off for long periods just out of boredom and sitting in one place for such extended periods.

One day, Mouse happened to catch her husband's eye. "With all the research, what will you do, write a book?" She was joking, of course. "Stranger things have happened, but that is a good idea. I have a lot of material. Besides, what else is there to do during this quarantine? The kids won't let the grandkids visit, and when they do, we must stay at a distance and can't even hug them. How can you stand six feet from a one-year-old when they reach out to you and not pick them up? The grandkids don't understand." Greg grumbled.

"You write a book?" That comment almost floored Mouse. "You don't even read for pleasure anymore."

"Maybe I am more of the screenplay writer-type."

"Hah! Now it's a movie! Okay, Santa, who will play you in your movie?"

"Please stop calling me Santa, and I do read for pleasure, sometimes. Brad Pitt played Dr. Fauci on Saturday Night Live. He can play me in the movie, although he would have to get in shape."

"Get into your shape? By drinking beer every day?"

"Precisely, it takes years of training. I didn't get into this shape overnight. It's not easy being me; Brad will probably win an Oscar."

"Well, if Brad Pitt plays you, I am playing myself in the movie. Your screenplay will need a lot of Mouse and Papa love scenes."

"Perfect. It will give you something to do outside of the house."

"You won't like it if I'm hanging out with Brad. All the long hours on a movie set, just me and Brad!"

"If you are happy, I am too."

Mouse said, "No, really think about it—you're talking about movie scripts, Brad Pitt, and wasting time and money on finding your long-lost ancestors — when will you ever stop dreaming?"

"Don't complain about money; we haven't spent a dime since this pandemic started. I will stop dreaming when I win the lottery.

"So, how is your research coming?"

"I hit a brick wall; I found one branch that goes back to Europe in the 1500s but nothing of import. I'm almost out of ideas. I will see if the Saint Nicolas Basilica in France can help me.

After months of sitting in front of his computer, Greg had reached an impasse in his ancestry research. He was frustrated and knew he needed additional help in his genealogy pursuit. So, he decided to contact anyone who could help him, and he focused on the support staff of the Basilica of Saint Nicolas website in Saint Nicolas-de-Port, France.

By now, Greg thought the name Nicolas was a good luck charm for him, and the Basilica must hold the key to unlock the next piece of the Klass puzzle. Greg never questioned why a stranger would give him a morsel of aid; he just bulldozed onward in his merry way.

He repeatedly wrote and revised his email inquiry to the purely anonymous "support@basilica.com" address. In his request, he tried to sound intelligent, even scholarly, not the goofy daydreamer Mouse regarded him. He painstakingly explained his quest, what he had found so far in his amateurish pursuit, and the critical need for professional expertise and assistance.

Mouse asked, "What are you going to ask them?"

Greg said, "I want them to do a DNA test on St Nick's bones. There are stories of harvesting marrow from Saint Nick's bones and using it to cure sick people."

"That's gross; they will think you are nuts and will never answer you."

"I bet they give out the DNA to help pull in revenue." Greg believed that 95% of religions existed to take your money to sustain an excessive lifestyle for church leaders. And that the remaining religions are extinct. Greg had little faith in organized religion.

"But will you do me a favor?"

"Sure, what's that, Mouse?"

"Don't you dare ask them for the DNA from the bones of some long-dead Saint; especially, don't ask for Santa Claus's DNA."

"And why not? I bet people make that request all the time."

"I bet people NEVER request that. They will think you are nuts, and you are not going to embarrass me by asking." Mouse thought, "When I met him, Greg was a young bank executive, good-looking, well-educated, and in shape; he did not make much money, but he had potential. We did okay over the years, but when did he become a moron?"

Fourteen days had passed since Greg sent his email request. He checked his email three times a day, searching for a response from the Basilica. He opened his junk file folder in case Yahoo misfiled it. In his mind, "the Basilica" began to take on a human persona. He was sure that although "the Basilica" did not yet contain the hint of a person's name, it had a strong, beating heart ready and willing to join in his passionate search. Greg careened through these days of waiting like the proverbial bull in a China shop. Mouse avoided her sullen-faced husband by watching HGTV in the sunroom far from their dining room. It worked for both.

On the fifteenth day, Greg was finally smiling. In all his months of research, figuratively "walking" alone up and down the myriad footways of the Alsace-Lorraine region, he hoped he might soon find a person to communicate with about his elusive gene pool, even if his gene pool turned out to be shallow. A person who might help to connect the dots of his heritage. A person who would appreciate his quest back through time to unravel his ancestry. A person who would go about their work and not mutter porky phrases under their breath while walking past the dining room doorway. And that person seemed to be one Emmanuelle Chasteté.

Emmanuelle Chasteté's initial response was brief and professional:

Dear Mr. Klass,

I appreciate your interest in the Basilica of Saint Nicolas-de-Port. While I thought your inquiry was intriguing, unfortunately, here at the Basilica, we maintain the heritage of the Basilica, and the Basilica does not offer genealogical services other than providing our records to the various genealogy companies. However, if you would like to donate to support the activities of the Basilica of Saint Nicolas-de-Port, please click on the corresponding link noted below. Thank you in advance for your generous financial assistance.

Amities,

Emmanuelle Chasteté
Associate Director of Museum Studies and Development
The Basilica of Saint Nicolas
City of Saint Nicolas-de-Port
Lorraine, France
Donations.basilica.saintnicolas.org

Getting hit up for a donation bothered Greg, especially in the initial contact, but he finally had a contact name. He was curious to know if Emmanuelle was the person he was looking for; if not, she could point him in the right direction. If she couldn't help, he could always ask for Santa's DNA and give the French one more reason to despise Americans. Emmanuelle's title was impressive; Greg needed to figure out what an Associate Director of Museum Studies and Development did during one's workday. He liked to imagine that she carried a lot of clout at the

Basilica. Greg assumed soliciting donations was a constant thing for them. He surmised that was the first thing the Church taught.

He thought about sending a $100 check to the Basilica of Saint Nicolas. Still, Greg—being highly superstitious—feared that if he were stingy with his money, Emmanuelle Chasteté would be cheap with assistance. He had a better idea. He decided to donate online. Online would be much faster, even though it took Greg an hour to figure out how to do it.

Along with the donation, Greg went into much greater detail in the Note Section, giving Emmanuelle an expanded version of his many months of research. He summarized his genealogical lines, a list of the towns his ancestors came from, and a generational run down on who begat who. Or is it who begat whom?

He hit several historical stumbling blocks before the mid-1800s, depending on the family branch he was tracking down. His primary issue was the need for more research databases, as the online stuff for European lineage was challenging to access, and he needed to speak German or French. The sites require monthly fees too, but Greg was tight with a buck.

The European side of Greg's family was difficult to trace. He discovered a family branch in the 1500s, but that was an online post from another researcher. He hoped Emmanuelle understood the gist of his message. He listed as many family names, dates of birth, and hometowns as he could. "I bet this will impress her." He said out loud to himself.

He made sure to reference his great-great-great grandfather Nicholas Meyer, and great-great-great grandfather Nicholas Schuster since the very name "Nicholas" might catch her eye, being the same name as her place of employment and its very-great Saint. He signed it 'Klass from Elsass, ' playing on the German spelling of Alsace. He hoped she didn't complete the rhyme the way his childhood friends would. "Klass from Elsass is an a..."

Emmanuelle's response to Greg was as brief as her first one. Of course, Greg read more into it. He thought it was warmer in tone and character. Unless his imagination ran away with him, he felt her email was gracious and courteous. She signed off as:

Amitiés sincères,
Emmanuelle

Greg went to Google to translate 'Amitiés sincères.' He wondered, "Is Emmanuelle trying to make a connection with me?" Greg's chest puffed out a little bigger at that thought. After this response, Emmanuelle asked Greg to provide even more family history, including any family myths, characteristic traits, or morsels of gossip, no matter how seemingly insignificant. She concluded her email message with a request for him to 'please stay in touch.'

Greg smiled at the thought of having an international friend. Greg's mind replayed what he read in her email, that Emmanuelle had explicitly agreed to help him trace his heritage but cautioned him not to tell anyone since 'it could mean her job.'

Emmanuelle's factual reply was, "If I find some spare time, I will try to locate some resources that you might investigate. I am busy now."

Over the next few weeks, Greg sent many emails to Emmanuelle and had yet to receive a response. Things changed several weeks later. Greg received an email from Emmanuelle. "My project concerning Covid-19 protocols just finished. I am working from home with spare time on my hands. I will see if I can help look into your family records." Greg, who lived in a fantasy world, was enthralled by the covert aspect of their relationship. He didn't tell Mouse — wherever she might have been hiding in the house. Greg and Emmanuelle were soon corresponding across the Atlantic weekly.

Even in Greg's blurry mind, this was not a hanky-panky-seeking, sleazy relationship with a young, hot French babe. Though he had no basis to believe she was young or hot. The association was platonic and professional; he would tell Mouse about Emmanuelle when the time was right.

He thought that an objective viewer might construe their association as that of a professor towards her less mentally adroit student, but that wasn't quite it either. Perhaps Greg and Emmanuelle were friends with an eccentric bond that intersected centuries ago. They may be kindred spirits able to connect in the ether of the internet. Greg knew that was an odd thought but a pleasant one.

Finding corresponding by email to be both slow and awkward, they soon began to talk on the phone. Emmanuelle and Greg were relaxed and friendly in their real-time conversations now. She had the most delightful accent, and Greg knew he sounded like an old guy from the middle of the U.S., which he was.

"I'm thirty-three years old, but most people say I'm an 'old 33'. I'm not sure what that means, but I like older music like Pearl Jam and Radiohead," Emmanuelle confessed in one of their early calls.

"I have never heard of them. Are they new bands? My music is older. Are you thirty-three? Wow! Any age where the two digits are the same is a fine age. You have your whole life in front of you, ready to explore. How lucky for you, Emmanuelle." Greg replied and immediately thought, "Why are you blathering? Any age where the digits are the same? How is that relevant? How stupid am I?" He was glad she could not see sweat forming on his forehead. "Of all places, how did you end up working at a church in Lorraine? Many of my ancestors were from a small town in Lorraine called Ippling, and other nearby villages, like Sarreguemines, whose name I can't quite pronounce."

"Sarreguemines is a charming town. I have driven through Ippling, but it's more rural and less quaint than Sarreguemines." Emmanuelle continued, "Well, it is not easy getting a job in France these days, especially if one has a degree in Antiquities and Library Sciences, even if it is from the University of Paris. But I have been here at the Basilica for about 15 years, so I think of it as a second home now."

"You went to the University of Paris?"

"Yes, I graduated from the Sorbonne."

"Oh, I thought you said you went to the University of Paris."

"Yes." Emmanuelle thought, "How dumb are Americans? I will let him wallow in his stupidity for a bit."

There was a pause as Greg, trying to sort through this exchange, thought, "She's French and doesn't understand simple English. And I don't understand a word of French. We will have these moments, I guess."

"Right, well, what do you do for the Basilica besides helping people like me?"

"I'm usually too busy to help people like you. But things slowed once we put in the protocols for the pandemic. We last had services or events a few months ago. I'm the only one that even comes into the office these days."

"Do you get many requests like mine?"

"Nothing related to genealogy. I do get weird requests now and then. Once, someone asked me for some of Saint Nicolas's bone marrow so that they could conduct DNA research. What a creepy request that was. What is wrong with some people?"

"No kidding? Americans, I bet. Some people have no manners; that's so obscene." Greg immediately thought, "I'm not the only one; wait till I tell Mouse." Quickly changing the subject, Greg said, "What do people your age do for fun in France, so far from Paris?" Honestly, he only asked this question because he liked listening to her French accent.

"Since I work indoors for my job, I try to spend every free moment outside. I love to hike anywhere, anytime. We have local mountains and big hills nearby; hiking is manna for my mind, body, and soul."

Greg said, "That sounds wonderful. Do you usually hike by yourself or with a group?"

"Oh, I have a group of friends — all girls — who are my hiking, how would you say, buddies? When we hike, our usual topic of conversation is that there are few available good men around here." Laughingly she added, "It is sad but true!"

"We can go hiking anytime!" Greg quipped, hoping immediately afterward that he didn't sound like some old guy.

"Ah, oui. Do you like to hike?" said Emmanuelle with a laugh.

"Not really, but I have thought about it."

A few weeks later, Greg asked Emmanuelle, "Perhaps our next conversation could be via something called Zoom."

"Of course! Please send me the link."

"Ahh, I'm not sure how to do that. Can you send me a link?" Although he worked in tech startups for the last few years, technology was difficult for Greg.

The next morning Mouse noticed that Greg had shaved his awful, ugly, scraggly beard.

"Where are you going today? You shaved."

"Um, I have a video call with Emmanuelle. I told you; she's helping me with my family research in France. Um, do you want to join?"

"You said someone from a French church was helping you. I assumed it was a priest. You never mentioned that 'someone' was named Emmanuelle. I have a lot of work to do around the house before I start in my garden. It needs my attention desperately, too. MY WORK never ends."

"Oh, she's been there forever. I think she's old. Have fun in your garden." Greg was obviously in a good mood. He completely missed Mouse's not-so-subtle dig.

The Zoom call started at noon CST. The video picture was sharp, and the audio was as clear as if they were next to each other; this was astonishing, Greg thought, considering their connection was over 4,000 miles long.

Emmanuelle and Greg were getting their first view of each other. Greg's immediate thought was, "Emmanuelle is a beautiful young woman." She had an oval-shaped face, long chestnut-colored hair, and deep green eyes. "She has the most expressive face." Greg thought to himself. Greg hoped that he looked better now that he was clean-shaven.

After the usual pleasantries were out of the way, Greg started the conversation by saying that he was so glad to have found Emmanuelle and that "his problem was now her problem." The joke instantly fell flat. He told himself to stick to the facts and not try to be a comedian for Emmanuelle.

"Greg, please tell me exactly what you've found in your genealogy research. Don't leave anything out. Most people don't realize that it's the smallest, forgettable details are most helpful in some cases."

That was all the encouragement Greg needed. Without taking a breath, Greg reviewed his family tree and shared more details about his ancestors as best he could. He held up his research notes with all the arrows drawn in every direction, hoping to impress Emmanuelle with his diligent research.

"That's very impressive," Emmanuelle said as soon as Greg paused to take a sip of water. "Tell me more about why you're doing all of this."

"Well, that's just it; I am not sure. I dabbled in researching my family tree before we got our ancestry DNA results. Then my DNA results showed a very diverse ancestry. I never imagined it was so varied. Then a silly idea popped into my head, and I couldn't shake it. I was never interested in this stuff before. But now, I am obsessed with it, and I've never been obsessed with anything before. My research generates more questions, and my answers generate more questions. All these questions demand more research. It's as if puzzle pieces are arranging themselves in my mind, but I am unsure what the puzzle is about or how big it is."

Greg continued, "Emmanuelle, you probably won't understand this, but during my genealogy research, I came across references to the Camino de Santiago de Compostela in northern Spain. I instantly had this incredible desire to walk the Camino de Santiago. I haven't even mentioned it to Mouse yet. I read that one doesn't decide to walk the Camino but that the Camino calls one to it. I've been thinking about this for a couple of months, but the pandemic set international travel back to Biblical times. I don't know why I want to walk the Camino, but I must. Have you ever heard about the Camino de Santiago?"

"Of course, I know about The Camino. Many of the oldest routes start way up here in northern France. All the French routes merge at Saint-Jean-Pied-de-Port in southern France before the route continues through the Pyrenees."

"I thought the walk started at some small town in the Pyrenees, not up in Lorraine. Strange, but somehow, I knew you'd know about The Camino before I mentioned it. Emmanuelle, it's almost like we're kindred spirits. Can you relate to why I want to walk The Camino?"

"Certainly, I know exactly why you must do the walk. I know this very well, this feeling. I've walked the Way many times myself."

"You've walked what way?" a perplexed Greg inquired.

"The Way of Saint James. Camino de Santiago means The Way of Saint James. Many pilgrims call it The Way."

"Oh. Did the Pilgrims walk it before they sailed on the Mayflower?"

"Remember that I told you I was a hiker, Greg? People who walk the Camino are called pilgrims, but they are not the same pilgrims that sailed to America."

Mouse was hiding around the corner from where Greg was sitting in the dining room with his laptop the entire time. She listened to every word, and since the volume was so loud, she heard every bit of that girl's French accent. It must be a fake accent, thought Mouse; Mouse was in a very irritable mood hearing Greg's almost sickeningly sweet banter with this Emmanuelle woman.

"If you can figure out how to get to France, I could be your guide on your Camino or at least part of the journey, as many people prefer to walk alone. I can easily get time off from work, especially since things are so slow. We haven't had visitors at the Basilica all year and have no funds to do anything extra anyway."

Greg was dazed and smiling and just about to answer when he heard the not-very muffled phrase "OVER MY DEAD BODY!" coming from somewhere in the house. Mouse must have left the T.V. on in the living room, Greg thought as he continued his conversation with Emmanuelle.

"Let me think about that, Emmanuelle. But can you help me dig further into my Alsace-Lorraine ancestors? Do you speak German?"

"Of course, I am fluent in German. I'm an Alsatian myself. But tell me one thing."

"Sure."

"You said your DNA results and ancestry research put a silly idea into your head. What was that silly idea?"

"Besides walking 500 miles on the Camino, you mean? It's all crazy, and you may think I'm nuts; Mouse sure does. My last name is Klass. I discovered that Klass is a derivative of Nicolas. Sinter Klaas is the Dutch version of Saint Nicolas. For some reason, I can't get it out of my head that I am related to Santa Claus,

Saint Nicolas, Sinter Klaas, Father Christmas, or whatever it is you call him. But it's so clear in my mind's eye; I don't know what to think."

Upon hearing this, a puzzled expression came over Emmanuelle's face. She then asked, "Do you remember what name you were researching when you got the feeling that you were related to Saint Nicolas?"

"Well, I can't recall, but it happened when I researched either my mother's or Mouse's family. Everyone migrated to Buffalo about the same time as my family; a section of Mouse's family was from Bavaria."

"When did your family migrate?"

"Around 1850."

"In 1850, Bavaria bordered Alsace, Germany consisted of many independent states and kingdoms. Several kingdoms, like Prussia and Bavaria, had territories that were not contiguous with their main territory. Western Prussia bordered northern Alsace, while the largest part of Prussia — East Prussia, was further east next to Poland. There were hundreds of miles between the two states. The kingdom of Bavaria was split into two as well."

"That may explain why the ship manifests listed my great-great-grandfather as Prussian, yet we know he was Alsatian."

"There was tremendous upheaval throughout Europe around that time. Many democratic movements exploded into revolution in 1848. The revolutionaries were called the 48ers. Many revolts failed, which fueled a large migration to Russia, Australia, and the U.S. over the next few years. In 1849, Alsace fought a revolt to secede from France. There were several small battles before France overwhelmed Alsace. Maps of Germany in 1850 are online; they will help give you a better understanding.' Emmanuelle paused and asked, "When did this desire to go on a Camino hit you?"

"It was all at the same time; I must walk the Camino, and I am related to Saint Nicolas, Sinter Klaas, and the others."

Emmanuelle's voice became quieter, and she hesitated to talk. Greg felt like there was a sudden tension in the air, though, for his life, he didn't know why.

Greg realized that he never understood women, even after being married to Mouse for so long.

Emmanuelle replied softly, "I need to...to...um..., speak to somebody and get permission first. It may take a few weeks. I need to think. You mentioned a mouse several times. I must ask, why does a mouse think you are nuts?"

"Mouse is my wife's nickname; the grandkids call her Mouse. I can tell that you think I am nuts."

"You also said Saint Nicolas, Sinter Klaas, and the others; what does that mean to you?"

"I am unsure what it means; I have a premonition that Santa may be many different people. Hearing myself say that I am starting to think I'm nuts too."

"No, no, not at all. I was expecting something else. I must go somewhere, and I will get back to you when I can, but please be patient; it may take me a while."

The Zoom call cut off abruptly, and Greg looked at his reflection on the darkened screen. He was bewildered at how a conversation going so right could end so wrong.

Greg emailed and called Emmanuelle every week. He left her voice messages, but there was no response. Greg redirected his energies to learning more about the Camino de Santiago. He wasn't looking for research on what to see on the Camino or the spiritual aspect of a pilgrimage. He tried to figure out what it would cost, how to get started, and if they had beer stops along the way. He spoke out loud. "I could walk from Spain to Siberia if beer stops lined the way. The Camino is a long distance, but it can't be that difficult of a trek if people have been doing it for over 1,000 years. I need to get started, and the rest will figure itself out. The online material said to pack light and buy a comfortable pair of walking shoes."

Greg and Mouse never over-planned a trip. They felt experiencing the local culture was essential, and if you see every museum and attraction, you miss the people. Greg had never been on a guided tour, a cruise, or a tour bus and didn't want to start now. He would do random and rudimentary searches on the internet and then plan accordingly. Sometimes, he would pick up an outdated travel book at the library and set off on an adventure. Many people like to arrange hotels, meal plans, baggage transport, etc. Inevitably something went wrong, and the traveler was left angry and frustrated. Greg believed overcoming challenges while traveling was part of the adventure. He would make few plans and enjoy whatever worked. Greg probably should have told Mouse that's how he went through life before proposing marriage. But that just happened too.

Greg discovered exciting details of the Camino, like scallop shells that identified a pilgrim are still in use. There were many routes to Santiago de Compostela from Spain and Portugal. One of the shortest routes was from Finisterre, the westernmost point of Europe. Finisterre means 'The End of the World.'

Greg made a note to himself to learn more about the scallop shell symbol. He was busy thinking about getting into shape for his marathon walk in Spain. Greg had a long way to go in building up his physical strength, endurance, and mental perseverance if he hoped to have any chance of completing the 500-mile trek from France to Santiago de Compostela.

11

Old God, New Religion, Mediterranean Sea, 6 BC

Cleopatra, the living incarnation of the Goddess Isis[1]

---

1. Source: Cleopatra as Isis Top 10 Amazing and Fascinating Facts about Cleopatra VII Last updated: May 29, 2022 by Saugat Adhikari

THE VIXEN LEFT PORT during the predawn hours, while the early sun lightened the eastern sky with a showering of orange, red, and yellow streaks. Hessulah and Assab concluded that Petrus and his Roman friends had no reason to suspect they had acquired a boat. Still, they hastily made their escape. Once in open waters, Hessulah steered the ship north toward Elaia, the river port that supplied Pergamum, the inland stronghold and center of learning in Anatolia. Petrus and his Urban Cohort compatriots could look forever; Hessulah knew the Mediterranean would cover their tracks.

As dawn approached, Hessulah spoke with Assab. "All my life, you have told me stories of 'your Queen.' They were stories of her beauty, intellect, kindness, cunning, and glory. Yet you never mentioned 'your Queen's' name. I assumed 'your Queen' was a fable you told to inspire me. Now you say that 'your Queen' knew the man whose family's crest is on the dagger that killed my father."

"The stories I told you of 'my Queen' are all true. She was all those things that you said, beautiful, smart, fearless, and more. She was also a goddess; Egypt built temples in her honor and worshipped her. But she was more than a Queen. She was Pharaoh. Her name was Cleopatra, Pharaoh Cleopatra."

"You served Cleopatra? How could you never mention that to me? I always thought you made up those stories about 'your Queen.'"

"I did not make anything up."

"How did you come to serve Cleopatra?"

"I was young, maybe 15, when I joined the army. My parents had died before I was twelve, and I lived with an aunt. My older brother served in the army. I don't know if he is alive; I hope to hear from him someday. I was thirteen when he left, I left at fifteen, and like my brother, I never returned home. Cleopatra was a few years older than me, and she taught me many things. As a young girl, she was married to her younger brother Ptolemy XIII; surely you know that story?"

"Not as well as I should; please tell me everything from the beginning. Where did you meet King Herod?"

"Let me start, and you will understand my concern about Herod. He has played an integral role in the life of my Queen."

"Indeed! I am listening."

"Three hundred years ago, Alexander the Great conquered Egypt. Shortly after that, Alexander died without an heir. His generals split the empire split into many kingdoms. Ptolemy Soter, Alexander's ablest General, took Egypt, North Africa, Syria, and the Levant; then, he declared himself Pharaoh. Cleopatra descended from Ptolemy; their family ruled Egypt until Augustus Caesar defeated Antony and Cleopatra twenty-five years ago.

"Everything I told you about Cleopatra is the truth; she was the most learned person I ever met. She was proficient in mathematics, oratory, cosmetics, languages, agriculture, politics, astronomy, and fashion. She was a shrewd businesswoman and a capable leader."

"But how did you meet her?"

"As a new Pharaoh, she needed guards loyal only to her. Cleopatra reviewed all the recruits to the army and sought out men she could trust. Cleopatra was the first Pharaoh to speak Egyptian since Alexander executed the Egyptian Pharaohs three hundred years ago."

"Egyptian Pharaohs don't speak Egyptian?"

"Not for the last three hundred years, until Cleopatra, that is. When she addressed the recruits, she spoke one question in different languages asking, "Anyone who understands what I am saying, take one step forward." She first asked the question in Nabatean. I spoke some Nabatean, but very little. The few phrases I mastered I learned from my uncle, who had labored on a Nabatean caravan. I thought Cleopatra said to take two steps backward. I was in the last row, and when I stepped backward, I stepped into a pile of camel dung. I was barefoot and swore an oath, a very loud oath. Fortunately, her officers did not execute me because Cleopatra laughed heartily. When Cleopatra laughed, everyone laughed, my commanders and the other recruits; I was completely embarrassed. After a few minutes, she continued asking that question in at least ten other languages. She took pity on me and selected me and a few others who understood one of the languages she spoke to serve on her guard."

"Why did she select you and those that spoke other languages to her guard?"

"Cleopatra was very clever. As Pharaoh, she threw opulent parties for visiting dignitaries and tribal leaders. At the party, these guests often spoke privately among themselves, out of her hearing, and in their language. She arranged the seating for the parties and assigned guards that spoke the guest's language within hearing of the guest. Cleopatra trained us to stand guard and to look and act dumb. Cleopatra would mock us in front of the guests and insult our intelligence. The guests assumed we were ignorant and felt free to have private conversations believing the guards would not understand. We overheard many things while pretending to be deaf and dumb; afterward, Cleopatra asked us to recall the conversations. She never apologized for calling us names, but we enjoyed our role. One always wanted to please her; you and Cleopatra are very much alike in that way."

"In what way are we alike? That you want to please us?"

"You are alike in that I'd never want to disappoint either of you."

A tear came to Hessulah's eye, or some sea spray splashed onto her face that she quickly wiped away and asked, "Did you ever learn Nabatean?"

"No, I still can't speak it well. But I learned Greek, Aramaic, and Latin. Her guards learned at least three languages, and our military training was second to none. We were the elite in her army, the strongest and most ruthless."

"What language does Herod speak in private? I assume you overheard him at one of these dinners?"

"Herod speaks Aramaic and Greek. But the first time we met was not at dinner. And I thought you wanted to hear everything from the beginning?"

"Yes, I do."

"Then let me go back to the beginning."

"Yes, Assab, please continue, but first, I have another question. How is Pharaoh different than being a king or queen?"

"Kings and queens are rulers of their land. A Pharaoh is a king or queen, but they are also gods. The Egyptians worshipped Cleopatra as the Goddess Isis incarnate."

Hessulah smiled—enjoying the conversation with old Assab, fully understanding what her father saw in this man for the first time.

"Cleopatra was 18 when her father, Ptolemy XII, died almost fifty years ago. Over the next twenty-one years, Cleopatra led a fascinating life. She wed her 12-year-old brother, Ptolemy XIII. Ptolemy XII hoped Cleopatra would guide her brother until he possessed the judgment of an able ruler. Ptolemy XIII's chief advisor, a eunuch named, Pothinus, and Cleopatra's sister and rival, Arsinoe, conspired together and poisoned Cleopatra's standing with Ptolemy.

"About a year after their marriage, Ptolemy tried to assassinate Cleopatra, which failed, and a power struggle ensued. Cleopatra fled to Anatolia with her guards, and we moved from city to city, staying one step ahead of Ptolemy's assassins. At that same time, the Roman Civil War raged between Julius Caesar and Pompey Maximus. Cleopatra kept up with news of the war, hoping, at some point, to use it to her advantage. She kept several steps ahead of everyone with her strategic thinking. News of Caesar's victory at the decisive battle at Pharsalus reached us, and Cleopatra instinctively knew her opportunity to return to Egypt and claim the throne was close. No one could have predicted what would happen. Cleopatra seized her destiny, and Ptolemy, Pothinus, and the Roman Senate all underestimated Cleopatra's cunning and bravery.

"Word reached us at an island off Anatolia that Pompey fled to Alexandria. Ptolemy owed Pompey a vast debt, enough of a debt that Pompey could raise another army to continue his fight with Caesar. Pothinus saw an opportunity to preserve the Pharaoh's wealth from being wasted by the Roman leader. Pothinus convinced Ptolemy to betray Pompey. Ptolemy sent his men to greet Pompey when he landed on the shore in Alexandria. Pompey thinking the soldiers were there to greet him, had entered a trap. Ptolemy's men beheaded Pompey on the spot. Caesar was at sea closing in on Pompey with a small army when he received Pompey's head as a gift from Ptolemy."

"Did Caesar thank Ptolemy for killing his rival?"

"Not at all; Caesar was infuriated with Ptolemy. Caesar landed in Alexandria with 3500 men. They joined a small Roman garrison stationed at a palace in the city. Ptolemy tried to convince Caesar to join his fight against Cleopatra, but Caesar resisted. He would not help the man that killed Pompey Maximus, a Roman and Caesar's former son-in-law (even though Caesar was six years younger than Pompey). Soon, Ptolemy's army of 30,000 surrounded Caesar's Palace and 4,000 Romans.

"That was when I again witnessed the true genius of Cleopatra. Cleopatra set sail and quietly landed near Alexandria to take advantage of Caesar's predicament. We stealthily entered the city as the Egyptian army was watching Caesar. Cleopatra left nothing to chance. She called three of us to her quarters and laid out the plan. Cleopatra disrobed before us and covered her body with silver and gold dust. She laid down on the end of a silken rug. We rolled the rug and carried her, hidden inside, through the streets. I told Pharaoh's forces surrounding the palace the rug was a gift for Caesar from Ptolemy. Fortunately, they let us pass."

"If Cleopatra and Ptolemy were Greek, were the Pharaoh's forces made up of Greeks or Egyptians?"

"The officers were Greek; the soldiers were Egyptians. Fortunately, I had learned Greek by then and spoke it well enough to convince them to let us pass. Please, allow me to continue. We walked to the palace gates; I was the only guard that spoke Latin and talked our way in. We reached General Marc Antony, and I explained, "General, we have a gift and an important message for the great Caesar from Pharaoh Cleopatra. My instructions are to deliver it personally."

Antony asked, "Where is Pharaoh Cleopatra? Everybody is fighting over her, and no one has seen her."

"I can assure you, General, that she is quite close."

"Antony relented and led us to Caesar's chambers. Antony and several guards stood by with swords drawn as we laid the carpet down. I whispered into the carpet, "You are now before Caesar." I slowly unrolled the carpet; she had barely enough room to open a bottle of her favorite perfume. She poured it on her body as the carpet unrolled. I stood and announced, "Caesar, may I present Pharaoh Cleopatra." Cleopatra popped out of that carpet wearing only the perfume and the silver and gold dust. Every man in the room was overwhelmed by her presence.

Cleopatra never looked more youthful, vibrant, or radiant. The light from flames in the fireplace and wall torches turned the silver and gold dust into flaming glitter. The perfume's aroma filled the room. Her breasts jiggled as she stood; it was an intoxicating sight. And no one was more entranced than Caesar. She had him in bed within minutes while we all watched."

"Don't you mean he had her in his bed within minutes?"

"I meant what I said. The poor man never had a chance. He was completely in her power when she stood before him. Within moments, the most powerful person in the world was at her complete mercy."

"So how did Caesar get out of Alexandria, and where does King Herod fit in?"

"Caesar owes a great debt to Herod and his father, Antipater. Mithridates, Caesar's ally in Pergamum, is the bastard son of King Mithridates of Pontus, the Greek king that fought three brutal wars with Rome."

"Why didn't Caesar ask Rome for help?"

"Caesar had few allies in Rome. Many in the Roman Senate supported Pompey. Rome awaited Caesar's return to see where the power tilted. Mithridates of Pergamum was Caesar's ally and the closest one to Alexandria. Mithridates raised a Greek force of 13,000 men from the interior of Anatolia and marched south to Alexandria.

"On his way south, after passing through Anatolia and Syria, Mithridates added 4,000 Jewish troops under Antipater, the governor of Idumaea. Idumaea is now part of Judaea. Antipater's two sons, Herod and Phasael, joined the expedition.

"Mithridates and Antipater fought several battles on their march to Alexandria while the Egyptians kept Caesar surrounded. Although, I don't think Caesar minded his confinement as he and Cleopatra seldom left his bed chambers."

"Indeed."

"Antipater's Jewish contingent distinguished themselves and saved Mithridates' army from defeat at the Battle of Pelusium and again a short time later at the Battle of Jews Camp.

"Though outnumbered and surrounded at the palace, Caesar rejected Ptolemy's requests for an alliance. But the noose was tightening, and Caesar had to move.

"Ptolemy divided his forces; the majority went to fight Mithridates, and the remainder watched Caesar's palace. Under cover of darkness, Caesar left behind a small Roman contingent to guard the palace while he escaped the city to the west with 4,000 men. Mithridates and Antipater were east of the city on the far side of the Nile. I remember it was February, and I celebrated my 16th year. Caesar led us on a forced march, and we circled back east and united our force with Mithridates' 17,000 soldiers. That army met the Pharaoh's army in a decisive battle on the banks of the Nile.

"Ptolemy had 40,000 troops and held a solid defensive position that forced Caesar to the attack. The Jewish troops distinguished themselves yet again and broke the Egyptian flank. This time Caesar personally witnessed their ferocity.

"The Pharaoh Ptolemy, and his eunuch Pothinus, watched from the Pharaoh's barge close by on the Nile.

"Once the Egyptian flank broke, a rout ensued. The Egyptian forces trampled one another as they tried to escape on river barges carrying Ptolemy and other Egyptian nobles. Once the rout was on, the Romans showed no mercy, and a terrible slaughter ensued. I can't count how many Egyptian countrymen I slew that day.

"That was when I first met Herod. The Egyptian barges became overloaded with fleeing men, and many barges sank during the chaos. Even the Pharaoh's barge capsized from the weight of the fleeing soldiers, and Ptolemy fell overboard, landing in knee-high water.

"Herod led a company of men laying waste to the fleeing Egyptians. He saw the Pharaoh struggling to escape the river and raced toward him. I ran as fast as I could but was fifty meters behind. Herod flung himself on the Pharaoh and held him underwater until he drowned. I could not save the boy. Not that I would have saved him, as Cleopatra had ordered me to kill him."

"Surely you wouldn't have killed the Pharaoh—he was just a boy."

"I had orders from Cleopatra. And yes, I would have killed the Pharaoh. And once I had killed him, my soldiers had orders from Cleopatra to kill me. Since Herod killed the Pharaoh, my soldiers spared me."

"Why would Cleopatra have had you killed?"

"Caesar was robbed of his prize when Ptolemy beheaded Pompey. If I killed the Pharaoh, Caesar would lose his prize again, and the blame would fall on Cleopatra. My death was important to protect Cleopatra from Caesar's wrath."

"And you knew this would happen to you?"

"Yes, I was serving my queen."

"So, what happened?"

"After the battle, Caesar held a party to celebrate his victories over Pompey and Ptolemy. In less than a month, he had ended two significant civil wars. Caesar and Cleopatra hosted his Roman officers and all the allied military leaders. The report spread that Ptolemy drowned trying to escape on the Nile River on his barge. The official statement said that Ptolemy drowned in the chaos, and a few knew the true story.

"Later, I learned from a servant that after the battle, Antipater, Phasael, and Herod stayed in the home of Pothinus. Antipater asked Herod, "Tell me exactly what happened when you reached the Pharaoh."

"His barge had taken on too much water and was listing. We waded into the water and slew all his soldiers and crew. Ptolemy was in the water, crying, still dressed in royal clothing. Phasael slew the eunuch Pothinus. I ran to the little Pharaoh, grabbed him, and put his head underwater. I held him under until he stopped squirming."

"You wanted to teach him a lesson? We will be lucky if Caesar doesn't teach us a lesson. Who witnessed this?"

"My men witnessed this, but they will keep their silence. But one of Marc Antony's centurions witnessed it, and Cleopatra's guard that fought beside us. What do you think Caesar will do if he finds out?"

"There's no telling. This whole mess with the Romans started because Ptolemy decapitated Pompey. You saw how Caesar reacted even though Pompey was his enemy. Caesar slew every Egyptian that was present and then fought for Cleopatra."

"But we helped save him and win this war!"

"Do you think that matters in the mind of these Romans?"

"Should I go back to Idumaea?"

"No. Just say that you tried to save the Pharaoh, but you were too late. It will be your word against Antony's centurion, as I doubt Cesar will believe that Egyptians' word. Let's hope we can get by with that. It's time to go; we can't keep Caesar and Cleopatra waiting."

"Antipater and his two sons, Herod and Phasael, walked into Caesar's palace, not knowing if they would leave alive. They immediately tried to read the atmosphere in the room to understand their fate.

"Marc Antony sat on Caesar's right while Cleopatra lounged on his left. She was probably pregnant with Caesar's child. Cleopatra wore sheer silk garments that revealed all the curves of her body and more. Her black hair was radiant, drawn back tight, showing her elegant cheekbones. A hieroglyphic crown with a golden asp's head in the middle rose atop her royal head.

"But what all those assembled never forgot is the fragrance of her perfume. The aroma wafted through the room and left everyone entranced. Cleopatra used more than the five senses to conquer her 'victims.' She was a master of using sight, smell, touch, taste, and sound to overwhelm them.

"Cleopatra's greatest weapons were her wit and charm. She assaulted those that she wanted to possess with everything that she had. She had conquered Caesar and would conquer Marc Antony in a few years. At that moment, I remember how she left Antony and Herod awestruck. Her breasts were fuller being with child, but her taut stomach muscles had yet to reveal any sign of the child."

Caesar appeared relaxed, almost cheerful. For the first time in years, he was not planning a battle. He was celebrating the end of the Roman and Egyptian civil wars.

Antipater and his sons Phasael and Herod stood before Caesar. Caesar spoke first, "Cleopatra and I are deeply indebted to you, Antipater. You and your men saved our army on more than one occasion. They reminded me of my 6th Legion that fought with me in Gaul. I have issued a decree making all Jews citizens of the Roman Republic. Furthermore, I am ending the taxes that the Jews pay to Rome for their protection."

"That is most gracious of you, Caesar." Antipater bowed as he replied.

"Which son of yours led the charge that finally broke the Egyptian defenses?"

"That was my eldest son, Herod, Caesar."

Marc Antony bent over and whispered something into Caesar's ear.

"Is it true that Herod was there when Ptolemy met his unfortunate end?"

"Yes, Caesar, Herod did all he could to bring the young Pharaoh to you alive, Caesar."

Caesar's brow wrinkled, "Did he? That's not what I understand."

Cleopatra quickly interjected, "Caesar, I believe Herod did us a favor." She leaned over and spoke quietly to Caesar in Latin for a moment. "If Ptolemy had lived, he would be a threat to you, me, and our child. And if you killed Ptolemy, half of Egypt would seek revenge. If Ptolemy drowns falling off a barge, that is his fate and the will of the gods."

"I suppose you are right." Caesar, unused to receiving counsel, especially from a woman, welcomed the advice and relaxed as he turned to Antipater, "Very well, Antipater, it seems we owe you and your sons a debt of gratitude."

"Hail Caesar! Hail Cleopatra!" cried Antipater as he bowed from the waist, and the tension left the room.

Caesar had his wine glass refilled and said, "I have given Cleopatra the rights to the asphalt harvested from the Dead Sea. It's a very lucrative business. Cleopatra asked that we share that with Herod, who fought bravely and did us a favor."

Antipater motioned for Herod to rise and speak. "Thank you, Caesar. And thank you, Pharaoh, you are most gracious."

Cleopatra smiled and spoke to Herod in Aramaic, "You may call me Cleopatra now that we are in business together. I will have one of my scribes draw up a charter."

Herod bowed, "Thank you, Cleopatra. I am honored."

Cleopatra addressed Antipater in Aramaic, "Antipater, you are the governor of Idumaea, are you not?"

"Yes, Pharaoh, I am."

"What of your sons? Should they not be governors too?"

"Yes, they would make excellent governors, but that is beyond my power."

"Well, it's not beyond my power." Cleopatra turned to Caesar and asked in Latin, "Caesar, you need strong advocates in Palestine. Don't you think Antipater's sons would make excellent governors? Besides, if I am to be in business with young Herod, he must have a title."

Cleopatra's beauty enthralled Caesar, but he was amazed at her mind and her accomplishments in medicine, debating, linguistics, math, logic, and science. She understood politics, flattery, and imagery. Cleopatra was a Pharaoh, an author of books on cosmetology and healing, and a well-respected ruler. By speaking to each person in their native language, she protected Caesar from having to contradict her in public should he choose not to follow her advice. It also enabled her to frame questions and suggestions that met her objectives. Caesar, like most men, soon found himself looking to her to translate and almost always following her advice.

Caesar replied to Cleopatra in Latin, "Yes, I see your point, Cleopatra. What is a reasonable offer?" Without answering Caesar, Cleopatra turned to Antipater and switched to Aramaic, "Antipater, what two provinces do you recommend that we award your heroic sons?"

Antipater paused and replied, "Why Galilee and Perea are both close to Idumaea and would be excellent choices." Antipater thought, "As governors, we will have the power to levy taxes. The governorship will give my family control over three of the four provinces of the kingdom of Judaea. Our power will be greater than the king of Judaea."

Cleopatra relayed that to Caesar. "So be it." proclaimed Caesar and ordered his scribe to draw up the appointments.

Marc Antony, staring at Cleopatra the entire evening, stood, and exclaimed, "Caesar, may I propose a toast to Antipater, Herod, and the Jews? They fought as bravely as our best Legions in Gaul. The outcome could have been very different without their heroics today and at the battles of Pelusium and Jews Camp."

It was unlike Antony to be so brief. He was famed for his orations and always liked to hear himself speak—at length. His eulogies lasted a lot longer. But he was distracted by the beauty of Cleopatra. He understood that he would have to keep his admiration under control, especially in front of Caesar. However, like most men at the party, he found it difficult not to stare. Cleopatra took notice of Antony's glances—she noticed everything—but she gave her undivided attention to Caesar. The party lasted early into the morning. During the party, Antony took the time to speak at length with Herod. They would become close friends.

I watched and moved within hearing as Cleopatra became involved in a deep conversation with Caesar. Caesar summoned Antony away from Herod and asked him to listen in. Cleopatra's suggestion involved declaring Caesar a god when they returned to Rome. Cleopatra was worshipped as Pharaoh and descendant of Isis and as the personification of Isis on earth. Isis is the most powerful goddess in Egypt. Temples of Isis and cults to Isis had spread throughout the territories of Rome.

Cleopatra began, "What's interesting, just before we met when I was in exile in Anatolia trying to recruit forces to assist you, I met a Zoroastrian High Priestess, a Magi, her name was Usiris. She told me the core strength of the old Babylonian Empires was enhanced when the people believed the emperor was an earthly representative of their god, Ahura Mazda. The Egyptians believe the Pharaohs descend from the gods. I think you have an opportunity to recreate yourself into a Roman god. You may build a Temple to yourself."

Cleopatra told Caesar, "Being declared a god binds the populace to you. You control their hearts and minds when they worship you—controlling temples and priests and teaching people what to think and interpret signs is always in your favor. It's because of my divinity that my people obey me. It keeps rivals from challenging me. Ptolemy was the personification of Osiris, the husband of Isis and chief Egyptian god."

Caesar reflected, "I see your point. Besides, if you are a divine goddess, I certainly am a god. I am of the house of Julia, and we are direct descendants of Aeneas of Troy. Aeneas was the son of the goddess Venus."

Cleopatra was always a step ahead in every conversation. "Mithridates," she called out, "tell Caesar about your name."

Mithridates replied, "Mithridates means 'gift of Mithras. Mithras was an important Iranian (Persian) God. Later, Ahura Mazda, the god of Zoroaster, was widely acknowledged as the one true god, and the worship of Mithras declined as the Zoroastrian god grew in importance."

Cleopatra turned to Caesar, "Mithridates told me of a secret Persian cult slowly spreading from Babylon. This cult worships Mithras, the God of Light and War. Perhaps there is something there that we can use."

Caesar continued, "I like that idea, Cleopatra. Antony, what if we commandeered this cult and recruited military commanders from the Legions and Navy? We could use the cult to extend our influence over legions that are not under our direct command. At the same time, we can build a Temple of Caesar and use that to influence the general populace. Together they will be a great counterweight to the Roman Senate."

Antony readily agreed, "Let me work on the cult Caesar. I agree that we must keep it exclusive. But why limit it to high-ranking military commanders? We should allow the wealthy in as well. It would be an excellent way to keep tabs on them, and our Temples will be a safe place for them to keep their gold and silver."

Caesar was excited, "I see your point. Let's put it in motion. Let's invite Mithridates, Herod, and Antipater to join. We can recruit Roman commanders deployed outside of Rome. We can expand our influence throughout the military. It will be important to keep the cult secret and thus more exclusive. We can develop a strong set of oaths, rules, and rituals. But we must keep it hidden from the general populace; we should build underground temples. We can 'resurrect Mithras' and use him as the god of the cult."

Cleopatra called me over to enact the rest of her plan. She told me which guests to send home and who should stay. "Caesar, I agree it is important to have rites of initiation into the cult. May I suggest initiating those we have selected as new members later tonight? I have an idea that should leave quite the impression on them."

Cleopatra sat back and watched her idea take root in these ambitious men. She knew that Antipater, Herod, and Mithridates were equally ambitious and would readily do as instructed. Caesar was her lover, and Cleopatra believed he would do anything to keep her happy, primarily when it benefited him. She planned to make the Temple of Caesar and the Temple of Isis the most important temples in Rome. Antony stared at her again with complete adoration; she shifted, revealing more of her body to him until he had to look away lest Caesar caught him. She thought that in different circumstances, he might be someone that could be of use to her. He was not as bright as Caesar, but he looked better and was closer to her age.

Later that evening, she noticed Antony and Herod in another deep conversation. She could use both to her advantage. As she approached, she saw them stare at her body, everything visible beneath the sheer cover she wore. She knew she cast spells on men, and she teased them accordingly. She spoke in Greek so Antony and Herod could understand their conversation. "Herod, I want to thank you personally for looking out for my brother Ptolemy in the battle. I always cherish men who do me such favors.

"My younger half-sister Arsinoe took up arms with Ptolemy against me. Caesar is sending Arsinoe to Rome. I would have preferred that she joined Ptolemy at the bottom of the Nile, but Caesar is Caesar, and I have no influence over the man."

Antony laughed, "Cleopatra, you have more influence over Caesar than anyone who ever lived. No one, not even the rich Crassus, could influence Caesar the way you do."

"Me? I do not influence Caesar. Everything is his idea."

Antony smiled again, "Everything that you suggest becomes his idea."

Cleopatra smiled conspiratorially and changed the subject. "Herod, what are your plans now that you are a governor? Surely you will not be happy just being a governor?"

Herod answered, "I have no plans, Pharaoh. I will serve my king."

Cleopatra said, "It seems to me that an ambitious governor can best serve Caesar with a royal wife by his side. That governor would get preference should any opportunities arise."

Herod said, "But I am married, and my Jewish faith does not condone divorce."

"Faith and ambition are often imprinted on the same coin. My coins have my face on the front and Isis on the reverse; they represent Power and Faith. Those in power make and change the rules. Powerful people get forgiveness from their gods, especially if they are the center of the religion. Speaking of coins, you will need a symbol of your family's power. What will you choose for the two sides of your coin?"

Herod had not thought that far ahead and stood numbly thinking about what Cleopatra suggested about another wife and furthering his ambitions. He finally exclaimed, "Jews cannot imprint a face on a coin; it is against our religion."

Cleopatra asked, "What is your family's symbol?"

Herod replied, "We don't have one yet."

Antony interjected, "Herod, I am sure Caesar will have an idea once he hears Cleopatra's suggestion: to bestow a final gift for the hard-fought victory you helped secure. Cleopatra will likely suggest you take an eagle, like the Roman Eagle, as your family's symbol."

Cleopatra was amused and smiled at Antony, knowing that her smile would drive him crazy, "Yes, that is an excellent idea. I will suggest it to Caesar right now. It's a great way to commemorate the power of the Romans."

The party continued into the early morning. Cleopatra spiked the wine with myrrh, enhancing the mind and the room's mood. By early morning only Caesar, Antony, a few of Caesar's top officers, Mithridates, Antipater, Herod, and Phasael remained. I donned my armor and led a bull into the middle of the room. Cleopatra had the fires dimmed. Four servants lifted the bull onto a high table. A large urn was placed on the floor directly beneath its head.

Cleopatra stood, "Caesar commands that Cleopatra initiate everyone into the cult of Mithras. Mithras—the god of Light, Mithras—the god of War. You will be reborn into the Mysteries of Mithras by the bull's blood."

"Mind you, Cleopatra was early in her pregnancy, and her breasts had begun to fill with mother's milk, and she was more voluptuous than ever. I jumped onto the altar and sliced the bull's throat as it gave out a bellow. Its blood began to spray. Then I quickly cut off the head as its blood rushed into the large bowl below. A servant caught the head before it fell to the floor. A circle of men stood around the altar and watched. Cleopatra walked next to the bowl, unpinned her dress, and let it fall to the floor. "Disrobe!" She commanded all of them. She stood before them wearing just her asp-crown. They stared at the beautiful Pharaoh and stripped at her command.

A female servant came over and put a linen cloth into the bowl; she bathed Cleopatra's face and body with the bull's blood. Her black hair and golden crown offset the crimson blood that washed her body. I held the bull's severed head high above her as she praised the god Mithras, asking him to overpower all our enemies. She then swore an oath to protect Caesar and Caesar's offspring. The exact words have faded from my memory. She bid each man step forward, one at a time. A naked servant girl would bathe each in blood as they repeated the prayer to Mithras and took the oath to protect Caesar and his heirs. I am sure she was thinking of the future of her unborn child as she had these men make an oath. She was always thinking of the future.

"The servant washed Cleopatra in more blood as each man spoke their oath. Herod and Antony were the last two in line. Another servant bathed each of them, and they followed, reciting their oaths. Cleopatra was breathless as she made them affirm their loyalty. Caesar became aroused by the rite and Cleopatra's power over the men. He disrobed and laid Cleopatra on the altar and took her in front of everyone present.

"It was a fantastic performance by Cleopatra. No one who was there will ever forget it.

"That night, Caesar celebrated his victories, but in a few years, tragedy would follow him. Caesar was making plans for a Triumph upon his return to Rome. He would use that Triumph to make himself Emperor of the Roman Empire, or Dictator, as his rivals in the Senate would declare him. Cleopatra would not be Empress, but her goal was for their son, Caesarion, the true son of Caesar, to be first in line to the Roman Empire. That was her plan, but things changed dramatically once news of her pregnancy reached Rome.

"The Roman Senate was in disarray with the defeat of Pompey, and even the supporters of Caesar were fearful of his new power. As Caesar's power grew, the Senate weakened. An Egyptian queen held sway over Caesar, and the Senate feared Caesar would move the power from Rome to Alexandria. The Senate obsessed over Cleopatra and Caesarion; they saw Caesarion as a Greek and Egyptian heir to the Roman Empire."

"That's quite a story, Assab."

"Yes, those were remarkable times."

"Did you meet Herod again?"

"Yes, Cleopatra and Herod had many business dealings. Most of those happened after the death of Caesar when she was with Marc Antony."

"This is all very interesting, but it doesn't answer the question, 'Why was a knife with Herod's insignia used to kill my father?'"

"If Herod is involved, we have to tread carefully. Not only does he have powerful Roman allies, but he is, as Zalman attested, utterly ruthless. I will finish the rest of my story about Herod tomorrow."

It was a clear, quiet evening with a gentle breeze; Hessulah stood the first watch while Assab slept. Progress would be slow but steady. She tried to make sense of the little she knew of Herod and her brother. How would Petrus have met Herod? He was always attending Roman parties and worshipping at Roman temples. Why was Herod in Ephesus? No doubt it had something to do with his new port at Caesarea. Her mind turned to Assab's adventures as a young man and how Hessulah would have loved to have known Cleopatra, the most powerful woman in the world. Twice she had shaken the world's mightiest empire, and her power was her brain. No matter how powerful, she never let a man hold her back from her destiny.

As the night progressed, her mind shifted to her father. Timo had taught her everything about trading. Standing watch between the rudders that night, she recalled what her father had taught her about captains. He had told her to study each ship as it docks to find the best pilots. He said, "It is the pilot's skill that guides the ship into its moorings and keeps both the ship and the docks safe. Winds and currents inside a harbor can get tricky. The currents in Ephesus are especially tricky, especially where the river current mixes with the sea."

Timo told her to study each ship and watch the crews to find the best captains. "A good captain will have a tidy ship; it will always be clean, everything stored properly, and nothing out of place that could cause an accident. A captain is responsible for the crew. You can tell a good captain by looking at the crew. A good captain has a well-fed crew. It is easy to tell by how they walk and the sound of their chatter. Sometimes the captain is the best pilot on the ship. Other times, a good captain finds and trains a good pilot, someone he can trust to dock his ship safely. And a truly great captain creates new pilots and captains."

When she was younger, he told her, "When you command a ship, there are three things you must be vigilant for pirates, storms, and wind." Hessulah replied, "I will command ships someday, father."

Timo looked down at her, smiled, and said, "I believe you; you are my little Spartan."

Her childhood memories of Assab mainly were that of a teacher. Assab trained her to hunt, sail, and fight. When she asked him to teach her to hunt, he taught her how to make arrows and skin a squirrel. When she asked him to teach her how to sail, he gave her a length of rope and said, "I will teach you to sail when you know how to tie the four knots used on every ship."

She recalled her conversation, "Assab, why did father call me his little Spartan?"

"When Spartan soldiers go to war, the city of Sparta is left vulnerable to attack. Spartan women grab their spears and shields and defend Sparta from those attacks. They are as formidable as Spartan men. When the soldiers are away, Spartan women manage the farms and businesses. If their husbands die, Spartan women inherit and own the property."

"Will you teach me how to fight like a Spartan woman?"

Assab answered, "What was the greatest battle the Spartans ever fought?"

She quickly replied, "Even though they lost, it was against the Persian King Xerxes at Thermopylae."

Assab came close to a smile and said, "Philip of Macedon, the father of Alexander the Great, had raised a mighty army and invaded the Greek city-states, which lay to the south of Macedonia. Quickly, several city-states surrendered to him without a fight, swelling his army's ranks with their soldiers. Philip's army was the mighty army that Alexander would inherit and conquer the world.

"Philip, to avoid battle with Sparta and substantial depletion of his army, sent a letter to the Ephors, who oversaw the city of Sparta. He asked for the city's surrender, knowing that a battle would also cost many Spartan lives. The letter said, "Should I come to your city as a friend or as a foe?"

"The Ephors sent Philip a one-word reply, "Neither."

"Philip became enraged and sent another letter. "You are advised to submit without further delay, for if I bring my army into your land, I will destroy your farms, slay your people, and raze your city."

"The Ephors responded with another one-word reply, "If."

"It was with those two words that Sparta defeated the army that would conquer the world. Neither Philip nor Alexander ever set foot in Sparta."

"Always try to avoid a fight if possible. Tomorrow, I will teach you how to use a bow and sword. It is one thing to shoot game with an arrow; it is quite another to kill someone who is also trying to kill you.

12

AZOFRA, MAY 2020

I AM SURPRISED TO see Emmanuelle approach the town. Her visit is unexpected but not unwelcome. I just returned from the villages and parked my motorcycle beside the barn. I have not had time to put the cover over it, so I will lead Emmanuelle in the opposite direction to prevent its discovery.

I appreciate Emmanuelle more each time we meet. Her eyes are very expressive. We can have long, nonverbal conversations, and I will understand everything she thinks by reading her eyes. As she approaches, those eyes tell me that we must talk in private.

A few townsfolk are within earshot, and Emmanuelle knew to speak carefully in their presence. Emmanuelle opened the conversation, her voice loud so others may hear, "Brother John, don't tell me that you forgot we arranged to walk the Camino today?"

"Of course not. How could I forget? Let me get my provisions."

"You won't need provisions. I brought enough for us."

John thought, "Emmanuelle arrives unannounced. The eyes watching us will be on high alert, and word will travel fast." I exclaimed loudly to minimize the situation, "Well, let's be off then!"

We had walked about one kilometer toward Burgos when she began speaking. "John, do you recall the last time we spoke, and I mentioned that the Basilica had an inquiry for Saint Nicolas's DNA sample?"

"I remember something about that. Is this what initiated this unexpected Camino?"

"No, I doubt it's related. But Covid has interrupted people's travel plans. With people unable to travel, I doubt I will find the next Santa walking the Camino."

"That's probably true. I had not thought about it in that light. But that's not the reason you are here, I assume?"

"Someone from America, in the United States, sent a note to the Basilica. Management passed it to me to answer. The American sent a note to the website looking for genealogy assistance. I politely declined to help."

"Why did you decline to help?"

"I declined at first. I was busy establishing protocols for the Basilica to deal with the pandemic. When I completed that, I had nothing to do as we had no functions or visitors. He contacted me again, and we started to correspond."

"So, you are helping him with his genealogy?"

"Yes, he is mostly of Alsatian descent, and it seems we may have matching ancestors if we go back several hundred years."

I teased, "Do you like this man? Are you worried that you are too closely related?"

"What! Oh, you are joking. No, no, it's nothing like that. He's old, just like you."

"My dear, no one is old like me. Besides, there is nothing wrong with liking older men." I laughed.

"That is so true. Well, we were on a Zoom call and..."

I interrupted, "A Zoom what?"

"A Zoom call, it's a face-to-face video call over the internet. You see the face of the person you are talking to, and they see yours."

"Well, that's quite the miracle if you ask me."

"If you used technology, we could have a Zoom call sometime."

"I think I'd rather see you in person," I spoke the truth.

She smiled at that. "Can I get back to my story?"

"Indeed!" I replied.

"Greg, that's his name, Greg and his wife received their DNA results from one of the DNA sites. His DNA is primarily Alsatian but has other DNA characteristics from Italy, Jewish, north African, and western Asia, probably around Turkey."

"I am sure many people have similar DNA characteristics. It sounds as if his ancestors got around quite a bit."

"John, will you please take me seriously for a minute."

"Of course, go on."

"During our call, he said that since his results arrived, he had a premonition that he's related to Saint Nicolas."

"Why would he think that? Perhaps he just a dreamer."

"His last name, Klass, is a derivative of Nicolas."

"Emmanuelle, Millions of people's last name is derivative of Nicolas, millions."

"I know that. As we talked, Greg brought up the Camino and that he's being 'called' to it. His calling started when he received his DNA results as well."

I asked, "Did his calling happen over Zoom too?"

"No, and why are you being so difficult, John? You are never like this."

"I'm sorry, my dear. Please continue. I'm just not myself today."

"I wonder if the pandemic is preventing people from walking the Camino, and here's someone with a premonition and a calling. Could he be the one we seek? The pandemic is preventing them from walking the Camino and finding us or us finding them."

"Perhaps you are getting impatient because you have not found Santa yet?"

"Possibly. I have been looking for fifteen years."

"Well, I have been looking for my answers for two thousand years, so join the club." I continued, "His name is Greg Klass, you say. Is there anything else Greg mentioned?"

Emmanuelle replied, "Yes, he seemed to know that Saint Nicolas, Santa Claus, Kris Kringle, Father Christmas, Ded Moroz, and Sinter Klaas are all different people."

"It is interesting that he would say that, Emmanuelle."

"I thought so too. Greg and his wife are from Saint Louis in Missouri, wherever that is."

I teased, "It's near Kansas, Dorothy."

"Ah, the Wizard of Oz."

"Well, if he is a Santa, and I don't think he is, he will find his way to the Camino."

"I was wondering if I should help arrange to get them here?"

"What do you mean help 'them'."

"Greg and Mouse, should I help arrange for them to walk the Camino?"

"How could you arrange that Emmanuelle? What does a mouse have to do with this?"

"Oh, Mouse is his wife. Their grandkids nicknamed her Mouse."

"Grandma Mouse?" I was momentarily stunned as my mind raced back all those centuries. I paused, then explained, "A long, long time ago, Alina had a pet mouse. As you may recall, Alina was Nicolas's sister. She called her pet mouse 'YiaYia Pontiki.' It's Greek for Grandma Mouse." I paused and thought aloud, "Yes, I think I should like to meet this new Grandma Mouse."

Emmanuelle offered, "Well, here's my idea...."

13

Translation, St Louis, MO, 2020 AD

Three weeks after the Zoom conference with Emmanuelle, and with no further contact from her, a UPS package arrived on the porch of Mouse and Greg's house in Saint Louis. It looked worn, with a crushed corner on one end and torn mailing paper on the other three corners. Greg assumed many hands and postal machines handled this package.

"Hey, Mouse!" he called into the home. "Are you around? UPS left a package on the porch. The return address is from a place in Spain called Burgos. Hey Mouse, where are you?"

"This better be good. I was upstairs cleaning. Running up and down these stairs is killing my back." Mouse was always terribly crabby when her back hurt. Greg ignored her complaints; his interest focused on the package in his hands.

"It's a package from Spain, some town called Burgos. Did you order anything from Amazon?"

"No, who is it addressed to?"

"It's just addressed to Klass and our address."

Greg ripped open the heavy brown paper wrapper while Mouse watched. He was baffled after he discarded the packaging tape and wrappers, and he looked inside the box. The box contained photocopied pages of what looked like an antique manuscript. Greg could not tell if its Latin or Greek, but that was only a guess; it could be Sanskrit for all he knew.

Mouse and Greg look at each other, bewildered.

"What is it?"

"I have no idea."

"Who sent it to you?

"I have no idea. It has something to do with Emmanuelle, but I am still waiting to hear from her. I don't get it."

———◆———

Mouse and Greg were fortunate to live in a city with two great universities. Retired professors frequently choose to stay in their town after retirement because of the reasonable cost of living. Greg took it as a personal challenge to find a university teacher, working or retired, who could help unravel this mysterious manuscript. Greg sought assistance in the university setting to little avail; he never took failure well and felt he was earning a Ph.D. in Rejection.

"I'm so sorry I haven't been able to help you, Greg. Oh, um, do you mind me calling you Greg?" said the young teacher's assistant he had met at the library during his quest.

"Sure, please call me Greg. What can I call you?"

"I am Noelle."

"That's a nice Christmassy name. Were you born on Christmas Day?"

"The night before, actually, on Christmas Eve."

"I have heard that birthdays around Christmas are not great for a kid."

Noelle laughed, "No, they are not. It's not fair. We only get clothes for our birthday. The toys came on Christmas Day."

"That's bad luck, for sure." "For sure?" Greg thought. Nobody with a brain says for sure. Greg continued his conversation with the cute TA, "I'm at the end of my rope on this text, and I don't know what more I can do."

The young teaching assistant's face lit up. "I have a suggestion. Why don't you post a picture of a couple of the paragraphs on an antiquity website? I think that's how Google quickly solved the Dead Sea Scrolls a few years back. They posted the scrolls online, and collaborators from across the globe took part in the translation. It saved decades of research time in translating the work when they had input from a worldwide research community. Researchers may help with the translation if they find your document interesting."

"Genius, simply genius," replied Greg with a big smile. "And I'm sorry if I've been impatient with you. I'm usually not like that." He said with a twinkle in his eye.

Looking up, the young assistant smiled back at him. "He seems like a nice, old guy," she thought.

Greg went home and told Mouse of the teaching assistant's suggestion. Mouse liked that idea and helped Greg with the wording of the posting request and how to find antiquities websites. They decided to post what looked like the first few paragraphs and see what would happen. Greg searched for the websites using keywords like 'antiquity,' 'ancient Greek,' 'Latin,' and 'translate.' Soon Greg was busy researching websites and figuring out how to submit his request for translation to the largest circulation of readers. "If it keeps him out of trouble." was the extent of Mouse's thinking. She had to figure out what to make for dinner, and soon. Google turned up a dozen pages of antiquity websites in various languages. Greg thought he figured out a way to post the text, including the request and his email address, to a half dozen sites but was never quite sure if he did it successfully.

———— ◄○► ————

Weeks had passed since he posted his request, and he had not received a response. Greg reminded himself of Aesop's fables, "Remember the tortoise flew too close to the sun. Be patient." Each day he looked at the manuscript and sighed with frustration.

Finally, a random email popped up in his inbox. The sender had some innocuous email address, goj212025@gmail.com. The email contained a copy of the page they submitted and what appeared to be its translation. "Mouse, Mouse! I got an answer!" Greg was yelling from behind the dining room door.

"Huh? What did you say? The dishwasher's running, and I can't hear you."

Greg went into the kitchen. His eyes lit up like he had won the lottery.

"What's going on? I'm babysitting the kids later this afternoon."

Greg walked to the fridge, got a cold can of beer, and then sat at the kitchen table. He began, "Mouse, I just got an answer to our posting. It's from one of the websites that I didn't think had any readers at all! Isn't that incredible? I can't figure out who answered my question, but I think it's somebody smart."

"Okay. What did the smart guy say?"

"There's a brief note before he starts with the translation; here's what he says: I haven't read an ancient Greek text in a long time. The text is archaic Greek from around the time of Christ. The story was told to the author by three women: Mary, Salome, and Hessulah. The story begins a long time ago in Ephesus, which, at that time, is a major city in Anatolia."

"Wow." Said Greg, "I bet it's difficult to translate modern Greek to English; I am sure it takes much more work to translate ancient Greek. He says the story begins in a city called Ephesus. Have you ever heard of a place called Ephesus, Mouse?"

"No, I've never heard of Ephesus. But we haven't been to many places, you know."

"Any idea where or what Anatolia is Mouse?"

"How often do I have to say that you haven't taken me to that many places?"

"Hmm, I wonder if Ephesus has anything to do with the Ephesians, you know, from the Bible. I recall something like that from my days as an altar boy." Greg continued, while ignoring Mouse's travel jabs, "Well, he says it's written in Greek and starts in Ephesus. It's a story by three women named Mary, Salome, and Hessulah."

"Hessulah, what kind of name is Hessulah, and what's an Ephesian?" Mouse asked.

"I don't know, but it sounds like an ancient name. I'd think an Ephesian is a person from Ephesus. Do you remember the Epistles in the Bible, the Letter to the Ephesians, written by Saint Paul?"

"Yeah, I guess so. Who is this guy who's doing the translation? What do you know about him?"

"I haven't a clue. I wonder if it's even a guy; the person didn't sign a name or anything. The translator is a complete mystery."

"Did he translate what we sent? What did it say?"

"Yes, oddly, it begins with a quotation from the Bible, from the Gospel of Luke. Let me read it."

> "In those days, Caesar Augustus published a decree ordering a census of the whole world. The first Census took place while Quirinius was governor of Syria. Everyone went to register, each to his own town. And so, Joseph went from the town of Nazareth in Galilee to Judaea, to David's town of Bethlehem—because he was from the house and lineage of David—to register with Mary his espoused wife, who was with child."

> -- Luke 2, 1-5

"Next, he writes:

> "The proclamation noted it was the 27th year of the reign of Caesar Augustus. This edict, the counting of heads conducted by civil servants, set off a chain of events that would be remembered through future millennia.

I transcribe this chronicle as it is told to me by my mother, Salome; my aunt Mary, who is Salome's sister; and Hessulah of Myra, who is known to Salome and Mary. These three women testified truthfully to me while on a ship sailing for Finis Terra—the end of the world—on the far coast of Spain. We are passengers on a funereal ship to bury my brother James, whose headless body has been anointed with oil and myrrh, according to our custom. His body is carefully wrapped in shrouds and is safely stored in the ship's hold. The testimony of the three women took place eleven years after my beloved Master left to join His Father. King Herod Agrippa of Judaea ordered my brother's death during the reign of Emperor Claudius of Rome.

Everyone has heard the story of my beloved Master's birth—that these women witnessed—everyone listened to my story of the events that followed His birth—that I attested. The testimony of these women is known, by me, to be true. This is how their story begins; this is the book of Hessulah."

Greg reread the translation. Mouse and Greg stared at each other. Greg uttered a quiet "What the hell?"

Mouse said, "What does that mean? 'Everyone has heard the story of my beloved Master's birth—that these women were witness to—everyone listened to my story of the events that followed—that I witnessed.'"

Mouse continued, "What is 'my story'? What did 'who' witness?"

Greg said, "I have no idea. The only ones I knew that wrote about Augustus Caesar's decree for the Census were Matthew, Mark, Luke, and John. I am not sure which Gospel writer wrote about the birth of Jesus. Who are these three women: Mary, Salome, and Hessulah of Myra? Hessulah is not a name from the Bible that I remember."

"You must read the Bible to know who or what's in it."

"Good point."

"Can you run upstairs and get our Bible, Greg?"

"We have a Bible?"

"Yes, it's in one of our bookshelves in the spare bedroom upstairs."

A minute later, Greg shouts from upstairs, "There are a lot of books up here!"

Mouse shouts, "Look for the one that says, 'THE BIBLE' You should try reading it and any of those other books too."

Greg scampered back and returned with the family Bible that had not seen much use. The first few pages were full-page pictures, including the Madonna and Child, The Crucifixion, The National Shrine of the Immaculate Conception, The Holy Family, and one of Pope John Paul II, who was pope at the time of its printing. There were two blank pages for the family to fill in the husband's and wife's genealogy—dates and places of birth, including parents, grandparents, and great-grandparents. Eight sections followed for baby names and their related information. Greg thought, "Obviously, this was before birth control was popular." He exclaimed, "Look, I can fill in some of that genealogy information from my research."

Mouse ignoring Greg's genealogy comment, asked, "Do we have to read the whole thing?"

"I think we can skip the Old Testament and start with the four Gospels in the New Testament. At least one Gospel mentions the Census. Let's start with the Gospel according to Matthew and work our way to the Gospel of John to see what they say about the Census."

Mouse skimmed the beginning of each of the four Gospels. "So, the Gospel of Matthew talks about the birth of Jesus, the Magi, Herod, the Holy Family's flight to Egypt, the murder of the Innocents in Bethlehem, and the Holy Family's return from exile to live in Nazareth. After that, it jumps about 30 years when Jesus meets John the Baptist. But Matthew's Gospel does not mention the Census at all."

Mouse flipped to the Gospel of Mark. "The Gospel of Mark doesn't say anything about the birth of Jesus; it begins with Jesus's meeting John the Baptist when they were both adults."

Opening the Gospel of Luke, Mouse says, "Chapter 1 of Luke's Gospel talks about Mary and Joseph getting married and their trip to Bethlehem. Chapter 2 of Luke starts with the census quote in the translation. It also has the shepherds tending their flocks in Bethlehem, as well as the circumcision, which I still don't understand why we still do that."

Mouse continued, "Lastly, The Gospel of John is like Mark as it starts with John the Baptist, again, when Jesus was about 30 years old."

Marge summarized, "So Matthew and Luke wrote about 'His birth or beginning' while Mark and John started with His life as an adult?"

"It sure looks that way."

"So does that mean Mark or John originally wrote this story of Hessulah or whatever the translation refers to?"

"Mouse, I have no idea."

"What do you think?"

Greg continued, "I think we need more information before we think anything. There are a lot of books that the Church never validated and declared heretical. They were called the Agnostic Gospels or something like that. Maybe this is just a copy of one of those books."

"Should we bring these pages and the translation to the Saint Louis Bishop?"

"And just what would we say to the Bishop? 'Hey Bishop, have I got something you need to see!' If these documents are real and contradict Church Canon Law, the Bishop will take them, and they will never see the light of day. If it's one of the agnostic gospels, again he will take it, and again, it will never see the light of day."

"You wouldn't trust a bishop?"

"I don't trust anyone in the church hierarchy. If this is real, why did it get sent to us? Why wouldn't they send it to the Church? They must not trust the Church, and who could blame them? The Church covered-up child abuse, scandals at the Vatican Bank, and all that other nonsense. You complain that the Church abused women for 2,000 years and still treats women as second-class citizens. Suppose the story is about this Hessulah, and it sounds like she is one of three, Salome, Mary, and Hessulah. The Church would probably declare her a whore, just like they did to Mary Magdalene to tarnish her name."

"Okay, Greg, maybe you're right. But I have one question?"

"What's that?"

"Why, in God's name, would anyone send this to you?"

"I have no earthly idea. It's not like I'm Indiana Jones!"

"Everything isn't a movie reference Greg."

Mouse and Greg continued to stare at the pages. Suddenly Mouse asked Greg to read everything aloud again. Greg began, "In those days,"

"No, before that."

"Oh, you mean the note that the translator wrote." He says, "I haven't read ancient Greek texts in a long time. The text is ancient Greek from around the first century A.D. The story was told to the author by three women named Mary, Salome, and Hessulah. The story begins a long time ago in the city of Ephesus, which was a major city in Anatolia."

Mouse said, "Yes, that's it. Afterward, he translates everything that we sent, correct?"

"I assume so. It's difficult to say, as my ancient Greek translation skills have lapsed recently."

"Quit trying to be funny."

"Okay, so what's your point?"

"Let's assume that he translated everything that we sent, which in length looks to correspond to the same number of words as the translated text he returned."

"Okay, so he translated what we sent, hopefully accurately.

"Well, what he translated does not mention Ephesus or Anatolia."

"It doesn't appear so, but I'm unsure how to spell either in ancient Greek. So, what's your point?"

"If this translation is accurate, and it doesn't mention Ephesus or Anatolia, and he translated only the text we sent, how does he know the story starts in Ephesus?"

Greg attended a socially distanced, mask-required training session for the 2020 Census at a south Saint Louis community center a week later. Upon filling out the appropriate paperwork and receiving his Census supplies, including a black canvas shoulder pack, a government-issued cell phone, and paper pads of tear-off notices, "Sorry, we missed you," with instructions to complete the Census online. A white background covered one side of the pack and the United States Census Bureau in blue lettering.

The area Supervisor, Elmer Stunkel, asked Greg and three other prospective Enumerators to stand and recite the Oath to defend the Constitution of the United States.

"I, Gregory Klass, will support and defend the Constitution of the United States against all enemies, foreign and domestic; that I will bear true faith and allegiance to the same; that I take this obligation freely, without any mental reservation or purpose of evasion; and that I will well and faithfully discharge the duties of the office on which I am about to enter. So, help me, God."

Greg approached Elmer after the meeting and struck up a conversation. "Hey, Elmer, I have questions about how we work together."

"Sure, it's Greg, correct?"

"Yes, that's what my name tag says anyway."

"Ha, I wasn't looking at it. How can I help you?"

"So, I am retired and want to ensure I don't have to work 40 hours a week. They just opened some golf courses, and I'd like to get out whenever it's not too hot. You should only count me for about 20 hours a week."

"That's fine. I understand; I am retired as well. What did you retire from?"

"Kind of hard to describe; I was in banking and telecommunications, mostly involved in technology that I didn't understand."

"Interesting; I was a history professor at a local community college."

"What kind of history?"

"Oh, mostly old stuff. That's a history teacher's joke. I taught U.S. and World History."

"Interesting, I read something interesting about some Greek city-states in Asia Minor shortly before the birth of Christ. Augustus Caesar's Census, mentioned in the Bible, is part of it."

"That's a fascinating time."

Greg elaborated, "It seems to start around 10 B.C. in Ephesus. That was Rome's capital for Asia Minor."

"Yes. It was. It's a bit to the north of the Bible story about the Census."

"I don't know much about the historical period, and I'm unsure if the story is true."

Elmer volunteered a quick synopsis, "Well, the Romans conducted a census every five years. The main purpose of their Census was to help levy taxes and ensure the population went to Roman temples to worship Roman gods and pay tribute. Rome's interest in Ephesus and that region started around 125 BC after the last Punic Wars with Carthage. Rome's interest in Palestine heated up around 64 B.C. If you need background, look up Pompey, Cilician Pirates, Julius Caesar, King Herod, Cleopatra, and Marc Antony."

"King Herod? Why Herod? I know the Bible mentions Herod, but he's certainly not on the level of those others."

"Oh, you'd be surprised. Without Herod, you can't tell the story of Caesar and Cleopatra or Antony and Cleopatra."

"I will have to look into that."

"Sure, if you need any help, let me know."

"I will, thanks. I'm sure we will be talking."

Greg and Elmer spoke for about another 20 minutes on the 2020 Census and the Roman Census.

Mouse was cleaning the wood floors when Greg came in the front door. "How was your Census training?"

"It went pretty basic, as expected. The Census Bureau gave us a phone with an app that guides us through each interview. We fill in the information on the phone and press a button to upload the info to a database. It will be hard to mess anything up."

"When do you start?"

"I start on Monday. I must fill out a schedule on the app for the hours I want to work each day, and they download a list of houses and apartments that I should visit during those hours."

"That sounds easy enough."

"Yeah, I can set my schedule and only work up to eight hours a day. You get fired if you work over eight hours without documented permission. Four hours a day is enough for me anyway.

"Do you have a boss?" Mouse asked.

"I do. My boss is a retired history professor named Elmer. We had a long talk after the training. I asked him what he knew about Augustus Caesar and his Census. I did not tell him we were working on a secret document."

"What did he have to say?"

"First, Roman Censuses were about more than counting people. During the earlier days of the Republic, they were also in charge of morals. The words 'censor' and 'censorship' comes from Census. The head of the Census was a critical position during Julius Caesar's time. The Censors controlled morals and taxes. The power of the position declined after Augustus Caesar, as Augustus and the Emperors that followed assumed that power to control tax revenue. Roman morals, which weren't high, took a big hit once that position lost its power."

"That's something I never knew."

"Elmer had a few suggestions if I was interested in that census and era."

"What do you mean by suggestions?"

"It was nothing dramatic. Elmer said to understand Rome's role in Anatolia and Judaea, you had to start around 64 B.C. with some pirates and Gaius Magnus Pompey. Magnus Pompey is 'Pompey the Great,' and Gaius is his first name. He fought a civil war against Julius Caesar. Elmer said that civil war brought Caesar and Cleopatra together, which led to Cleopatra and Marc Antony. Another Roman civil war between Antony and Caesar's nephew Octavius followed. Octavius renamed himself Augustus Caesar and ordered the Census at the time of the birth of Christ."

"Sounds like something a History professor would say."

"Yeah, but Elmer did say something else that I found interesting. He said that one person profoundly impacted the events of that time and led a violent and fascinating life that most people ignore today."

"Jesus Christ?"

"No, and you shouldn't swear."

"I was only answering your statement, and you know it."

Chuckling, Greg said, "Elmer said one of the most influential, violent, and fascinating figures was King Herod of Judaea. Herod ruled for decades, and his shadow spread over the land for over a hundred years after his death. He bankrupted the country to finance his massive construction projects. The resulting poverty in Judaea led to a failed Jewish insurrection, the destruction of the city of Jerusalem, and the Second Temple of Solomon, followed by the eviction of Jews from Jerusalem in 70 A.D. That first-century revolt preceded the diaspora of the Jews from Palestine by 135 AD."

14

ELAIA, RIVER-PORT OF PERGAMUM, 6 BC

A SLIGHT EVENING BREEZE and calm water convinced Hessulah to remain out to sea and forgo sanctuary in a deserted cove. On the first night watch, she used the stars and a faintly visible coastline as guides to keep the small ship pointed north. Assab woke to relieve her halfway through the night. Before she turned in for her sleep, she asked, "There is something that I never understood. After Alexander conquered everything there was to conquer, the generals split his Empire into three parts, Greece, Persia, and Egypt. Greeks have ruled in Persia and Egypt for the last three hundred years. Why didn't all the Greek kingdoms join King Mithridates VI of Pontus when he fought his wars with Rome? Surely a united Greek force would have beaten the Romans."

"Because they are Greek, that's why. Alexander united the Greek cities, but after his death, the city-states continued to fight each other. Alexander's father, Philip of Macedon, conquered or forced most of them to join him. Alexander conquered the remaining after his father died; some say Alexander poisoned Philip. Once Alexander died, the city-states returned to their sovereignty and began their wars again.

"After three hundred years, alliances changed, and Greece never had another king strong enough to unite the city-states. Mithridates tried, but the other Greek cities did not trust him. The Seleucids ruled Persia, including Anatolia, Syria, Babylon, Afghanistan, and the eastern portion of Alexander's Empire.

The Seleucid kings waged war against Ptolemy's' Egypt and tried to expand into Greece. Greek kingdoms from Anatolia allied with Rome to expel the Seleucids from Anatolia and pushed them east of the Tarsus Mountains. About 60 years ago, just before Caesar, Pompey defeated the Seleucids. The Pharaohs of Egypt indeed were Greek, but the Greek Pharaohs did more business with Rome than with the Greek city-states. So, in answer to your question, sometimes Greeks are reluctant to get involved in someone else's war, and sometimes Greeks like to fight other Greeks as much as they want to fight anyone else.

"Now go get your sleep, Hessulah, and we will talk more about Cleopatra and Herod in the morning."

Nemi sliced the cap off the bottom of the pomegranate. He scored the ridges on the sides and held the fruit flat with the skin facing up above a large bowl. He paddled the top of the peel of each section with the flat of his knife, releasing the tasty seeds into the bowl. With incredible quickness, he had prepared enough fruit to fill the bowl. He tossed the seedless peels into the water. He scored and separated a final pomegranate. Instead of releasing the seeds, he pulled the sections apart and handed a section to Hessulah, Assab, and Priam. Everyone sucked the seeds from their peel and used the acidic membranes in the peel to cleanse the sleep from their mouths. He tossed the fifth section to Priam, saying, "Your breath is so foul it needs two sections this morning." Then he passed around the bowl of life-giving seeds for breakfast.

Hessulah and Assab stood at the stern, with Hessulah manning the rudders. Assab stated, "We should see the Caicus River before long; it's not far from the mouth of the Caicus to the port; we will be in Elaia by mid-day."

"Assab, are the stories true about Antony and Cleopatra? Did Cleopatra seduce him too?"

"We fled Rome after the death of Caesar. Cleopatra feared the Senate would try to execute her and her son, Caesarion. Antony aided our escape, and we sailed to

Egypt. Antony and Octavian joined forces and formed a triumvirate with Marcus Lepidus. Antony led the war in the east against Caesar's assassins - Cassius and Brutus. Octavian quelled opposition forces in Spain and then forced Lepidus to retire. Octavian and Antony then split the Empire between them. Octavian held Rome and the western Empire, while Antony ruled Greece, Egypt, and the east.

"The Roman Senate would never accept Cleopatra or Caesarion as rulers. Cleopatra knew she needed a formidable Roman army behind any claims they could make to Caesar's throne. She seized the opportunity to capture Antony's heart just like Caesar's. Antony was in Tarsus on the southern coast of Anatolia, north of Syria. She outfitted a river barge with large purple and gold drapes above an oversized bed. We rowed the barge up the Tarsus River near Antony's palace and maintained a pace at the oars to keep the barge from moving. Cleopatra opened large vats of perfume on the barge, and the breezes floated the fragrances into the city. All Tarsus came to the riverfront to see the ornate gala. Antony stood on the riverbank and saw Pharaoh Cleopatra naked, except for her crown and jewels waiting for him on the makeshift bed. Like Caesar, Antony had no chance. He rowed out to meet Cleopatra, and they made love on that bed in front of the city.

"Antony ruled the eastern Empire for the next ten years, and Cleopatra ruled Egypt. Octavian consolidated his power in Rome. As co-rulers of the eastern Empire, Antony and Cleopatra led an idyllic life and raised many children. They formed a drinking society amongst the elite called "The Indelible Livers." That was the only time in Cleopatra's life she was in love. They were both very much in love, and Antony began giving Cleopatra gifts of lands that Rome had conquered, including Cilicia and its vast northern forests.

"Meanwhile, Octavian's power grew. He had Julius Caesar declared a god and built a great temple for him in Rome. The Temple of Caesar made Octavian stronger among the Roman populace; naming Caesar a god was astute as Caesar previously named Octavian, his son. Octavian would claim he is the son of a god. Civil War pitting Octavian against Antony and the east became inevitable.

"Why wasn't Antony more careful?"

"Antony wanted to please Cleopatra, his gifts became grander, and they had convinced themselves that their combined power insured their safety. Twenty-five years ago, Octavian beat Antony in a sea battle near Actium. Antony and Cleopatra fled from the fight to Alexandria and their final fate. Many say Cleopatra was afraid to commit her naval forces on Antony's behalf at Actium. That's not true. Antony knew the Roman Senate would never accept peace if Cleopatra defeated Octavian's navy. The Senate would continue to raise new legions to fight him. Antony had to defeat Octavian, Roman versus Roman, for the Senate to capitulate. The Senate always feared Cleopatra. Antony sent word for Cleopatra to return to port, where we received word Octavian defeated Antony. We made haste to Alexandria, where Antony planned to regroup, use Cleopatra's naval forces as a buffer, and rebuild his army.

"That was a mistake, and Octavian bottled Cleopatra's navy in Alexandria. As Octavian advanced, Antony and Cleopatra drank heavily. Cleopatra passed out from the drinking to such an extent that she was unconscious. Antony, also very drunk, came into her room and assumed she was dead. He fell on his sword, thinking Cleopatra had committed suicide. Cleopatra awoke in time to find him dying. She contemplated suicide, but she could not abandon her children. She devised a plan to woo Octavian, but Octavian was much younger than Cleopatra and Cleopatra no longer was the beautiful, young Pharoah that had seduced Rome's two most powerful men. Childbearing and drinking had taken a toll on her looks, but Octavian rejected her simply because he did not need Cleopatra to become Emperor.

"Cleopatra's plans to seduce and possibly kill Octavian fell apart. She hid an asp in her bed to use on Octavian, but when Octavian would not sleep with her, she went to bed knowing the asp would take her life. I would have stopped her had I been there, but she had sent me on some fool's errand."

"Their story is as tragic as Helen of Troy and Paris."

"Yes, Hessulah, maybe even more so. They were madly in love and had a real family. Octavian, now Augustus, has been in power ever since, and Rome controls the Mediterranean world."

"Where does Herod fit in all of this?"

"Cleopatra had a fondness for Herod. She nurtured and used him to develop her asphalt, copper, and forestry businesses. Cleopatra advised Herod to build Caesarea as a city for the rich to play. She convinced him to make Caesarea Maritima and helped him gain financing from Zalman. Herod planned to name it Cleopatra Maritima. She instilled in Herod the importance of using religion to gain the support of the people. That is why Herod built a Temple for the Jews in Jerusalem. And she taught him the importance of protecting his power. It wasn't until after her death that Herod would take that lesson to the extreme. Had Cleopatra lived, she would have controlled his worst impulses.

"After the deaths of Antony and Cleopatra in August twenty-five years ago, Herod found himself in a precarious spot. He supported Antony in the civil war against Octavius/Augustus. Herod sailed to Rome and pledged himself to Augustus Caesar. His friends implored Augustus, reminding the Emperor of Herod's family's support in Egypt for his uncle/father, Julius Caesar. Seventeen years earlier, Herod joined the group of fighters that helped save Julius Caesar. Augustus was generous and allowed Herod to rule as Governor in Judaea, Samaria, Galilee, and Perea. Augustus gave Herod several hundred of Cleopatra's Celtic bodyguards as a gift to commemorate the appointment. Herod added them to his contingent of 2,000 bodyguards. In addition to Cleopatra's Celtic guard, Herod's guard consisted of Jewish, Roman, and Germanic troops. I left Cleopatra's army before they assigned me to Herod.

"Rome controls their client kingdoms by installing local rulers loyal to Rome. Rome maintained a tight grip on these rulers whose chief responsibilities were to keep order, collect taxes and defend Rome when called.

"Herod's rise to power coincided with the death of many of his rivals, including within his family. About 30 years ago, Herod took Cleopatra's advice and cast aside his first wife, Doris, and his eldest son Antipater. Herod married Mariamne I, the beautiful granddaughter of the Judaean King Hyrcanus II. This marriage to Mariamne gave Herod a royal claim to the throne. It was a bonus that Mariamne was beautiful, and Herod fell madly in love with her. Madly was the operative word. His first signs of insanity manifested in his jealousy over Mariamne.

"On several occasions, Herod ordered his ministers to kill Mariamne if he failed to return from a trip abroad. He would not allow anyone to be with her, even after his death. Mariamne became furious when she heard Herod ordered her conditional death, and in retaliation, Mariamne refused to sleep with Herod. Herod believed the palace lies that Mariamne was unfaithful, which fueled his jealousy and inflamed his mental unbalance. Herod accused Mariamne of an affair punishable by death, but she convinced him of her faithfulness, and he spared her. Before Herod and Mariamne reconciled, someone accused Mariamne's mother, who was of royal blood, of trying to overthrow Herod. The mother tried to deflect blame and accused Mariamne of infidelity to save herself. Herod executed Mariamne and her mother.

"Years later, two of Mariamne and Herod's sons were accused of plotting to assassinate Herod. Herod needed Augustus's permission to execute anyone listed as a successor to the Judaean throne with Caesar Augustus. As these sons were first in line for the throne, Herod sought Augustus's approval to execute his two sons."

Assab took a deep breath and continued, "Augustus, knowing the Jewish custom not to eat pork, said of Herod, 'I would rather be Herod's pig than Herod's son.' Augustus spoke this as a rhyme in Greek, which had similar sounding words for pig (hys) and son (huios). Besides building the most powerful Empire the world had ever seen, Augustus became known for his sense of humor and his enterprising use of homonyms.

"Herod spent tremendous amounts of taxpayer money on his building projects. Herod built the Second Temple in Jerusalem, Caesarea Maritima (Harbour) and the city of Caesarea, the city of Sebaste, the fortresses in Masada, Herodium, Alexandrium, Hyrcania, and Machaerus."

Hessulah asked, "Is Herod bad because he executes his family? Or is his family bad for trying to kill him?" But before Assab could answer, Hessulah interrupted,

"There on the bank is the marking for the Caicus River. I hope it's true that we can acquire parchment here."

"I thought you said Artemis, and Athena assured you that we would acquire a load of parchment in Pergamon."

Hessulah said. "Well, they didn't exactly say anything. Maybe it was just wishful thinking. Please don't tell Priam or Nemi. They need to think we have the favor of the gods. I am sure we will find something that we can acquire for trade. We have no choice."

Assab's face turned stern, "You led us here on wishful thinking? Just waiting for an opportunity to present itself?" He paused, "You are just like my queen. Sailing with you is going to be an adventure. A new plan for every port is exactly like your father." Assab burst out laughing.

15

CARDINAL O'ROURKE RESIDENCE, ROME, 2020 AD

Mithras Sacrifice, Tauroctony
Creative Commons
Attribution-Share Alike 3.0 Unported[1]

---

1. English: CIMRM 181: Tauroctony fresco in the mithraeum of Santa Maria Capua Vetere, 2nd century. Vermaseren notes that the face was damaged in 1947 by playing children. Author: Dom De Felice

His Eminence, Timothy Cornelius Cardinal O'Rourke, ignored the pain the metal prongs of the cilice inflicted on his thigh as he walked through the underground tunnel. He suffered the pain from the cilice as atonement for the sins that he could not confess, even to a priest. The tunnel connected the underground Mithraic Temple to the basement of his residence outside the grounds of Villa Albani in Rome. Workers reinforcing the foundation of his residence stumbled upon the passageway several years ago. They immediately alerted the Cardinal to the discovery. Accompanied only by Monsignor Thomas White, they traced the passage to the Mithraeum.

Archeologists discovered hundreds of underground Mithraic Temples (Mithraeums) in Rome, Italy, Germany, Anatolia, and Eastern Europe. Like the other discoveries, this Temple housed a marble relief of the god Mithras wearing his iconic Phrygian cap standing over and slicing the throat of a bull. The ceiling was a fresco of the sky depicting the constellation Perseus with the Taurus Constellation below it. Their Phrygian caps forever linked Perseus and Mithras.

The tunnel, dimly lit by a string of construction lights, revealed the Cardinal was naked except for a pair of sandals covered in blood. Monsignor Tommy acquired the bull's blood at a farmer's market about 60 kilometers from the residence. The Cardinal performed the ancient bull's blood ritual on himself whenever Monsignor Tommy procured enough blood.

The Monsignor waited for the Cardinal to finish in the basement with a robe. "I don't know why your Eminence reenacts those pagan rituals. You are a Roman Catholic Cardinal, for God's sake!"

The Cardinal tried to laugh it off as if it was a joke. "I am just playing the odds, Tommy. What if Mithraism had survived and Rome had forever banned Christianity? It would be a very different world today if Emperor Constantine had sided with the Mithrians, not the Christians. The stories of Christ and Mithras are extremely similar; they were born of a virgin on December 25th. Shepherds and wise men witnessed their births. Jesus was born in a stable, and Mithras was born in a cave. They healed the sick, performed miracles, and were Saviors; both died and rose from the dead. After Christmas Mass, I wish the parishioners a Merry Mithras. They assume I had too much wine and thought I said Merry Christmas."

"That doesn't tell me why you do it." Tommy retorted.

The Cardinal smiled and thought, "Power comes from the ancient god. The similarities between Jesus and Mithras are too hard to ignore."

Later, after a thorough shower, the Cardinal sat in the parlor of the residence. Tommy joined him, each sipping a glass of Kentucky Bourbon on the rocks. "Any news on the internet today that I should be aware of?" asked the Cardinal.

Tommy shifted uncomfortably in his seat, knowing the following conversation would be difficult for the Cardinal to hear. He replied, "There was another article about you in the Sunday Saint Louis Post Dispatch."

Timothy Cardinal O'Rourke grimaced. "Why can't they just leave it alone?"

Tommy, who studied law before finding his vocation, answered, "Well, let me recap, you excommunicated devout parish priests, loyal parishioners, and the board of a parish church over their Building Fund. It was money that they raised for a specific purpose; repairing the church their immigrant ancestors built. They revolted at the idea you could steal their money and use it to pay off the legal fees and the settlements of abusive priests. I advised you against it, but you were too stubborn and went ahead anyway. You excommunicated Catholics that are in good standing simply because they opposed you about a financial issue. It's not like they worship a pagan god, for Christ's sake."

"Well, I was their Bishop, and they defied me. What else was I to do?"

"Nothing. You were well-advised by me to do absolutely nothing. Instead, you made matters worse when you gave the abusive priests jobs in the Archdiocese or re-assigned them to other parishes. You excommunicated the good and rewarded evil. It is the antithesis of the Christian ideal."

"The Laity has no say in church matters. What I say is the law."

"What the law says is the law. Cannon law does not justify your actions. So, live with it."

"I don't know why I keep you around. You never agree with me, Tommy."

"I agree with you on plenty, Your Eminence, just not this. And you keep me around because I know where you buried the bodies."

"Well, make sure you don't join them soon." Timothy Cardinal O'Rourke chuckled.

They exchanged banter like this for years, thought Monsignor Thomas White, but recently the Cardinal's veiled threats had become more menacing. Time to make sure I have options and protection.

The Cardinal returned to his study and re-read the notes of the report the Spanish priest had provided over the cellular phone. It was worth noting that this was the first time in decades, if not centuries, the subject altered his routine. The first order he gave Tommy was to outfit the Spaniard with an encrypted phone for all future calls. The second order was to convene a series of private phone calls with the conservative representatives of the other major faiths. The Spaniard had reported the movements of 'The Writer' had taken a subtle change.

Cardinal TC O'Rourke was Prefect, or head, of the Supreme Tribunal of Apostolic Signatura. The 'Signatura' is a powerful Roman Catholic organization whose declared purpose is to adjudicate civil and canonical suits within the Church. As its Prefect, O'Rourke used the Signatura as a tool to consolidate his conservative power base. His goals were to protect the church from women, who sought (1) a more significant role in religious affairs; (2) to internalize the trials, punishment, and forgiveness of priests accused of horrendous personal misdeeds; (3) to protect and control church wealth, and, most importantly, (4) to use that wealth to forward their liberal feminist agenda. When the Cardinal was appointed Prefect, he and Pope Bartholomew shared a strict interpretation of church law and tradition—until vociferous public outrage at the decades, if not centuries, of abuse of young men, nuns, and women forced Pope Bartholomew into retirement. Bartholomew's blind eye, or outright acceptance, of the abuse, left him vulnerable. He reluctantly gave up his power. Unknown to all but a select group, Bartholomew was in the early stages of Alzheimer's.

The Cardinal's plan quickly fell into disarray. He exerted his influence with Pope Bartholomew to appoint Cardinals loyal to their conservative viewpoint and personally loyal to the Cardinal. When Bartholomew's pontifical reign ended, the Cardinal would control enough votes in the College of Cardinals to become the first American-born Pope.

The abuse issues would not disappear and anyone remotely involved was toxic. The Cardinal did not yet control enough votes when Bartholomew announced his retirement. A French Cardinal was elected and took the name Pope Edward James the First. To O'Rourke's disgust, Pope Edward James I shepherded the Roman Catholic faithful from a position of love and forgiveness.

O'Rourke's role as Prefect ended when Pope Edward James demoted him to an ordinary member of the Signatura. Other posts soon slipped away, and now his only official power was that as a stand-alone Cardinal with no archdiocese or essential responsibilities. O'Rourke always believed his calling would lead him to glory. In his early seventies, he was still young and knew the pendulum of fortune would swing back to him. Still, rather than wait for the fates to decide his future, O'Rourke took matters into his own hands. He was confident he would lead the Church of Rome; he just needed to figure out a way to swing the pendulum.

In 2014, Pope Bartholomew's final act before retirement was to assign O'Rourke to a covert, secret interfaith team whose mission was to identify and intercede in any mystical or extraordinary events that threatened the churches or the current order of religions. Pope Bartholomew provided detailed intelligence to O'Rourke of a man referred to as 'The Writer.' The Pope told O'Rourke that the Writer's existence was a further testament to the Word of the Lord. The Writer had vanished for centuries but turned up in Spain when an anonymous monk published The Little Flowers of Saint Francis of Assisi. Only someone that was on the Camino de Santiago with Saint Francis could have published the book, and the book was published two hundred years after Saint Francis walked his Camino.

There had been persistent rumors within the Church over the centuries that the Evangelist was still alive. A Minister General of the Franciscans had confided as much to a Pope who had whispered it to others. Whispers became rumors. When the book was published the Church assumed that John the Evangelist was the author. They forced the Minister General to reveal what he knew, and John has been watched ever since. Pope Bartholomew told O'Rourke that for the last seven centuries, each Pope kept a watchful eye on The Writer.

O'Rourke thought it was important for the secret interfaith team to have a shared identity. He knew most men enjoyed the privileges of a private club. He revived some of the rituals of the Mithraic Mysteries and slowly converted the members of the interfaith team. It was quite an achievement since all were in leadership positions within their various faiths. It was essential to downplay the worship of the ancient Persian (Iranian) God, Mithras. O'Rourke laughed off the initiation rites as simply his invention to help form a bond between the men on the secret committee. He silently hoped the team would come to worship Mithras as he did.

Cardinal O'Rourke acquired his current residence with that appointment, and for the last six years, he received the same report from the Spaniard. The Writer had made no unusual movements, met no new associates, and showed no unusual activity. He kept to his small church, tended the garden, and took walks on the Camino. Today's report, however, was different.

"The young woman, Emmanuelle Chasteté, who has walked the Camino with him in previous years, arrived unannounced. We lost sight of them for several days; they reappeared on the Camino outside Burgos. We are checking local villages to see where they may have been. They stayed one night at a pilgrim's hostel in Burgos before continuing their pilgrimage. While in Burgos, the woman stopped at a package shipping facility. We found out later from the clerk that she sent a package to America to someone in the city of Saint Louis. We are trying to find out who the recipient is. After that, they continued their pilgrimage for another week, cutting it short and returning home. In previous pilgrimages, they always reached de Compostela."

The Cardinal mulled this information over in his mind. At first, he thought the assignment was a waste of his time and talents. Perhaps His Holiness had received divine guidance when he chose him. The Writer kept the same routine for decades, maybe for centuries. I must keep the other team members informed for now. The first call will be to Daniel Jack, the second in command of the Church of Latter-Day Saints and one of three members of the "First Presidency." The First Presidency is the team that guides the LDS church.

The Writer played a critical role in the early days of the formation of the LDS church. Daniel Jack could help interpret the significance of today's report.

His next call was to Rabbi Hillel YaVaz Meierson, the lead Rabbi of the Haredi Jews. The Haredi have proclaimed for ten years that the arrival of the Messiah is imminent.

Calls followed to the leading Imams of the Muslim faith. He called Monsignor Tommy into his office to line up the conversations.

"Tommy, I want a secret communication channel with the other Mysteries members. We must protect everything we say."

"That's not a problem. We can switch to encrypted satellite phones and encrypted texting apps. What are we keeping secret?"

"Something is afoot with The Writer, and we need to find out what it is before anyone else. We may need to intercede and control the event."

"How can we control events from here? We no longer control powerful committees and have little influence or access to money."

"We must change that at all costs. Once we remove Pope Edward James and reinstate Bartholomew, we can appoint three more cardinals loyal to me. Then I will have enough backing to get elected should an opening occur."

"Well, there are two problems with that; first, Bartholomew has Alzheimer's, and second, Edward James is as healthy as a horse."

"The Pope is elected for life. Bartholomew can serve even with Alzheimer's. We will use his mental condition to our advantage. Once Edwards James I is eliminated, I can reclaim my position as chief secretary and make all appointments in Bartholomew's name. The Curia is within reach. Only I will limit access to Bartholomew. Once the majority in the Curia favors us, we will let Bartholomew's health decline, and I will safely be elected. As for Edward James, well, he wouldn't be the first Pope to die from mysterious circumstances. And as Pope Bartholomew's primary assistant, I will direct the investigations."

The Monsignor let that sink in.

Rabbi Hillel hung up from his call with the Cardinal. He knew enough not to trust the Cardinal and would not follow the Catholic's order. That the Writer was acting unusual for the first time in centuries only meant one thing. The Messiah is coming. His first call is to Joshua, his contact in Mossad. The Rabbi told Joshua, "The Writer will seek an extraordinary baby boy. We must abduct and raise that boy. You cannot fail."

Mithraic relief with original colors (reconstitution)

c. 140 CE–160 CE; from Jona Lendering - Livius.org[2]

---

2. Provided under CC 0 license (notice under the photograph in the description page of the photograph).

Strasbourg-Koenigshoffen, Second-Century Mithraic Relief, Reconstruction ca. 140 CE–ca. 160 CE

16

The Boy in the Phrygian Cap, 4 BC

Girl in Phrygian Cap[1]

————•○•————

FOR THREE YEARS, HESSULAH, in disguise, plied her trade in the eastern Mediterranean Sea along the Anatolia Coast. Her route went from Byzantium through the Straits of the Dardanelles, then south along the Anatolian ports to Syria and further south to Samaria and Judaea. There were islands within reach, including Cypress, Rhodes, Crete, Lesbos, and Kos. Hessulah's trading territory encompassed a range of 1,000 nautical miles.

She built and continually refreshed her business plan in her mind. Transportation of goods by land was possible as Rome built roads throughout the Empire, but transport by sea was always faster and less expensive. Land transport had added burdens of theft from highwaymen or tribute demands by local tribes and kings. Transportation by sea had perils, with pirates and storms, but a good captain and gods' favor can overcome those and, as Hessulah believed, if you have Artemis' favor.

The Vixen was an old sturdy craft, almost 14 meters long and 4.5 meters wide. Its square sail pulled the vessel effortlessly, even with a light wind. The boat's pilot stood in the stern between the two parallel rudders to guide the craft. Now that she owned her boat and had money saved, Hessulah added a small sail near the bow called an artemon that helped the craft safely navigate inside a port with tricky winds or strong river currents. The Vixen was small enough to be manned by three sailors and a pilot. The largest shipping vessels at the time could handle up to 400 tons of cargo. Those massive ships crisscrossed the Mediterranean, but only to the larger ports. The Vixen could handle between six and eight tons of freight. It was ideal for hopping between the small and medium ports along the Greek coasts. Hessulah felt safe supplying these smaller ports as it kept her from the eyes of her brother Petrus and his Roman friends.

Hessulah was the Vixen's captain. No one else gave orders. While she listened to Assab and the two mates and valued their knowledge, she maintained order and was the final decision-maker. Assab helped manage the crew and represented

Hessulah in business matters when necessary. Her business plan followed her father's initial business model; build a reputation based on honesty and reliability. Hessulah completed her first strategic goal — to acquire a boat and crew that could service small to midsize ports. She believed that dependability and honesty would overcome the fact that she was a woman. In time, she envisioned expansion to larger boats and ports.

Like most old boats, the Vixen needed plenty of maintenance. Hessulah had spent the last two months in port making repairs and adding the artemon. Hessulah maintained her disguise on land, but whispers were growing in a few ports that the captain of the Vixen was a young woman. Those stories also noted that the Vixen had a most capable captain.

Assab suggested the name, The Vixen. Like many names, Vixen held a double meaning. A female fox was the everyday use, while a sly, crafty, dangerous woman was the other. Hessulah thought the name appropriate for the old vessel. She assumed Assab named the Vixen after the fox and never realized his true intention.

Hessulah handled business deals with a harbor master or a street vendor in various ports while maintaining her boyish disguise. Still, Assab was presented as captain when they dealt with Romans, Greeks, and Jews. She attended those meetings as Assab's servant but remained silent (sometimes). She found that difficult, especially if negotiations hit an unexpected snag. Hessulah's temper repeatedly got the better of her, leaving the other party confused as to why a servant was a more difficult negotiator than the master of the ship.

Once, sailing north, she passed the cliffs that enveloped the ruins of the fabled city of Troy. The land has been reclaiming the city for over a thousand years. That city, and its final battle, were immortalized in Homer's epic poem, The Iliad. Her eyes fixed on the legendary walls still faintly visible from the sea. It was an awe-inspiring sight for a young woman in charge of her sailing vessel with visions of future glory.

The adventures of Odysseus (Ulysses) in Homer's poem, The Odyssey, were retold by sailors in every port on the Mediterranean. Hessulah imagined herself akin to the great Odysseus in every sense of the word. She faced the same dangers at sea that he faced. She harnessed the same wind that he harnessed. He fought gods and demons, and she had her demons to fight, the power of Rome and the animosity of her brother chief among them. It took Odysseus two decades to win back his Penelope. She would win her father's business back even if it took her entire life.

———◆———

Today, they unloaded their cargo in Isthmia, a small port on the western end of the Saronic Gulf that supplied Corinth from the east. Assab walked westward over the 6.5-kilometer road from Isthmia to Corinth to acquire 50 amphorae of olive oil. He hired a local carter to help transport the olive oil back to the ship.

While waiting for the olive oil to be loaded, Assab ventured into the Corinth agora, to see if he could acquire more supplies for the ship. He came across a vendor with an unusual item that he decided to get as a gift for Hessulah. It was an elaborate double convex bow made from wood, antelope horn, sinew, and glue. It took most of Assab's strength to string the bow.

Hessulah had stayed in Isthmia with the crew unloading the cargo. Another larger vessel, with a ten-man crew, was at the dock. Their captain, Leonidas, was in a foul mood and caused trouble with the harbormaster. A two-week delay in his promised cargo left his crew hungry, angry, and grumbling about their pay. During the day, Leonidas eyed the Vixen, a smaller vessel with a slight teenage boy for a captain and two crew members, as an idea formed in Leonidas's head. Sometimes boats would never reach their destination. Although Pompey wiped out the Cilician pirates 60 years earlier, there were small bands of pirates everywhere. Leonidas thought, "Maybe there was an easy way to change our fortunes."

When Leonidas saw Assab return with a wagonload of amphorae, he sent a crew member to help load the cargo and to find out what was on the Vixen and its next destination. Assab and Hessulah were thankful for the help but kept a watchful eye on the sailor. Hessulah noticed the sailor initiated a conversation with Priam, but all seemed on the up and up. They transferred the fifty amphorae jugs of olive oil into the Vixen's belly. It took them about sixteen trips each, as a loaded amphorae jug weighed 38 kg (84 lbs.).

While the crew loaded the olive oil, Assab fashioned a pulley and lever system enabling Hessulah to string the bow herself. First, she strung the bottom of the bow and set it in a wedged position between two wood pieces that Assab fastened to the deck. The lever and pulley allowed Hessulah to bend the bow far enough to string the top while she built the necessary strength to string it herself. In time Hessulah built up the power to string the bow, fully draw it, and hold the bow and arrow in position as she aimed at her target. Out of habit, Hessulah collected pieces of obsidian to sharpen into arrow points in the various ports they visited. Hessulah made a collection of wood-tipped arrows for practice at sea that she would shoot over the ship's bow at the pesky seagulls. She quickly became deadly proficient even in differing wind conditions.

Hessulah watched as Leonidas's ship left port. The ship rode high in the water, attesting to its empty holds.

Four hours after the Vixen set sail, its course set to bypass Piraeus, the busy port of Athens, and head past the southern end of the Attica Peninsula at Cape Sounion. The imposing Temple of Poseidon sat high on the point overlooking the cape where it had guided Athenian sailors home for a thousand years. In Attica, they acquired a load of almonds and about 100 more amphorae filled with highly sought-after Attica wine. Hessulah intended to sell the wine along the Anatolian coast. Hessulah's trading operation filled a niche in the coastal trading market as it moved products from the large vessels to the Vixen's smaller hold, and she traded those products in the smaller ports up and down the coast. The commercial products they handled were olive oil, almonds, dyes, and wine. Trade was abundant around the Mediterranean, and all ports were busy. From Sounion, they planned a brief layover in Ephesus to unload the olive oil. After Ephesus, she designed a short layover in Halicarnassus before a stop in Heracleum (Hercules' City) on Crete. In Heracleum, she planned for Zalman to meet Hessulah for the 'first time.'

Heading slightly north, then west to Ephesus, they saw a ship with a half-sail unfurled looming in their path at the end of the straights of Kea. The boat was riding high in the water. She asked Priam, "Priam, what did that sailor who helped load the olive oil, say to you."

Priam answered, "Nothing really; he asked which gods I worship. I told him I was fortunate that I would visit my favorite Temples soon, Poseidon and Artemis. Why?"

Hessulah turned to Assab, "I need help stringing that new bow. Something about that crew made me uneasy in Isthmia; we will make them wish they didn't play with us. I will get our quivers."

As they approached Leonidas's ship, Assab asked, "What's the battle plan?"

Hessulah, setting one quiver at her feet and strapping another to her left hip, replied, "We will attempt to sail around her; if she turns to block us, we will know their true intent."

"Then what do we do?" he asked.

"Then we fight; they will soon discover the sting of a fox bite." Hessulah continued, "I will steer toward their stern; if they turn to port and circle to block us, we will know. String your bow and have Priam and Nemi ready to take on boarders if they get that close."

Assab, showing little concern, asked, "Is there more to the plan?"

"I am sure their captain is thinking that they are lighter and faster than the Vixen. He saw three sailors and a young boy, an easy mark. He will try to intimidate us into turning over our cargo. After we do that, he must kill us to dispose of witnesses. Perhaps the three sailors will join his crew. He expects that we will try to run from them and once we are caught, we will only put up a little fight."

"Is that why you brought your quiver of wooden training arrows?"

"I need some practice with the new bow."

"Those arrows don't fly as far as your obsidian-tipped arrows."

"I know, and they float too. He will think he's fighting a child and the battle will be over in minutes. His over-confidence will be his downfall."

Assab, soaking in Hessulah's plan raised an eyebrow, "I think that's a very good plan."

Hessulah guided the Vixen toward the stern of the threatening ship. As Hessulah anticipated, the ship turned to port to block the Vixen as they sailed on an eastern course.

Hessulah and Assab walked to the bow of the Vixen, and Priam manned the rudders keeping the Vixen on its course.

Hessulah pulled a wooded tipped arrow, strung the bow, and fired the heavy arrow on a high trajectory toward the ship. As expected, the wooden arrow fell short, landing in the water, surfaced, and silently floated toward the ship. She fired two more wooden arrows with the same results; the last arrow bumped against the ship's bow.

Yelps of laughter came from the ship as the crew sensed an easy victory.

Hessulah told Assab, "The wind moves the arrow about one meter to the right."

"Sounds about right," answered Assab. "They seem very confident right now." They both strung an obsidian-tipped arrow.

Leonidas stared at his prey. He expected more commotion on the Vixen; he expected the smaller ship to try to outrun him, though he was the faster ship without cargo. He did not expect to see the boy and the older Egyptian standing on the ship's bow, calmly discussing the weather. They were waving their hands as if debating the flight of a bird. The Egyptian's hand made a long slow line through the air, while the boy's hand was more of an arc, going high then low. Not worried about the two on the bow, he shouted to his men, "I want four archers on the stern. We will make quick work of them."

Assab said, "I can hit my target with a maximum height of ten meters." Hessulah countered, "I will shoot first, on a high arc, maybe 25 meters high, to get their attention. I'll shoot on the count of two; you shoot on three. They will watch my arrow while yours comes hard and fast. Mine will strike a second after yours."

Hessulah cried, "Let's give them something to think about."

In unison, "Ready one, two," Hessulah fired, "three," Assab fired.

Hessulah's arrow sailed high. Leonidas yelled, "Here comes one." The entire crew watched Hessulah's needle. Then Assab's arrow struck first, hard and fast, and hit the wood rail inches from Leonidas's hand while Hessulah's found the shoulder of the sailor who helped with the loading. Another volley quickly followed as Assab and Hessulah fired their shafts in unison. Two of Leonidas's archers were down, and two others were ducking for cover. Volley followed volley, and soon half of Leonidas's crew was wounded, dying, or dead. The rest cowered in fear from the onslaught. Hessulah's cap had fallen to the deck, and her long curly black hair framed her determined face.

Leonidas peeked above the railing he used as cover. He saw Hessulah standing with her bow outstretched. He shouted to the crew, "It's not a boy; it's Artemis. Let's get out of here." Blaming the defeat on a god was readily accepted by the men. They could never admit defeat at the hands of a girl. Leonidas ordered the sail raised, and they drifted out of range of the Vixen. Leonidas collected the bodies of his dead sailors, wrapped them in canvas, weighed them down, and dumped them into the water. He grumbled, "Artemis or not, she is a sea witch, that's for sure."

Whispers travel with the wind. Those whispers evolved into rumors. Rumors become folklore, and folklore claims the goddess is amongst us. Artemis had returned, and the goddess would deliver the people from Rome. Folklore repeated often enough grows to legend. In the seaports of Anatolia, enemies whispered stories about the sea witch; friends whispered tales of Artemis. Conflicting truths can both be true.

———◄○►———

Seven days later, the Vixen docked in Ephesus, and Hessulah donned her Phrygian cap and old tunic. She told Assab, "I will run by my father's shop and check to see if Petrus is in town. I will visit the Temple of Artemis if he is out of town. But I will immediately return if he's here; we will unload and set sail as quickly as possible.

THE BOY IN THE PHRYGIAN CAP, 4 BC   161

While in her boyish disguise, she hung out nearby her father's shop. That day, the shop was busy, so she suspected Petrus was close by and returned to the dock.

She thought her disguise and the short layover provided sufficient cover. She knew she could outwit and outfight Petrus. It was the Urban Cohort that concerned her. They were renowned for their brutality. It was common knowledge that many Greeks arrested by the Cohort vanished. The Roman Centurion Quintus led the Ephesian Urban Cohort, whom she suspected of aiding her brother after her father's murder.

Back at the Vixen, she told Assab. "Petrus is in town; let's make this a quick one-night turnaround. We will sleep on the Vixen tonight. In the morning, we will pick up our cargo and depart."

Once she completed her duties, her mind turned to her father, brother, Quintus, the Urban Cohort, Herod, and Rome. She believed the Romans and her brother had conspired in her father's death. She had kept the dagger as a reminder and as evidence. She couldn't prove anything - yet. She could not name what she sought; it was somewhere between revenge and justice.

Petrus was firmly entrenched with the Romans and abandoned the commercial business that Timo had so carefully built. It left a vacuum that Hessulah was determined to use to her advantage. But with minimal access to Ephesus, she needed to find a port to call home. She could expand rapidly with larger ships and a busier home port. She planned to gain access to Ostia. From Ostia, every port in the Empire would open to her vessels. She mused that if all roads led to Rome, all sea currents led to Rome's hectic port of Ostia. Hessulah dreamed of having her base in Ephesus, but that would wait until she solved her Petrus problem. Until then, she needed another base of operations.

Over the last three years, her business had been moderately successful. The Vixen was limited in its capabilities, and she had kept mainly to Greek ports, the Greek Islands, and the Anatolian Peninsula. She needed outside investment to have a chance to achieve her father's dream of building the largest merchant fleet in the Mediterranean. Hessulah set sights on her first expansion, including the ports south of Anatolia. The Levant region had the Syrian ports of Byblos (papyrus) and Tyre (silver), the Judaean ports of Akko (dyes), Jaffa (oranges and soap), and the beautiful, recently opened, Samarian port city of Caesarea (silk and spices from the east, passengers for leisure and sport).

Hessulah was a meticulous planner, and through a series of letters, she arranged to meet Zalman the Nabataean when he traveled to Heracleum. She hoped to persuade him to help her acquire a larger boat and gain access to the largest artificial port in the Mediterranean, Caesarea Maritima.

Returning from her father's shop, Hessulah stopped at the Roman Temple of Neptune. It was important for Roman authorities to see the Greek merchants and traders at Roman Temples. The Romans demanded sacrifices in the form of money or goods. Crews required the captain to make such sacrifices to ward off ill omens. Today was the Nones of Junius (the fifth day of June). The Mediterranean waters were warm and clear. Later that evening, a one-quarter moon would lighten the night sky. Meanwhile, the winds in the harbor became gusty, blowing inland.

A stiff breeze blew in her face as she stood at the rail. The crew stowed the supplies as she watched the other ships pull into the docks. She wore her weathered Phrygian cap according to Phrygian custom, with the conical end pushed forward atop her head. Its soft wool made it easy to change its shape. Donning the look of a farm boy, she garnered no interest from Romans or Ephesians. Her skin was golden brown after months of sailing along the eastern shores of the Mediterranean. Her arm muscles were taut after weeks of practice with her new bow. Her eyes took on the color of the sea; today, they were a rich green, while her dark, curly hair rolled up under her cap. Gazing at her face, one could easily see the intelligence and sense of adventure she held within her. Hessulah was athletic, energetic, and (unknown to most and herself) quite beautiful. She kept her looks hidden away, even from herself. She always dressed as a man and never thought of herself as beautiful. Those thoughts were for other girls. She thought of herself as captain. Besides, it was unsafe for a woman to parade around in Mediterranean harbors and ports. And no Roman port was safe for Hessulah of Ephesus, daughter of Timo.

Hessulah followed a routine as captain. She entered the cargo hold and double-checked that nothing would get loose and roll about in a turbulent sea. She checked the provisions as they came aboard. She always made sure that bandages and medicinal herbs were in place. She constantly reinforced the crew on their responsibilities.

Back on deck, she watched as a large vessel steered toward moorings two piers away. In her mind, she placed herself as the ship's pilot. The Cayster River flowed into the harbor, making the currents difficult. Docking a large boat could be tricky if unexpected winds cropped up at the wrong time. A harsh west wind was blowing that day. She knew that docking that big of a ship safely, the pilot should lower all his sails and only use rowers to maneuver to the dock. She thought it must be a new pilot; the artemon unfurled, and the mainsail was not entirely down; it was still catching the wind. Suddenly, a strong wind gust blew, and the ship picked up excessive speed.

She knew that the ship's rowers could never compensate in time. There was going to be trouble. She pointed and yelled to Assab at the end of the dock, "That ship's coming in too fast. Get those people off the dock."

She jumped from the Vixen to the pier and ran down the dock, yelling. Assab looked up and stared at the boat coming in. He quickly realized Hessulah's warning. He ran to the other pier waving his arms and shouting, "Run, clear the pier, run!"

A few people on the doomed pier looked at him, trying to understand the commotion. One of them turned and saw the ship moving fast toward the dock. He yelled to get everyone running toward the shore. The vessel bore dead aim at the pier. A few people jumped into the opaque waters. The ship was uncontrolled and collided with the dock, ripping up the wooden planks for about 5 meters before it came to a shuddering halt.

Those at the end of the pier nearest the shore appeared to have made it safely. Hessulah ran up the next dock that was across from the damaged pier. As she surveyed the damage, she saw a man in the water struggling to stay afloat. She ran up the dock to get closer to the man, threw off her tunic, and dove. She knew to swim behind the flailing man. She put her arm around his neck as he went underwater for the final time. The maneuver caused both to submerge. Underwater, she secured her grip and kicked upwards with all her strength. The man was dead weight, and she struggled to surface. With several strong kicks, their heads emerged, and Hessulah drew several deep breaths.

She scissor-kicked with her legs and paddled with one arm toward shore while keeping the man's head above water. As she neared the dock, someone threw her a rope, and the crowd pulled them both to safety. They lifted the man onto the landing and administered aid. Someone helped Hessulah from the water and stood nearby the man she saved to catch her breath. She watched as the man spit up water and began to cough. Amid the chaos, she lost her Phrygian cap and invisibility when she dove into the water.

The collision attracted people's attention from all over the port. Petrus, the centurion Quintus, and a few guards were at Petrus's shop, not far from the docks; sounds of the collision startled them while the commotion drew their attention. They left the shop and hurried to the scene. Petrus felt a premonition as he had a ship due that day.

Petrus stood before the half-destroyed pier and recognized the captain on the bow. The captain instructed the rowers to pull the vessel from the wreckage. Petrus muttered, "This will cost a small fortune to repair both the ship and the pier." As a small crowd gathered across the way, he heard more commotion on the next pier. Men gasped as they pulled Hessulah from the water. "It's a girl. She saved him." He looked over to see a tall thin drenched girl pulled from the water. She was taller and skinnier than the girl he remembered, but once he saw her eyes, there was no denying it was Hessulah.

As if she felt his stare, Hessulah looked across the other dock and locked eyes with Petrus. Petrus, thinking Hessulah would run when she saw him, was disappointed. Instead, Hessulah stood defiant and stared at him. He could feel her hate from sixty feet away. Petrus was the first to turn away and yelled to Quintus, "Bring the guards; that's my sister Hessulah." He caught Quintus's attention and pointed at the dock where Hessulah had stood, but she was gone.

Hessulah moved as soon as Petrus turned away and called to Assab, "We must go - now! Petrus saw me." Assab pulled his sword as they returned to the Vixen. They threaded their way through the group of onlookers and hurried down the dock to their mooring.

Hessulah quickly gave orders, untied the boat, and shoved away from the dock. The bow faced the sea, and the stern faced the shore. The crew manned long poles to maneuver the ship into the harbor, where the wind could do the rest of the work.

But the breezes that caused the accident blew them toward the dock. There was no breeze to carry them to safety. They floated a few feet away from the pier. Hessulah watched and saw Petrus and his accomplices approach her dock. She went below and retrieved her bow and quiver of arrows from the hold. Standing at the stern between the rudders, she strung the bow without needing the pulley. Her hatred of Petrus fueled her strength.

The crowd that pulled Hessulah and the drowning dock worker from the waters followed Petrus, Quintus, and two Cohort guards onto the Vixen's pier. Petrus and the Romans ran toward the floating Vixen. When they were about 20 meters from the end of the dock, Hessulah fired an arrow that intentionally landed at their feet.

"Anyone takes another step, and the next one goes through your black heart Petrus." She had another arrow notched and ready to fly, aimed directly at his heart.

The four men pulled up and stared at Hessulah, who stood defiant. One of the Cohort began to move forward, but Petrus stopped him, "As I recall, she is an excellent shot. She missed with the first arrow on purpose." Just then, one of the men from the crowd who had thrown the rope to Hessulah a few moments earlier hurriedly came up the pier. Oblivious to the confrontation, he yelled, "Hey miss, I have your cap."

Petrus turned and grabbed the Phrygian cap, quickly realizing the extent of her deception.

Feeling little wind and Hessulah trapped, Quintus ordered a guard, "Get back to the barracks and bring me an archer on the double." The guard took off running.

Petrus yelled, "I will get you. You are not safe anywhere on the sea."

"You can try." With a resounding thud, her arrow embedded itself in the wood plank just inches from his foot. The crowd, realizing that Hessulah had just saved one of them, started taunting Quintus and Petrus. Quintus turned, "Silence lest you want to feel the tip of my blade."

Hessulah yelled to the crowd. "I am Hessulah of Ephesus, the daughter of Timo. My brother Petrus, with the help of his Roman friends, murdered my father three years ago. You all knew Timo as a good man and a man of his word. His son is his murderer."

Petrus yelled at Quintus, "Put an end to this!"

Quintus replied, "My archer will be here shortly. He will make quick work of this business."

The Vixen was slowly moving away from the dock as the crew poled them through the water; a slight breeze kicked up that helped to pull them further away. The man that brought the cap overheard Quintus call for his archer. He returned to the end of the dock, asking for a couple of volunteers.

"Quickly, she saved Zander; we need to help them."

Eight of them crewed two small rowboats, four men per boat. They rowed to the bow of the Vixen. Nemi tossed each craft a line. They towed the Vixen away from the dock deeper into the harbor. They were about 100 meters away from the pier when the archer arrived.

Quintus called him to the end of the pier, "Bring her down," pointing at Hessulah.

The archer walked deliberately to the end of the pier and focused on the ship, Hessulah unmoving defiantly on the stern. He declared to Quintus, "She will be fish food in a minute."

He glimpsed Hessulah with an arrow notched in her bow that pointed down to the sea. Unfazed, the archer slowly aimed. He looked to the sky, gauging the distance and wind. As he pulled the bowstring back past his ear, he saw a flicker of light flash in the sky and paused for half a second, trying to determine what caused the glint. He released his string as Hessulah's arrow pierced through his throat, its point emerging from the back of his neck. His bow arm moved, and his arrow released sideways and flew harmlessly into the water. The archer fell backward into Quintus, his life's blood spurting out from his jugular. The archer's blood splattered Quintus's face. Quintus swore and tossed the dead archer into the water, the archer's bow falling to the pier.

The crowd stood silent and watched the archer's body splash into the water with the arrow through his throat. They realized the whispers and rumors were true, and a woman's voice above the muffled crowd sang: "Art-e-mis! Art-e-mis! Art-e-mis!" More voices joined the chant: "Artemis! Artemis! Artemis!" Finally, a thunderous refrain emerged from the crowd **"Artemis! Artemis! Artemis!"**

Hessulah heard the chanting and lifted her bow high overhead as a light breeze caught the sail and pulled the Vixen deeper into the bay. The morning sun threw her larger-than-life silhouette onto the Vixen's square-rigged canvas sail unfurled behind her. The crowd cheered at the backdrop of this courageous girl with her bow extended high overhead. The cheer continued until the Vixen sailed deep out of the bay. Hessulah replayed the scene in her head. Her arrow splicing through the archer's throat reminded her of Odysseus killing Antonius, Penelope's suitor, when Odysseus returned home from his twenty-year Odyssey.

She moved between the rudders as the wind pulled the boat to sea. She slung the bow over her shoulder and laid the quiver at her feet. Assab stood beside her, and they set their eyes forward, looking for pirates, wind changes, and storm clouds.

As was her custom whenever she left Ephesus, she turned around to commit the cityscape to memory. She'd recall everything she knew about her city and noted the changes that were taking place. This time the visual felt different. The people knew her. Her last glance took in the Artemision, Artemis, her goddess, the goddess of the hunt, the protector of children and young girls. She pledged to be Artemis's warrior to protect her city, children, and young girls.

She could no longer see into the harbor but knew she had another threat besides Petrus. It was the Roman centurion. She had felt the hate emit from both Petrus and Quintus as they stood at the end of the pier watching the Vixen and Hessulah and committing the scene to memory.

Assab watched Hessulah survey the city and said, "It will be a while before we are back in Ephesus."

"I understand. I needed to get a last look." After a pause, Hessulah continued, "City historians contend that a band of Amazon warriors founded Ephesus; they built the first Artemision over a thousand years ago. A nomadic tribe, they traveled on horseback from grassy plains north and east of Babylon near a great sea. Images adorn our new Artemision of those fabled female warriors fighting the ancient Greek warriors. The carvings on the Temple walls attested to the Amazon's strength and courage.

I am a descendant of the Amazons and ancient Greeks. I was born a warrior like them. You taught me how to hunt using the atlatl, a spear, and a bow. Now you must teach me how to kill using the dagger. I must be ready to kill someone up close to avenge my father."

They sailed west until the shoreline was out of sight, then the Vixen turned south to Halicarnassus and Hessulah's destiny.

17

QUARANTINE, ST LOUIS, MO 2020 AD

GREG POSTED THE FOLLOWING 30 pages of the Greek text and a week later received about a dozen translated pages in return. Over the following week, the translation sporadically showed up in email, one page here and there and then 4 or 5 pages at once. After the initial correspondence, the Translator only sent translation, no other type of notes or messages.. Mouse and Greg set up a process each time a new translation arrived. Greg would print two copies, and they would read them at the same time.

"Mouse, what do you think?"

"I think I like this Hessulah girl."

"She does seem independent and sure can handle things."

"Her brother is a monster."

"That was the way they did things then. Men had to watch out for themselves."

"I can't believe that you are taking Petrus's side! He murdered his father, and he's trying to set up his sister."

"I'm not taking his side; we just don't know how things worked back then."

"Well, let me clue you in, murder is still murder, even then.

"I get it. Hessulah is resourceful. Do you think she was hot?"

"Ugh, you are such an idiot. When will you ever grow up?"

"What do you think of Petrus's mother, Vissia? Is she going to put the moves on Petrus? Is this an updated story of Oedipus?"

"It's his stepmother, not his mother, and she was his age; sounds like she's just trying to survive."

"I need to read up on my ancient history. This story reads as if the writer is present. I don't know much about Ephesus besides its fabulous ruins; frankly, I don't know much about those."

"I just don't see where this story is leading."

"Me neither. So, I've been thinking about walking the Camino de Santiago de Compostela when we go to Europe. Pilgrims have been walking the Camino for more than 1,000 years." Greg tried to show that he was introspective after all his research. He not only wanted to find his roots and complete his connection somehow with his ancestors, but he also wanted to 'enhance his spirituality,' something he neglected during his business career. Greg read that phrase in one of his Camino de Santiago research articles. Now he only had to figure out what 'my spirituality' was before he enhanced it.

"I know what the Camino de Santiago is. I read books." Mouse's frustration came through loud and clear. "It's a 500-mile hike and takes over a month. I was wondering when you were going to hit me with this. On your Zoom call, I overheard you plotting with your French girlfriend, Emmanuelle."

"She's not my girlfriend. I haven't even met her. Besides, she's half my age, and I haven't heard from her in almost six weeks."

"Good."

Greg wondered, does Mouse mean good - I have yet to hear from Emmanuelle, or good - Emmanuelle's half my age? "Would you like to walk the Camino with me?" Greg offered, knowing that was beyond Mouse's physical ability.

"You know I can't."

"What if we rent a house in Provence for a month and have the kids and your sisters visit while I walk the Camino?"

"So instead of our 'honeymoon' trip to Paris, we will spend a few days in Paris, and then I am stuck in a villa in Provence for a month. The kids and my sisters can visit me, and we will explore Provence, its history, restaurants, and vineyards while you are on a long dusty hike across Spain?"

"Yes, that sounds about right. We can meet at the end of my walk, then go to San Sebastian for a few days and eat. I heard that they have some of the best restaurants in the world. I should be plenty hungry by then."

"If you can arrange all of that, I'm all in. Where are you getting the money for all of this?"

"We will figure that out."

Greg's spirits remained sky-high. He continued exchanging documents, via email, with the anonymous Translator. The manuscript's translation occurred consistently but slowly, sometimes only a paragraph or two. Greg could not complain since he would be at a complete standstill without him. Greg said aloud, "This guy - whoever he is - even if he is male, is a godsend! How can I ever thank him?"

Greg couldn't thank him since this 'Translator,' as Greg mentally named him, never answered any of Greg's questions. Greg thought his questions could have been more intrusive and impolite. Greg complained to Mouse often. "I'm not asking much from the Translator. I want to know his name, where he lives, what he studied in school, and what school he attended. What does he know about the manuscript, and why does he think it ended up in my hands? And who wrote it, and where has it been? How old is it? Why did they send it to me and not to the Church?"

Greg tried a friendly approach with Translator to draw him out. But Translator never slipped up; he never revealed personal information about themselves. Still, the translations continued, slow and steady. It was puzzling, very puzzling.

However, even with Translator's odd behavior, or rather non-behavior, the Translator disclosed the text sentence by sentence, paragraph by paragraph, and page by page. Greg's immersion into the story deepened with every new reveal from Translator. Rather than being in *'in a galaxy far, far away'* like his favorite sci-fi movies, this story transported Greg back in time, geography, and society. Greg waited for an email from the Translator with childlike anxiety, like a child trying to sleep on Christmas Eve. As much as Greg wished to find out how the story ended, he hoped it would continue.

It was fortunate that Greg was engrossed with the Translator's work since he'd been waiting to hear from Emmanuelle since their Zoom meeting a month ago. Her sudden and complete withdrawal from any communication left him bewildered. Greg wondered if he inadvertently hurt her feelings, but he couldn't recall anything too rude or unduly disrespectful. Luckily, he avoided asking for Santa's DNA, though he didn't understand why someone might think that offensive. Everyone knows that DNA research solves more and more crimes these days. It would help solve his issue. He could make another run at that.

He was depressed at the thought of being left hanging, and Greg was uncomfortable in that state of mind. Trying to distract himself, Greg refocused on his plans to walk the Camino. Selfishly, he needed Emmanuelle for this as well. He needed answers to practical questions like 'what should I pack or not pack,' 'should I stay in hostels or hotels,' 'how much money should I carry or is a credit card better,' 'how much training must an old guy like me do to get ready?' And, importantly, 'where can you get a cold beer along the trail?'

The conversation with Mouse that day returned to the Camino.

"Greg, why on earth would you want to walk 500 miles to something that is not near anything? My bunions hurt just thinking about it."

"I'm telling you - it's speaking to me – I've read a few first-hand accounts of the pilgrims - historical ones from centuries past and modern pilgrims from before the pandemic. You already think I'm crazy, but I will be a traveler on this path. They say people don't choose to walk the Camino; the Camino chooses them."

"Is that the only reason you want to do this silly walk? Because you are a new-age nomad?"

"Well, I would also like to lose my beer belly."

"Why don't you just stop drinking beer?"

"That makes no sense. Why would I want to do that?" asked a puzzled-looking Greg.

"Just saying, it might be easier than walking 500 miles, but who am I to question your motives?"

"Well, I am going to do it," Greg said confidently. "It should take about 30 days, probably a little more, but not much more. I don't expect you to join me. Stay in Provence, as we talked about the other day. That's been on your bucket list. The kids can join you in France for a few weeks while I'm walking. That's not a hard sell to any of our girls."

"I can guarantee you will wish you were relaxing with us, enjoying an Aperol Spritz before your journey is over!" chuckled Mouse, happy to know her participation in this ridiculous quest was unnecessary.

The translations continued coming from goj212024@gmail.com. Whenever a new translation came in, Greg printed off two copies and went to find Mouse. They agreed it was an exciting story about an orphan and her brother—but where was it leading?

Greg studied topics he had never heard of, nor thought of before, archeology, ancient societies, migrations, ancient battles, old gods, and mythology. Mouse let the house grow messy and ignored the mountains of laundry in the basement. Her garden looked a little weedy. But her knowledge of Provence, French food, wine, and agriculture increased exponentially. Greg continued his abysmal home maintenance routines, so their residence remained in its usual sorry condition.

Together they learned about life in ancient times, not prehistoric, but rather in the centuries preceding and after the birth of Christ. They learned of the fearsome power Rome held over the Mediterranean world from the time of Pompey and Julius Caesar, Antony and Cleopatra, Jesus Christ, and Herod, through Augustus Caesar until Emperor Constantine. They read for the first time about local political leaders who, though not necessarily Roman, were horrific in their brutal decrees.

Greg and Mouse scrutinized ancient maps between 500 BCE and 500 AD and learned about the common trading routes to India and China through the deserts and around the Mediterranean Sea. Teas, spices, and silk were brought west from China, while pottery and pearls moved west to east. They learned of ancient seaports, kingdoms, and kings. Religion, critical in the ancient world, was more intertwined with daily life. The ancients prayed to their gods much the same way people prayed today. Their daily routines began and ended with prayer and rituals. Religions had their genealogical traits as parts of every religion had borrowed stories, legends, and miracles from others. Greg mused, "If people wanted 'that old-time religion,' they should take up Zoroastrianism."

People were isolating and social distancing this year, and that was that. All anyone wanted to do was stay healthy. Due to these strange new days of social isolation, Greg and Mouse didn't have to explain their newfound scholarly quests. If asked by family and friends to explain what they were up to, no one would believe them.

The Translation was affecting their lives, but Mouse and Greg had no way of knowing that this was just the beginning.

Conversations at dinner often revolved around the Translation they received or research about that period. "Mouse, I have been looking into Ephesus. Did you know that the Virgin Mary retired there?"

Mouse asked, "What do you mean retired? Did she stop being a Virgin when she got old and move to the retirement home for old virgins?"

"Ha, that's almost sacrilegious. I doubt Mary's friends and family called her the 'Virgin Mary' to her face. She left Nazareth with the disciple John eleven years after Christ died. John the Apostle wrote "The Gospel of John." He moved to Ephesus and brought Mary with him. She lived her last few years outside of Ephesus on the side of Mount Koressus. It's about 15 miles from Ephesus. There's a very nice Catholic Shrine on the spot where she lived."

"I've never heard of it."

"Me neither; it has a replica of her home that they converted into a quiet chapel. Outside the chapel stands a stone wall where visitors can write a note to Mary and stick the note between the stones. The notes ask Mary to intercede for health, family, or blessings. People write the notes and stick them on the wall and wait."

"What does the church charge for that?"

"It is free, which, in and of itself, should qualify as a miracle. There is one more thing I learned from my research."

"What's that, Greg?"

"It's this 'Virgin' thing. The Old Testament and Zoroaster predicted a Messiah would be 'born of a virgin.'"

"That's right, so what about it?"

Greg answered, "In Biblical times, they didn't have the phrase or words for 'pre-marital sex.' If a woman who was not married became pregnant, they said the child was 'born of a virgin.' The Church announced Mary was "a true virgin" hundreds of years after her death. The whole virgin thing sounds like something a bunch of priests invented. Just another instance of the Church using mysticism to put awe or fear in the congregation."

"Well, mister-know-it-all, then how did the Virgin Mary become pregnant?"

Greg quipped, "The old-fashioned way is my guess."

The Translations kept coming in, and the story was unfolding. Mouse and Greg continued to be intrigued by Hessulah's story.

"This is a fascinating story Mouse, but what does it have to do with us."

"Why does it have to do anything with us? Can't you enjoy the story?"

"Everything happens for a reason. I only wonder why we are getting these Translations. Especially, why us?"

18

THE CALL OF THE MAGI, HALICARNASSUS, 3 BC

The Tomb of Mausolus, Halicarnassus, Caria (Present day Bodrum, Turkey)[1]

⊷◆⊶

THE VIXEN TURNED EAST after it passed the northeastern side of the island of Kos and entered the Ceramic Gulf. The Tomb of Mausolus dominated the view

---

1. Credit: Mausoleum of Halicarnassus Encyclopædia Britannica.

of Halicarnassus. Halicarnassus was a small port town whose safe harbor set back on the idyllic bay. It was late afternoon when they docked. Hessulah bought cooked fish and vegetables for the crew from the lone street vendor still operating that late in the day. She returned to the Vixen and spent the night aboard.

Two silhouetted figures, deep in conversation, stepped onto the upper roof of the Tomb of Mausolus. The younger male acolyte carried the old priestess. He had carried her up more than twenty flights of stairs without complaint. He spread his robe on the flat stone roof, and they settled to watch the stars. It was past midnight, and aside from the active rodent population below, the two figures are the only two beings awake in Halicarnassus. The young male left his oil lantern inside so light could not disturb their viewing. The roof of the Tomb was 160 feet from the ground and overlooked the harbor. The Tomb sat atop the tallest hills forming the town's eastern border. Their perch gave an unobstructed view of the stars. Usiris was an old Magi priestess, and Melchior was her promising young Zoroastrian disciple. Melchior was in his mid-20s, of average height, with a solid but thin frame. His wavy dark hair and the beginnings of a beard, several years away from being successful, framed his youthful face. He was considered good-looking but had no discernible features except a friendly smile and a genial countenance. Usiris was old and wrinkled, mainly consisting of skin and bones. Her bright, dark eyes overwhelmed her thin nose and thin lips. Her eyes lit with an intensity when she spoke, and tonight's stars mirrored deep in her dark pupils. She displayed an energy that belied her age and her physical condition. She understood her time was at hand. She used her remaining strength to convey instructions to her disciple.

Halicarnassus was the capital of the small kingdom of Caria on the central west end of the Anatolia Peninsula, 150 nautical kilometers south of Ephesus. The region of Caria was renowned for its magnificent rock and stone tombs. The Tomb of Mausolus, the most famous Tomb in Caria, if not the known world, towered over the small port city. Tonight's night sky and the view from the top of the Tomb were unusually brilliant. Gazing at the multitudinous stars, they felt the weight of the cosmos pressing down from the firmament. Melchior believed that the luster of the heavens brought him closer to Ahura Mazda, the God, and only God, of the Zoroastrians. Usiris directed his gaze to the far eastern quadrant of the heavens, where they could detect a faint, flickering light seeming to enter the universe.

Usiris said, "Look at that small beam of light above that cluster of stars. Do you see it?"

Melchior said, "Yes, it's small, but clearly, there is a beam."

Usiris explained, "Zoroaster's sacred texts identify this light as the cosmic signal of the beginning of the prophecy he foretold almost fifteen centuries ago. Magi have been waiting and watching for Zoroaster's sign for millennia. That time is now upon us, and the event he foretold will unfold. My time is over, Melchior. You must fulfill my role as High Priest and fulfill the role of the Magi in the prophecy."

Melchior said, "I am not yet a priest; how can I fulfill the role of a High Priest? You should fulfill that role."

"I have waited and prepared for this sign my whole life. But my time is over, Melchior. I am entrusting that responsibility to you."

"How can that be? You look healthy enough to me." Melchior lied, knowing that such a lie fulfilled the Zoroastrian principle of speaking Good Words.

Usiris smiled sadly, "My body is old and frail. I have been passing blood for ten days now. I have been drinking draughts of wine laced with opiates to dull the pain. I know when one's time ends, and my time has arrived. I am grateful that Ahura Mazda has allowed me to live long enough to see this sign and send you off on your destiny. All praise to Ahura Mazda." She paused, "You will travel to Babylon to join a conclave of Magi. When you arrive, your training will be over. They will confirm you as a Magi. I have high hopes for you, Melchior, you are special, and Ahura Mazda selected you to follow Zoroaster, and he sent you to me for this reason."

Usiris was from the Medes tribe that lives in northeastern Persia. The Magus priests recruited her into the fabled sect of Zoroastrian scholars, theologians, mathematicians, astrologers, military tacticians, and court counselors. This priestly clan evolved into a sect within the Medes called Magus. At times, gifted disciples, like Melchior, were recruited from outside the Medes tribe and trained to be Zoroastrian priests. Exceptionally bright priests ascend into the Magus sect and are individually known as Magi. Magi are universally well respected and received by the royal courts in Asia Minor, northern Africa, and the eastern Mediterranean. Magi are highly educated religious diplomats and well-trained astrologers. Melchior learned everything about the Magi, Zoroaster, and Ahura Mazda, the supreme god. He knew that for over 500 years, Magi had served as court counselors and advisors to great kings, emperors, and Pharaohs, including Xerxes the Great, Cyrus the Great, Darius the Great, Nebuchadnezzar, Alexander the Great, Pharaoh Ptolemy I, and many more. These last moments with Usiris were the completion of his studies. This final quest that she offered was breathtaking.

As the third son of a small trader from Myra, Melchior would not inherit his father's business. His options to lead a successful life were limited. He could learn a trade and start his own business. Like most Greek youths, Melchior received early training as a soldier and could continue in the army. He could not marry into a prosperous family because a third son would not inherit the family business or farm.

As was common in a Greek city-state, Myra hired an old Spartan commander to train their home guard. Sparta's military prowess as a powerful city-state had long declined, but the military training and acumen of Sparta were second to none. Their soldiers and officers often became mercenaries for other armies. Calyx served Sparta until his military service was up in his late fifties. Now a mercenary, Calyx must return part of his earnings to Sparta. Calyx had a full beard, now heavily sprinkled with grey. In Spartan fashion, he shaved above his mouth, giving his gaunt face a lion-like appearance. His body was lean but hardened from years of military service. If he lived that long, he could retire from military service when he was 60. His demeanor is stern but sometimes uncommonly subtle.

He trained Melchior and the other recruits in a martial art called Pankration. The name pankration comes from two words meaning 'All Force.' Pan means

'All,' and Kratos, the Greek god of strength, means 'Force, Power, or Strength.' Pankration included boxing, wrestling, locks, throws, kicks, and anything else that could subdue an opponent. Pankration roots went as far back as an early Olympic sport. The Spartans withdrew in protest from the Olympics when the Greek governing council modified Pankration rules and outlawed eye gouging, castration, and disembowelment. The committee continued to allow the dislocation of limbs, breaking bones, and suffocation to force an opponent to submit.

Once recruits were proficient at Pankration; fighting with their hands, elbow, knees, feet, and teeth; they trained as teams with swords, spears, knives, and shields. Learning to fight as a unit followed team training. Their final training included riding, running, and forced marches. Each unit marched over two hundred miles in full armor in three days and arrived ready for battle. Full armor weighed almost seventy-five pounds.

Calyx trained his recruits hard and instilled the Spartan virtues of honor and duty. He used few words and resorted to the whip to reinforce what words he did use.

During their third year of training, while resting for a water break after a forced march on a hot summer day, Melchior asked Calyx. "What was the greatest battle the Spartans ever fought?" Calyx stared hard at Melchior. Melchior knew he had overstepped his rank by asking an uninvited question and expected some menial punishment or the whip. He had not expected the answer he got from the stern, old soldier. Calyx came close to a smile as he told the story of Phillip of Macedon and the Ephors of Sparta.

Melchior's training started when he was fourteen years old. He could join a Roman Legion or a Lycian home guard when it ended. Military life required a mindset that limited Melchior; it was fighting and following commands. Calyx saw something special in Melchior and sought him out when the training was complete. "Melchior, what do you intend to do with yourself?"

"I will probably stay in the Lycian army. Which should I join? Rome or Lycia?"

"Neither. You will waste your talents in either army. Besides being my best student, you have a brilliant mind. You should not waste that in the military, and especially not under Romans."

Melchior was taken aback by this blunt assessment from his commander. "My options in life are limited. What are you suggesting?"

"I have a sage friend that you should meet. She is a Zoroastrian High Priestess. Her Temple is in Halicarnassus. I will give you a letter of introduction; go and speak with her."

"A Zoroastrian priestess? I don't understand."

"You are formidable and can become a great soldier, but to continue as a soldier is a waste of your mind. You can use the religion of the Persians to broaden your knowledge of the world, study the stars, and lead a great life. Zoroastrian priests are taught military tactics but also writing, languages, mathematics, philosophy, and astrology; some even become a councilor to a King or Emperor."

Melchior took Calyx's advice and traveled to the small harbor of Halicarnassus, where he presented his letter to Usiris. She was surprised to receive a letter from this old lover she'd met many years earlier. Though they developed a close personal bond, they never corresponded once they separated. Calyx's first mistress was fighting, and he followed her call. In all the years since Calyx had never contacted her; she was surprised he still lived. She looked over the letter and the prospective student. He was young and lean. She recalled the Spartan tradition, where they fed their new soldiers very little food, forcing them to forage or steal food. They were whipped if they caught them stealing. If they did not steal, they starved. Calyx would not send someone to her unless he felt the young man was exceptionally talented. This young man, not yet twenty, was lean and fit, with clear brown eyes and no facial hair.

Usiris stated, "This letter says your name is Melchior." Melchior nodded. "Why does Calyx send you to me? Do you believe in Ahura Mazda or the Greek gods?"

Melchior, unsure what answer Usiris wanted to hear, recalled his conversation with Calyx, smiled, and responded, "Neither."

"Well, I am a diseased old woman. If you are willing, I will teach you some of the things I know before I am gone."

Believing that Usiris knew the Spartan story of Philip II of Macedon, he assumed to reply with the word "if," might sound impudent; Melchior replied, "Gladly."

Usiris shortly realized Melchior was not an ordinary student. She was amazed that Melchior remembered everything. He remembered, word for word, everything he had read. He was advancing at a pace that overwhelmed his teachers. Without Melchior's knowledge, Usiris expanded his curriculum to include training as a Magi. She sent letters to other Magi and told them of her new acolyte. Usiris was old and had a wasting disease. Four years after Melchior arrived, she neared death.

Usiris instructed Melchior on his duty to fulfill the prophecy. "You must travel to Babylon and join a gathering of Magi who are now moving to assemble there. All Magi watch the skies searching for that distant light. It is the beginning of the prophecy. That sign calls the Magi to assemble outside the sacred Gate of Ishtar. In my room, you will find chests of silver and gold and four empty wooden boxes with a Faravahar symbol carved on the lid. The wood is from a branch of the Tree of Zoroaster. You are to take them and be on your way."

Melchior said, "I accept this responsibility. Please tell me all that I must know."

Usiris was confident that all Magi, trained to read the cosmos, would recognize the signs she saw. "Now is the time of the prophecy. The arrival of the Messiah is at hand. You must attend the gathering of the Magi; the stars are calling us. Magi use the Gate of Ishtar for all important ceremonies. The great King Nebuchadnezzar of Babylon built the Gate nearly 600 years ago."

Melchior kept his eyes on Usiris, amazed at the juxtaposition of her fiery passion and waning spirit. He felt overwhelmed by his role in the prophecy. Melchior adopted her belief that the celestial event and the arrival of a Messiah would change the world. He was awed that he, Melchior of Myra, would be at the center of it all.

Usiris and Melchior sat all night studying the cosmos, looking for other signs that might guide his journey. During the night, Usiris had imparted her remaining knowledge of the prophecy and detailed Melchior's duties and responsibilities. Usiris said, "According to Zoroaster's prophecy, the Messiah will be born of a virgin. The Magi will learn of the location of the Messiah while in Babylon, but it's unclear how that revelation will occur. You shall look for other signs that will guide you. Ahura Mazda chose you, Melchior. You will attend the Magi gathering as the High Priest from the Zoroastrian Temple of Caria at the Tomb of Mausolus."

Usiris handed Melchior her chain with a silver medallion that contained the Zoroastrian symbol of the Faravahar. "The figure on this medallion represents the tenets of Zoroastrianism. The circle around the man's waist signifies the universe's eternity and the soul's immortality. The male figure represents humankind. He points to heaven to signify the way to heaven through Good Thoughts, Good Words, and Good Deeds. The large wings represent those three concepts. The two spokes represent a Zoroastrian's daily choices between Good and Evil. The small wings between the spokes represent Bad Thoughts, Bad Words, and Bad Deeds; a Zoroastrian should strive to rise above them."

Faravahar. (2022, December 29).[2]

---

2. In Wikipedia. https://en.wikipedia.org/wiki/Faravahar

———◆◇◆———

Melchior replied, "I accept this as my life's guide."

With that, Usiris's spirit gave out. Melchior allowed himself a moment to grieve. Usiris had been training him for four years. He vowed to follow through on his promise.

At dawn, Melchior walked out of the Tomb to see a vibrant reddish-orange sunrise to the east beyond the hills that overlooked the small harbor. After the long night, Melchior was exhausted but exhilarated, his body running on adrenaline. He knew he must arrange a Zoroastrian Sky Burial for Usiris. But his priority was to arrange transport to his home city of Myra on the southern part of the Anatolia coast. From Myra, he must organize a small caravan and travel to Babylon to convene with the Magi.

Usiris had provided Melchior a chest of silver and gold, her silver Faravahar medallion to use as a credential to confirm that he was a Magi, and four empty ornate boxes 24 inches long, 12 inches wide, and 8 inches deep. Each box had a tightly fitted wooden lid with a carved, brightly painted Faravahar symbol on top, cut from a branch of the Tree of Zoroaster.

While in Myra, he must harvest and fill the boxes with myrrh. Myra lay on Anatolia's southern coast; it would take many weeks to get there over land but only a few days by sea. Though the Persian Empire was defunct, Zoroastrianism was still the largest organized religion in the Mediterranean world. Like other Zoroastrian disciples, Melchior learned the basic tenets of Zoroastrianism, including life after death, re-unification of the body and soul, heaven and hell, and a belief in angels. The overarching principle taught by Zoroaster and preached by his followers for almost two thousand years, a life filled with good works is the pathway to heaven. Melchior embodied the precept that one must bring happiness to others to achieve health and happiness.

Usiris's instructions to Melchior were simple but demanding, a perplexing mixture to the young disciple. Simple instructions, he thought, but it was an epic mission to travel 3,000 kilometers to Babylon across rugged mountains and desert, then have faith that at the end of the journey a group of Magi would have convened in. the same spot. He anticipated that the Magi would hold a ceremony that would reveal the location of the Messiah. They would organize a team of emissaries to greet the Messiah and travel thousands of kilometers back home. Simple? Yes. Demanding? Absolutely. Epic? Unbelievably.

Melchior was very aware of the immense responsibility placed upon him. Another complication was Babylon itself. Two thousand years ago, Zoroaster believed that Babylon would become the center of the world when he foretold his Prophecy. Babylon was now n ruin, a treacherous, dirty, decaying expanse. Melchior thought, "the Prophecy will be fulfilled, and all must do their part." Zoroaster had prophesied it. Melchior's mind raced as he formulated his plans. The logistics were daunting. First, he thought, I must get to Myra and collect myrrh. Myrrh gave Myra its name, growing in abundance outside the city. Myrrh paste was collected from small, thorny Commiphora trees and dried, then finely ground into a resin.

Melchior promptly set out to find a merchant vessel sailing to Myra or hire a small boat and crew. Halicarnassus was more of a marina than a port, especially compared to Ephesus, Tarsus, and Myra, the largest port cities along the coast. Halicarnassus supported local fishermen and minor trading vessels. Melchior worried if adequate transportation was available.

He walked hurriedly into the marina, searching for the harbormaster to ask about options. Not looking where he was going, Melchior roughly bumped into a young sailor. Both stumbled and almost fell to the ground. The collision knocked the hat off the sailor.

Melchior regaining his balance bent over to pick the cap up. As he stood to hand the cap and apologize, he became utterly dumbstruck; the sailor, also recovering their footing, was the most beautiful girl he had ever seen. While exhaustion seeped through him after the long night, his adrenaline had increased thinking of his mission; the impact of the collision left him at a complete loss as to what to say or do. So, he just stood, staring. Words would not form in his mouth, and time froze. He did nothing; in fact, he—just—stared—at—her.

Hessulah, with a slightly pained look on her face from the force of the collision, had no such issues. She scolded the young man for running into her, not apologizing, staring, and saying nothing.

"What's wrong with you? Have you never seen a girl before? You could apologize, at least. I pray Poseidon drowns you!" She walked over and ripped her cap from his hands.

The more she shouted at him, the more frozen he became. Finally, he mumbled, "I'm sorry."

"Well, you should be!" answered Hessulah. She tucked her hair under her cap and transformed into a sailor again. She turned on her heels and was gone. Immediately she felt terrible; the collision had been an accident and did no real damage. Also, the boy was visibly startled and entirely obsessed with her. That may have upset her the most. She had no use for men and did not want one in her life right now.

However, that young man had unnerved her. She quickly walked away from him, trying unsuccessfully to think of something else. She reorganized the cargo in the hold when she returned to the Vixen. It was a task that had been completed and did not need redoing.

Assab had watched the encounter from afar and ribbed Hessulah when she returned, "Is that how you meet all your men? You will never marry if you scare them half to death."

Hessulah swore at Assab, "May Poseidon cut out your tongue!" She moved on, trying not to get caught in one of his verbal entrapments. While growing up in a port, Hessulah learned to swear like a sailor. It did not matter which God, Egyptian, Greek, or Roman, Hessulah invoked them all, and often. She tried to put the encounter with the young man out of her mind, but her thoughts quickly returned to the incident.

Melchior stumbled off in search of the harbormaster, talking to himself as he walked away, "What an idiot you are. You sound like a fool; why can't you speak up? I didn't ask for her name. How can I find out her name? I must undertake the quest of Zoroaster, but why can I only think of her?"

As he was berating himself, he found the harbormaster. He discovered that The Vixen was the only ship leaving soon and headed toward Myra; he should look for an old Egyptian sailor.

Melchior headed back in the direction he came to where the harbormaster said he would find the Vixen moored. He saw what appeared to be the ship and walked up to the Vixen's master, the Egyptian by his looks. The Egyptian stood at the stern and watched the last cargo loaded. Melchior asked, "Are you headed to Myra? Can you take on a passenger? I am willing to pay."

Assab looked at Melchior, trying to size him up. Finally, he grinned and said, "You must speak to the captain."

Melchior replied, "Okay, but aren't you the captain?"

With a wry smile, Assab replied, "No, but I can fetch the captain for you if you would like."

Before Melchior could respond, Assab yelled loudly, "Hey, captain! Someone wants to speak to you!" And then Assab just broke out laughing. Melchior was puzzled as to why this man was laughing at him.

"What's so funny?" Melchior asked Assab.

But suddenly, that girl emerged from the cargo hold. Hessulah, who was always in charge of every situation, was again surprised. She followed her natural inclination whenever she was caught off guard and yelled at Melchior, "What do you want now?" Hessulah immediately regretted being so harsh.

Melchior was stunned. He could only stammer, "I'm looking for the Vixen's captain, but he," pointing to Assab, "must be playing a trick on me."

That added to Hessulah's irritation, and she yelled, "Why? Who says a woman can't captain a ship and do it as well as any man? Aren't the Amazons feared as warriors and captains of their ships? Artemisia, a woman, was the greatest admiral in Xerxes' Navy. Didn't Cleopatra command an entire navy, an entire Empire?"

Again, she thought, "Why can't I say something nice to this boy? He will think I am the goddess Eris who sows chaos, strife, and discord." Her thought continued, "I don't care! But why do I? Ugh."

Melchior wanted to run away. He had had few interactions with young women and never one in public. A beautiful girl had never challenged him. He honestly did not know what to do.

The Egyptian and a few others watched with bemused looks, and he felt all their eyes upon him. But his mission was too important to jeopardize simply because he was embarrassed. He had to find the courage to speak to this girl.

Suddenly, he spoke faster than he had ever spoken. "My name is Melchior—I am a Zoroastrian disciple at the Tomb of Mausolus—I need passage home to Myra—as quickly as possible—I'd prefer to sail with the most capable female captain there is—I will pay whatever you ask—Please—can you take me?"

Then he stopped and tried to draw a breath. There was complete silence between them. Their eyes locked on each other in that silent, electric communication of mutual attraction. A smile began to form on Hessulah's mouth as they both broke out laughing. Hessulah's mind mused, is this Cupid at play?

Melchior, slightly troubled, explained to Hessulah, "There is another issue, though. Usiris, the High Priestess, died last night. I must bury her today. Is it possible that you can wait a day before we leave? I left her body covered in my robe at the foot of the Fire Altar in the Temple. I can pay extra for the added delay."

Hessulah explained, "We must stop in Heracleum for a night and will reach Myra the day following if that's okay with you."

Hessulah agreed to the extra day delay for half her regular price and offered to help with the burial. "I have waited months for my meeting in Heracleum; it can wait a day more."

Assab lifted one eyebrow and gave her a quizzical look when she told him of the arrangement and the discounted rate. Assab teased, "He has fuzz for a beard. He looks like a baby goat."

She said, "Oh, mind your own business. The day delay will give you time to finish those repairs I have been asking about." She tossed her head high and walked away with a strut.

She felt sympathy for Melchior; burying his priestess seemed essential to him. They went into the hills and collected four long branches for wooden poles and a bundle of shorter branches. He cut several branches from a Cypress tree. Cypresses are green coniferous or fir trees with long pine needles.

He caught her staring at his unshaven face. "Why are you looking at my beard? "You call that a beard?" she teased.

"My beard will grow. The men in my family all have proper beards; mine will grow with time."

Hessulah laughed and lied, "Well, I think it makes you look distinguished."

Melchior, confused again, nodded thanks, and explained, "Cypresses represent everlasting life in my religion. Zoroaster chose Cypresses as an important symbol because they can grow for over a thousand years. Zoroaster planted the Sarv-e Abarkuh Cypress tree in eastern Persia. It was almost 2,000 years old before you and I were born!"

On a hillside overlooking the harbor, Melchior, with the help of Hessulah and others from the Temple, built a burial "Sky Tower" called a Dakhma or Tower of Silence. It is a circular tower about 2 meters high with a flat top. He explained to Hessulah, "The unwrapped body of Usiris is placed on the flat top and exposed to the elements. In time, the birds will have cleaned the bones. Then after the sun bleaches the bones, they are collected and cast into a lime pit and the circle of life will be complete."

Melchior raised his arms in prayer as they placed Usiris on the Dakhma. Quietly, Hessulah asked Artemis to watch over Usiris.

Although the skies were clear the following morning as they left Halicarnassus, there was talk in the marina of a storm coming from the south and west. Hessulah hoped they would catch a good breeze and beat any storm to Heracleum. The stop in Heracleum would delay Melchior's arrival in Myra by a day, but it was necessary for her future. She thought that whatever adventure this young man was up to can wait a day for me to complete my business.

Melchior was on the deck near the stern, trying to keep his balance. He had the unsure footing of one new to the sea but was athletic enough not to fall on his face. And he was, after all, trying very hard to impress Hessulah. Hessulah stood at the stern between the two rudders keeping the Vixen on course. She stared into the distance, looking for pirates, wind changes, and storm clouds. The clouds were getting heavier, and the blue had left the sky. The sea had begun to chop, and the water's color changed from deep blue to green.

When she caught Melchior looking at her, she turned her gaze directly at him, challenging him. He quickly diverted his eyes. She'd let her eyes return to search the horizon for sail or storm. Soon she'd find herself studying the young man. When he caught her staring, he turned his gaze directly at her. She quickly diverted her eyes back to the horizon. This game of cat and mouse went on for some time. Neither was experienced with the other sex to know what to say or do; however, they enjoyed each other's presence.

Assab observed this juvenile flirtation by walking around the deck, mumbling aloud in his native tongue. Neither Melchior nor Hessulah understood his mumbling, but they realized he was making fun of them. That was the price of their inexperience.

Finally, Melchior found some courage, "Thank you for taking me to Myra."

Hessulah shrugged indifferently, "Well, you are paying twice the going rate."

Melchior apologized, "I am sorry for running into you yesterday. It was very kind of you to delay leaving for me and help me bury Usiris."

It was Hessulah's turn to apologize, hoping to de-escalate the dialogue, "It was unfortunate that I snapped and took your head off. It caught me off guard, that's all."

"Why do you disguise yourself as a man?"

Unwilling to trust Melchior with the real reasons for her disguise, she answered, "It's difficult to be a woman in most ports." Not a lie, though not the whole truth; I don't want him to think I am a fugitive, she thought. Hessulah changed the subject,

"Why the big rush to go to Myra?"

Melchior, thankful for the change of subject and a more conversational tone, answered, "Well, it's a long story, and it may sound rather strange."

Hessulah, thinking, I hope he's not crazy, offered, "We've got time, and neither of us will be leaving this boat anytime soon."

Melchior told his story as an acolyte of Zoroaster, rising to the rank of a disciple, the Prophecy of Zoroaster, astrology, and something about a messiah or adventure. He kept looking at Hessulah to see if his outlandish story was convincing. Hessulah politely listened to him, but he couldn't tell what she was thinking. Melchior worried that she believed him to be crazy. But I must always tell the truth; Good Words are one of the three principles of Zoroaster.

Hessulah thought, "Hmm, maybe he is crazy, but he is a good kind of crazy. I like him; he is good-natured and seems honest."

Hessulah was used to crude men who worked for her father, like Nemi, Priam, and other sailors. Though they were mostly honest, they lacked refinement and education. Her brother was wicked and treated her, and others, with contempt. Men around the ports were vulgar, and she did her best to avoid them. Romans were arrogant and rude.

Melchior was none of that. It was refreshing to meet a man who was both kind and intelligent. Her father was kind and clever, but he had rough edges that years of sailing forged into his demeanor. She liked that Melchior tried to impress her, but not by braggadocio. It was little things like trying not to lose his balance. He didn't need to boast or swear to prove his manhood. He was content being himself. He seemed genuine and competent, and he was handsome.

Hessulah took in everything that Melchior was saying. It was a fantastic story if true. She asked, "How are you certain the Prophecy is true? What is a Messiah? Will the Messiah overthrow Rome?" She had so many questions it started to detract from the story he was trying to tell. So, she stopped asking questions and just looked at him and listened.

Suddenly Hessulah swore, "Neptune's balls! I don't believe it!" Melchior started apologizing for telling such a tale, and then he followed Hessulah's eyes fixed on the horizon. A very dark storm with lightning bolts was far off in the distance but approaching fast. Immediately the wind picked up, forming white caps while they felt light vibrations from the thunder booms. She commanded Assab, Priam, and Nemi to take down the sails and latch everything that could latch down. Melchior asked, "What can I do?"

"Go down below and pray to your God while I ask Artemis for help. We may need them both!" said Hessulah. Melchior took confidence in Hessulah's expression that showed concern but no fear.

The storm was ferocious. It tossed the boat as heavy waves crashed over the sides. Lightning flashed all around, illuminating the cargo hold where Melchior stood hanging onto a rope. The crew and Assab joined him. The crew took turns handling the bilge pump as the sea water came in fast.

Hessulah was alone on deck in the storm, manning the two rudders and keeping the boat pointed into the teeth of the storm.

Melchior tried to pass Assab as the storm raged to be on deck with Hessulah. Assab held him back.

"You can't go up there. She must do this alone. If you go up there, you will be in danger, and she will try to save you; then, we will all drown,"

Melchior shouted at Assab. "Will she be okay out there by herself?"

His response did not answer the question, "Hessulah is the fiercest captain I know."

Melchior thought of pushing Assab; instead, he asked, "What can I do to help?"

Assab replied, "If you want to help, start pumping."

After he finished, Melchior knelt in the water in the hold of the reeling boat and raised both arms and prayed. "Blessed are thee, Ahura Mazda, may you grant us safety. Grant Hessulah the strength she needs to weather this storm. Watch over us, oh blessed God!" Soon, the wind subsided, and the sea calmed. He went on deck as soon as it was safe and found Hessulah standing between the rudders.

She had tossed her tunic aside as the storm hit in case she had to swim. The tunic and her cap were swept away in the storm. Her undergarments pressed tight against her lithe body. The wind blew her wet hair across her face. Feeling like Odysseus tied to the mast of his Galley to hear the wail of the sirens, Hessulah wore a bold and triumphant look on her face.

Melchior and Hessulah locked eyes, standing two feet apart, transfixed on each other. Hessulah stood leaning forward into the strong breeze, her undergarments soaked from the storm, pressing tightly, almost invisible, against her, enhancing her youthful feminine form. Her muscles were hardened and taut from the fight with the sea; her nipples were cold, wet, and excited. The water on her face was fresh from the rain and slightly salty as it mixed with the blowing seawater. The taste of the water, the smell of the sea, the blowing wind, and Melchior standing before her, coupled with the magnetism flowing between them overwhelmed her senses.

She was victorious as she fought the furies to save her vessel, her cargo and crew, and the man that would be hers. Melchior stood staring unabashed, but this time his attention was not unwanted. Both stood staring, intensely looking at the other, realizing they were each other's destiny.

Assab emerged from below and took in the scene. His wry quip did not escape his lips. Silently he went to the bow to assess any damage. He knew that one was lucky to have such a moment once in a lifetime. Hers was a hard life; he would not deny Hessulah even a second of that moment.

Hessulah and Melchior remembered that moment for the rest of their lives. It was as intense and pure a moment as they would ever know. Once the moment was over, a calm certainty replaced nervous tension. Love replaced uncertainty.

The crew emerged once from the hold, most of the water pumped back to the sea, and Hessulah began giving commands. In awe of the gods, the superstitious male crew immediately thanked Melchior for saving them with his prayers. Melchior answered them by looking at Hessulah and thundered, "Thank you, Hessulah, for saving all of us."

His words were the only words she heard. She ordered Assab to take the rudders and make for Heracleum as she walked into Melchior's embrace.

———————◦◦——————

The Vixen slowly sailed into Heracleum (Hercules City), the major port for the island of Crete. A statue of Hercules wrestling a bull stood in the center of the port. The Vixen lost some of its lead sheathings that covered the bow during the storm. The sheathing provided a watertight seal so the cargo hold would remain dry. Melchior accompanied Hessulah and Assab during their inspection of the bow.

She pointed at the bow, "Here's where the pitch is applied and where the lead sheathings should cover it. The black pitch is lathered between the boards and worked into the seams to provide the seal. The result is extremely thick and blunts the bow of the ship. Then we must reapply the pitch after a few months at sea as the saltwater erodes the bond. It is a constant challenge as the seal erodes, water seeps, and we continually operate the bilge pump. The lead covering is placed over the pitch to help extend its life, but it's not perfect."

Melchior mentioned, "I have read about black tar. It's been in use for over 1,000 years. Persians called the tar - asphalt - and used it extensively on roads, walls, and shipbuilding. The Zoroastrians keep an incredible library of thousands of documents on religion, history, astrology, plants, animals, and minerals. I believe the Persian application of asphalt delivered much better results than this."

Melchior was always interested in learning how things worked. He was a voracious reader, and Usiris gave him access to all Zoroastrian scrolls. When he was not studying, he liked experimenting with plants and minerals and seeing how they reacted under different conditions, especially heat. Fire was at the heart of many Zoroastrian rituals, and a Fire Altar was in each Zoroastrian Temple.

Hessulah said, "I promise to get you to Myra as quickly as possible once I conclude my business. Normally, I would stay and fully repair the Vixen, but that will take many days. I will have the shipyard apply some pitch to the damaged part of the hull. We can cover the pitch with an extra canvas. Calm seas and good weather should see us safely to Myra. But it will mean more time operating the bilge pump, but we have an extra hand with you aboard. We can put the Vixen in for full repairs in Myra."

"I appreciate everything that you are doing for me. I hope I can repay you someday."

"There is something you can help me with if you don't mind me asking a favor."

"Please ask me anything; I would love to help."

"I am here to meet with Zalman of Caesarea on business. I want Assab to stay with The Vixen to oversee the repairs. Would you represent my interests? Zalman is a Nabataean and married to a Judaean, he practices Judaism, and Jews are forbidden to negotiate with unmarried women. I need someone to speak for me. I will be in the room and promise to remain silent even if that is difficult." Hessulah's frustration that her sex made her unequal was evident. "I can explain the details of the negotiations on our walk to Zalman's place. He is staying with his wife's sister, Esther."

As they walked to Ester's several times Hessulah replied, "That's a good question."

Melchior asked pointed questions on costs, timeframe, interest, etc. He then asked a strange question, "What would be the advantages of making the ship watertight with a pitch that's not as thick, eliminates the need for lead sheathing, and lasts longer?"

"That's easy, the ship is lighter without the lead, and it would be less blunt, so it cuts through the water easier, allowing it to sail faster. If it spends less time in drydock for repairs, it can make more trips each year. Also, if it is watertight and faster, there is less cargo spoilage and less time on the bilge pumps."

Melchior added, "I am all for less time on the bilge pump; my arms are still sore."

He isn't the tongue-tied youth she met in Halicarnassus. "Why were you so silent when we first met?" she wondered aloud. Melchior was about to reply when she caught herself and said, "Never mind!" Simultaneously, they thought he better get used to being spoken to like this.

After their conversation, Melchior recalled what he had read of pitch, asphalt, water, and Bitumen. Bitumen was a naturally occurring mineral that was the main ingredient of pitch and asphalt. There was something about the Persian application that was superior. He wondered if it had something to do with the asphalt or the pitch process.

On the walk to Zalman's, Hessulah explained, "I am anxious about this meeting. It took months to send couriers back and forth to arrange it. Zalman was my late father's business associate. I wasn't sure he remembered me. My father, Timo, spoke highly of Zalman as a man of faith, integrity, and good character."

She failed to mention she met Zalman three years earlier to exchange her mother's jewelry. She did not say how her father died or that Roman authorities wanted her for the killings of a Legionnaire and archer. She did not want to burden Melchior with those troubles, nor did she say anything about the disguise she used to deceive Zalman. She was not in disguise now and prayed Zalman did not recognize her from that earlier meeting.

She continued. "Word has spread about the quality of the ships made in Caesarea. They are faster and hold more cargo than equivalent-sized ships in the eastern Mediterranean. I need the best ships to fulfill my father's, I mean, my dream. But there are two issues: I only have ten percent of the money needed to purchase a new ship, and I am a woman. We must convince Zalman to build me a ship and lend me the money to buy it. I could not secure financing anywhere in Anatolia."

"That's all?" Melchior stopped walking and asked incredulously. "Build a big, fast ship and give you the money to buy it? Why would he do that? You said you are a woman, and they don't negotiate with women."

"That's why I am bringing you. Assab is a terrible negotiator. Besides, you said you would do me a favor, and this is what I am asking. I will not let the fact that I am a woman get in the way. I have a burgeoning reputation in these waters, and my father's past relationship with Zalman should help me overcome these obstacles. Zalman responded to my letters that he and his son Michael, the shipbuilder, would be in Heracleum in June. The meeting is now; I need you to make the deal happen."

"I will do my best, but I can't guarantee anything."

"All I can ask is that you do your best. Negotiations are in Greek and are more like verbal warfare than negotiations. We must be willing to walk away at any moment, over any point, no matter how insignificant, but never walk away. You must show complete indifference to what they are selling, curse its quality no matter how well constructed, and always complain about the price, or else they won't respect you. You must hate the product that we so desperately want."

"Are you sure that is how you want me to do this?"

"Trust me; there is no other way."

They arrived at the home of Esther, Zalman's sister-in-law and one of Herod's many daughters. A servant led them into an open-air courtyard. Zalman was present and greeted them warmly. With Zalman was a younger version of himself; Michael was tall and thin, black hair, a black beard, and dark olive skin. Hessulah thought, "If it weren't for his brown eyes, he would look like Petrus." Melchior opened introductions and introduced Hessulah as the daughter of Timo of Ephesus. Zalman introduced himself and his son Michael. Women rarely spoke directly to men and were never present for negotiations, so Hessulah nodded to Zalman and Michael.

Melchior, speaking Greek, began, "Zalman, Hessulah's father, always held you in the highest esteem."

"And I held him in great esteem." Zalman acknowledged, "Timo was indeed a good friend and associate; we all miss him." Zalman taking the offensive bluntly, added, "It is difficult for men of my faith to do business with a woman."

Prepared and not intimidated, Melchior replied, "Hessulah has a fine reputation as a ship's captain and trader; her father trained her well."

Michael turned to Zalman and said in Nabataean, "Father, it doesn't matter. We can't do business with a woman. What does she know of ships, the sea, or commerce?"

Zalman replied in Nabataean and told Michael, "I understand, my son. We will listen to what they propose out of respect for my friendship with Timo. We can end this talk once we hear the proposal."

Hessulah did not understand Nabataean and became concerned that the negotiations had taken an adverse turn. She told Melchior, "Ask them to speak Greek; I need to hear any objections that Zalman may have and catch any nuances to the negotiation."

Melchior ignored Hessulah and began to speak in fluent Nabataean, "There is no finer ship's captain on the Mediterranean than Hessulah of Ephesus. We were in a dangerous storm on the way to Heracleum. The experienced crew sheltered in the hold while she was exposed to the elements and bravely manned the rudders herself. She kept the ship pointed into the teeth of the fierce storm; large waterspouts formed on both sides as lightning flashed everywhere. The storm ripped the lead sheath off the bow, but Hessulah was unfazed. I staked my life and would, again, on her ability as a ship captain. Experienced sailors seek competent captains who pay a fair wage and treat them respectfully. Sailors volunteered to sail with Hessulah, a woman, because she is trusted." He continued, "Zalman, you say you knew her father. I understand that Timo was a man of faith and an honorable man. Hessulah carries her father's honor as her shield. Like her father, she has never broken her word, ever, and her reputation in business grows by the day. Hessulah will fulfill her father's dream of building the largest fleet of merchant ships in the Mediterranean, and you would be wise to support her. As sure as she stands here, her father's will and determination live within her. Nothing will stop her from completing this dream."

Zalman, continuing in Nabataean, asked, "What is your relationship to Hessulah."

Melchior wished to say more, but his mission conflicted with their relationship. He hesitated and said, "I am just a passenger and, hopefully, a friend."

Zalman said, "You sound like you more than a friend." Zalman and Michael both sensed that there was more to the relationship than Melchior admitted.

Trying another tactic to ascertain Hessulah's competence and commitment, Zalman, knowing that doing business with an unmarried young woman was a liability, said curtly, "Can you tell Hessulah to find a husband to speak on her behalf? We can bargain with a husband, but we cannot bargain with an unmarried woman."

Melchior hesitated and said, "I have not known Hessulah for long, but I don't think any man can tell her what to do, least of all a husband. Hessulah would rather be a beggar if you, I, or anyone told her she must find a husband to do her business. But I will certainly ask."

Melchior turned to Hessulah and said in Greek, "They think doing business with an unmarried woman is bad luck and that you should return when you are married. What do you want me to tell them?"

Hessulah was enraged, but she knew better than to show it. Instead, she stepped forward and addressed Zalman and Michael directly, saying in Greek, "Zalman, I trained by my father's side for many years. You saw me with him many times. I grew up learning this business; his dream became my dream the day I found him murdered. My brother Petrus, who has taken over my father's business, is using my father's merchant fleet to support Imperial Rome's military. You once told my father that Zalman of Nabataea would never finance Roman military operations. I intend to take up the vacuum created by Petrus' decision to leave the merchant business. I can guarantee my ships will never carry supplies for the armies of Rome. As far as being a woman, Amazon warriors founded Ephesus. The goddess Artemis, a woman, is the guardian of Ephesus. I am an Ephesian woman, the daughter of Timo and Hestia. I am the daughter and a woman of Ephesus. You are a Nabataean that married a Judaean. Israelites have had many women of courage lead them throughout their history. I pledge to conduct myself with that same courage and determination. My word is my life."

Zalman, Michael, and Melchior stood silent after she finished. Their conversation continued in Nabataean for quite some time. Melchior quizzed Michael on shipbuilding techniques, especially about the pitch. They switched to Greek at the end of the conversation, Zalman thanked Melchior, bowed to him, nodded to Hessulah, and ended the negotiations. Melchior and Hessulah were escorted from the house by a servant. Michael looked at Zalman and said, "Why did you agree to finance the ship for her?"

Zalman turned to Michael and said, "I can't lose. She has her father's determination and her mother's spirit."

Once they were outside, Hessulah asked, "What just happened?"

Melchior replied. "The negotiation is over. You agreed that you wouldn't speak to them directly."

Hessulah protested and turned back to go into the house, "Artemis be damned! By the gods! I will change their minds. I must get that ship!"

Melchior held her up and looked at her with a smile, "You don't need to go back; the ship is ours, er, I mean, it is yours. We are to bring 1,500 silver pieces to the harbor tomorrow. The boat will be ready in eight months at the shipyard in Caesarea. Zalman will lend the remaining 8,500 pieces of silver. You will have three years to pay him back, plus another 1,500 pieces. He said he may finance more if you demonstrate profitability within a year."

"Really?" shrieked Hessulah, "You must have bartered like I asked and complained mightily about the price for them to agree to those terms."

Melchior, "No, I did not have to. Zalman immediately offered the terms after your speech. Michael will start building the boat when they return to Caesarea."

Hessulah inquired, "Then what was that long Nabataean conversation about?"

Unwilling to tell Hessulah all he had said about her, Melchior replied, "We spoke about religion. I had to find out if they had an insight about the Prophecy or news of any Magi."

Melchior and Hessulah now referred to his quest as his 'adventure.' Melchior's focus on his adventure and Hessulah's desire to succeed in business was at complete odds with their growing feelings for each other. She asked cynically, "So, have they seen the cosmic signs too?"

Melchior, ignoring the sarcasm in her voice, said, "No."

Hessulah inquired, "By the way, where did you learn to speak Nabataean, and who are Magi?"

Melchior said, "My grandmother taught me Nabataean. Her father traded with caravans when she was young. She learned the language and taught me. I told you that I was studying to join an elite group of Zoroastrian priests. This adventure is the completion of my training to join that elite group. They are called Magi."

They inspected the black pitch and an old canvas wrapped around it the following day. Melchior spent extra time examining the pitch and collected several wooden buckets filled the compound from the shipyard. Assab said, "This short-term fix will get us safely to Myra, I think." They left that day around noon. A strong wind followed them toward the Anatolian coast. The Vixen sailed into the port of Myra in the middle of the afternoon, two days after leaving Heracleum.

19

Return of Emmanuelle, Saint Louis, MO, 2020 AD

Mouse and Greg put the future out of their minds, transfixed with the pages flying off the printer. The story of Hessulah, an orphaned girl, meeting Melchior, one of the Magi, the three kings, the Wise Men! They read the last pages of the translation.

"Wow, can you believe that!" Greg exclaimed, "She shot the archer through the throat, and she was on a rocking boat in the middle of a bay."

"Is that hard to do?"

"Are you kidding? That's like a hole-in-one, even better."

"I like how the crowd cheers her."

"Yeah, I bet that pissed off Petrus and Quintus. Hessulah was an interesting story before. It might be better than that."

"You think it's more interesting because she shot someone with an arrow?"

"It is more interesting because she shot someone with an arrow *in the throat* from the stern of a rocking boat at a very long distance. Nobody does that."

Greg continued his take, "Mouse, did you know that the Magi weren't just three guys that happened to follow a wandering star? The Magi are from an Iranian tribe that thrived for hundreds, perhaps a thousand years as philosophers, advisors to kings, astrologers, and all-around smart people."

"We weren't taught that. Our traditions display them as three guys who met in the desert and eventually arrived in Bethlehem."

"If they taught about the Magi, they'd have to teach about Zoroaster - no religion class ever mentioned he predicted the birth of a Messiah, by a virgin, no less. I had never heard about Zoroastrianism in all my years in Catholic grade school, Jesuit High School, or Jesuit University. Shouldn't they teach their students that many of our beliefs are from religions outside the Old and New Testaments? Ironically, Zoroastrianism was the major religion in Babylon during the Jew's exile. Judaism adopted many Zoroastrian concepts, added them to the Jewish faith, and passed them to Christianity.

"You weren't exactly an A student Greg. Are you sure they didn't teach you those things?"

"Thanks for the reminder, but if they did teach that, they didn't stress it enough. Besides, it's more than a coincidence that the Magi were a religious sect waiting for the Messiah. The Wise Men didn't just happen for a star to follow; they were watching and waiting for the star to appear. They knew it was coming; they didn't know when. Maybe we should turn our book into a book about Zoroaster."

"Greg, nobody will want to read a book about Zoroaster. Zoroaster is very ancient history; nobody reads history anymore, and no one reads ancient religious history."

"Well, it's not all about Zoroaster. It's about Hessulah too—and bows and arrows."

"You're hopeless; I give up."

"Well, it just happens to start with Zoroaster. Will you write it for me?" asked Greg.

"I am going to write *your* book for you! I must admit that I didn't see that one coming!"

"You know I can't write. I'll dictate the story, and you key it all in and add everything you need to turn words into sentences, sentences into paragraphs, and paragraphs into chapters, until we have a book."

"I can't keep up with the work here and become your secretary too!"

"Michener and Clive Cussler use others to do all their dirty work, besides you have always wanted to write a book."

"Yes, I have always wanted to write my book."

"I will give you half billing. I'm not greedy. You can go on Oprah and her book of the month thing. Oprah can introduce you as Grandma Mouse!"

"Oprah hasn't been on for years."

"Really?"

Greg admitted he couldn't understand much of what was happening lately. Mouse would never write a book for him. He couldn't understand why Emmanuelle, whom he thought was his new friend, would disappear. And The Translator — Greg had so many questions about him (or her) he could hardly keep them straight. Where did she (him) come from, why was she (him) helping him, and why did he (she) refuse to answer any personal questions? How did he (she) learn ancient Greek? How did a manuscript about a Greek girl and a Zoroastrian Magi land in my lap?

"It doesn't make sense," Greg would say quietly in the dark of the night. "None of this makes sense."

Greg had spent the last week in a crabby mood. Then there was an email from Emmanuelle, all happy and cheerful as if weeks without a single word were normal. He reread it to ensure he wasn't missing anything, like a hidden message. His mind was working overtime with riddles lately. Her email read:

Hi Greg!

I just got back from a spur-of-the-moment hike on the Camino. What's new with you?"

E.

What's new with me? Greg thought. Nobody takes a spur-of-the-moment walk on the Camino. Greg put protocol aside and dialed Emmanuelle, unsure if the time was convenient for her or if it might awaken her. He hoped it would wake her, payback for her behavior towards him for the past many weeks.

Emmanuelle answered the call with a quick "Bonjour!"

Greg started with a rhyme he remembered from his childhood years. "Where've you been, Bridget O'Flynn?" Greg started with this because he dialed without thinking about how to begin the conversation. And he knew if he started the conversation, he would sound offensive, desperate, or pathetic. Greg had never learned to talk to women, which showed in spades. He hoped Emmanuelle would get the drift, start talking to him, and tell him what was happening.

Emmanuelle replied in heavily accented French, "This is Emmanuelle; *Bridg-eeet* is not here. I don't know *Bridg-eeet*."

"Hi Emmanuelle, this is Greg; I know you are not *Bridg-eeet*; that's just an old family expression."

Emmanuelle started laughing. "I know. I was pulling your leg. I hope you are not mad at me for disappearing on you."

"I'm not mad. But I am a bit confused." Greg confessed.

Then she began talking about her hike as if nothing unusual had occurred. Say, you've fallen off the planet for the past month or two, and you don't bother to say sorry, thought Greg. She's not getting my goat, he said to himself, so Greg acted like the long silence was nothing abnormal. I'm not a fool; he thought as he continued to fool only himself.

"Emmanuelle, I have to ask you something. Things have been strange here ever since we last spoke. You may know what's behind it, or maybe not. About three weeks after our Zoom call, I got a mysterious UPS package from Burgos, Spain. What's going on here? Did you possibly have anything to do with it?"

"Well, Greg, I have a long story to tell you."

"Great, I'm all ears."

Emmanuelle continued, "Yes, it's why I've been out of touch all this time. I didn't have access to Wi-Fi. You could say I've been living off the grid."

"Okay, I'm not sure what "off the grid" really means but go on."

Emmanuelle took a breath. "Well, during our last conversation, I was excited to help you research your genealogy. One of your ancestral names sounded familiar, and I thought it could match one of my ancestors. If they matched, we could be distant relations, and it would be interesting to see where our families intersect and if we had similar family stories or traits. Maybe see how those traits changed, as one side of the family moved to America, and the other stayed in Alsace-Lorraine."

"Yeah, I remember that conversation. That's the one where you hung up on me." Greg thought but held himself in check and said, "So you're saying we're related? I didn't see that one coming, *cousin*."

Emmanuelle smiled at the cousin's comment, "Yes, *cousin*, but you said more than that, which was quite important. I couldn't say anything to you then, but I knew I had to act on it. That's why I've been gone so long and was incommunicado."

Greg hated it when women used foreign phrases like 'incommunicado' with him. He knew Emmanuelle had left him high and dry, leaving him bewildered.

She proceeded to talk. "When you told me that, I knew I had to speak immediately with Brother John. Unfortunately, it takes several weeks to walk to Brother John's church."

"When I told you what? Do you have a brother? Do I have another cousin?"

"No, Greg. John is not my brother. He's a religious brother, like a monk."

"Like Frere Jacques, in the nursery rhyme?"

"Yes, in Spanish, Frere Jacques, Brother John, or El Hermano Juan. Please, let me finish. My story is important!" Momentarily, Emmanuelle's heart felt for Mouse. Greg was a nice guy with a heart of gold, but mentally he was all over the place all the time.

"Anyway, I knew I had to speak with Brother John. The first time I hiked the Camino about 15 years ago, I had a revelation like yours; that my need to hike the Camino was related to Saint Nicolas. Brother John invited me to walk the Camino with him. Now I stop to see him every time I hike on the Camino. Each time the walk and discussion with Brother John renew me, it restores my soul; you understand, don't you, Greg?"

"Sure, I do," Greg lied while wondering how old Frere Jacques was.

"Well, I had to talk to Brother John about you. He asked me to send that manuscript. That's what this is all about; remember the package from Burgos, Spain?"

"Emmanuelle, I'm not quite sure where this is all heading."

"What don't you understand, Greg? I've been clear this whole time."

"Clear as mud, as we say in America. I still need help following the story; first, you say we might be cousins. Next, you hike with a monk on the Camino. Third, you send me an ancient Greek manuscript. I need a little more detail."

"Okay, Greg, Brother John is a monk; he lives in the small town of Azofra in the La Rioja region of Spain. It's on the Camino. Certainly, you've had many delicious red wines from La Rioja, haven't you?"

"Maybe a few, but I'm more of a beer man myself."

"No matter, since he's so old, Brother John is not assigned to any particular parish or religious duties, but I know that I can always find him at the church, Nuestra Señora de los Ángeles in Azofra.

"Emmanuelle, slow down. I'm lost again."

"Translated from Spanish, it means Our Lady of the Angels. Isn't that the most wonderful name? But I had to walk the Camino to speak with Brother John. Brother John only speaks with people who walk or bicycle to see him. He claims it's part of his vows. Some people would call him an eccentric, but it's because of his all-encompassing love for Mother Earth and her people. You meet incredibly fascinating people on the Camino."

"That's nice. But I want to know why you and Brother John sent me an ancient Greek manuscript when I only asked you for some background help with my ancestors. I'm not the most sophisticated guy, but I don't get this. I don't understand where Frere Jacques comes in at all."

Greg heard Emmanuelle take a deep breath. Then she took another one, even deeper this time.

She said gently, "It's all about your ancestors, Greg. When we spoke a few months ago, you mentioned having this strange feeling you can't shake."

"Yeah, that. I almost forgot; the translation has taken over my life." Greg interrupted. Emmanuelle's slow pace was driving him crazy.

"Wait, you are translating the manuscript?" she asked.

"No, I'm not. Someone is helping me, and I hope you know who it is."

"I don't know anything about that. What is the manuscript about?"

"Don't you know? I'm not even halfway through it yet. It's about a girl from Ephesus named Hessulah and Melchior, one of the three Magi."

"Oh, my God!"

"No kidding. I have no idea where this is leading, so, *cousin*, what were you saying about my ancestors?"

"It's our ancestors; we are related to someone named Nicholas Meyer around the 13th or 14th century."

"Awesome! So, you and I are cousins," said Greg sarcastically. Was Emmanuelle finally trying to shake me down for some money, coming up with this crazy lost ancestor story? Greg listened on, wondering where this conversation was going.

"The name Meyer is derived from the word Myra. Myra was a Greek city where myrrh was grown. A long time ago, someone from Myra moved to Alsace. This person's descendants took on the last name of Meyer, Maier, Meier, and the like. Our many-generations-ago-shared-ancestor, Nicholas Meyer, is somehow related to Nicolas of Myra."

Greg knew instantly. "You're telling me that we are not only related, but we are related to Nicolas of Myra through Nicholas Meyer?

Emmanuelle said, "Well, yes, but to be more accurate, we are related to Saint Nicolas of Myra, as in Santa Claus."

Greg thought he smiled for the briefest of seconds before his vision faded to black, and he passed out cold. Mouse found him on the dining room floor on her way to the kitchen.

"What are you trying to pull now, Greg?" she mumbled before seeing Greg's eyelids flutter.

20
Love and Marriage, Myra, Asia Minor, 2 BC

"By all means marry.
If you get a good wife, you'll be happy.
If you get a bad one, you'll become a philosopher."
— Socrates

The Rock Tombs overlooking the ancient Myra Amphitheater[1]

---

1. https://upload.wikimedia.org/wikipedia/commons/c/c7/Myra_Tombs_T
emples.jpg

MELCHIOR SAID, "HESSULAH BEFORE we disembark, there is something that I need to explain about Myra. Our dead hold a special place of honor in Lycian culture. A necropolis surrounds the city and features rows atop of rows of tombs built into the rocky hillside. These tombs overlook the city's amphitheater. One could say that the Lycian dead have special seating for all events. Sitting in the seats and watching a play with all the tombs quietly watching from behind you is a little eerie. But we are very respectful of our dead. Myra is just that kind of place."

"Why is myrrh a gift for your Messiah?" asked Hessulah.

"Myrrh has many uses; physicians use it to treat everything from fever, cough, lung infestation, leprosy, and almost anything else that might ail someone. Myrrh is also mixed with oil to anoint the dead."

Melchior explained one of his reasons for going home to Myra. "Myrrh is harvested in Myra. It's a substance that grows inside the bark of small local thorny trees. A sticky gum seeps from its bark when sliced with a knife. The gum is collected and dried, and ground into a resin. Some people mix it into their wine, which has an overall calming effect; put too much myrrh in it, and you can start to lose your mind."

Once in drydock, further checks of the Vixen showed more damage than first revealed, and the repairs would take several weeks. Old boats thought Hessulah, always need work. She arranged for another merchant ship to deliver her cargo to Paphos, Cyprus.

Hessulah was thrilled that the delay gave her an excuse to remain in Myra and see more of Melchior. Hessulah had to admit that she found him fascinating and, surprising herself, she often daydreamed about him. Many of the daydreams ended when Assab caught her not paying attention to her task. He knew it was not in her nature to miss something.

"Thinking about your prince again?" Assab jested.

She would swear oaths at him as she continued to daydream, and he continued to jest. Soon she just ignored him.

"Somebody is in love!" Assab teased.

Upon arriving in Myra, Melchior thanked Hessulah and Assab, then walked towards his home. He was in love but completely unprepared emotionally and did not know what to do about it. His epic task required his full attention and was too important to ignore. His desire for Hessulah consumed him. Why now? Melchior wondered. As he planned his trip to Babylon, he thought of visiting Hessulah.

Magi had been creating records for centuries, first in cuneiform on wax and wooden tablets, then on papyrus scrolls. For the last 500 years, Magi across the old Persian Empire had transcribed their records onto scrolls and translated them into Greek. Alexandria, Pergamum, and Ephesus had the most extensive libraries.

As an acolyte, Melchior read all the scrolls in the nearby temples of Zoroaster. He had a voracious reading ability and the unique talent to recall everything he had read. Usiris, knowing that it was a rare and wonderful gift, made sure Melchior always had hundreds of scrolls to read and set up an exchange with temples and libraries throughout Anatolia, Syria, Egypt, and even Babylon.

While in Heracleum, Melchior watched the workers apply the hot pitch to the Vixen. He recalled a scroll of how Babylonian shipbuilders used asphalt. Over six hundred years, asphalt was crucial in walls, roads, and keeping the Euphrates rivercraft watertight. The scrolls explained how the Babylonians had heated their asphalt and burned out the impurities leaving a thick but smooth paste. He had brought a couple of buckets of pitch onto the Vixen and thought he would conduct some experiments when he reached Myra.

The Zoroaster Temple in Myra was a perfect place to conduct the testing. Each Zoroaster Temple had a constant fire at the Fire Altar. Soon Melchior fell into a routine. When he wasn't with Hessulah, he was at the fire altar. When he wasn't at the fire altar, he was with Hessulah. He brought the pitch he obtained in Heracleum plus other minerals, including tree bark and resins. Although the fire altar constantly burned throughout the year, the local Zoroastrian priest wondered why Melchior kept his fire so hot during the day. It is summer, after all.

Hessulah's and Melchior's relationship flourished, and each tried to spend time with the other. Hessulah learned more details about Melchior's adventure, family, and Zoroastrianism. Melchior found himself zealously teaching Hessulah about Zoroastrianism. He tried to explain all the philosophies of Zoroaster and explain the role that Ahura Mazda plays in everyday life, the attainment of heaven, hell, and the angels. Melchior explained, "It's a complex religion based on a simple premise. For your soul to achieve everlasting life, you must lead a life based on three things."

He saw a frown on Hessulah's face, caught himself, and rephrased, "There are only three things that one must do to reach heaven. First, you attain heaven by leading a life of good deeds. People that perform good deeds for others without thought of reward will go to heaven."

Hessulah said, "So you helped me with my meeting with Zalman so that you could get to heaven?"

Melchior stammered, "No. Yes, it was a good deed. But no, I did that because you asked me and would take me to Myra. One who does good deeds receives health and happiness in return. They should desire no other reward."

Hessulah teased, "But you just said you helped me so I would take you to Myra? Your reward for your good deed was the ride to Myra, was it not?"

Melchior began to sweat; why do I get so flustered around her? "I did it because you asked me. I would do anything for you."

Hessulah loved winning these arguments, and she moved closer and rubbed a hand on his arm and chest. "What are the other two things I must do to reach heaven?"

"The next thing is to think Good Thoughts."

"Like the one I am thinking right now?" she looked at him lustfully.

"I um, I um, I don't know what you are thinking now." Again, he quickly lost control of the conversation, and she stood there grinning. "Good Thoughts are, um, are just that, Good Thoughts." That makes no sense; how does she do this to me? "Just think positively about people, yourself, and others."

"Okay, I will think more good thoughts like the one I am thinking about you, and what's the last rule?"

"You have to use Good Words. You should not lie, curse, or swear."

Hessulah's brow furrowed, "I am going to have a hard time with that one, Melchior. Will I not go to heaven?"

"All in good time, Hessulah; let's concentrate on the first two, and we can work on the last one."

"Are you certain about the Good Word rule? What else about Zoroaster should I know? Does he treat women as viciously as the Greeks treat their women? Women are nothing more than slaves to the Greeks, and Athenian treat their women the worst. Did you know a Greek wife cannot eat meals with her husband?"

Melchior boasted, "There is no difference to Zoroaster who prays to Ahura Mazda, be it man or woman. Women are equal to men in the eyes of Ahura Mazda. In Persia, women and men must do their daily tasks, but women own property, worship at the Temple, and become priestesses. Many Persian women are rich and powerful landowners."

Hessulah mentioned, "Do you remember the story of the famous Admiral, Artemisia, that I told you? She was a powerful Greek woman who lived under Persian rule. She fought for Xerxes against the Greeks because she was free to choose. She would not have been allowed to own anything or fight in Greece. Greek women are not free. Even though I am capable, I needed you to represent me at my meeting with Zalman. And now, it's getting worse for women with the Romans. They are spreading Greek practices everywhere they go. Maybe I should be a Zoroastrian. Better yet, I should find a Zoroastrian man to marry so my husband would allow me to be a trader." She searched his face for a reaction to her threat to find a husband.

Melchior was tongue-tied and didn't know how to respond without revealing his love for her. He committed to completing his mission, and Hessulah could unravel it. His pounding heart made him afraid to speak. He studied under Usiris, who was brilliant, but Hessulah emotionally challenged him. He was wholly unprepared and unnerved.

Hessulah was in love with Melchior, and she knew he was in love with her. She realized, "I will have to lead the conversation until he realizes he must ask me to marry him. Getting him to propose will be child's play. Besides, his journey to Babylon will keep us apart for far too long. Such a long journey was dangerous; he needs me to protect him. It will take one or two more dates before he dares to propose. Melchior is brilliant, but he has a child's emotional makeup."

The next day they were walking in the hills around Myra, and Melchior demonstrated extracting myrrh from the trees. He took his knife and cut wounds into the bark. Slowly, the gummy myrrh oozed onto the open wound of the bark. He scraped it off and let it dry in the sun. "You can touch it," he said. Hessulah felt the gummy substance. "Once it dries, we can grind it into a fine resin."

Hessulah decided it was time, first, though; Melchior must know everything about her. It would be unfair for him to propose without knowing her whole story. She asked, "Do you recall when I told Zalman how my father died?"

"Yes."

"You never asked for an explanation."

"I knew that you would tell me when you were ready."

"My mother died when I was born." She told Melchior about her father and brother; she left nothing out. She told him about the archer she killed and deceived Zalman when she sold her mother's jewels. She told Melchior about her love for the sea, "Since I was a child, my father protected me from my brother. He took me everywhere. I spent as much time at sea as on land. The sea gives me peace and brings me closer to Artemis. Even the storms are simply a test to ensure that I belong there. That is how I came to meet you. I wanted you to know everything."

Melchior leaned to Hessulah and kissed her forehead. They moved closer and embraced. They started to kiss profoundly and longingly.

She put her head against his chest and asked, "How much longer before you leave for Babylon?"

"I am not sure. The mountain ranges between here and Syria are formidable. I must be sure of the supplies that I will need. I will be traveling in hot weather initially, then freezing temperatures over the peaks, and hot again on the plains on the other side of the mountains. It may take 150 days to get there. I don't know the plan once I get to Babylon or whether I shall return immediately." He explained, trying to answer the question both have been avoiding - when will we see each other again?

Hessulah found herself saying, "Didn't they teach you geography at that Temple of yours?" Hessulah thought that was a bit too harsh; she must learn to use good words with him. She continued in a more conciliatory voice, "Why don't we sail to Caesarea and organize the caravan there? Traveling to Babylon from Caesarea will cut the distance over land by a third. You will avoid most of the mountains and the cold. Most caravans that travel east originate in Samaria and Judaea. We will easily find the animals and supplies that you need there. We can be in Caesarea in a few days by sail."

Melchior was excited by that idea, especially when she said 'we,' 'Why don't we sail.' and 'We can sail.' Any time spent with Hessulah was time well spent. He wondered if Hessulah had become more important to him than his quest. Melchior pushed that thought out of his mind knowing the vow he had made. His love for this girl could not cause him to go back on his word. Did I admit I am in love? If only I could have both, was his fleeting silent wish.

He asked, "I could not ask you to take me to Caesarea. I am so indebted to you already."

Hessulah replied, "I don't have any cargo to deliver right now, and while I am in Caesarea, I'd like to visit Michael and tour the shipyard." Undaunted, Hessulah quickly added, "We can acquire what we need for our caravan there."

Melchior, for once, was quick to pick up on her points; smiling, he repeated, "We can acquire," "What we need," "For our caravan," He stressed, 'we,' 'we' and 'our.'

Hessulah sighed, "Yes, We! We! Ours! I can't let you walk to Babylon by yourself. Someone must look after you."

Melchior, with a smile on his face, "But we are not married. Would you travel in the caravan as a servant or in disguise as a man?"

Hessulah beamed, "Neither."

"Would you travel in the caravan if you were married?"

Hessulah smiled, "If."

"Well, I could not allow a beautiful, young, single woman to travel alone in a caravan."

"I agree. You certainly cannot! It's not proper. So, what do you propose to do about it?"

"Will you go to Babylon with me as my wife?" They held each other close and kissed for a long time.

Hessulah inquired, "Will the Zoroastrians accept me as your wife if I am not a Zoroastrian before marriage?"

"That is not necessary. Zoroastrians can have wives that are not followers of Zoroaster. I would only ask one thing of you."

"What is that, my love?"

"That you follow the precepts of Zoroaster and practice Good Deeds without thought of reward, train your mind to focus on Good Thoughts and try your best to use Good Words."

"I promise that I will try my best. I want to train to become a Zoroastrian and pass through the Homa ceremony one day."

The next day Hessulah approached Assab in the shipyard. Assab quickly read Hessulah's face and knew what this conversation would be about. Instead of teasing her, he smiled and said, "It looks like someone has something to tell me."

"How do you know?"

"It's the first time I have seen you truly happy in a long, long time," he said, not wanting to bring the death of Timo into the conversation at this moment.

"I am thrilled, Assab. Will you be my sponsor at the wedding?"

"Nothing would give me greater pleasure." He hugged her tightly. "I told your father long ago I would always protect you if you were ever in need."

"I can't thank you enough for your friendship and everything you have taught me, Assab."

They embraced, and both cried silently.

The next day Melchior and a young girl arrived at the room Hessulah had rented. "Hessulah, this is my youngest sister, Kashmira. She can help prepare you for our wedding rituals. Kashmira married last year, and she is very knowledgeable about our rituals. I thought it best that she helps prepare you for everything."

"It's so nice to meet you, Kashmira."

"We are so happy for both of you. The bride's family arranges most Zoroastrian weddings, but we will easily adjust since your family is neither Zoroastrian nor from here. Everything will be fine. It's not unusual that a Zoroastrian male marries someone outside the religion. Indeed, Zoroastrians practice good thoughts, words, and deeds, but one does not have to be a Zoroastrian to be the beneficiary."

"Kashmira, please tell me everything that I must prepare for."

"Tomorrow, my mother, sisters, and I will visit you here. Please light a lantern as a sign of welcome and have a little food and wine ready. Mother will place a few coins by your lantern. We will drink the wine and tell you stories about Melchior that he wishes we don't tell. After the food and wine, you will return to our mother's house with us. Mother will light a lantern for you, and you will place a few silver coins on it. We will have more wine, and you can tell us some stories about yourself that Melchior doesn't know. You and Melchior will give each other a ring, and you will be engaged."

"That sounds wonderful; I can't wait for us to be sisters."

"You will visit again three days before the wedding. We will present you with gifts of clothing and jewelry. Our relatives, neighbors, and friends will join us for a traditional feast of boiled eggs and bergamot oranges."

"Please, may I bring the oranges?"

"You don't have to, but that is a nice gesture. The next night, you and Melchior will plant a mango twig by your front door. It will be a full moon that night, which means good luck. Mango is a Zoroastrian fertility symbol. You, Melchior, my sisters, and I will go to the rock tombs in the morning. We will start a small fire and burn myrrh so the incense smell will waft throughout the tombs. We honor each other's family and ancestors through these rituals."

When they were alone the day before the wedding, Hessulah asked Melchior. "How old is Kashmira? She seems so young to be married."

"She's 14 now. She was twelve when she married."

"How old is her husband?"

"I think he is over 30. Why?"

"Did she choose her husband?"

"No, the families arranged it."

'Isn't she too young to marry a man she doesn't know?"

"Not really, and she knew him before; he is our cousin."

The night before the wedding, after all the family events had ended, Hessulah stood outside her room, staring at the heavens, and thought about the last few weeks. She tried to find the light Melchior talked about but needed to figure out when or where to look. Everything had changed. She had set aside her ambition to follow her father's dream and decided to run off on an adventure and *marry* a young man she had just met. She knew that it was the right thing to do. Melchior was everything that she hoped to find in a husband. He was educated, caring, and selfless and promised not to interfere with her pursuing her dreams.

They had the BIG conversation the evening before. Hessulah started, "Melchior, I must be your equal in the marriage. I cannot accept a servant role. Lastly, we haven't talked about children. I only had a brother, and he despised me. But I want you to know I will welcome children when they come. I am sure Artemis will know the right time for us to have a child in a few years."

Hessulah continued, "I don't fully understand the prophecy you are following, but I will play whatever small role you need me to. Prophecies have explained every great event that has happened in Greek history."

"Hessulah, it is important to me that you are happy. If you want to build a fleet of trading ships, that is what you should do, and I will always support you. Ahura Mazda and Artemis will probably decide when we will have children, and I, too, will welcome them."

She slept that night excited for her future and what marriage would bring. She was content that she had made all the right decisions, even those Melchior thought he had made.

•◦•

Jer, Melchior's mother, greeted the wedding guests at the door. A small procession with flute music led Hessulah to the home. Hessulah wore various white garments earlier that evening after taking a ceremonial bath at home. Melchior dressed in his finest garments. Kashmira greeted Melchior at the door and made a long red mark with local dye on his forehead. The wedding guests were seated on carpets and cushions arranged throughout the main room. Lit candles encircled the room.

Hessulah and Melchior sprinkled each other with barley they picked from a cup. Then Melchior took a quail egg and encircled his head with it three times. He then smashed it on the ground. He explained to Hessulah, "The egg collects my bad thoughts when I circle it around my head. Smashing the egg destroys the bad thoughts."

Hessulah laughed, "I may need a couple of eggs."

Melchior and Hessulah sat next to each other, facing east. Kashmira and her husband stood behind Melchior, while Assab stood behind Hessulah, serving as witnesses. Two priests recited prayers as Kashmira wrapped a ribbon of long cloth around them and their chairs seven times. They held right hands, which were tied together with a ribbon. A priest placed a large piece of fabric between them. They picked up a cupful of barley in their left hand. When the curtain separating them dropped, they dumped the barley on each other. Both laughed as Hessulah 'won,' as she was quicker with her cupful.

The elder of the two priests stood in front of the couple and recited, "May the Creator, the omniscient Lord, grant you a progeny of sons and grandsons, plenty of means to provide yourselves, heart-ravishing friendship, bodily strength, long life, and an existence of 150 years!"

Melchior and Hessulah each recited their consent to the marriage. Jer brought a tray, and they shared a few bites from a typical barley dish to complete the ceremony. Jer laid out a simple feast for family and friends. Bowls and plates presented on serving trays were passed around to all.

The dinner began with trays of local cheeses, olives, nuts, and barley bread. Hessulah dipped her hard bread into the watered-down wine to soften it. A salad followed, made with romaine lettuce, oil, vinegar, cheese chunks, and walnut shavings. The women passed around a barley and lentil soup. The main dish was fresh fish, squid, prawns, olives, nuts, and raisins. Pomegranates, figs dipped in honey, and plums completed the dessert.

Melchior served wine to all the guests and toasted Ahura Mazda, the Zoroastrian Fire Temples, and Hessulah. Friends and family laughed and talked about their daily lives. Hessulah only experienced brief interludes of a family gathering as she grew up. Her father tried, but he traveled frequently. Her brother was rude and sullen. Vissia was more of a sister than a mother. She sat back and enjoyed the banter and the normalcy of family ritual. She felt melancholia without her father at the wedding. She'd long reconciled life without her mother. A blessing in that she could focus on her husband, a curse as Timo could not share in her joy.

Tears ran down Assab's face as the ceremony played out. He had promised Timo that he would watch after Hessulah if anything unfortunate ever happened to Timo. As he stood behind Hessulah, he silently repeated that promise. He vowed to keep that promise for the rest of his life.

Hessulah was free to choose her husband, just like many ancient Ephesians. Marrying into a religion that recognized a woman's equality was essential to her. Artemis would approve, she thought. Thinking back to Ephesus's history of equality between men and women, Hessulah vowed to change that pattern with her children. Her children will equally share anything she and Melchior left, regardless of sex or rank of birth. She immediately caught herself; I have thought of children two nights in a row! How can I be thinking of children? What has happened to me?

However, her plans for a shipping business would wait until their adventure was over. They would be back in Myra in a few months, her new boat would arrive, and she would pick up where she left off.

The repairs were completed two days after the wedding, and they left Myra for Caesarea. They pulled into a cove along the Syrian coast on the first night and waited out a small storm. By morning the sea settled down, and a constant breeze carried them onward. When they pulled into Caesarea Maritima, Assab pointed out that two of her brother's ships were unloading what looked like military supplies. Hessulah sailed to the dock furthest from her brother's ships. With such a long journey ahead, now was not the time to stir up trouble. However, Eris, the Greek god of chaos, had other ideas.

21

Frere Jacques, Dorme-vous, 2020 AD

I am a forest and a night of dark trees:
but he who is not afraid of darkness
will find banks full of roses under my cypresses.
Thus spoke Zarathustra (Zoroaster)
– Friedrich Nietzsche

The Cypress of Abarkuh 4,500 years old (Persian: Sarv-e Abarkuh)
Yazd Province, Iran

The Cypress of Abarkuh 4,500 years old (Persian: Sarv-e Abarkuh)
Yazd Province, Iran

MOUSE AND GREG HAD agreed that everything would stay normal until it wasn't. The invisible elephant in the room would remain hidden.

Mouse lamented, "We are not back to this nonsense again. You are not Santa Claus."

"I'm not saying I am. It's just what Emmanuelle confirmed: I am a distant relation to him."

"You and half the world are probably related to Nicolas of Myra. Genghis Khan's DNA is in about one-sixteenth of the world's population. And Genghis was born much later than Nicolas."

"I believe Genghis Khan was more prolific than Santa Claus."

"How do these juvenile conversations get started? Is it a man thing?" Mouse was losing her mind. "You understand nothing about genetics. How could you research your family's genealogy and know nothing about genetics?"

"What do you mean? I know genetics."

"You know nothing about genetics."

"What does that have to do with anything?"

"It's got like everything to do with what we are talking about." Mouse started the sentence with 'It's got like' to emphasize the irony of the idiotic.

"You just don't believe in Santa Claus, do you?"

"What???? I don't believe in Santa Claus. Is that why you are fighting me on this? How could YOU claim to be Santa Claus?"

"He's my great, great, great-something grandfather."

"YOU, who have never wrapped a present, you are Santa Claus! REALLY? Every Christmas gift the kids opened was a surprise—to them and you. Who decorates the house for Christmas? Not Santa! Who cooks the Christmas dinner? Not Santa! What cookies did Santa bake last Christmas? Who puts up the Christmas tree and decorates it? Certainly not Santa; he's too busy watching football. Who cleans the house for Christmas? Some elves? Now you have the gall to think you are special because some French girl says you are related to some old forgotten Greek saint. Have you completely lost your mind?"

"You just don't get it, do you?"

"Okay, Wise Man, let's change the subject. What did your precious Emmanuelle say about the manuscript?"

"She did not say much."

"You were on the phone for an hour and learned nothing?"

"Well, she said the manuscript came from a Spanish monk named John, or as Emmanuelle says, 'Frere Jacques.'

"'Frere Jacques, Frere Jacques. Dormez-vous, Dormez-vous', that Frere Jacques?"

"No, he's just a Spanish monk or something named John. I think the monks in his order are called Brothers. So, he's Brother Juan of 'Brother John' in English or Frere Jacques in French."

"What did she say about the manuscript? Did Brother John give it to her, where did Brother John get it, and why was it sent to us? Does she know anything about the Translator? You know, did you ask her about all the stuff that we have been speculating about for months now?"

"We never really discussed it."

"How could you not discuss it?"

"We talked about being related to Santa Claus."

Just then, the Mac dinged, signaling a new email. This one had about 20 pages. The conflict over the phone call immediately ended. Greg opened the document, selected Print from the File Tab, entered '2' in the window for the number of copies, then pressed the 'PRINT' button. The printer whirred as it spun out both sets of the document. Mouse and Greg started reading the story of the Gathering of the Magi. They were in a daze.

"Mouse, if this is going where I think it is going, this might be the original story of the birth of Jesus. Why else would someone write about the Magi?"

"I don't know. This section puts a whole new perspective on it for me. According to this, the Magi expected a celestial sign to take them to the Messiah. Unbelievable, especially since the manuscript appears from that period. Whoever wrote this was probably there or knew someone who was there."

"Remember how I said I was researching Zoroastrianism? Zoroastrianism was the largest religion in Persia for over 1,000 years. They believed in one god, called Ahura Mazda. Zoroaster predicted a Messiah to be born right around the time Christ was born, so it makes some sense that they would be watching for a sign.

"Many other Zoroastrian fundamentals overlap with Judaism and Christianity. Cypress trees are one of their symbols of everlasting life. Cypress trees in Anatolia are fir trees, just like our evergreens or Christmas trees. There is a Cypress tree in northeast Iran called the Tree of Zoroaster. Legends say Zoroaster planted it. It is 4,500 years old."

"That's pretty old for a tree."

"Zoroaster kept asking his followers to make the right choices, to choose light, not darkness, to choose truth; he preached goodness over evil. Zoroastrians believed good people went to heaven and bad people went to hell. They were a lot like Christians, except Zoroastrians believed in science, ecology, and women's equality. Then there is the Queen thing."

"What Queen is that?"

"Not what, Queen, the band, Queen."

"What are you talking about now?"

"Queen, the band, Freddie Mercury, was a Zoroastrian."

"What does that have to do with anything?"

"Nothing, it's just a simple fact that interests me."

"Are Zoroastrians still around?"

"Christianity and Islam pretty much wiped them out by 700 AD. But a small number fled to a city in India. That's where Freddie Mercury's family is from; his parents eventually immigrated to England."

"Any other interesting facts you care to share?"

"Yes, a Japanese auto company was looking for a universal name for their corporation. After researching Zoroastrianism, they named their company after the god of Zoroaster, Ahura Mazda, Mazda Car Corporation."

"You are right; that is another fact that interests only you."

Frustrated at a lack of answers, Greg had sent a series of questions to the Translator, trying to establish a line of communication. No text, just a simple question in the subject line. There were finally some answers to his questions; the email reply read:

From: gklass@me.com
To: goj212025@gmail.com
Subject: Are you Brother John?

<Yes.>

Emmanuelle said your church in Azofra, Spain, is on the French route of the Camino, south of the Pyrenees. Can I visit you if I walk the Camino de Santiago?

<I am usually at the church. There is only one.>

Why did you send me this manuscript?

<We will talk when you get here.>

There is a travel ban because of the virus. Can we speak online or on Zoom?

<We will talk when you get here. Emmanuelle will help. Trust no one else.>

Greg yelled, "Mouse, its Frere Jacques!"

"What's Frere Jacques?"

"Brother John, the monk, is the one that sent the manuscript and is doing the translation. Look!" Greg showed the text thread.

Mouse summarized, "Well, he never actually said any such thing. He just said he's Brother John and will talk to you if you meet him at his church on the Camino."

Greg sighed, "Yes, that's what he replied, but he would not have done so unless he was the Translator."

Mouse said, "Are you sure this isn't an elaborate con?"

"So, you accuse Emmanuelle and Brother John of being con men? That's a little harsh. What do we have that they could want? Wouldn't con men go after someone with money?"

"You have a point there, Greg. But this sounds fishy. What are you going to do? Walk the Camino when there's a virus going around? How will you get to France? Will Spain let you cross the border from France? Or do you want to meet your girlfriend Emmanuelle, who didn't speak to you for almost two months?"

"Do you think she digs me? Emmanuelle is half my age; you have nothing to worry about; I need to speak to Brother John to get to the bottom of this."

"Get to the bottom of what?"

"Everything. Everything must be linked. The manuscript, Saint Nicolas, Melchior, you know everything."

"I think you imagine things. There's some logical explanation to all this; you just aren't seeing it."

"Well, you can help explain it to me. Are you coming with me?"

"I won't travel during this pandemic, and you shouldn't either."

"Well, let me talk to Emmanuelle and see what she can arrange, if anything."

Emmanuelle started the next Zoom call, "Greg, I spoke with Brother John. He said you and Mouse are coming to visit. I can help arrange everything. We can get you here on a special cultural mission visa. Quarantines have some compliance issues, but it's not too bad."

"Whoa, Brother John said Mouse is coming?"

"Yes, he insisted that she come."

"How does he even know Mouse?"

"I must have mentioned her when I spoke to him about you guys."

"Does he say anything when you talk to him? I can barely get two words out of him, and that's after months of trying."

"Brother John? Oh yes, he never stops talking."

"Really? Well, I need to check how much this will cost first."

"I can help with all of that too. Flights are cheap as no one is flying. I can get you upgraded to business class. Then two weeks at the hotel in Paris for quarantine won't be that much as they are mostly empty now."

"Two weeks in quarantine? I can tell you right now that Mouse won't come."

Undeterred, Emmanuelle kept talking, "You can start your Camino right after quarantine. It will take about 12 days for you to reach Brother John's in Azofra, then another three weeks to finish the Camino."

"Can't we drive there quicker?"

"No, you have to walk. Remember I said Brother John wouldn't talk to people that ride to see him? I always walk to Azofra, and then we walk together for another three weeks to Santiago de Compostela."

"Mouse can't walk that far."

"That's okay; Mouse and I are driving."

"You just said he won't talk to anyone that doesn't walk to him."

"He will make an exception for Mouse."

"What will Mouse do when I am on my walk?"

"I will show her France from the Assistant Director of Museum Studies perspective. She will love it."

"I like your optimism, but I doubt this will fly."

<hr />

"Mouse, I spoke with Emmanuelle; Brother John insists you come to Spain."

"Why do I have to go to Spain?"

"I don't know, but he's insisting."

"How do you know he's insisting? He never says a word to you."

"I don't know, but why would Emmanuelle make it up?"

"Why would they send you the manuscript?"

"I don't know."

"That's my point exactly."

"What's your point exactly?"

"You believe everything anyone tells you."

"Why would someone lie?"

"Have you always been gullible?"

"I guess so."

"So, Einstein, what's the plan?" Einstein was a term of endearment Mouse used for Greg.

"Emmanuelle can get our tickets upgraded to Business Class. We will stay at a hotel in Paris for two weeks under quarantine. Then we will see Paris as you have always wanted to. We will visit Alsace-Lorraine and look at the bones of Saint Nick, and with any luck, I will get something I can get a DNA trace on. After that, I will start my Camino in the French Pyrenees.

"Emmanuelle will show you France for a couple of weeks, and then you and Emmanuelle will meet Brother John and me in Spain. After we meet, I will finish my Camino. You and Emmanuelle will do more sightseeing this time in Spain, and after that, she will drop you off to meet me in Santiago de Compostela. We can take extra days to do more sightseeing, eat and drink, and then fly back."

"Who's paying for all of this?"

"We are."

"Okay."

"Okay, what?"

"Okay, I'll go."

"You will?"

"Sure, just to see this nonsense finally end."

Mouse settled into her seat in Lambert Saint Louis Airport bound for Newark, "What's the itinerary?"

"We fly from Lambert to Newark and then from Newark to Charles de Gaulle."

"We don't have to go to JFK?"

"No, we will get into Charles de Gaulle at 6 a.m. local time."

"That's not bad. I thought we'd have to hop 3 or 4 flights like you made the kids do when you paid for their tickets to fly to Europe."

"That was when they had economy carriers in Europe. I saved so much money on their tickets that we can now afford a direct flight. Besides, they were young and got over it in time."

"What time is the hotel check-in? We can get a good meal when we get there."

"We paid for a room starting tonight, so we can check in as soon as we arrive. We must go straight to the room from the airport and start our quarantine."

"Greg, you're kidding me?"

"No, they are serious about this quarantine thing. We go to jail if we break it."

"What will we do if locked in a room together for two weeks?"

"Pray that the other doesn't have a gun?"

Mouse said, "I think we should re-read the manuscript on the plane and again when we quarantine. We need to prepare for our meeting with Brother John."

"Why, what's to prepare for?"

"We must have our questions well thought out to get the answers we need."

"What answers do we need?"

"We should assume that Brother John read the manuscript before we emailed him the pages. We want his perspective on the themes that run through the translation to understand better what the author meant."

"What themes, Mouse? And why would Brother John know them?"

"He must have some insight."

"What else do we need answers for?"

"Everything that involves you. Why did Brother John send this to you? Why does he live on the Camino? How does Emmanuelle fit into this? Are you writing this down, Greg?"

"I have to write it down?"

"Yes, Einstein." There's that term of endearment again.

"Suppose Brother John hasn't read the manuscript and has no answers?"

"It will be a short meeting, and you will have a long walk ahead of you."

"Okay, you start reading the manuscript. I am going to have a screwdriver. When we fly out of Newark, the drinks are free in Business Class, you know."

The bump from the landing gear woke Greg. He looked over at Mouse, who was in the middle of the manuscript writing notes.

"Are we in Paris?" Greg asked and yawned at the same time.

Mouse ignored him, giving off a major case of annoyance.

"What's the matter, Mouse?"

"You."

"Me, what did I do."

"Don't tell me that you don't remember."

"I don't know, or else I wouldn't be asking." A feeling of guilt and dread built up in Greg's voice.

"Well, just apologize to the flight attendants on your way out."

"I took a sleeping pill, only had one drink, and slept."

"You took several pills and fell asleep."

"It's against the law to sleep now?"

"You snored the entire trip. No one else was able to sleep you snored so loudly."

"Really? When did this happen?"

"The entire flight. Everyone was looking at us. Let's just get our stuff and get off the plane as quickly as possible."

22

The Caravan, Caesarea to Babylon, 2 BC

If one would have a friend, Then must one be willing to wage war for him. And in order to wage war, One must be capable of being an enemy.

– Zoroaster

A model of the Gate of Ishtar built in c. 575 BCE by in Nebuchadnezzar II in Babylon. Displayed at the Museum in Berlin.[1]

---

1. Gryffindor, . "." World History Encyclopedia. Last modified July 03, 2012. https://www.worldhistory.org/image/735/model-of-the-ishtar-gate/.

———◆◇◆———

ZALMAN AND MICHAEL STOOD in the shipyard when a servant brought word that Melchior and Hessulah docked in Caesarea. Zalman said, "Melchior and Hessulah are here and are asking for a meeting. Where is your brother Jacob?"

Michael replied, "He's looking at some camels for our caravan. May I mention again that I am wary of the risks involved in investing in a woman?"

Zalman replied, "I know your feelings, but Hessulah's speech in Heracleum moved me. I owe her this out of respect for her mother and father. And I know my feelings are not enough justification for risking such an investment."

Michael responded, "We must decide how to handle her brother Petrus. He has sent numerous letters requesting financing for his ventures with Rome."

"Yes, I have been trying to formulate a path forward on Petrus. I don't trust him, but he has the backing of Herod and the Roman authorities. We must be careful; we cannot keep him at bay forever."

"What do you have against Petrus?"

"Well, let's start that he murdered his father and tried to have his sister executed for it."

"There is that!"

"You will learn, Michael, that you will get bit when you do business with a snake. I learned that lesson from supporting Herod. I don't need another client like him. I was very impressed with Hessulah when she came aboard our ship in disguise. She was probably thirteen years old and fearless. Her father was like that, and her mother was an impressive woman."

"I didn't know that you knew her mother too. When did you meet her?"

Zalman's tone was curt, "That was long before I met your mother."

Michael turned up an eyebrow and wanted to follow up, but he knew to do so would not sit well with his father. "Well, I am firmly against working with any woman in business. I agree that Hessulah is remarkable, but can women be trusted to run a business? Their minds are fickle."

Zalman disagreed, "Hessulah was correct, and there was nothing fickle about Cleopatra or Ruth and Esther from the Bible. I want to give her a chance to prove herself. I don't know how to do that—ah, here they come now. Let's greet them by the keel of their new ship."

Zalman began. "Welcome to Caesarea. Here is the keel of your new ship. We are on schedule and can't wait until the launch."

Hessulah, as was her way, spoke first. "Hello, Zalman and Michael. It's a pleasure to see you again. Before we get down to the reason for this surprise visit, I wanted to let you know that Melchior and I married recently."

"That is joyous news, except that it means you will not be able to wed one of my sons."

Hessulah smiled, "We are on an urgent mission. Melchior must join a Zoroastrian conclave in Babylon. We must find passage on a caravan or assemble one."

Michael started to speak, but Zalman interrupted, "It's the middle of summer, and no caravans are operating." Michael's eyes widened, and he looked sideways at his father but knew better than to interrupt.

Zalman continued, "However, if you and Melchior can assemble a caravan, you could provide us with a great service. I have several loads of goods that are ready to ship east. I need someone to take them. I can reward you handsomely if you would help."

Hessulah replied, "We are honored to help. Melchior constantly says helping others is the way to heaven. Don't you, Melchior?"

Melchior stammered, "Of course, we'd be happy to provide any service. But I don't understand how we can assist?"

"Melchior, we cannot refuse Zalman; we will do whatever is necessary." added a gleeful Hessulah.

Zalman smiled, "Great, we agree. Michael will help you procure the camels and servants."

Once they left, Michael asked, "Why couldn't they have joined our caravan? It should be ready in a week."

Zalman said, "Yes, but I needed something to test Hessulah's competence, and this is perfect. Hessulah will pass the test if she is as good a captain as Melchior claims. If not, we will sell this ship to Petrus. Get your brother Jacob; he is going as their camel steward. He can take over if anything goes amiss."

Knowing what his father was scheming, Michael started laughing at the thought of Jacob as a camel steward. Looking for signs of Jacob in the compound, Michael began shouting, "Hey, camel-boy!"

Melchior and Hessulah obtained all the supplies, mainly from Michael. One evening, Hessulah was preparing food for the crew, and she pulled her dagger to open a sack of grain. Michael noticed the markings on the dagger's hilt but said nothing. Later that evening, Michael told Zalman that he was suspicious of Hessulah, "She carries one of Herod's daggers."

The next day Zalman approached Hessulah in the courtyard. "Hessulah, would you show me your dagger?" he asked.

Concern showed on Hessulah's face, and she countered, "Why do you want to see my dagger?"

"Please," he said.

She slowly withdrew the dagger and handed it to him. "Where did you get this?" he asked.

Not sure where Zalman was going with his questioning, she asked, "Do you recognize it?"

"I do," he said, pulling out a matching dagger.

"Where did you get that?" Hessulah asked.

"From someone, I do business with," Zalman replied. "I'd like to know where you got your dagger?"

Hessulah said, "It belonged to whoever killed my father. Assab and I pulled it from my father's back."

Zalman reached into his money purse and retrieved a coin. He handed it to Hessulah. Inscribed on one side were the Greek words for King Herod, and on the reverse was a full-breasted eagle with the letters KP.

"What does this mean?" Hessulah asked nervously.

Zalman replied, "Whoever killed Timo does business with King Herod. Herod presents these as gifts to commemorate business deals." He handed the dagger back to Hessulah. "Be careful and do not show this to anyone in Judaea. You will draw suspicion. Let me make inquiries, and we will talk when you return."

"Who are you going to ask about the dagger?" Hessulah inquired.

Zalman thought aloud, "Well, I doubt that Herod killed Timo. And I doubt he will remember to whom he gave these daggers as a gift. Then again, if he did remember, he is paranoid about divulging any information, and he would want to know why I am asking. But I know someone that works for Herod, who will certainly know who in Anatolia received a dagger as a gift. I will get a list and see what names turn up."

Several days later, Hessulah said in the shipyard, "Good morning Zalman; Assab asked to stay in Caesarea and help build the boat. He's a sailor and does not relish the idea of a long journey through a desert on horse, camel, or foot."

"Excellent, we can put him to work. I have questions about your father's murder, if you don't mind."

"No, not at all."

"I understand that you found your father."

"Yes, I went to the shop at daybreak as father did not come home the night before. A soldier from the Roman Urban Cohort was hiding in the shop, expecting me to arrive that morning. Assab saved me from certain death."

"Hessulah, do you know where Petrus was during all this time?"

"Vissia told me that the night before the murder, he attended a party given by the Roman Governor. It was the beginning of the feast of Artemis."

"No doubt Herod would have been at that same party." Zalman paused, "Hessulah, do you think Petrus had anything to do with your father's murder?"

"I think he had everything to do with his murder, Zalman. I can't prove it - yet. Who else could have sent the Urban Cohort to detain me? Petrus deeply desired to work with Rome and rise in Roman society. He married my father's wife, Vissia, shortly after the murder. Petrus's goal was to ingratiate himself with the Roman elite. You probably heard that I killed a Roman archer in Ephesus's Harbour. No one knows that I missed my target. I was aiming for Petrus."

"I suspected that it was you. My associates in Ephesus told me a wondrous story about the return of the goddess Artemis and how she had saved a drowning dock worker and then struck down a Roman archer from a rocking boat 400 meters offshore. The people of Ephesus will do anything for her; she is a hero to them. But in the meantime, I have a business decision to make. Petrus has been asking me to help finance his ventures. He has Herod backing him. I will put off those two vultures as long as possible. We will talk more when you return from Babylon. May you have a safe and prosperous journey, and may Artemis protect you. Although, if you can shoot an arrow like the Ephesian goddess, I am not certain you need her protection."

Hessulah helped fill out the rest of the caravan; five camels, a guide, two camel drivers, six servants, and several bodyguards. They burdened one camel with grains to feed the animals. Another carried food and wine for the travelers. The next camel was ladened with camping, cooking, and hunting gear. Another camel has the medicine, Melchior's ornate boxes of myrrh, soaps, spices, and extra clothing.

Zalman's goods increased the caravan by seventeen camels, six camel riders, fifteen servants and their families, and a youthful camel steward. Zalman gave Hessulah detailed instructions on his merchandise. He told her where to deliver, what to acquire, and when to sell and buy. Hessulah requested several large bundles of yarn and knitting needles. Their route would take them east from Caesarea to the King's Highway, then south past Rabbah. Once they pass Rabbah, they turn east onto the Silk Road towards Babylon.

The day before they were to depart, Assab asked Hessulah. "Where is Melchior? I have not seen him this morning."

"He went to buy some horses. I told him I was not walking or riding a camel to Babylon. He should be back soon."

"When will you get to Babylon?"

"I am not sure. It should take about 70 days to get there. We will return in winter if we leave tomorrow, and the ship should be ready. That is if we leave tomorrow. Jacob comes up with something that delays us whenever we're about to leave. I can't quite figure him out. Sometimes the delays seem intentional."

"What have you said to him?"

"Nothing; Melchior is in charge. It's like home; they don't appreciate women."

"When have you let that stop you, Hessulah? Has Melchior ever managed something like this? You are a ship's captain; you should use your talents."

"I understand what you are saying. I must give Melchior a chance."

"Well, this operation needs a captain, Melchior is a good man, but he is not a captain. And I'd keep an eye on Jacob."

"Yes, I have been watching him. Something isn't right."

Assab said, "Here comes your Melchior. Let's look at your horses."

Melchior said, "Hessulah, I got us two Persian horses. The man I bought them from said Persian horses don't mind saddles and are easier to ride than Roman and Arabian horses. Mind you, though, these two Persians are unique. I bought them from a carnival troupe on the outskirts of Caesarea. The troupe leader said he had to sell them to raise funds to pay Herod's taxes. The horses have unique talents. My horse, Farrokh, likes to twirl. Your mare, Bulsara, likes to parade, taking high steps and almost skipping as she walks."

Hessulah walked around admiring the horses. She took Bulsara's bridle and stroked the horse's forehead saying, "We are going to be great friends, Bulsara."

They left two days late and made 6 kilometers on the first day and barely 6 kilometers on the next. Everyone complained about the poor organization. Issues with loading the baggage prevented leaving by first light, and the caravan departed by mid-day. They stopped every time a load fell off a camel's back. Hessulah noticed that each time the cargo fell off the camel, the camel quickly jumped forward a few feet. With all the chaos, it seemed as if the camels were complaining - if they could complain more than usual. It seemed odd to Hessulah the camels appeared more frustrated than the riders. Soon everyone in the caravan, except the riders, showed frustration.

As they were setting up camp, Jacob spoke with his lead rider. "Tell the other riders to keep up the mayhem. One more day, and I will take charge. This caravan was Zalman's idea to put them to the test. He asked me to test Melchior and Hessulah, but I don't think I must wait for her to make a bigger mess."

Hessulah spoke with Melchior that night and suggested he ride ahead to meet with the next village chief to arrange food and water. Melchior agreed and called Jacob over. "I will ride ahead and obtain some more food and water. We need it to account for the food and water we used during the delays."

Jacob said, "That's a good idea. I will take charge."

Melchior said, "No, Hessulah will be in charge. You will take orders from her."

"But—but she is a woman. Surely, she doesn't know how to lead a caravan. Men will not follow a woman."

"You would do well not to underestimate Hessulah."

After Jacob left, Hessulah told Melchior, "After you have arranged food and water, don't ride back to the caravan. Stay there until we arrive, even if it takes a few days."

———————◦◦◦———————

Back by his campfire Jacob told the lead rider. "Melchior should have placed me in command. He is a fool to entrust this responsibility to a woman. Let's make sure this charade ends today. Nothing must go right. Move the goods around so the weight on each camel is unbalanced. Tell the others to continue to use knots that won't hold. I am tired of getting nowhere. Zalman's test will be over soon; I will take over and get things moving."

Hessulah knew she was facing an insurrection as soon as Melchior was out of the camp. Hessulah did what Assab and her father had taught her, and she took command. Hessulah managed men, a ship, and cargo; a caravan was no different. She gathered Jacob and the camel riders.

"Tomorrow is a new day, and we will start afresh. Load all the camels at first light, and let's see if we can make a great distance. Jacob, please report to me when we are ready to move."

She heard grumbling in response, but she said nothing more. She sat down and drank a cup of wine. She expected tomorrow to be an eventful day and formulated her plan.

When Hessulah dressed that morning, she added several pieces of weaponry underneath her outfit. She set her bow and quiver on Bulsara's saddle. Three hours after sunrise, Jacob reported to Hessulah, "The camels are in line, and we are ready to march. But the men are uneasy and will not follow a woman."

Hessulah said, "I agree that they won't follow a woman. They won't have to." Jacob raised an eyebrow, appearing confused by her statement.

Hessulah mounted Bulsara and rode to the front of the caravan. Instead of giving the order to move out, she wheeled Bulsara around and rode the length of the caravan. No one moved. When she reached the end, Hessulah looked over the cargo and knew the knots holding the cargo would fail. She adjusted the knot on the trailing camel to expose it and set it on top of a wooden box. She rode slowly to the front of the caravan, where Jacob waited. Stopping by each camel, she used her sword and manipulated each knot. The camels were lined one behind another in a perfect row. Each camel's cargo hung off on both sides.

She reached the front and glared at Jacob and the camel riders, "Many of you have heard the stories in the port that a woman pilots a ship. Some call her Artemis; others call her the Sea Witch. You can call me Hessulah, Artemis, or the Sea Witch, but know that I am the captain of this ship, and you will obey my orders. Now pick up the cargo that has fallen off the camels and load it correctly."

The men looked around, and laughter ensued. Jacob's lead rider looked back at the caravan and laughed, "The cargo is secure on the camels."

At that, Hessulah reached for her bow and quickly loaded and unleashed an arrow that split the knot she had set atop the furthest camel. Its cargo fell to the ground; then, the camel leaped forward, causing a chain reaction, and a load fell from the next camel, then the next until most of the cargo was on the ground.

Hessulah stood in her footholds and opened her tunic, revealing her sword and dagger, "I will accept the challenge of any man. We can fight with bow and arrow, sword, or knives. Know this; I am more skillful with a sword than a bow. I am faster than lightning with a knife. I will make your wives into widows."

The men stood in stony silence as Hessulah stared them down. The desert wind quietly whistled.

"Load the heavy cargo on the young, healthy camels. Load the bulky but light supplies on the older camels." Pointing at the fourth camel in line, Hessulah said, "Leave the camel whose belly is swollen with calf here with a servant. They can catch up in two weeks after she gives birth."

Hessulah then pulled a small length of rope from her saddle. "If you tie two bundles together using a rope from each bundle, use a lashing knot like this." She quickly tied a lashing knot, knotting each end. If you lash a bundle to frame, use a sailor's knot like this." She demonstrated a bow knot. If you connect two frames, you can use any damn knot that works, but not those useless knots you tied this morning. Anyone that uses those knots will walk back to Caesarea and explain themselves to Zalman.

"Everything will be stowed and tied down properly. Step forward now if I must train you to tie a proper knot." No one moved as Hessulah continued, "Jacob, have them balance the loads with equal weight on each side of the camel. Redistribute the load from the pregnant camel among the rest."

Everyone stood in silence. Hessulah finished, "Those are your orders. Are there any questions? If not, be about your work." The camp women began to whistle excitedly. They were glad that a woman stopped the nonsense that was going on.

A few hours later, Jacob approached. "The caravan is ready to move."

Hessulah responded, "Let's see." She reviewed each camel load and noticed a few loosely tied bundles. "They need more practice with their knots. Unload all the cargo. We will stay here tonight and try again in the morning."

Jacob responded, "As you say, Hessulah."

She called Jacob over and spoke. "I know you felt you should be in charge, but that responsibility has fallen to me. You are right, they will not follow a woman, but they will follow a captain. I expect everyone to follow my orders. If you have a problem with that, leave now."

Jacob just stood there stunned. A woman had never spoken to him like that.

She woke before the first cock's crow and exited her tent. It was still dark as the early light emerged from the eastern hills. She was about to call for Jacob to get everyone up and to start packing as her eyesight adjusted to the dark. The caravan was ready; all the camels were loaded, in line, and prepared to move.

Hessulah knew better than to test the knots. Jacob led the first camel and said, "We are ready to sail, Captain."

Hessulah smiled and said, "One more thing, Jacob, no one is to bother Melchior with any questions about the caravan."

Jacob smiled and replied, "That won't be a problem, Captain." He turned and shouted at the caravan, "Sail ho!"

Hessulah could hear cheers and whistles from primarily women's voices. Everyone was stunned. The servants had never seen a woman in command, especially one so comfortable giving men orders outside marriage. Hessulah reminded the men of their wives! Jacob decided to cease his mayhem, thinking. "Maybe Zalman was on to something!"

Hessulah quickly and quietly assumed leadership over the caravan without speaking to Melchior. Progress and morale improved, and they began to traverse large amounts of territory.

Hessulah's management style was direct, unambiguous, and fair. A few days later, she had an idea and decided to try it at dinner that night. Hessulah knew there were few secrets in a caravan. Everyone knew if someone heard something said in 'private,' in no time. Hessulah made sure that at least one servant was within earshot. "Melchior, when I saddled Bulsara today, I noticed that Joshua, who is in charge of the feed for the horses and camels, had put a poultice on Bulsara's leg. He must have noticed where a branch had cut her. Would you say something to him tomorrow? It was very thoughtful, and I appreciate his care of the animals."

Each night it was a different servant and a different story. The servants appreciated this unfiltered feedback and realized that someone had their back. The servants responded and began to treasure Hessulah.

———•◦•———

East of Rabbah, they camped at the first caravanserais. Caravanserais are places of respite that sprung up along the trade routes. Over the years, many grew into small towns. Melchior claimed the spirit of hospitality towards strangers, integral to the region's culture, sprouted from Zoroastrianism.

Melchior settled into his role, meeting with local leaders and determining if there were any dangers in the area. He bartered with the leaders for water, feed, and protection. Water was always at a premium, as a thirsty camel can drink up to 25 gallons.

When they were halfway to Babylon, Melchior told Hessulah, "I am pleased that my caravan operates so smoothly."

Hessulah acknowledged, "Yes, all due to your fine leadership skills, no doubt!" Melchior took note of the sarcasm as he quietly finished his cup of wine.

The caravan settled into its routine. Each day was remarkably similar, break camp, march, rest, march, set up camp, eat, and sleep. The days became weeks and the weeks months. Hessulah estimated they had traveled about 80 days.

"Hessulah, have you noticed that the villages are poorer as we get closer to Babylon? Poverty is an after-effect of the downfall of a civilization."

"Yes. I am out of the clothes I brought to hand out to the needy. The money I brought for the poor is almost gone as well."

Melchior said, "I appreciate everything you do for them. Your selflessness embodies the Zoroastrian philosophy that you can only be happy if you help others. The scouts said we will be at the Gate of Ishtar in two days."

————◄○►————

Melchior and Hessulah led Farrokh and Bulsara on foot at the head of the caravan. Melchior told Hessulah the history behind the Gate of Ishtar as they approached it "The Gate of Ishtar was commissioned by King Nebuchadnezzar about 600 years ago when Babylon was at the zenith of its power. There is an inscription from the king on a cornerstone dedicating the Gate to the Babylonian god Marduk. As you can see, the towers connect to the city walls that encircle all of Babylon. Thirty-five years after the Babylonian king dedicated the Gate of Ishtar, Cyrus the Great conquered Babylon. Cyrus was known as a Zoroastrian emperor as the religion spread throughout the mightiest empire in the world. Magi were Cyrus's chief advisers.

"The front portion of the Gate stands 15 meters tall and 10 meters wide; two taller square towers frame it. It's wide enough that a legion of soldiers eight-abreast can march through the Gate. In bas-reliefs, one hundred twenty golden bulls, dragons, and lions overlay on the bright blue bricks. They represent the three gods of Babylon."

Hessulah replied, "The Gate is stunning."

"I am sure the Magi will hold a procession through the sacred Gate and re-create its pomp and glory. Zoroastrian priests led all new Persians Kings, victorious armies, and religious festivals through this Gate for hundreds of years. Let's find a place to pitch our camp."

After their three-month journey, they united with a collection of Zoroastrian priests, priestesses, their families, and servants. Everyone camped outside the city. Melchior found a suitable location to make his camp. Once settled, he went to see those in charge. He met people from all over the world as he walked through the camps. They came from as far as Ethiopia and Tunis in Africa. Others came from Goa, India, and Carpathia. Still more came from Rus and other places to the north. All told, about 150 priests and priestesses were there. Over 1,000 people were in the camps when counting families and servants. It was a loud and colorful collection.

Hessulah exclaimed, "Look at all these people. Where do they come from?"

Melchior replied. "Zoroastrianism began, without political influence in Persia, more than 1,000 years before Cyrus. Once Persia fell, the Egyptian, Greek, and Roman empires tolerated Zoroastrianism, and slowly, our faith spread as far north as Byzantium. From there, we reached north into the land of the Rus. To the east, you will find our temples in the lands of the Afghans and India. Some stories claim Zoroaster was born in the Afghan mountains. To the west, we have temples throughout Egypt, Ethiopia, and northern Africa."

Melchior's campsite sat nestled between two older Magi's camps. Balthazar came from Ethiopia, a kingdom south of Egypt. The other Magi came from the Kaspari tribe that settled southwest of the Caspian Sea. His tribal name was difficult for others to pronounce, so he was called Kaspar.

Melchior walked through the encampment, trying to find someone in charge. He told Hessulah, "I have walked the entire encampment and spoken to many Magi. No one is in control or knows what to do next.

The Magi have no structure or means to form a consensus. The assembly has yet to set rules of conduct. After a few days of debate, they broke into smaller groups, and each group must present two or three organizational ideas at the next assembly. The conclave will vote on which ideas to accept, discard, or debate as a group. I am joining Kaspar and Balthazar's group. Everyone agrees the comet is our guide, but no one knows its path."

Nightly, Melchior worked with other astrologers, taking measurements of the comet's distance from other stars, trying to plot its speed and direction. Melchior used the map of the stars drawn 130 years earlier by Hipparchus of Rhodes using Hipparchus's mathematics (trigonometry) to calculate the comet's path.

Late one afternoon, Kaspar asked Melchior and Balthazar for support when the assembly reconvened. Kaspar said, "I don't believe sitting in Babylon is wise. We should send teams in all four directions. Once the comet's path is clear, the closest team will have a chance of finding the Messiah."

The assemblage debated ideas and proposed rules. Some Magi wanted to wait by the Gate of Ishtar until the comet revealed an exact path. Kaspar stood and made his suggestion. He added, "Each team will carry the same tribute. The rest of the Magi may remain at the Gate and continue the study of the comet; scouts can be dispatched to the other teams once the comet's path reveals itself. By spreading the Magi in four directions plus with those in Babylon, we will be in five places at once and can better react to any event."

Balthazar heard some rumblings from the contingent that wanted to remain behind. He stood and suggested, "We can make a fifth set of tribute to leave with the Magi in Babylon if the comet heads here." That quelled the dissent of those in fear of missing out. The assembly answered with murmurs of approval.

Melchior then stood before the assembly and said, "Usiris, the high priestess of Halicarnassus, instructed me to bring five boxes of myrrh as gifts for the Messiah. Many of you knew Usiris. It is my duty, and with profound sadness, to report that she died before she could join us on the quest."

Gloom permeated throughout the camp when news of her passing spread. A group of older Magi who had known Usiris for a long time held a vigil in her honor at the Fire Altar at the Babylon temple.

Melchior brought the boxes of myrrh forward. Gold and frankincense had been chosen as the other gifts and were collected from the assembly and then split into five equal parts. A team of Magi divided the treasure into equal portions and outfitted each team with three boxes containing gifts of gold, frankincense, and myrrh.

The four teams formed, and Kaspar was selected to lead the westward team. Melchior pulled Kaspar aside, "I believe the comet is headed west, but further calculations are needed to confirm that. I have been consulting the map of Hipparchus and using his mathematical calculus."

Kaspar replied, "I want you and Balthazar to join me. The westward route coincides with your path home. Combining our caravans will make us large enough to fend off bandits, and you are good company. This assembly is over; we must get ready to move out."

Kaspar, Balthazar, and Melchior returned to camp, satisfied with a shared purpose. Melchior was anxious; he had to convince Hessulah this next adventure was also in her interest. Hessulah was visiting with Movared, the wife of Kaspar, and Aimilia, the wife of Balthazar. When the men returned, they found the women in a cheerful mood. It was apparent that the women had enjoyed each other's stories and, perhaps, a secret or two. The men told the women they would break camp in the morning and head west.

"What were you women so secretive and happy about in there?" Balthazar asked Aimilia when they were alone.

"Not for me to say," Aimilia responded quizzically.

Hessulah was silent on the way back to their campsite. Melchior sensed Hessulah's apprehension and worried this new journey would disappoint her. He felt selfish for involving her on this quest, though he knew he could not stop her from coming. It was a difficult trip, and now they would return on a different route to Caesarea and Myra than he had promised. "Hessulah, I know you want to return to the sea, launch your new ship, and chase your father's dream. But I am equally drawn to my quest. Usiris selected me, and now I am chosen by Kaspar. I believe in my heart that this quest is our destiny."

Hessulah's replied in a non-accusatory tone, "Why did you volunteer to go on this new quest without consulting me first? Haven't I done everything that you asked? Do I have no say in any of this?"

It was more of a plea than a complaint. Melchior momentarily silently said, "I'm sorry, but I had little choice. I was selected, and I could not refuse." He then tried to make it sound like this was the best option, "I also thought it was more or less on our way back, and we could use the company for protection."

Hessulah countered more accusatorily, "Don't try that nonsense on me! You knew this was not what we agreed; you never thought to consult me." Then Hessulah's countenance lightened, and she pouted, saying, "Besides, I want our child to be born at home and not in some caravan camp."

Still unused to Hessulah's flair for the dramatic, Melchior paused to let that statement sink in. Then, with a huge smile, he grabbed Hessulah, holding her tightly; he leaned back to look into her smiling eyes and said, "I love you. Let's go to bed."

Laughing, she pushed him away, saying, "Haven't you done enough already?"

Melchior said, "I can't tell you how happy you make me."

Hessulah said, "I know you make me very happy, love. There is no one I'd rather go on an insane adventure with, but you must promise that we can return to Myra once we get near a port. This adventure is about more than you and me now."

Melchior, "Yes, love, I promise."

23

EUROPEAN VACATION, PARIS, FRANCE 2020 AD

I like your Christ; I do not like your Christians.
Your Christians are so unlike your Christ.
— Mahatma Gandhi

CHARLES DE GAULLE AIRPORT was almost half empty as a testament to the virus. Upon clearing Customs, they saw a driver with a sign that said 'Klass.' Greg tried to introduce himself by speaking English in the Google Translate App and showing the driver the results. The driver was several inches shorter than Mouse. He ignored Greg's attempt to communicate and motioned for them to follow.

The driver led Mouse and Greg out of the terminal to a waiting car, but he never verbally engaged with them nor helped with their luggage. Mouse and Greg were crammed together in the back seat of a tiny Fiat with their carry-on bags between them. Their two pieces of full-size luggage took up all the room in the hatchback. Mouse sat directly behind the driver, who drove with both hands atop the steering wheel. All Mouse could see were the driver's hands.

A thirty-five-minute ride through the empty streets led to a lovely boutique hotel with a French-sounding name in a charming downtown district. Greg made several attempts to communicate with the driver, but he paid him no attention. The driver was nervously staring out the side and rearview mirrors. Neither

Mouse nor Greg realized a large black Citroen with darkened windows followed their car.

The driver kept peering nervously behind him when he left them off at the entrance. Mouse and Greg walked through the lobby to the Front Desk, where a Plexiglas barrier separated the desk staff from the guests. To Greg's relief, the clerk spoke English. The clerk slid the keys to Greg and "You must stay in your room for two weeks. We will leave clean linens outside your door every three days. Your meals will arrive at 7 a.m., 11:30 a.m., and 7 p.m. Do not leave your rooms; no guests are allowed. Hope you have a great stay." The clerk instructed Greg to carry his bags to the room.

"What do we do if we start coughing or have a fever?" "Ouch." Greg cried as Mouse's elbow rammed into his side. Mouse said, "Can't wait to see your wonderful city. Get going, Greg, and quit embarrassing me."

After the door to their elevator closed, the driver of the black Citroen approached the front desk. "Yes, Father, how may I help you?" The clerk inquired of the tall, young priest.

"Can you answer a question about the American couple that just checked in?"

"I will do my best, but we have strict privacy policies for our guests."

"I understand. I met the couple on the plane from America and wanted to see if I could show them the remains of the Cathedral at Norte Dame and some of our other great churches. We get so few visitors these days. I didn't get a chance to ask them on the plane."

"Well, all new arrivals are in quarantine for two weeks."

"Of course, I forgot about quarantine."

"Would you like to send them a note? I can have that slipped under their door."

"Yes, thank you, their name was Claus, correct?"

"No, Father, not Claus but Klass."

"Yes, of course, I misunderstood them. On second thought, I am only in Paris for a few nights; I may see them when I return in two weeks. Merci"

Greg dropped the bags on the floor and said, "So this is our cell for the next 14 days."

"You wanted to make this trip. I do not want to hear one complaint from you. Besides, we have a lot of work to do?"

"Work? What work do we have to do?"

"I re-read the manuscript while you were flirting with the brunette flight attendant. There's more to the story than Hessulah shooting someone full of arrows or the Magi visiting Bethlehem."

"What story were you reading?"

"What's Hessulah's major complaint throughout the first few chapters?"

"Petrus killed her father."

"Greg, that's not a complaint. That is the backdrop. Hessulah constantly laments that women can't run a business and are subservient to men."

"When did she say that?"

"Like almost every other page."

"How'd I miss it?"

"It's ingrained in our nature, men, especially."

"I don't get what you are saying."

"I want you to re-read the manuscript from cover to cover. And I want you to pay attention to anything that draws attention to the equality, or inequality, of men and women."

"Okay, any other themes?"

"Yes, Zoroastrian beliefs emerge in Judaism, Christianity, and Islam. In that sense, the story is almost a genealogical book of religions, like Judaism adopting the story of Noah from another ancient culture. It describes a genealogy of empires in Anatolia, including the Amazons of Scythia, Egypt, Persia, Greece, Rome, and Byzantine. Then, there is the extensive treatise about Greece and how Greek civilization influenced the Mediterranean world. The whole Hellenization concept is laid bare."

"You read that in the manuscript?"

"Yes, and if you pay attention, you will find all of it. I'd like to hear a male perspective.

"What are you going to do while I read this? Are you sure about that Noah thing?"

"Me? I am taking a nap. I didn't pass out from drinking on the plane."

Mouse fell asleep in about 5 minutes. Greg read about three pages and was asleep 5 minutes later.

———◆———

Mouse brought several books and zipped through them as the days and nights passed slowly. She took the Bible from the bedside drawer during the second week. Mouse concentrated on Saint James and his brother Saint John as she read the four Gospels.

Mouse said, "Jesus was John's first cousin. John didn't write about the birth of Jesus probably because he wasn't there; John was the youngest disciple, born after Jesus."

"John and Jesus were cousins?"

Mouse replied, "James and John are brothers and were Jesus's cousins. Salome was their mother; she is the sister of the virgin Mary."

"I doubt she called her sister a virgin after the birth of Jesus."

"Do you have a one-track mind?"

"Just saying. So, Saint James, of the Camino de Santiago, is John the Gospel-writer's brother?"

"Yes, Santiago is Spanish for Saint James. Camino de Santiago is "The Way of Saint James."

"Does 'de Compostela' mean Apostle as in Saint James the Apostle?"

Marge tutored, "No, Santiago de Compostela means Saint James of the Field of the Star. According to legend, a peasant discovered his tomb when he saw a star land in his field. Don't you know anything about the Camino? You've been researching it for months."

"I was looking for beer stops."

Mouse admonished Greg, "You are some Einstein. Jesus called James and John 'the sons of Thunder.' I guess they were pretty loud."

"He should have met my great-uncle Foghorn Meyer. He was loud and a boisterous sinner."

Mouse said, "I shouldn't show you this, but there's a strange passage at the end of the Gospel of John."

"What's so strange about it?"

"You read it and tell me. Jesus has just finished telling Simon Peter that he would be bound and die a gruesome death in service to the Lord. Peter was confused and probably a little hurt by the conversation. He noticed John following Jesus and asked Jesus what would happen to John. This conversation occurred after Jesus arose from the dead, so the phrase 'until I come' literally means the second coming."

The Beloved Disciple. Peter turned around at that and noticed that the disciple whom Jesus loved was following (the one who had leaned against Jesus' chest during the supper)and said, "Lord, which one will hand you over?" Seeing him (the beloved disciple), Peter was prompted to ask Jesus. "But Lord, what about him?" "Suppose I wanted him to stay until I come," Jesus replied, "how does that concern you? Your business is to follow me." This is how the report spread among the brothers that this disciple was not going to die. Jesus never told him, as a matter of fact, that the disciple would not die; all He said was, "Suppose I wanted him to stay until I come (how does that concern you?)."

Conclusion. It is this same disciple who is the witness to these things; it is he who wrote them down and his testimony, we know, is true. There are still many other things that Jesus did, yet if they were written about in detail, I doubt there would be room enough in the entire world to hold the books to record them.

Greg said, "Wow. So, Jesus said that John the Apostle, the Evangelist, might not die. He didn't say he wouldn't die, just that he might not let him die. That's unbelievable. Jesus wasn't known for telling jokes."

"Yeah, it's all there in the last chapter, Chapter 21."

Excitedly Greg said, "Mouse, where's my PC?"

"It's in front of you."

"I need to check something. Look, the Translator's email address is goj212025@gmail.com"

"Whose email address is what?"

"Frere Jacques, the Translator, his email address is the scripture from Gospel of John chapter 21 verses 20 to 25 or goj.21.20.25. Could our Frere Jacques be John the Evangelist? According to the Bible, John may never have died."

"Get a grip on yourself, Greg. Think about what you are saying. You are saying that John the Evangelist uses Gmail?"

"Well, it is odd. Either Jesus has plans for John beyond the 1st century, or Jesus played a terrific joke on John that spooked the other apostles."

"This whole adventure is odd if you ask me."

"Well, only a few more days of this quarantine, and we will be out of here."

———◦———

Greg and Mouse continued for the last few days of quarantine, surviving together in Paris with nowhere to go. Greg was doing his usual random searches on the internet when something popped up. "Mouse, do we have a Mormon Bible in the room?"

"What do you want with a Mormon Bible?"

"You are not going to believe this."

"No, we don't have a Mormon Bible. We are in France, a Catholic country, and we are not at a Marriott."

"Remember when we lived in Buffalo, and I used to do business in Rochester? The town of Palmyra was just outside of Rochester. I told you once that I drove by Hill Cumorah, where Joseph Smith is said to have found the Golden Plates of Mormon. Those plates are the basis of the Church of the Latter-Day Saints."

"I know about Hill Cumorah being in Palmyra."

"Well, a few years after Joseph Smith found the Golden Plates, he moved to a farm in Harmony, Pennsylvania, where he translated the plates into the Book of Mormon. Do you know who visited Joseph Smith in Harmony in 1829?"

"Not really, and please stop with the dramatics."

"John the Apostle visited Joseph Smith, John the Evangelist, or John, the Beloved Disciple, whichever name you want to call him. According to the Mormons, John was, get this, 'translated,' which meant he was changed, or translated, from a human being into an immortal being."

"Greg, now you are saying that John the Evangelist is a vampire?"

"No, he's not a vampire. Don't be ridiculous."

"Me, I'm being ridiculous? Have you heard yourself lately? Twice this week, you said that John the Evangelist is still alive, and he is sending you notes on Gmail."

"Yeah, but no one ever documented that John died. Jesus said he might not die in THE BIBLE. The Book of MORMON, from the Church of Latter-Day Saints, says that John doesn't die but that he became immortal. I can't make this up. That's two documented sources that say that. Two documented sources, the Book of Mormon and the Catholic and Christian Bibles, are highly respected works. Highly respected! That's enough confirmed sources for the New York Times to go to print."

"Please stop, or I will have you committed, and they are no longer called Mormons."

"When did that change?"

Finally, the day arrived for Mouse and Greg to leave their hotel. Emmanuelle was to meet them outside, but first, they went to a pastry shop around the corner. They returned to the hotel and waited on the front steps.

"You are acting like a school kid."

"What are you talking about, Mouse?"

"You. You can't stand still waiting for your Emmanuelle to get here."

"That's not true. After two weeks, I'm glad to be out of that hotel room."

"Tell me about it; I had to spend them with you. Why are you pacing all around?"

"I'm not, I just have a cramp in my leg, and I'm walking it off."

"Yeah, right."

"I think that's her."

"Pull yourself together. You are with your wife."

Marge stepped in front of Greg, "Hi, you must be Emmanuelle; I'm Marge, Greg's wife."

Greg thought he heard an over-emphasis on the words 'Greg's wife,' maybe he was just out of position.

Emmanuelle smiled, "Hi, Mouse; I am so happy to meet you; Greg has told me so much about you." In French fashion, Emmanuelle leaned over and kissed Mouse's cheeks.

"I bet." Mouse half-smiled.

Emmanuelle and Mouse looked at Greg, expecting him to greet Emmanuelle and say something. Instead, he stood there with a goofy look, not knowing what to say.

"Oh, he gets like this sometimes. Just ignore him until he gets his wits about him."

Greg emitted a feeble "Hi."

Emmanuelle embraced Greg, kissed his cheeks, and said, "We finally meet face-to-face. I can't believe it." Greg continued standing, looking goofy.

Mouse looked at Emmanuelle and said, "He gets like this when he's excited. We best get a drink into him. Beware, though, after two drinks, he won't stop talking. It's like putting oil on the Tin Man."

Emmanuelle laughed, "I know just the place. It's around the corner, and we can arrive in two minutes." She looked at Greg and wondered, "what is with this guy?"

Entering the friendly environs of a bar worked wonders for Greg. He offered, "How about we start with a round of Aperol Spritzes? It's too early for a beer."

Emmanuelle and Mouse said simultaneously, "Sounds wonderful." Emmanuelle called the waiter over and ordered the three of them in French. "I also ordered fromage and some bread."

"Do they have any cheese? Ouch! Why'd you kick me, Mouse?"

"You are acting stupid."

Emmanuelle started to laugh.

Mouse offered, "Please don't encourage him."

Emmanuelle began, "I hope your quarantine wasn't too much of a burden. We must all be careful these days. Knuckles said the ride from the airport was peaceful."

"Knuckles? Who is Knuckles?" asked Greg.

"Your driver, we call him Knuckles. Didn't Knuckles introduce himself?"

"He didn't say a word. Why is he called Knuckles?"

At which Mouse started laughing, "Because all you can see from behind him is his hands on top of the steering wheel. It's like two handfuls of knuckles are driving the car."

"Oui, Oui," shouted Emmanuelle. "That's right, that's Knuckles! But he should have introduced himself."

Mouse offered, "He probably doesn't speak English, and Greg's French is horrid."

Emmanuelle said, "He speaks perfect English; he lived in New York City for years."

After the waiter brought the drinks and food, Greg offered, "Potens un toast. Here's to wives and girlfriends; may they never meet. Ouch! That hurts."

Mouse started the interrogation, "So Emmanuelle, tell me about yourself. Are you married?"

"You don't have to answer that, Emmanuelle."

Emmanuelle laughed, "You are both exactly as I imagined. And no, I am not married; I haven't been lucky to find someone like Greg."

"Lucky you!"

Greg interrupted, "Emmanuelle, why don't you tell us about the itinerary you cooked up?"

"Sure, you two would like a few days in Paris to start. I've got two tickets to the Louvre for you. Greg said you are not much for heights, Mouse, so I arranged a city tour on a guided bus that runs by the Eiffel Tower but not up it. I can recommend some nice restaurants for your dinners."

Mouse said, "That sounds wonderful. I can't walk much right now, but I will make an exception for the Louvre. The bus tour sounds ideal."

"Sounds good to me; who needs another drink?" Greg asked while he eyed the waiter and pointed at his drink, hoping that was a universal sign to bring him another.

"After your two-day tour of Paris, we will meet in the morning. We can take a train to Nancy in the Grand Est and drive to the Basilica of Saint Nicolas. I'd love to show you the Basilica and around the City of Saint Nicolas. It's very quaint. We can drive to nearby towns like Ippling, where we all had ancestors.

"The next day, I'd like to take you to an out-of-the-way place in southern Alsace in the Jura Mountains. It's a two-and-a-half-hour ride from Saint Nicolas to this town near the Swiss border. The Swiss in that region are also Alsatians. We can visit a quaint mountain village that has mostly stayed the same over the years. I first found this place on a hike about fifteen years ago."

Mouse offered, "That sounds ideal. Our favorite trips are visits to out-of-the-way places and meeting the locals."

"Then this would be a perfect stop. You would say the villagers are all from small families." Emmanuelle said.

"Well, nobody has a lot of children anymore." Mouse offered.

"Oh, they have lots of children." Emmanuelle responded.

"I thought you said they were small families."

"Yes."

"Must be lost in translation," thought Mouse.

Greg asked, "Does the village have a pub?"

"Of course. Do you think we are barbarians?"

"I will let you know once I taste the local beers. Speaking of which, does anyone want another?"

"I think you shall like the local beer." laughed Emmanuelle. "After we visit the Jura Mountains, we can send Greg by train to the French Pyrenees, and he can start his Camino. Brother John will meet him in Azofra about nine or ten days later. Mouse and I will explore Provence and meet you and Brother John in Burgos in about two weeks."

Mouse and Greg agreed that sounded perfect.

"Mouse, I rented a villa for you in France, near San Sebastian's border. You can stay there and rest and see the countryside."

"Well, I am looking forward to this," Mouse said. "Thanks for all of your help Emmanuelle."

"It's my pleasure Mouse. It's so nice to meet you finally. You will love it here."

"Excuse me." said Greg, "I have to use the little boy's room." Walking past the bar, he told the waiter, "Bring me another, por favor."

The waiter, in English, rolled his eyes and said, "That's Spanish."

"Excelente! Gracias."

A small Citroen, with blacked-out windows, sat outside the café. The Citroen followed the party for the next few days; its driver made two phone calls on an encrypted satellite phone. The first was to the Cardinal. "Your Eminence, I wanted to report that Emmanuelle Chasteté has made contact with an older American couple from Saint Louis in Paris."

"Do you know their names?" asked O'Rourke.

"Margaret and Gregory Klass."

"Never heard of them. I will check them out with my contacts at the Archdiocese in Saint Louis. Keep on them and let me know if anything peculiar happens."

"Certainly, your Eminence."

The second call was to Joshua in the Mossad, where he made the same report. Joshua asked, "Have you reported this to the Cardinal."

"Yes, those were my instructions."

"Okay, very good; from now on, you will contact me before you contact the Cardinal. We need to keep a tight rein on things from here on out."

"Yes, sir."

24

Winter Solstice, Silk Road, East of Jerusalem, BC

KASPAR LED THE LARGE caravan west, following the comet whose path now led westward. He convened the three families and spoke. "Upon reaching Jerusalem, we will either turn south to Egypt and Alexandria or north through Syria to Anatolia and Byzantium unless the comet does something mysterious."

Melchior said, "Hessulah and I will stay with you until Jerusalem. There we will head northwest to Caesarea. From Caesarea, we will sail home to Myra."

Kaspar said, "I understand. Mothers prefer to have their first child at home."

Balthazar proclaims, "Movared and I will turn south toward Egypt after Jerusalem. Byzantium is too cold for us."

The caravan traveled fifteen to twenty kilometers each day.

On one uneventful day, the three Magi rode ahead of the caravan. Melchior rode Farrokh, his white Persian horse; Balthazar sat atop a reddish-brown Arabian stallion while Kaspar towered above them on a drab, insolent camel. Camels, the preferred beast on the Silk Road, were famous for their ill temperament. Kaspar's mount was no exception and continually made his displeasure known.

Melchior, Kaspar, and Balthazar were discussing their trips to Babylon. Melchior bragged, "Toward the end, we were covering almost thirty kilometers a day."

Kaspar remarked, "Only a well-organized caravan can cover such distances. That's impressive, especially as you are so young and inexperienced."

Melchior replied, "Truth be told, Hessulah maintains order. I took charge at first, but I failed miserably. Hessulah lets me think I am in charge, but she runs everything. I let her think that I believe I am in charge, but we both know I am not. The servants go to her for everything. The smartest thing I ever did was to fail miserably at leading my caravan!"

"Aimilia runs my caravan too!" Balthazar laughed.

Kaspar nodded in agreement, saying, "Yes, in my tribe, they say a hard-working wife is worth three good camels, and a wise man marries a hard-working woman."

Melchior chimed in, "I think we are all wise men!" They all chuckled. It was a Magi joke.

Hessulah was early in her pregnancy, and aside from morning nausea, she felt great. The baby would not begin to show till nearly the fifth month as her stomach muscles were very taut, and this was her first child.

She was riding on Bulsara when she felt an ant crawl on her arm. She flicked it off, thinking, "These damn bugs, how I long to be at sea. I miss its smell and can do without camel stench. I can't tell which smells worse, the camel, camel dung, or the camel riders. I wish I could feel the fresh air and sea breeze. Stiff breezes keep the bugs away. I hunger for a freshly cooked branzino, filleted, covered in herbs, and cooked with olive oil over the small fire in the Vixen's galley." Crickets chirped in the distance. "Well, we will have something crispy for dinner tonight." Immediately she thought, "There I go complaining again. I will start thinking good thoughts tomorrow."

The days stretched into weeks, and the roads were long and dusty. Villages were few but friendly. The men spent the cold nights watching the stars, tracking the comet, and trying to interpret changes in its path. Over the last few days, the comet altered course and picked up speed. Its course was heading toward Jerusalem. Melchior told Hessulah, "We think the new course holds promise. It leads towards Jerusalem. I will honor my promise to you. I instructed Jacob that we would leave the Magi caravan in Jerusalem and head to Caesarea."

Hessulah countered, "You did this without consulting me?"

"We spoke about this before."

"We agreed you would consult me on any decision."

"I'm sorry I thought this was what you wanted."

"I want us to be a happy family. You will not be happy if we cut short your quest. How can the family be happy if the father is not happy?"

"But don't you want the baby to be born at home?"

"Yes, but Movared and Aimilia are competent midwives. They have become like sisters to me. Let's continue the quest if you agree, that is."

"Yes, of course, I agree. Thank you, my love. Let's call Jacob over."

Melchior spoke, "Jacob, we are near Jerusalem. When we get there, you are to return to Caesarea with Zalman's camels. Hessulah and I will stay with this caravan."

Jacob replied, "I think that is an excellent idea. My father will be grateful to both of you. Good luck on your quest."

Jacob walked away, looking for servants to help him. Melchior was baffled and asked Hessulah, "What will the camel-steward's father be grateful for?" Hessulah was unsure but always thought there was something familiar about Jacob.

Kaspar, Melchior, and Balthazar agreed that the comet's change in direction was a good omen. Their hopes grew that they were on the right path to greet the Messiah. But that night, the comet moved on and rapidly exited the skies. Unsure where to go, they headed to Jerusalem and sought counsel with the leaders of the Jewish Temple.

The Magi met the Temple elders and offered sacrifice to their god as a custom of respect. Five hundred years earlier, Magi crossed paths with the Hebrews held captive in Babylon for seventy years.

At the Temple, the Magi and Jewish Elders discussed that Jewish and Zoroastrian prophecies foretold the coming of a Messiah, born of a virgin. The Magi learned that the Jewish prophecy predicted the Messiah would be of the House of David. The Zoroastrian prophecy only foretold that a Messiah would come. The Jewish Elders advised the Magi to meet with Herod, as he would be interested in their news and might help their cause.

The Magi were renowned as councilors of Kings and Emperors. It was appropriate and customary to introduce themselves to the ruler whenever they traveled to another kingdom. The Magi agreed and sent an emissary to the king requesting permission to visit his court.

Kaspar, Balthazar, and Melchior discussed the day's event that evening. Kaspar noted, "It is very significant that the Jew's prophecy is similar to ours. It increases my confidence that we are on the correct path."

———————◆———————

The next day the trio attended the court of Herod. The three travelers left their mounts outside the palace walls and entered the courtyard, where Herod sat in an oversized chair. Several advisors and servants attended to him. He was old, as his reign had lasted for almost forty years. Herod's court seemed subdued, with no laughter or joy. Kaspar spoke first and told Herod about their group and mission. "We are Magi from the Temples of Zoroaster, the religion of the Great King Cyrus of ancient Persia. We have journeyed from Babylon and beyond to pay homage to the birth of a new King, the Messiah, which our great prophet Zoroaster foretold in prophecy two thousand years ago."

Herod replied, "I am the king of Judaea. Who is this new king that you speak of?"

Kaspar answered, "Our Prophet foretold that a Savior would be born to punish the wicked and renew the world. We followed the signs in the cosmos to this place. We beseech you to help us find the new king."

Over the years, Herod's insecurity and paranoia grew. He recently executed his third son, another wife, and over 300 of his top military officers. Herod was not of royal birth, and that preyed upon his mind. His hold on the throne of Judaea was always tenuous. The mention of a new king sent his mind to a dark place.

Herod's reign was complex. There had been significant civil accomplishments and successful business ventures. However, the heavy taxation required to fund his massive building projects left the people extremely poor. Personal atrocities offset his achievements and fed his paranoia. He did not trust the leaders of the Jewish Temple or the Romans, but he trusted his family the least.

The visit from these Magi was a new threat he must meet with swift and decisive action. He used the Magi as bait to find this newborn king. "Once you have found the new king, please return to me so I may pay homage from one king to another."

Kaspar agreed and left the required tribute for the audience with the king. Once the Magi left, Herod called for his servant, Jethro, "Follow these Magi and their caravan and report back on their movements."

Returning to camp, Kaspar called the three families to meet by the central fire. The days had grown short and cold; snow flew at night. They brought rugs to sit on and blankets to keep warm. Kaspar said, "We have journeyed far. We have reason to believe that the Messiah is close. The Judaeans have a prophecy that a Messiah will deliver them. Their king asked us to return to him once we found the Messiah so he might pay homage."

A sudden chill went through Aimilia, and it aroused her paranoia. A mother of five children has finely honed maternal instincts. She asked, "Does their king have ulterior motives in wanting to know the location of the Messiah?"

"Strange that you ask that," said Kaspar. "Throughout our meeting, I sensed things at this court are not as they appear. Only their king spoke. The rest stood around as if in a state of fear."

Melchior added, "That was my sense too. No one looked at us; everyone averted their eyes whenever I glanced at them."

Balthazar said, "We must do all we can to protect the Messiah. We must be cautious and attract little attention."

Jethro watched from a distance under cover of some date trees. The families socialized around a community fire, but he was not close enough to hear a word. He left as the meeting ended and decided to return the following day.

The families returned to their tents for the night. As he and Hessulah reached their tent, Melchior noticed something peculiar in the sky.

"Look, Hessulah, just above the horizon, those two moving stars. They weren't there yesterday. It appears that they are moving close to each other. I wonder?" He called a servant, "Saddle Farrohk, and bring me some blankets."

Melchior walked to Kaspar and Balthazar's tents and called them together. He pointed out the celestial display. Balthazar asked, "What do you think it means?"

Melchior responded, "I'm not sure, but I think we should follow it and see where it leads."

"I agree, let's go, and we will take a servant to send back to have the caravan follow us."

After about an hour's ride, the stars dipped below the horizon. Kaspar said, "Let's camp here and see what tomorrow brings. We can bring the caravan forward once we know we are onto something."

———————◦○◦———————

Watching a camped caravan for six or seven days was monotonous. Jethro became lax as the days wore on. He had not seen the three Magi for a few days, but the caravan was here. Jethro would do as instructed and follow the caravan. He returned to the caravan camp each day after a good breakfast, usually when the sun reached its zenith. On the sixth day, Jethro returned to the caravan camp. He was shocked to find everyone, and everything gone. Local people went about their daily work and their steps covered the tracks from the caravan.

Jethro asked if anyone knew where the caravan was or when it had left. But no one had seen or heard anything. It was as if it had disappeared. Returning to Herod and saying he lost a caravan would mean his death. Instead, he began to search. He rode to Caesarea first, knowing Zalman had business with many caravans. He rode to the gates of Zalman's compound and asked for entry on behalf of the king. Jethro waited outside for Zalman, who appeared in about ten minutes. "Greetings, Zalman. I hope you can be of service to your king today."

"Greetings, Jethro. How can I help you and be of service to my king?"

"A small caravan camped near Jerusalem about 10 miles from here. Do you happen to know its whereabouts?"

"Whose caravan?"

"There were a few Zoroastrian priests, Magi, I think; the king asked me to watch it."

Zalman smiled and said, "How could you lose an entire caravan, Jethro?"

Jethro left Zalman's compound with no new information and was slightly humiliated. Jethro continued his search, making a circle with the caravan campsite as the center. He was looking for the most recognizable caravan sign—great piles of camel dung, a sign you will undoubtedly smell before seeing it.

The Magi followed the celestial chase for six evenings. Each evening the showcase lasted an hour, and they had traveled only 6 or 7 miles from the caravan campsite. Kaspar said, "Let's move the caravan closer, and they can join us tomorrow evening."

A star was chasing a star, and they were chasing both. The star chase continued, and on the seventh evening, these dancing stars gave an extra show that night. As they watched the end of this night's dance, it was as if a door opened, and what appeared to be a tiny dot flickered on and off in front of the closest star, but they were not quite able to ascertain the import of that dot or even if they had seen it. Was it an illusion?

The furthest star had an elliptical shape and appeared to have rings surrounding its center. That night the three men had stopped outside a small village, waiting for the caravan to join them. They prepared hot mulled wine and settled down for the night as their caravan approached. Their chase would continue tomorrow when the celestial event re-appeared. They sat by a fire outside a quiet village where a small herd of cows and sheep grazed nearby. The wail of a tiny infant from a nearby shack broke the calm of the evening.

Joseph of Nazareth, of the house of David, walked into the early evening air. He stood in a pasture outside Bethlehem, about 10 miles from Jerusalem. The village sits among low fertile hills. His wife, Mary, had just given birth. It was just after sunset, and all was quiet on this crisp and clear winter evening, when two horsemen, a camel and its rider entered the pasture and set camp several hundred yards away. The travelers sat by a fire facing west, watching the skies as a caravan followed their path from the north. Joseph's gaze shifted to the western sky following the new visitors.

Low over the western horizon, the two wandering stars were visible, each star set atop the other. Joseph's mind etched the sight into his memory. The celestial chase culminated in a most fantastic display as if a door opened into the cosmos. He had watched the wandering stars' cosmic dance. Silently, one of the stars slipped below the horizon.

Joseph and Mary named their son Jesus.

25

TOWN OF BETHLEHEM, ANNO DOMINI

THE SERVANTS UNLOADED THE caravan and set up camp. Melchior walked around the village in the morning to better understand their surroundings. Slowly the day passed as everyone waited for the evening to see where the star would lead them. As evening approached, the Magi saddled their mounts and gathered at the campfire to await the two stars leading them onward.

As evening settled, murmurs weaved through the camp as everyone affixed their vision low on the horizon; but the celestial display did not appear. The three men sat on the camel and horses, watched, and waited. Their only plan was to fasten their path to the stars leading them, but the stars did not call that night. The three Magi sat quietly and pondered their next move. Their servants and wives knew not to interfere; the Magi would have a plan.

As the three men sat, the baby in the nearby shed started its tiny wail. The Magi discussed how to interpret the unexpected when they realized their stars would not appear. Melchior arose first and looked around with a troubled look on his face. Then he turned 180 degrees, and his vision rested on the shed, his ears tuned to the tiny wail. The shed was more like a wall with half walls on each side. A small ledge performed the role of a roof. One could not call it a barn. It was barely sufficient to blunt the fierceness of the winter winds.

Melchior stood and stared, listening to the cry. Balthazar noticed the change in Melchior's countenance as his troubled look changed to puzzlement. Balthazar stood and went beside Melchior, staring at the structure and listening. Soon Kaspar joined them. Melchior spoke quietly, "Perhaps we should trust in the Star and not let our assumptions guide us." The three stared as a feeling of hope welled within them.

Kaspar suggested, "Melchior, you speak Aramaic; you should approach the family and report back to us."

Balthazar said, "I agree. Maybe our expectations for a newborn messiah are inaccurate." Melchior walked alone to the open stable.

The wives joined Balthazar and Kaspar and waited as a group for Melchior to return. Melchior began, "They are named Mary and Joseph, from the Judaean House of David. Their child is named Jesus."

Hessulah asked, "Are you certain this is the family? That stable is hardly the birthplace of a king."

Melchior said, "As soon as I saw the mother and child, I knew. They are who we seek. The mother is not much more than a child herself; her husband is an older, quiet man who seems honest. The baby will rest tonight; we will visit in the morning."

After breakfast, Melchior, Balthazar, and Kaspar walked to the dwelling of Joseph, Mary, and the baby. Melchior addressed Joseph and Mary, "Long ago, our great prophet, Zoroaster, prophesized the birth of a Messiah. Magi have been watching the heavens ever since for the celestial event that would lead us to the Messiah. We came from an assembly of Magi and Zoroastrian priests in Babylon and followed a comet to Jerusalem. The dancing stars of the past few nights led us from Jerusalem to your stable."

Mary and Joseph were honored by the presence of the Magi. They acknowledged a visit by these distinguished men as part of an already magical and mystical experience, as childbirth is to so many new parents.

The Magi presented gifts of Gold, Frankincense, and Myrrh. Melchior told Mary, "Our wives want to speak with you and see the baby. Would you mind taking the child to the large tent in our camp? They have prepared breakfast for you."

"That is most thoughtful; I should like that," Mary responded. She wrapped the baby tightly in his garments and proceeded to the camp.

Mary joined the wives in the central tent, where the women sat in a circle on warm rugs. A servant placed a small round stool draped in cloth in the center of the women. Another servant who spoke Aramaic and Greek served as the translator for the women. Movared motioned for Mary to join and said, "Please sit here and join us. We'd love to see your baby."

Mary was a thin girl with brown eyes and a pleasant smile. She was not much older than thirteen and was delighted to have the company of other women, especially after traveling for so many days with quiet Joseph.

After introducing themselves, Aimilia explained, "Mary, we know that our husbands have provided you and Joseph with gifts fit for a king. We wonder if you could use some motherly help. Movared and I are both experienced mothers and midwives. We have been teaching Hessulah, who is also with her first child."

Mary replied, "Please, anything you can teach me is appreciated. I am the youngest daughter in my family, and I have not had to care for a baby. My sister Salome will join Joseph and me, but I don't know when she will arrive."

"That's wonderful that your sister will join you. Joseph is good, but what do men know about babies?" All four women nodded and smiled. Aimilia said, "Can you put the baby on the table so we can examine him?

Mary loosened the wrapping and gently laid Jesus on the table. The women did what all people do. They counted fingers and toes. The baby held Hessulah's finger and tried to direct it to his mouth. Hessulah asked, "Is He feeding, okay? Has He been able to latch on to your nipple?"

Mary replied, "Yes, but I am not sure my milk has arrived."

Movared picked up the baby's undergarment, "Well, this is wet. He must be getting some milk. How often does He wet? Has He pooped?"

"I have to clean his garments constantly. He didn't poop for the first few days but has pooped three to four times a day since."

Movared laughed, "Well, there is no worry. He is getting plenty of milk!"

Movared said, "Wrap Him tightly, especially on chilly days like today. It is better for Him. He will fight against tightness, but it is only necessary for a month." Movared demonstrated the technique by tightly wrapping the baby. When she had finished, Jesus opened His eyes. She exclaimed, "Oh, He is green-eyed, such beautiful eyes. Does Joseph have green eyes too?"

Mary replied, smiling, "No, Joseph and I have brown eyes. He has His father's green eyes."

There was a slight pause while that statement hung in the tent; Movared said, "Well, he has beautiful eyes."

Mary said, "Let me tell you the story. It may help to make sense of why you journeyed here." She paused and then began, "A traveler, a man of God, arrived at our dusty village of Nazareth, in the Province of Galilee, at the beginning of Passover about nine months ago. Passover is an important feast in our religion. The traveler walked a white donkey and came directly to our home. He knelt before our house and blessed our home before asking my father if he could stay for Passover Supper.

"My father agreed, and we prepared a seat for him at our table. He was a man of average height with radiant green eyes. His eyes were as green and as bright as yours, Hessulah.

"After dinner, he announced, "I am a Messenger of the Lord, and our Lord is amongst you."

Mary continued, "I was not fearful as I had always expected him. He prepared a draught of wine for my parents and mixed it with myrrh. My parents quickly fell asleep. I drank a small amount and felt strangely alert and relaxed. He took me into my room, where I disrobed for him. Afterward, he told me to follow Joseph to Bethlehem and await a visit from travelers. Joseph was a man in our village who had lost his wife to sickness a year before. When my father learned I was with child, he arranged for Joseph and me to wed. Joseph is a good provider and will look after the Child and me."

The four women formed a strong maternal bond, and the Magi wives were happy to help the young mother in her need. They knew not to question what had transpired to bring them to this place, but they marveled at the circumstances that brought about this gathering. Mary's story gave everyone an understanding of this mystery, and she was radiant in her new maternal role.

A few weeks after the Magi's arrival, Mary's sister, Salome, and her four-year-old son, James, arrived. Mary introduced Salome and James to Hessulah, Aimilia, and Movared. While the women chatted, James ran about the camp exhibiting his boundless energy. He went wherever he wanted; everything he saw was his to touch and immediately went into his mouth. He had a strong voice and was not shy about using it loudly and often!

As the visit ended, Hessulah and Melchior prepared their caravan to depart in the morning for Caesarea, the final leg of their journey, before sailing home to Myra. Hessulah was six months into her pregnancy, and it was time for her to return home. They would dismiss the servants, sell off the camels when they reached Caesarea, and then depart on her new ship. Balthazar and Kaspar prepared their caravans to move each to head home. Kaspar would stop in Babylon and inform the other Magi of the events that unfolded in Bethlehem and Jerusalem. The camp settled into tents for the night; the servants would pack the camels at sunrise.

Late that night, a Messenger visited the tents of the Magi. The Messenger sent a servant to awaken the three wives and told them to quietly assemble in a nearby grove, far from the tents, and not to wake the men. Following the instructions, the three women quietly made their way outside and walked to a grove of Terebinth trees. Overripe pistachio shells fallen from the branches crunched underfoot. Salome's solitary tent stood next to the pistachio grove. Inside the tent, Salome heard the crunching sounds. She arose and, unseen, she followed the shadowy figures silently.

The Messenger with vibrant green eyes stood in the middle of the grove. He invited the women to kneel. Salome knelt silently, undiscovered, behind a Terebinth tree.

Hessulah, Aimilia, and Movared knelt before the Messenger, filled with wonder. Bravely, Movared spoke, "What do you want of us?"

The Messenger said, "Be not afraid. I am with the Lord, and the Lord is amongst you." The Messenger continued, "It is by your words and deeds that the Lord has led you here."

Movared said, "We have done nothing special. We are just travelers. We followed our husbands."

The Messenger answered, "Is it not all of you that nurse those sick; comfort those in sorrow; cook to feed the hungry; make clothes to dress the poor; and provide shelter for those in need? You educate the young, administer to the elderly, midwife for expectant mothers, and raise your families. Your first thoughts are always for the health and safety of your families; and not for yourselves. You demonstrate love, teach values, and pass on family traditions.

"You brought gifts of love and necessity to the Mother and Child. You do these things without thought of reward. The Lord ingrained these virtues in your being. You advance the work of the Lord without complaint and with obedience in your heart.

"The Lord blesses all of you and your descendants for generations. The Lord blesses you for the gifts you brought His Son, the love and compassion you have shown to others, and the gifts you share with others." As the Messenger blessed them, a warm radiance flowed through the core of their beings.

The Messenger said, "Aimilia, on your way home, take the Family with you and flee Them to Egypt. The Mother and Child are in danger from Herod. Do all that you can to protect the Family. The Family shall remain in Egypt until Herod is dead, and only then is it safe for Them to return."

"Hessulah and Movared, do not return through Jerusalem. Find a new path to your home. Herod is a danger to the Child and each of you."

To all, the Messenger said, "Bless you and make haste."

The Messenger left, and the women slowly arose. Astonished, they looked at each other, sharing the experience in silence. An understanding took over the women, their minds accepting the mystical experience.

As they slowly returned to their tents, Hessulah turned and smiled at Salome, still kneeling behind a tree. Salome rose and went back and checked on her sleeping son, James. She understood that something special was afoot, as she had felt the radiance flow through her body. Salome believed Mary's son, Jesus, was sent by God. She would ensure that James stayed close to Jesus as they grew up together.

In a few years, Salome would give birth to another son. That son would be an unruly child, full of spirit. Salome named him John. Together, James and John were called the Sons of Thunder, and they would set out to change the world.

The women woke their spouses and told them of the Messenger's visit. Without question, the Magi acknowledged and accepted the commands. The servants packed the camels in the morning, and the caravans prepared to move out. Hessulah said her goodbyes to Movared and Aimilia. She approached Mary and the Child to say goodbye.

Mary spoke, "When He reaches a certain age, my Son shall need a great teacher. When He is ready, I want to send him to Melchior for learning."

Hessulah agreed, "Yes, that will be splendid; Melchior will be honored." Hessulah thought, "Who could be a better teacher than the wisest of the Wise Men?"

Hessulah sought out Salome. "If you or Mary are ever in need, please contact Zalman of Caesarea. He will know how to reach us."

Salome replied, "Thank you for your kindness Hessulah. I know we will see each other again." No further words about the previous night were necessary. The Messenger's blessing linked the women present that night forever.

26

Mouse and Papa, Alsace-Lorraine, 2020 AD

Having tea and croissants at a local café before Emmanuelle picked them up, Mouse remarked, "The biggest discrepancy between the Bible and the manuscript is the Angel appears to the three Magi, while in the manuscript, the Messenger appears to the Magi's wives."

Greg shrugged, "Why would an angel appear to the wives? Obviously, the angel appeared to the Wise Men."

Mouse responded, "Why is that obvious? Maybe it is, to a male author, in a male-dominant society, a man would write that the angel appeared to the Wise Men. But logically, the angel would have appeared to their wives."

"Why is that logical? Besides, are you saying that Matthew, Mark, Luke, or John lied?"

"The Gospels were written well after Christ's death, and John was the only gospel writer that was a disciple, and he didn't write about Jesus's birth. The others were second-hand accounts."

◆◆◆

Mouse and Greg got into Emmanuelle's car. "I loved the Basilica of Saint Nicolas." Greg said, "It was impressive. Too bad we could not see his bones, though. Do people ask for a sample of his bones to check the DNA?"

"Yes, can you believe that? Recently I received a request from someone in Saint Louis, Missouri, for his bone marrow. Isn't that where you live? Some idiots from Saint Louis sent me an empty FedEx box with no name, asked for his bone marrow, and to return the box to my local FedEx office."

"Well, that's a coincidence; it wasn't me." Greg quickly volunteered.

"What kind of an ASS would do that?" Mouse challenged, all the while glaring at Greg.

"Look, there's a reindeer." Greg pointed out the window.

The terrain seemed to rise on their way through the Vosges Mountains. About 20 kilometers after the city of Belfort in a valley between the Vosges and Jura Mountains, Emmanuelle pulled off the highway onto a small dirt road that hid their car from the other vehicles on the motorway.

Emmanuelle asked, "May I have your phones, please?"

"Why do you need our phones?" Greg inquired.

"Just to be safe, we think someone is following you."

"What do you mean followed? Who would follow us? We've been in quarantine for 14 days; a two-year-old could follow us."

"We believe you showed up on their radar when I sent the manuscript."

"Who's radar? Nothing you are saying makes any sense. I thought you and John sent the manuscript."

"No, John didn't want to send it to you, so I took it and sent it."

"Why didn't John want to send it to us?"

"He didn't want to send it to you. He only wanted to send it to Mouse. You will have to ask him why when you see him."

"I'm confused, but I will ask Brother John. And who is following us? And why would anyone follow us?"

"A secret religious group has been watching John for a long time. They latched onto you when you posted part of the text online. We think they are following you because of their interest in John."

"So, the Roman Catholic Church has yet another secret organization, and they are looking for Mouse and me?"

"It's a religious group, but it's not only Catholic; it includes leaders of Jewish, Mormon, Christian, and Islamic faiths. They are all watching John. A former Bishop of Saint Louis leads the group; he is now a Cardinal."

Greg yelled, "Not that nut job! He covered up the abuse by the priests in our diocese. He tried to steal money from one of his parishes to pay for the abusive priests' lawyers. The parishioners rebelled against his extortion scheme and refused to hand over the money. This Bishop, a self-proclaimed man of God, excommunicated the members of the parish council and the parish priests. The parish raised the money specifically to pay for renovations of their historic church. The press crucified the Bishop for his pathetic response. Many believe he is the personification of what's wrong with the church."

"Crucified? Greg! Couldn't you use a better term?" Mouse was perturbed.

"You know about this guy? His name is Bork or something like that. He is anti-gay, anti-women, anti-fun, and only concerned about his power and money. After all his nonsense, what did the church do? They promoted him and sent him to Rome, where he could do greater damage. Thankfully the current Pope re-organized him into a do-nothing position."

"Greg, let Emmanuelle speak."

"Well, some sects of the major religious groups collaborated and set up an organization to watch John. That Cardinal is the head of the group."

"Well, what can a bunch of priests and rabbis do to us?"

"I must tell you that they have already killed at least two of our people."

"Killed? And just who are your people?"

"You will see. We are on our way to meet 'our people.'"

"Are we in danger? We did not sign up for danger. I'm sure danger wasn't on the itinerary."

"Please, we need to keep moving. I need to disable your phones so they cannot track us."

Mouse and Greg handed over their phones.

"Hon, if you want to turn back, we can turn around now."

"No, Greg. Let's see what tomorrow brings. We don't need to make that decision today."

"Okay, it's your funeral."

Both women shouted in unison, "Stop Greg!"

It had been an overcast day. Emmanuelle returned to the motorway and turned off a few kilometers up the road. They drove for about 15 minutes before Mouse fell asleep. The local highway soon became enveloped in a fog. Greg asked, "Is it always this foggy?"

Emmanuelle remarked, "Every time I come here, it's foggy. I walked for kilometers in the fog the first time I found this place. It's where I first met John."

"What was he doing here, and are we still in France? Are we still in Alsace?"

"Yes, I think so."

"Well, we are not in Kansas, Dorothy."

"Who is Dorothy?" Emmanuelle questioned.

Mouse briefly woke up from the chatter between Emmanuelle and Greg, adding, "That's just Greg's attempt at humor. Ignore him."

"What was John doing up here? Besides getting lost."

"He said goodbye to an old friend who had passed on."

"We are sorry to hear that." offered Mouse. Greg kept trying to peer through the fog. They arrived after a slow hour or two drive through the heavy mist. Greg may have fallen asleep while Mouse had abruptly fallen back to sleep.

"Here is the first village," Emmanuelle claimed as the car drove into a quaint area of what looked to be a bustling downtown. People were riding bicycles and walking briskly by.

"Look at all the children," Greg remarked. "But some look a little older."

"Those are not children. They are the adults." Emmanuelle offered. "Remember I said they were from small families."

Mouse immediately understood. "You meant they were from short families, as short in height. Small families, to us, means there are only one or two children."

"Yes," exclaimed Emmanuelle, "short families. I always get short and small mixed up. English is so difficult sometimes."

Greg chimed in, "Well, I will like it here. I was never the tallest person in a crowd. Where's the pub?"

"Greg, it's not even 11 a.m." cautioned Mouse.

"Well, we are on vacation."

"Where are we, Emmanuelle?" asked Mouse. "This place is charming."

"It's just a little village in a secluded upper mountain valley between Switzerland and Alsace, not too far from Lorraine. There are several other villages nearby."

"Sounds like the center of Alsace."

Emmanuelle said, "Yes, it was once, I think. We should get out and walk around. But before we do, I must warn you that I told them you were coming."

Greg asked, "You told who that we were coming?"

"I told the people in the village. They don't get many tall people here, so I had to alert them."

"I was 5'10' in my twenties, I am not sure I am 5'10 now, and I am not considered tall."

"Well, you will be tall today."

"Why don't they get many tall people visiting here?"

"It's remote and difficult to find this place. It's challenging to get through the fog."

Emmanuelle, Mouse, and Greg exited the car. All the bustling and hustling around them came to a sudden halt. All eyes turned to Mouse, Greg, and Emmanuelle.

Greg whispered to Mouse, "They are all looking at us."

Mouse smiled, "They all seem very friendly."

A well-dressed older gentleman, who was not very tall, walked up to Emmanuelle and started speaking gruff German. Emmanuelle interrupted, saying, "Herr Meier, I'd like to introduce you to Margaret and Greg Klass."

Mouse offered, "You can call me Marge." then extended her hand.

Greg said, "Guten tag, I am Greg."

Herr Meier said a quick "Wilkommen," continued his conversation with Emmanuelle, and gesticulated at Mouse and Greg when he spoke. He finished what he had to say, gave a curt nod to Mouse and Greg, and walked quickly away.

Greg whispered to Mouse, "Well, they are not all that friendly. Who was that Emmanuelle?"

"That was Herr Meier; you would call him the mayor. He said welcome to the village."

"Well, the next time you see Herr Meier, the Mayor, tell him for me; it was nice to meet him too. Let's go to the pub; at least we can get a sandwich. Do they have Thüringen here? I'd love a Thüringen and cheese sandwich."

"I am sure they will have whatever you ask for."

"What pub are we going to?"

"Meier's Pub."

"Somehow, I knew you were going to say that."

Everyone stopped, turned toward them, and then slightly bowed or tipped their hat at them as they made their way down the street.

Greg had to duck as they walked through the door to Meier's Pub. It was dimly lit inside but seemed cheerful and was about half full.

Emmanuelle said, "Let's take that open table over there. Most of these are night workers. They stop here after the late shift."

Greg raised an eyebrow at that. "I like their work ethic already." Mouse and Greg nodded to everyone as they walked by. Everyone had stopped their conversations and looked at them, almost to the point of staring.

"Where do they work?" asked Mouse.

Emmanuelle said, "There's a large manufacturing facility and shipping complex that employs many from the neighboring villages too."

"Kind of like Amazon? Greg asked.

"Yes, it's something like Amazon. Did you notice the large building near where we entered the village?"

"Yes, the one with the green metal roof?"

"Yes, that's the village post office."

"That's a large post office for such a small village."

"Well, they get a lot of mail up here."

"Didn't the internet put a crunch into that? Nobody writes letters anymore."

"No, not their mail; they still get a lot of inbound mail."

"That's interesting."

Herr Meier came up to the table to take their orders. "Guten tag, I mean, good morning."

"Guten tag, Herr Meier." Having studied his German in isolation, Greg was finally getting to try it out. "Was für ein Bier hast du?"

"Viele Arten."

"What did he say, Emmanuelle?"

"He said they have many kinds."

"Drei pilsner, bitte." Greg had memorized 'eins, zwei or drie pilsner, bitte', almost the total of his German vocabulary. "I ordered for all of us." He said proudly. "What's his problem?" Greg asked as Meier walked off, shaking his head.

"He wanted to run down the menu of the beers that they brew here. They are quite proud of them. They grow their grain, malt, barley, and hops up here. They have some excellent local brewers."

"Oh, I was thirsty and needed something quick. I will ask Herr Meier when he comes back."

Mouse chimed, "What a quaint pub; how is the food?"

"I always get the cheese and meat platter; they have some of the best French, German, and Swiss cheeses."

"That sounds wonderful."

Greg dropped any pretense of being able to speak German and asked Meier when he returned, "Herr Meier, can you show us the beer menu? I'd like to know what your best local brews are. We had a long drive and needed this pilsner to 'whet your whistle' as we say in America. Mouse and Emmanuelle would like to order some food, especially anything local that you'd recommend. We could start with a nice cheese and meat platter if you have that."

Herr Meier's mood immediately changed. "Jawohl, I will be right back." Herr Meier's accent was thick, but his English was much better than any German that Greg could muster.

Herr Meier brought out a large platter of cheese, meat, various mustards, an assortment of olives, and two types of sliced artisan bread.

Mouse and Emmanuelle started cooing over the food. Greg remarked, "You two act like they just brought a baby to look at."

Mouse said, "Mind your own business; we're hungry."

Herr Meier handed Greg the beer menu. He and Meier had a lengthy discussion. "Mouse, they have several beers that Urban Chestnut brews. Emmanuelle, a local Saint Louis brewery, makes several beers and ales from old Bavarian and German recipes. They've been quite successful with their approach."

"Herr Meier, bring me your favorite ale as long as it's not too bitter or too high in alcohol."

"I know just the one."

Meier returned with Greg's ale. Meier said proudly, "This is called "Elsasser."

Greg laughed and said to Marge and Emmanuelle, "Germans simply add 'er" to the town's name to identify its beer." Turning back to Meier, he said, "We live in St Louis; it is the hometown of Budweiser."

Herr Meier tipped his head slightly toward Greg and said, "I'm sorry," as if he had not heard what Greg said.

Greg repeated himself loudly, "St Louis is home to Budweiser."

Herr Meier yelled, "I know; I said, 'I'm sorry,' I'm not deaf!"

Emmanuelle had her stein to her mouth and a mouthful of beer; Herr Meier's joke caught her at the wrong (or right?) moment. She snorted half the beer out through her nose. Mouse involuntarily slapped her hand on the table, immediately regretting the flare-up of her arthritis but kept laughing anyway. Greg thought the joke was hilarious and joined in the laughter. Greg's laugh was more of a titter-titter than a throaty haha. It wasn't an offensive laugh but not robust either.

The pub immediately went silent once everyone heard Greg laugh, and he heard himself laughing alone. "What did I do?" he whispered to Mouse.

"Nothing I could tell. That was quite an odd reaction."

After an awkward silence, Herr Meier told Greg, "We brew this beer the way Budweiser uses pieces of beech wood in the fermentation process. The difference is that we used pieces of cypress wood." Herr Meier's wife, Theresa, shouted something in German or Alsatian at Herr Meier.

Herr Meier winced slightly, sighed, and said what sounded to Greg to be the equivalent of "Yes, Dear." Greg took the opportunity to showcase his humor, referring to wives in general. "Don't worry, Herr Meier; wives get better with age."

Herr Meier responded with one word posed more as a question "Tatsachlich?" (Indeed?).

"Nein Herr Meier, das ist ein Witz!" (No Herr Meier that is a joke!)

Herr Meier laughed heartily, but when Greg joined in the laughter, a concerned look overtook Herr Meier, and he abruptly stopped laughing.

"Mouse, each time I laugh, everyone stops laughing and looks at me like I'm an idiot."

"Maybe you are not that funny, Greg?"

"I'm using my best material."

"Tatsachlich?"

Greg asked Herr Meier, "Isn't a Cypress tree like a pine or evergreen tree? Wouldn't that add too much pine flavor or creosote oils? Although this is delicious, I cannot detect anything in this ale but the hops."

"We import our cypress wood from a monk in Spain. He treats it with a resin that extracts the oils. The cypress odor is rather pleasant, and the chips help with our fermentation process."

"The monk's name wouldn't be John by chance?"

"Yes, I suspected you knew John," said Herr Meier.

"Only by reputation, we haven't met, but I'm going on the Camino de Santiago to meet him in Azofra."

"Why don't you drive there?"

"Well, you know, motor vehicles and all that."

Herr Meier looked at Greg quizzically and thought how odd Americans are, this one especially.

After a delightful lunch and a few more drinks, Greg asked for the check. "Emmanuelle, how much of a tip should I leave?" The age-old question most Americans ask when they are in Europe.

"No one works for tips here. Just pay the total."

"I love that. It's like a 25% discount."

"Is that a dad joke? Let's go outside and look around." Emmanuelle suggested.

Emmanuelle pointed out the post office again and some other points of interest.

"They also have a large communal farm over there. It runs for miles on the east and west side of the ridge that you can see over there." Emmanuelle pointed out the ridge to the south of the village.

"What do they grow?" asked Mouse. "I love gardening."

"Greg, you should have told me Mouse likes to garden."

Mouse sneered at Greg, "You never say anything nice about me."

"Sure, I do, and often."

Emmanuelle shouted at one of the nearby women, "Hey, Eloise. Do you have a minute?"

A friendly young blonde-haired woman walked over and said, "Hello, Emmanuelle."

"Eloise, this is Marge and Greg Klass. We were talking about the farm, and Marge loves to garden. Could you show her around the village farms?"

"Oh, that's not necessary, Emmanuelle; I am sure Eloise is busy. But it's so nice to meet you, Eloise."

"It's nice to meet you, Mrs. Claus. I have plenty of time and would love to show you around."

"That'd be lovely, but it's pronounced Klass, not Claus."

Eloise raised an eyebrow at Mouse's comment and gave Emmanuelle an odd look. "Sure, if you say so. Are you Americans?"

"Yes, we are."

"That explains it."

"Explains what," Greg interjected.

"Oh, nothing."

"We don't get many Americans up here," Emmanuelle noted.

Eloise, with an attitude, said, "Come with me, Mrs. KLASS."

Greg and Emmanuelle continued walking around the village together as Marge went off with Eloise. "What was that all about, Emmanuelle?"

"Nothing, I'm sure. Let me show off the rest of the village. This place is as Alsatian as Alsace gets."

Marge and Eloise walked towards the fields. It was late fall, and the farmers had harvested the crops. Marge said, "I see that you grow the hops on the ridge's eastern side and the vegetables on the western side."

"Yes, that's been the way for at least ten years. Why do you ask?"

"Oh, it's none of my business."

"Please, if you have an opinion, I'd like to hear it."

"Well, from my experience, at least in our climate in America, vegetables like the morning taste of the sun. The sun warms their root systems early and activates the growth process. At harvest time, the vegetables are fuller and more colorful. Meanwhile, hops appreciate the sun's last rays as it pulls their vines to greater heights while building more robust buds."

"So, you think you know more about how to farm than the men that have been farming here for decades?"

"Oh no, not at all. I didn't mean to sound like I knew anything at all. I am sure there's a perfect reason it's reversed."

"Well, it just so happens that I agree with you. The men here are stubborn-headed and think they know what they are doing. They are stubborn and very obstinate when they are wrong. It will be nice to have someone else on my side."

"I'm not on anyone's side. Thank you for showing me the farm, it's quite lovely here. We are just here for a short visit."

"You are not staying?"

"No, not at all; we head back later."

"That's strange." Eloise changed the subject. "Do you have any children, Marge?"

"Why yes, I have three daughters, four grandchildren, three grandsons, and one princess."

"I bet the princess is very demanding of everyone. Do they call you Nana or Grandma?"

"Oh, they don't call me either. When the first grandchild started to speak, he had trouble saying Marge, and Mouse popped out. So, the grandchildren have called me Mouse ever since. I always wanted a nice-sounding nickname, and Mouse was perfect. And yes, our little princess oversees everything."

"What do they call your husband?"

"Greg? Oh, they call him Papa. It was what our children called his father, and he likes tradition."

"So, the two of you are called Mouse and Papa?"

"Yes, Mouse & Papa."

Eloise tried it out slowly. "Mouse. And. Papa. Klass," She repeated, "Mouse and Papa Klass. Why that sounds well, almost perfect!" More excitedly, she said, "Mouse and Papa. Mouse, does Papa like traditional things?"

"Oh yes, he's very old-world like that. He still calls the Holy Spirit the Holy Ghost."

"We are a very tradition-based set of villages. He will like it here too."

"Oh, I don't think Papa is much for a small village."

As they walked closer to the village, Eloise called out to lady friends in a small circle and said something in what sounded like German. Mouse heard the words "Maus und Papa" as part of the exchange but could not follow it.

"What language are you speaking, Eloise?"

"Oh, that's an old Alsatian dialect that many of us still speak in the hills. I told them what your nicknames are."

Mouse turned to look at the group as they scattered throughout the village.

Mouse asked, "I've been wondering, do you mind me asking a question? Where do you go shopping for food and things?"

"Oh, if it's something we don't have here, there's an Aldi in the valley. Then there's always Amazon and eBay. We have the internet and everything. We are secluded but not isolated."

"Do you have Walmart's here?"

"No Walmart's and no McDonald's; we are very civilized."

"Lucky you!" Mouse added, acknowledging her agreement.

Greg and Emmanuelle were walking back through the village when they spotted Mouse and Eloise. Greg walked over to Mouse and said, "The strangest thing happened. We were walking along, and the villagers suddenly said, 'Hey, Papa.' Did you tell anyone the grandkids call me Papa?"

Mouse looked at Eloise and smiled, and said, "Nope."

"That's weird," replied Papa.

Eloise looked at Emmanuelle and asked, "Have you told them of our Cypress Tree?"

"No, I haven't. If you want to show it to Mouse and Papa, we have time."

Mouse winced and said, "I have done enough walking today and will have to sit this one out."

Eloise said, "We can take care of that." She turned to one of her friends and said, "Have Charlie hitch Farrokh and Bulsara to the carriage."

Mouse said, "Please don't go to all that trouble for me."

"Nonsense, I am doing it for me too. It's all uphill from here." Eloise laughed.

In 5 minutes, a dapple white and red bay horse came prancing up, drawing a small carriage. Charlie and his brother Teddy sat on the buckboard holding the reins. Two carriage seats faced each other and carried about six normal-sized passengers or about eight or ten of the locals.

Eloise yelled over for Freddy to join them. "Freddy is my brother and is in charge of decorations this year. He can explain what we are doing."

Papa asked, "tell me about the Cypress tree. I didn't know they grew this far north or high in the mountains."

Teddy offered, "They always grow in the mountains. But this one is special to us. It was brought here and planted by one of the early ancestors of our tribe. Our legend says she was the sister of Nicolas of Myra, the original Saint Nicolas."

Papa almost had the big one. "Mouse, did you hear that? Emmanuelle, why didn't you tell me? You knew our whole adventure started because of Nicolas of Myra."

Emmanuelle said, "I wanted this to be a surprise. It's one of the reasons why I brought you here."

"How old is the tree? If the sister of Nicolas planted it, it must be over a thousand years old, maybe more." Papa was furiously counting on his fingers.

Teddy answered, "We are not exactly sure, but we think it's 1,700 years old now."

"Can we cut it down and count its rings?" Papa asked.

"Papa, no!" Everyone shouted in unison.

"Okay, okay, just a thought."

As the carriage took them higher up the mountain, a dusting of the first snow of winter began to cover the ground. Charlie turned his head and said, "It's not much farther, about another half mile around the bend. The view is spectacular. It's always been called Alina's Tree."

"Who is Alina?" Mouse asked.

"No one remembers." laughed Teddy.

A towering Cypress, an evergreen, unfolded before them. The carriage stopped at the top of a bowl-shaped field that ran down to the base of the Cypress. On the horizon, past the Cypress tree, was a stunning view of mountains and valleys, slightly impaired by the light falling snow but very impressive, nonetheless. The mountain fell steeply away just past the tree.

Freddy said, "Each Christmas season, we decorate the Cypress with white lights; in the old days, they used white candles. We have games for the children, and groups break off for caroling. At the end of the season, we come back here and send the naughty children down the bowl on fast sleds."

"Freddy! Please stop with those awful jokes of yours." cried Eloise.

Charlie and Teddy couldn't stop laughing. "Good one, Freddy."

Papa laughed, "Do you wax the sled runners, so they slide fast?"

Back at the village, Mouse admired the postcard-like setting, it was a clear night, and soft light shone through the windows of the village homes. Mouse was about to remark on the peaceful setting when Greg said, "I can't believe the fog is so heavy. It's like the village disappeared. You can't even see the people; they were here a moment ago."

"What are" Mouse started admonishing Greg when Emmanuelle cut her off.

"Let's get Greg in the car. We have to return now." She told Mouse quietly, "I will explain in the car."

They put Greg in the passenger seat, where he fell asleep immediately. Mouse looked up one last time and waved to the townsfolk lining the roadway to say goodbye.

"What happened there, Emmanuelle? Why couldn't Greg see anything?"

"It's difficult to explain, Mouse. A force safeguards the villages. It allows some people, like you and me, to visit and return. For some reason, it allowed Greg inside just this once."

"Why will it allow me to return and not Greg? I don't understand."

"I don't know, Mouse. I hoped you both could return."

Emmanuelle drove clear of the mists an hour later and entered the valley. Mouse and Papa had both fallen asleep. Mouse woke and felt refreshed by her nap. Papa slept, as he might have had an extra pint or three.

They were on a highway when both were awake. An understanding took over in Mouse and Papa's minds; they acknowledged the mystical experience but accepted it as an ordinary event.

"That was nice of you to bring us there, Emmanuelle," said Mouse.

Papa interjected, "Yes, can you tell us more about the legend of the Cypress tree? That sounds pertinent, especially considering the manuscript John has been translating."

"I don't know much more than that. Legend says Nicolas's sister came here and planted it. It might have been in the 4th century CE."

"What brought her to Alsace?"

"According to legend, she fell in love with an Alsatian, but I don't know more."

"It ties Nicolas to Alsace and may help explain why his bones are here. I'd like to know if we could do a DNA trace with people in the village."

"Papa, stop!" cried Mouse and Emmanuelle.

"Okay, Okay, it was a joke."

"It's not funny." insisted Mouse.

"I bet Charlie, Teddy, and Freddy would laugh." Papa teased. "Emmanuelle, may I ask something that may sound insensitive?"

Mouse interjected, "Why are you asking permission to be insensitive?"

Papa ignored the comment and asked, "I couldn't help but notice that most, if not all, of the people in the villages are short. Doesn't that draw a lot of attention from people that don't live in the villages?"

"Well, many of the villagers have jobs throughout the area. There are many ways to exit the mountains, and the roads lead to Switzerland, Germany, Alsace, and other parts of France. People ignore, or pay little attention to, short people. As the workers spread out, no one puts two and two together that they all live in the same community. The ones that work in the villages make crafts sold throughout the Christmas Markets in the region."

"Fascinating," Papa continued, "they are hiding in plain sight."

"No one is hiding, Papa."

"Why are you calling me Papa all of a sudden?"

"Everyone calls you Papa now."

"Hmmpf. I'm going to start singing Short People by Randy Newman."

"Papa, No!" cried Emmanuelle.

"Don't sing; your voice will ruin the trip," demanded Mouse.

Emmanuelle said, "We have rooms near the train station. Papa will take the early train to Saint-Jean-Pied-de-Port to begin his Camino. You can pick up all your passes and maps tomorrow morning once you arrive there. It's best to spend a night in the town and get a fresh start first thing in the morning. If you leave too late in the afternoon, you might wind up on a mountaintop with nowhere to sleep. The trail is well-marked and easy to follow. There are plenty of places to stay along the trail. Few pilgrims are on the trail due to the pandemic; you won't need reservations. When you get to Azofra, ask for Brother John, someone will help you. Mouse, what if we relax for a day or two and do nothing? We can sit around and eat at the local cafes and try their wines?"

"That sounds wonderful to me."

"Can I sit around, eat, and drink for a couple of days too?"

"No, Papa!!"

After they checked into their room, Papa opened his laptop and connected to the Wi-Fi and internet to catch up on news, sports, and emails. The Buffalo Bills were winning again, which put Papa in a good mood. He checked his emails and found a large file from Brother John with a note.

<This is the end of the first Book of Hessulah>

———— ❖ ————

"Mouse, you should see this. We have some reading to do! I will call Emmanuelle to see if she can get the hotel to print this out. I can read it on the train tomorrow. Mouse? Mouse?" Greg looked over, and Mouse was fast asleep. Papa covered her with a blanket, thinking, I hope this trip isn't too much for you, Hun. I'll remind Emmanuelle to take it easy.

———— ❖ ————

The following day Emmanuelle dropped Papa off at the station. "Please keep an eye on her, Emmanuelle. She isn't in the best health and will need plenty of rest.

She insisted on this trip. We planned to honeymoon in France long ago, but we couldn't get the time off from work, nor did we have enough money."

"I understand. Mouse is in good hands. We will see you in a week or so. Enjoy your Camino; may it be the first of many."

"Let's get through one before you commit me to another. One question on Brother John, is he John?"

"You will meet him yourself, and then we can talk more. Goodbye, Papa." Emmanuelle pecked Papa a couple of times on each cheek.

"Aw, river." Papa waved goodbye and moved down the platform to the waiting train. He boarded and found a window seat after tossing his coat in the overhead storage; he pulled the papers from his backpack and settled in for a good read and a long ride.

Three rows behind, the tall priest settled in for the ride.

27
The Black Madonna, Sinai, 1 AD

The Black Madonna and Child[1]

---

1. Picture Source: The Black Madonna And Child Jesus From Russian Icons
Shalom

Scanner: Internet Archive HTML5 Uploader 1.6.3

———◆◇◆———

BETHLEHEM IS SOUTH AND east of Jerusalem. The three caravans left Bethlehem on two paths. One group went south toward Egypt, and the larger caravan went east. Jethro rode into Bethlehem from the north as the groups split and went in different directions. He saw them divide and go in two directions. As per his orders, he immediately returned to King Herod and updated him on the movement of the caravans. King Herod abruptly dismissed him after his report.

King Herod summoned the leaders of his guard. He dispatched a squad of fifty soldiers from Jerusalem to Bethlehem. His most loyal and lethal commander led them.

Jethro believed Herod wanted to pay homage to the newborn king. He was at the court when he saw the squad of soldiers march out. He asked Herod's chief councilor where the soldiers were going. Jethro was unnerved when the councilor informed him of Herod's order to the soldiers.

He immediately re-saddled his horse and set out to warn the caravans, knowing that would invite Herod's wrath upon himself and his family. It was a three-hour march from Jerusalem to Bethlehem. Jethro rode a path that brought him around and then in front of the soldiers. When he arrived in Bethlehem, the caravans were gone, but he could see the column of soldiers approaching from behind him. Jethro warned those nearby that soldiers were coming with evil intent. He followed a goat path heading east that was recently trod by camels. It led east for about 8 kilometers before turning north for 15 kilometers and then west towards the coast.

The Roman soldier created a unique sound as they marched. Caligae were the leather sandal worn by the typical Roman soldier. Each sandal has small iron hobnails tacked to the bottom providing traction in rough terrain. The caligae's sound had a secondary effect. The iron hobnails made a menacing sound when squads of soldiers marched on stone or paved roads. That sound carried ahead of the marching troops, and Rome's enemies usually heard the soldiers before they saw them. Each Roman sandal had about 100 iron bolts embedded in the leather. The constant beat of Roman soldiers' feet on the march created fear. The unending cadence of the sandals on the stone was in tune with the shield and spear slapping against the soldier's leather breastplate. The men that Herod sent to Bethlehem were called Hades Squad. They would follow orders, no matter how gruesome.

The soldiers methodically completed their diabolical orders to kill all male children under two in Bethlehem. It was wretchedness that would haunt them for the rest of their days. A sorrow haunted every mother in Bethlehem for the rest of her days.

The soldiers quickly accomplished their terrible business in Bethlehem. They retraced the slow-moving caravans' tracks and came to the spot where the groups divided. The soldiers split into two groups. One went east, following the trail of Melchior and Kaspar. The other group followed the southern path that Balthazar, and The Family, took toward Egypt.

Balthazar and Aimilia tried to make haste, but the Romans moved faster than the caravan, and they were getting closer each day. Balthazar sent a scout ride back to see how close the Romans were. He reported, "Balthazar, the Romans will catch us in two days."

They were still far from Egypt and freedom when Balthazar realized they could not outrun the Romans. Balthazar dejectedly approached his wife Aimilia, Mary, and Joseph and told them of their predicament.

Aimilia remembered that she had bartered with a merchant from the port of Akko for some purple dye. Aimilia said, "The Romans are looking for a Jewish family. I have an idea that might work." Upon hearing the idea, Mary said, "It is worth a try."

Aimilia quickly got her servants to start a fire and had the caravan make camp. She put the purple dye, blackberry juice, deep sea algae from Akko, and raw coconut oil in a large pot. After heating and stirring the concoction for about three hours, she molded the compound into a dark paste. The new mix was close to the color of her skin. Aimilia said, "Mary, please come inside my tent and bring the baby. Aimilia said, "I think this might fool the soldiers. Let me start with the infant."

Mary protested, "No, start with me first. I'd rather wear the mixture if it doesn't work." Mary undressed, and they applied the dark paste to her skin, careful not to color her lips or palms.

Aimilia stepped back and exclaimed, "Mary, you could be my sister!"

"Okay, Aimilia, let's do the baby now."

A dozen large candles stood on a makeshift table inside the tent. Aimilia lit the candles to provide light to apply the compound to the Mother and Child. Aimilia laid out traditional Ethiopian garments for Mary and Jesus to perfect the ruse on the Romans. Aimilia and Mary would dress alike to appear as sisters.

Mary's dress was beautifully ornate and laced with threads of silver. Aimilia set out a gold-laced outfit for the baby. Mary dressed while Aimilia applied the compound to the baby. Mary then dressed Jesus while Aimilia arranged the rags for Balthazar to use on Joseph.

Mary took the baby in her left arm and turned to face Aimilia. Mary's back was to the row of candles. Aimilia looked up and saw Mother and Child illuminated in marvelous light. A bright corona surrounded their heads as their darkened skin contrasted with the shimmer of the golden and silver garments. The visual aura awed Aimilia, and she fell to her knees before the Mother and Child.

Aimilia tried to comprehend the past few weeks' events, the delight as the comet appeared and brought them to Jerusalem, the dread the three women experienced after their husbands returned from the meeting with Herod, the unexpected awakening and blessing from the Messenger, who instructed them to take the Family and flee to Egypt.

Her mind will never forget this radiant vision of the Black Madonna and Child. She did not question what she witnessed; she accepted her fate to protect the Mother and Child at all costs. She will have artisans in Ethiopia remake the vision of the radiant Black Madonna and Child on paintings and wood carvings. Aimilia referred to Mary as La Negra Madonna from that moment.

After the women left the tent, Balthazar and Joseph went inside and covered Joseph's skin similarly. Joseph quickly donned his ragged clothing without complaint.

A servant sighted the twenty-five soldiers as they crested a nearby hill. Balthazar walked out to meet the soldiers hoping to diffuse a dangerous situation. The centurion said, "We are looking for a Jewish family." He signaled for his troops to inspect the camp. "We are all Ethiopians; there are no Jews here. You can tell from looking at us. These two sisters are my wives." Balthazar exclaimed while pointing at Aimilia and Mary. He flashed the Roman an amiable grin. The Roman troops rounded up the servants, families, and children for inspection. The centurion saw nothing but rich, dark African skin. He commanded his troops, "Move on, nothing to see here."

The dye would last several weeks as the caravan entered Egypt. Aimilia made several more batches of the paste. She instructed Mary and Joseph to re-apply the stain until the Romans had given up the search. They could let it wear off once they knew they were out of danger.

28

THE CAMINO, AZOFRA, LA RIOJA, SPAIN, DECEMBER 2020 AD

The Hermitage of Saint Bartholomew, Canon Del Rio Lobos, Spain[1]

As he now thought of himself, Papa left the Pyrenees and was in La Rioja territory. Yesterday he labored on the walk. He stopped for the evening at the first village

1. https://fascinatingspain.com/place-to-visit/the-best-of/most-curious-herm itages-in-spain/

in La Riojas and tried a bottle of local red wine. It wasn't as refreshing as a beer, but it helped dull his senses after the day's hike. The wine was delicious, and he decided a second bottle would completely dull those throbbing aches and pains, although he would suffer the consequences of that decision in the morning. He slogged through his walk the next day, drinking as much water as possible to counter the dehydration effects of the wine. He approached the village of Azofra, a small farming village of 200. It was easy to spot the church, Nuestra Señora de Los Ángeles, Our Lady of the Angels. As they said in the US, Azofra was a one-pony town. For the last ten miles, Papa rehearsed the critical questions for John that Mouse had coached him on. Preparation was essential, but he forgot every question when he saw the church. His mind could not get past the question, "Are you 2,000 years old?" He thought, "How can you ask a person that question and be taken seriously?" He became visibly nervous as he neared the church, where he saw an elderly man tending a small vegetable garden on the side of the church. A dozen small thorny trees grew near the garden. The man was old and frail, but his steely grey eyes shone fervently.

"Hola!" Papa said.

"Hello Greg," the old man replied, unenthusiastically. Immediately Greg's nervousness took over, and his poorly thought-out plan disintegrated.

"Are you Brother John?"

"I am called John."

It was not the answer Greg sought. "Are you Brother John, as in John, the Evangelist?"

"John the Evangelist lived a long time ago."

"I know, but are you him? Are you John, the Beloved Disciple of Jesus? John, the Apostle? John, the Gospel Writer? John, the brother of James? John, the son of Salome? John, the son of Zebedee? John, the cousin of Jesus, John, to whom Jesus entrusted the care of his mother?"

"That's a lot of Johns."

"John, the Translated? John and his brother James, who Jesus called the sons of Thunder?"

John answered, "Most people thought Jesus called John and James the sons of Thunder because they argued loudly, often, and about everything. Thunder was a reference to their father, Zebedee. Zebedee may have been the loudest man ever to walk the earth and that is why they were the sons of thunder."

Realizing that John did not deny that he was John, Greg asked, "Are you, Saint John? Is Zebedee your father?"

"How can I be a Saint if I am still alive?"

"Good point, but how are you still alive?"

"Exactly."

Greg persisted. "Exactly what?"

"Why did you come here, Greg?"

"The Camino called me?" Greg said more as a question than an answer.

"Why, specifically, did you come to see me?"

"Everything has led me here since I first contacted Emmanuelle. She directed me here. Why did you send me the document?"

"Emmanuelle sent it to you. That wasn't my idea."

"Now I'm confused. Why have I been led on this chase?"

"It's not about you, Greg; it has never been about you."

"I don't get it. So why have I been led here?"

"It's Mouse we led here, not you."

Greg was stunned. "Mouse? Why Mouse?"

"Did you think you were Santa Claus?"

"I know I'm not Santa Claus!" Greg, getting defensive, his self-importance minimized, and the reasons for his quest unraveling.

"Look, Mouse is practical, and Emmanuelle thought it would be difficult to get her to follow our trail. So, Emmanuelle used you to get Mouse to visit."

"To visit what?"

"We wanted Mouse to visit the villages in the mountains, of course. We need someone practical to run them. The last guy ran them into the ground."

"Who was the last guy?"

"Some people called him Santa Claus."

"What do you mean, Santa Claus? But why do you need Mouse? She's not well."

"Her health is not an issue. I can take care of that."

"What? How?" Then an understanding filled Greg's consciousness that what John said was true, that Mouse would be ok. When experiencing a mystical event, the mind accepts the event as reality. The mind doesn't question the event; it agrees with its reality. But Greg ignored his mind and plowed on unrelenting.

"So, you want Mouse to be Santa Claus?"

"No, we want Mouse to be Mouse Klass and in charge of the villages."

"But the doctors say that she doesn't have much time left. I'm worried this trip might take too much out of her."

"When she was in the villages, she seemed better, did she not?"

"Yes, we both felt remarkable. How did you know that?"

"As I said, her health is nothing to worry about."

Greg stood for a minute, trying to understand everything. John was, or at least did not deny that he was John, the brother of Saint James. He wants Mouse to be the next Santa, and I'm just a pawn. "Why didn't Emmanuelle just say that in the beginning?" He became deflated upon realizing his role was inconsequential. Without getting an answer, he asked, "Can I ask you a philosophical question?"

"Sure."

"Is there life after death?"

"I certainly hope to find out. I am more concerned about finding out if there is death after life."

Slightly puzzled, but then Greg realized he might be talking to a 2,000-year-old man. "What's been the greatest invention in the last 2,000 years?" Greg thought, "How did that question escape my lips? "

"Deodorant." John retorted while thinking, "what an idiot."

"Deodorant?! Well, I have been walking for days, and the hostels have low water pressure." Greg sniffed around himself and quickly changed the subject, "So if this has all been to lure Mouse here, what more do you need of me?"

"I'm not sure. Emmanuelle thinks you are useful, and so does Herr Meier."

Not much of an endorsement, a dejected Greg asked, "What's next for me? Should I finish the Camino de Santiago?"

"You did say the Camino de Santiago called to you."

"The bloom is off that rose. It doesn't matter if the Camino de Santiago called me; or Santiago, Chile called me." Greg said dejectedly.

"You can continue your Camino while we establish Mouse in the villages. Besides, there's something afoot."

"What do you mean?"

"Everything is coinciding with the re-appearance of the Star of Bethlehem. I have a feeling that something important is happening."

"What do you mean the Star of Bethlehem will reappear?"

"The Star of Bethlehem is a rare celestial event. The last time it occurred was two thousand and twenty years ago."

"When will it reappear?" Greg's questions continued.

"In less than a week."

"Are you going to Bethlehem?"

"No. That's not the place."

"How do you know?"

"I know. I am certain it's not the place."

Suddenly John pulled out a satellite phone, pressed a button, waited for the connection, and then spoke in German. "Herr Meier, where are Mouse and Emmanuelle now?"

As John spoke on the phone, Greg said to no one, "I thought this guy didn't use phones?" John ignored him, and Greg began thinking about recent events; now it's the Star of Bethlehem, John the Apostle, short people in Christmas villages, and the Camino de Santiago. What a couple of weeks, as his mind drifted and he began rambling aloud, "Most Americans have no idea that Santiago is Spanish for Saint James. Not that they know who Saint James is or where Santiago, Chile is. Half of them think Chile is a type of bean stew."

"What did you say? You have said it twice now." John asked expectantly.

Greg stared at the phone in John's hand, "I thought you didn't speak on phones and avoided technology?"

"Who said that?

"Emmanuelle."

"Well, sometimes they are useful. But please repeat what you just said."

"I thought you didn't use telephones?"

"No, before that."

Greg pondered what he had been saying, "I was just musing to myself that Americans don't know who Saint James is."

"Not that?"

"I don't know; I think I said I could just as well have walked to Santiago, Chile."

John shouted into the phone. "Herr Meier, that's it! It's not Santiago de Compostela. It's Santiago, Chile. I am sure of it." There was a pause as Meier spoke to John. John replied in German. "Er ist ein Amerikaner idiot, aber ein nützlicher idiot." (He is an American idiot but a useful idiot.) John continued after another pause, "The people in the villages want both Mouse and Papa?" Pause. "Let me think on that."

John turned to Greg, "Looks like you are coming with me, Greg."

"How far are we going? I've already walked 20 klicks today."

"I have a motorbike. We can ride there."

"I thought you didn't use telephones and walked everywhere."

"Who said that? Ahh, Emmanuelle! Well, have you met Emmanuelle? Would you rather speak to her in person or on the phone?"

"In person, of course."

"Would you rather walk with her for three weeks or ride in a vehicle with her for a few hours?"

"I think I see where this is heading."

"I didn't get this old without learning a thing or two."

"I like how you think. But aren't you a priest?"

"I can't say that I am ordained, although I have been married quite a few times."

Then Greg gushed several of Mouse's questions utterly unrelated to the topic they were discussing, "Why are women excluded from the priesthood? Why can't priests be married? Why is it important for priests to be celibate?"

"Those are good questions. I think the Catholic Church got most of that wrong and for all the wrong reasons. Celibacy harms the church much more than it helps. Priests can better relate to the challenges of a married couple if they speak from experience, and they could help demonstrate the sanctity of the unborn.

"Women were leaders of the early church, and there were many female priests in the beginning. Most of the early priests were married. We accepted anyone to spread the word of Our Lord who had the calling, regardless of sex or marital status. The early church would never have survived without the roles played by women as priests, and especially as investors."

"The relegation of women to a subservient role was a societal phenomenon. Hellenization spread Greek culture across the Mediterranean, Europe, and western Asia from Alexander's time to the end of the Roman Empire. That era lasted over a thousand years. Hellenization placed women in a minor societal role, below that of male slaves. The early Church was too weak to fight for women and grow simultaneously. Women were pushed into the background as males dominated the Church hierarchy in the second and third centuries. That dominance culminated at the Council of Nicaea in 324 AD, which codified male and female roles. Nicolas did what he could to stop it, but Nicaea and later Councils continued to push women aside."

"When did it change that priests could not marry?" Greg asked.

"Pope Urban banned married priests in 1100. He sold the wives of the married priests into slavery and orphaned their children—nice man, that one. In the life of the church, celibacy is a relatively new rule. The Church instituted celibacy 1,500 years after Christ. Plenty of popes had wives and children, as did most Apostles. Later, the church used celibacy to control money and inheritance. The church lost wealth when a priest died, as his family inherited his home and money. By enforcing celibacy, the church inherited the priests' entire estate. That is the principal reason the church required priests to be celibate. It had nothing to do with whether Jesus was celibate. And whoever says Christ was celibate has no idea what they are talking about."

"What about divorce?"

"Did you read John's Gospel?"

"I read your Gospel recently when I holed up in a hotel room for two weeks." Greg trying to get John to confirm his identity.

"Hmmph. Do you recall the story of Jesus at the Well of Jacob in Samaria?"

"Yes, Jesus had gone on ahead; you and the other disciples were trying to catch up to him. He met a Samaritan woman in a village at the Well of Jacob and offered her some water. That shocked the woman as it was unacceptable for a Jew to talk to a Samaritan or a woman, let alone offer a Samaritan woman water. The woman at the well had divorced five times and was living with another man. Jesus offered her a drink, and they spoke. After He told her that He knew about her past marriages, she acknowledged He was the Savior. Jesus stayed with her and the other villagers for a few days before going to Jerusalem and His fate."

"That's a good summary, Greg," John added, "And knowing she is divorced, living with a man while unmarried, he stayed at her home. He had no problem with her divorce, or that she is unmarried and living with a man, or her being a woman and from Samaria."

"Yes, I think He liked her. He offered her everlasting life. She spoke to Him frankly when she talked to Him." Greg opined.

John replied, "Yes, He offered her the water of eternal life because she believed in Him. Jesus loved to talk to women. He believes women are as important, if not more important, than men. He was against Hellenization because of its treatment of women."

"Jesus was political?"

"That's not what I said. He was more for women's equality."

"Then why did the church adopt such harsh policies against women?"

"After Peter, subsequent Popes found it easier to follow societal norms. As men took over the church, their thirst for power overshadowed the teachings of Jesus.

By making and keeping women subservient, they forced women to do whatever they wanted."

"What was Jesus's greatest miracle?" Greg's question of the moment.

"His greatest miracle? I have often thought of this. In retrospect, He performed three miracles. The first two are Love and Forgiveness. But I think His greatest miracle is Hope." John thought, "Maybe there is hope for this idiot?"

"John, I admit that I am not very religious. But one thing about religions in general always baffled me."

"What's that, Greg?"

"Zoroastrians call their God - Ahura Mazda, Christians call Him - God the Father, Jews call Him – Yahweh, though they can't say his name. Islam calls God – Allah. Allah, to the untrained ear, sounds like a knockoff of Ahura. Native Americans call God - the Great Spirit."

"Yes, what's your question?"

"Does God care what we name Him? We have been fighting wars for 2,000 years for the right to name God. I want to think that God doesn't care what we name Him."

"That's a good question." John never explained further.

"One last question, for now?"

"Okay."

"Did Jesus believe in science, or did he believe what the Old Testament said?"

"Two answers; first, Jesus answered that question when he answered the question on taxes."

Greg recalled, "Render to Caesar what is Caesar's and render to God what is God's."

"Yes, if asked about science, Jesus will say, 'Render to Science what is Science and render to God what is God's.' The more science discovers, the greater the glory of God's creation is revealed. Jesus never preached the Old Testament. At the beginning of the early Church, the Old Testament was used as the basis for Christ's teaching to appeal to Jews. Jesus proposed a way to live life humbly, love for thy neighbor, and pray to God. The Old Testament was about what not to do – Thou shalt not...." His was a very different message."

John led Greg around the building where an antique – somewhat rusted but operational - motorcycle stood. On the back of the bike was a worn-out license plate. There were three letters on two rows: rusted letters, DON on the first row, and DER on the second. A faded La RIOJA identified the province, while the date on the plate was missing.

"Hop on the back," John commanded.

"Where are we going?"

"We are going to an old Templar chapel, La Ermite San Bartolome de Ucero, The Hermitage of Saint Bartholomew in Ucero. It is a three-hour ride."

"Why there?"

John explained, "La Ermite San Bartolome de Ucero is about 160 kilometers south and west of Azofra. The Templars dedicated the chapel to three apostles, Saint Bartholomew, Saint James, and Saint John. Saint Francis walked a route of the Camino de Santiago that went through Ucero in 1213. On his return, He established a convent for his Friars at the Hermitage. The Templar's placement of the structure is stunning. The back of the chapel faces the mountain chaparral. The caves surrounding the chapel were inhabited 10,000 years ago. Many believe it is a mystical place, and the Romans used it to commemorate feasts to the god Janus. It's believed that the Templars built the chapel to house the Arc of the Covenant. The Templars always searched for something and planned to hide in their churches when they found it. They honored Saint Bartholomew, a martyr who was skinned alive. The chapel sits on the midpoint of the Iberian Peninsula, exactly halfway between Cape Finis Terra to the west and Cape Creus to the east. A line drawn from north to south through the chapel cuts the Iberian Peninsula in half, and the lines form a Templar cross with the line from Finis Terra to Cape Creus. The chapel is set back among stunning caves and surrounded by almond, fir, and juniper trees. We should be the only ones there as the park is closed to tourists for winter."

Greg Asked, "Did the Templars ever find the Arc of the Covenant?"

John's reply was non-committal. "The Templars were very thorough in their searches."

A thought popped into Greg's head and emerged as a question. "Didn't a monk write a book about Saint Francis and his Camino? If I recall correctly, an **anonymous** monk wrote the book."

"Yes, The Little Flowers of Saint Francis of Assisi. You should read it sometime." John thought, "My God, he has more questions than Emmanuelle."

"Everybody wants me to read something. I'll put it on my reading list. Any other books that you wrote that were published?"

"I didn't say that I wrote it."

Greg almost said, "you didn't say no," but instead asked, "Anything else I need to know?"

John offered, "Like the city of Myra, there is a rock-hewn necropolis nearby, and it's close to where they filmed, The Good, The Bad, and the Ugly."

"Clint was here? Now that's cool." Greg answered. "I have a question about when life begins and abortion. Can I ask it on the ride?"

"Absolutely!"

John started the motorcycle's engine, and it roared to life. It proved impossible to continue their conversation, which suited John very well. Greg was still confused about his role in this play, but by the sound in John's voice, he believed that he was still involved.

The tall priest had walked into the village a few minutes after Papa. He heard the motorbike roar to life and saw the pair head out of town. He quickly sought out a vehicle he could 'borrow.' Borrowing a car in this small village is simple. Everyone left the keys in the ignition.

In less than three hours, John and Papa entered the Canon of Rio Lobos, whose park road led directly to the Templar chapel. John drove the bike to the side of the chapel and parked. When Papa crawled off the motorcycle, he couldn't tell what parts of his body ached the most. The roar of the old engine concussed his hearing, his back was sore from the jolts every time they hit a bump, and his face felt frostbitten. He wondered how John, who looked much older, had survived the trip. He had felt nothing but skin and bones when he held onto John's shoulders.

John opened the side door and led Papa to the church's apse near the altar. To the right of the altar was a semi-hidden door. John quickly unlocked the door, which opened to a small dark room. John flipped a nearby switch, and a light revealed a dimly lit stairwell that led underground.

"What is this place?" Greg asked.

John was silent and led the way. A quiet figure slipped through the side door into the chapel as they walked down the stairs.

Downstairs, John flipped another switch and illuminated a large room. A tall marble table, or altar, stood in the center. It was about two feet wide, three feet high, and six feet long. The room had a couple of wooden chairs, an old writing table with various types of pens, and pieces of parchment. Rudimentary electrical wires that supplied the lighting littered the floor. Underneath the altar was an old wooden box with a figure carved on the wooden lid. Papa recognized it as the Zoroastrian symbol called the Faravahar. He recalled reading about the Faravahar in the book of Hessulah and started to ask a question. But John interrupted his train of thought.

"I use this place when I need to write. I prefer to write in solitude."

At that remark, Papa realized that John the Evangelist, the Gospel writer was, and still is, a writer at heart. The avocation had never left him.

"You still write?"

"Often, I meet interesting people walking the Camino. I talk to them and write down their stories."

"Did you publish their stories?"

"No, they are all here. I sent you the first story, the first book of Hessulah."

"There is more to her story! Did she walk the Camino?" Was this his first genuine admission? Greg wondered.

"Oh yes, there is more, much more, to her story; she was a remarkable woman. She told me her story when we sailed to Finis Terra to bury my brother in what is now known as Santiago de Compostela."

"Didn't James die 11 years after the crucifixion of Jesus?"

"Yes, that's correct. Herod Agrippa, the grandson of King Herod, ordered James's execution in 44 AD. Herod Antipas, one of Herod's sons, had my cousin John, whom you call the Baptist, beheaded in 30 AD. The Pharisees sent Jesus to Herod Antipas for sentencing, but Jesus refused to speak with him. Herod Antipas sent Jesus back to Pilate."

"It seems the Herod family had a lot to do with everything. What did you call John the Baptist?"

"Cousin."

"I see." Now he's just messing with me.

"Here, let me show you another room."

"Another light switch was flipped that illuminated a large room with wooden shelving that held hundreds, if not thousands, of scrolls." Behind them, the silent figure had followed them to the underground and hid in a dark corner, listening.

"These are stories from people that walked the Camino?" asked Greg.

"Yes."

Papa's feeble attempt at a joke, "Anyone I know?"

"Nicolas of Myra's story is here. Nicolas is a direct descendant of Hessulah and Melchior. He wasn't all that jolly but a good man all in all. Alina's story, she is Nicolas's sister, is intertwined with his. Alina was as remarkable as Hessulah. There is also a story of an Englishman who became known as Father Christmas. There is one about a Russian called Father Frost, known by the Russian name of Ded Moroz. Your relative's story, Sinter Klaas, is here somewhere. There are many more."

"You wrote all of these?"

"Yes, every life has a purpose. Eventually, mine was to write. Your life needs a purpose."

"I am not a writer. Why are you showing me this?"

"I need you to publish them."

"If you anonymously published, The Little Flowers, why didn't you publish these?"

"That book drew too much attention. For many reasons, I must stay hidden."

"Publishing all of these stories will take forever."

"I have said before that time is not an issue."

"Why me? Why now? And how is time not an issue? I'm in my late 60's."

"Why not you? Isn't it time you did more for Christmas than write a check and buy the wine?"

"Have you been talking to Mouse?... Okay, I guess, but why now?"

"Something important is happening. I can feel that my time on earth is almost over. I need you, Mouse, and Emmanuelle to find the Master. I believe He is to be born near Santiago, Chile. The Star of Bethlehem is about to reappear. The three of you must follow it. It will lead to Him, and He will need protection as he grows up."

"Shouldn't someone younger be doing this? I hardly qualify as a Magi. And I thought He was supposed to return on a white horse with a flaming sword."

"He said He would return. He never said anything about a white horse. You will do it; what else have you got going on?"

"Well, nothing." Papa paused, "Where are Mouse and Emmanuelle?"

"They should be here soon. Herr Meier is booking your tickets from Madrid to Santiago. You have no time to lose."

"Not four tickets? Aren't you coming?"

"I don't think I can make this trip."

"That's cruel. You wait for 2,000 years and are not there for the big event?"

"I have nothing to complain about."

Papa thought, my god, he is either John the Evangelist and 2,000 years old or one great imposter. Why would anyone go to this length to fool me?

They walked back into the first room. John said, "Grab that pile of scrolls; you can get started on them. Let's go upstairs and wait for Mouse and Emmanuelle."

Papa walked out to the fresh cold air carrying two armfuls of scrolls. Inside, the chapel was dry, cold, and dusty. He saw a car's headlights drive down the park road. Mouse and Emmanuelle emerged after the car pulled up beside John's motorcycle. He spotted another vehicle parked about 100 yards away. It wasn't there when they arrived.

Papa put down the scrolls, hugged and kissed Mouse, and gave Emmanuelle a bigger hug than Mouse appreciated. Emmanuelle kissed both his cheeks in French fashion. I could get used to this, he briefly thought before he saw Mouse glare at him. Quickly changing the subject, "How was your trip, Mouse? John and I have had some fascinating discussions."

"Where is John?" asked Emmanuelle.

As the three were saying their hellos, John silently turned around and hastily returned to the church. A dark figure emerged from the doorway and ran to the parked vehicle. A faint smell of smoke was in the air.

"Quickly," yelled Emmanuelle. The three of them chased after John as he disappeared into the church.

Papa followed Emmanuelle inside and down the stairs. Mouse moved as fast as she could toward the chapel. John opened the door to the inner room, where a fire was burning. Smoke filled the outer room. John went inside and tried smothering the flames with his coat, but the heat and smoke were too much. He continued fighting the fire but soon fell to the floor.

Papa grabbed John and passed him to Emmanuelle. "Look after him. Take him to Mouse; she's a nurse. I will see what I can do in here."

Emmanuelle dragged John to the outer room. John must have weighed less than 45 kilos. Mouse had made her way down the stairs, saw Emmanuelle dragging John, and shouted, "There's too much smoke; we have to get him outside." The two of them carried him up the stairs.

Papa went into the room and started to beat down the flames. He grabbed unburnt scrolls and threw them into the outer room. Soon the smoke and heat overtook Greg, and he retreated. He closed the door to the inner room, hoping to cut off the oxygen and starve the fire. He left the scrolls he had saved on the floor. Time enough to retrieve them once the smoke clears, he thought.

He found Mouse tending to John, giving him mouth-to-mouth and beating his chest, trying to resuscitate him. Emmanuelle stood beside Mouse, looking crestfallen. John's breathing ceased, and his color left him. Mouse checked his neck for a pulse. "He's gone."

Tears started to stream down Emmanuelle's face. "You did all you could, Mouse. I'm so sorry, Emmanuelle," said Papa. He looked down at John and said quietly, "I guess you will find out soon enough, my friend."

"Find out what?" asked Mouse.

"Oh, nothing, just something he said when I first met him."

The three milled around the body, trying not to look down at John. "What do we do now? How did the fire start?" asked Mouse.

Emmanuelle said, "I saw someone run from the chapel when we turned to look for John. There was another car, but it's gone."

"Who would want to burn his writings?" asked Papa.

"The Cardinal, I am sure of it," answered Emmanuelle.

"Bork?"

Mouse corrected Greg, "It's O'Rourke, and you know he's not named Bork. Now is not the time to trivialize things."

Greg said, "Just before you arrived, John said the three of us must complete a mission."

Mouse said, "A mission? After all of this, are you crazy?"

Greg, in a severe tone, "It's not a mission where you can say "No." But before I explain what I know, we must care for John's body. Any ideas?"

Emmanuelle said, "We need to anoint his body with oil and wrap him in a burial cloth. That is his custom. We picked up extra-virgin olive oil on our travels. It's in the car."

Papa said, "I think I saw a box that may contain some resin to mix with the oil in the outer room. Maybe you and Mouse can wash his body with that?"

Mouse said, "What's the matter with you?"

Papa replied, "Nothing is the matter with me. I believe it's a Jewish tradition that women wash the body."

"It's not a tradition in 2020; you are such a baby."

"Well, you're a nurse and are used to this sort of thing."

"Nobody is used to this sort of thing. Go get the oil and look for some garments or rags."

Papa grabbed the oil from the car and searched the apse, where he found some rags. Mouse and Emmanuelle moved the body to a blanket that Emmanuelle kept in her car. They straightened out John's limbs. Papa gave them the materials and poured the oil into a large bucket he had found. John's body looked small and worn. Just before the women dipped the towels into the oil, Papa remembered the box he had seen underneath the altar. "Wait a second." He ran into the outer room with a rag over his mouth as the smoke was still intense. He grabbed the old box with the Faravahar carved on the lid and carried it upstairs.

The box contained a small remnant of resin, perhaps a cupful. Papa mixed the resin into the oil. "There," Papa said, "I think this might be myrrh. This mixture should be as close to his custom as possible."

The women silently washed the body with the mixture of myrrh and oil. Mouse handed a rag to Papa and said, "You can do his legs." When finished, they carefully wrapped John in the blanket.

Emmanuelle said, "Let's put his body on the table in the outer room until we can arrange burial."

Papa and Emmanuelle carried the body down the steps to the smoke-filled room. Papa looked down and saw a pen on a piece of parchment. John had written "The Book of Mouse and Papa."

Papa stood beside the body, made the sign of the cross, and said a few silent prayers. When they saw what he was doing, Mouse and Emmanuelle stood on each side of Papa and linked arms with him. Together they quietly recited the Lord's Prayer.

Afterward, Papa said, "We all need fresh air."

Emmanuelle said, "We can't leave him down here, can we?"

Papa said, "The smoke can't bother him anymore."

Once outside, Mouse asked, "So what happens next? Can this crazy adventure finally be over?"

"Not quite," said Papa, "John thinks something mystical is happening, and it coincides with the Star of Bethlehem, which will reappear next week. Herr Meier has booked our tickets to Santiago, Santiago, Chile. I think we are three modern-day Magi."

"What do you mean? Can't we go home?" asked a worried Mouse.

"John said that we must see this through. He thinks the Lord is returning as a newborn child and that we must find and help protect Him. John knew he wouldn't make the trip. When you lived so long, you know when your time is up."

"But why us?" Mouse queried.

"I don't know but look what he started to write." He showed Mouse the beginning of their story.

29

CAESAREA, 1 AD

JACOB ARRIVED IN CAESAREA with Zalman's caravan many weeks earlier. He reported to Zalman on his remarkable trip to Babylon, "Hessulah's skills are beyond what I could have imagined. As you instructed, I did my best to create problems that only an experienced caravan leader could solve. It was easy to disrupt the caravan as Melchior was unprepared to assume that role. Hessulah made an excuse and sent Melchior to confer with some tribal chiefs while she assumed command. That woman, who had never ridden in a caravan, quickly reorganized and took control of everything. It was beyond belief. She won over the servants and camel drivers and stopped and helped the villages we passed with clothing, food, and medicine. Nothing escaped her attention. I would sail with her anywhere."

───────◆◇◆───────

Zalman and Jacob were in the courtyard in Caesarea when a rider on Bulsara approached. "The captain said they will arrive tomorrow in great haste and must leave Caesarea quickly. A rider, who appears frequently, follows the caravan. The captain believes Herod is looking for us. The captain said she would approach Caesarea from the east as she must circumnavigate Jerusalem."

Zalman and Jacob finished questioning the servant when a large transport vessel docked next to the new ship awaiting Hessulah's return. Zalman could tell from its markings that the craft belonged to Hessulah's brother Petrus. Zalman watched as horses, supplies, and soldiers unloaded. Then, he saw Petrus on deck. "Petrus is here!" Zalman turned to Jacob, "This could get dangerous. Jacob, find Michael and return at once. I will need you both." Zalman sent a servant to warn Assab to stay out of sight.

When Michael and Jacob returned, Zalman said, "I have been ignoring requests from Petrus for financing for many months. Now that he is here, it will prove difficult to ignore him. He has strong connections with Rome and Herod. Michael, collect the workers and go to the warehouse. I will speak to them shortly. Jacob, mount a horse and ride east to meet Melchior and Hessulah. Tell Hessulah that her brother is in Caesarea, and she must approach the shipyard carefully."

As Jacob left to find a mount, Petrus's servant arrived. Petrus's message was blunt, without the usual business courtesies. "Zalman, I will arrive within an hour."

Petrus arrived with two heavily armed servants and the Roman centurion, Quintus. A servant escorted them to Zalman's second-floor office. It was not customary to bring armed men to a business meeting. Zalman greeted Petrus cordially. "Welcome Petrus, son of Timo." Zalman knew that mentioning Timo's name was a source of irritation.

Petrus ignored the greetings and started in on Zalman. "Why have you ignored my letters? I am in dire need of financing. You always financed my father's ventures. You must continue and finance mine."

Zalman calmly explained, "Business has been slow since Augustus took the throne. There has been peace with Parthians and Greeks in the east, and it's been quiet in Gaul. War drives revenue, and that has dried up. My remaining funds are financing King Herod's projects. Herod tells me that you are serving Imperial Rome. If you have their business, why would you need my financing?"

"Why, indeed! Rome pays when Rome wants; I need funding until they release my funds," complained Petrus. Petrus looked over Zalman's shoulder and asked, "Whose new ship is that?"

"It's not mine. It belongs to a merchant from Myra."

"Did you finance it?"

Zalman would not practice deceit in business. Any direct question requires an honest answer. "I have only financed ships for your father's house." Zalman justified the non-truth; that's technically not a lie. It's just being evasive.

Petrus continued his query, "Who owns it then?"

Zalman said, "A merchant purchased it from the House of Melchior in Myra."

"Never heard of them," exclaimed Petrus.

"That will change soon enough." Zalman thought, then replied, "People in the Levant hold the House of Melchior in high esteem, but they are relatively new to trading."

Petrus walked over to the window and scanned the docks. He noticed an old merchant vessel that seemed familiar. Petrus turned and pressed Zalman about more financing. "I need money, Zalman, and you must get it for me."

Zalman was evasive, "Unfortunately, Herod has restarted his expansion efforts. He tied up all my resources. Once Augustus completes his census and reallocates taxes, Herod's finances will improve, Herod will be flush with money, and I can extend credit to the House of Timo."

"I will speak to Herod. My business is his business." Petrus was frustrated with Zalman's evasiveness. "I hope you are not misleading me; you won't like my response." He nodded toward Quintus putting a face behind the threat. To reinforce Petrus's words, Quintus put his hand on his sword hilt and withdrew the sword halfway.

Responding to the threat, Zalman quickly changed from the mild-mannered merchant, "Speak to Herod then, boy, but do not threaten me. You are not the man your father was, nor am I one to turn my back on you."

With that, Michael and several other armed men appeared outside the door.

Zalman continued. "Don't ever think that you can come here and threaten me. Now leave before I feed you to my camels."

Petrus ruefully smiled, "You misunderstood me, Zalman; I meant no threat. Let's go." He motioned to Quintus.

———— ◆ ————

At dusk the next day, Melchior and Hessulah arrived with their small caravan. Hessulah was six months pregnant and clearly showing a new mother's stomach. She led the servants, camels, and goods through the tall gate into Zalman's enclosed courtyard. Melchior led Farrokh. Jacob followed with his horse. Everyone seemed exhausted but in good spirits.

Hessulah and Melchior quickly sized up the situation for Zalman.

A servant ran up to Zalman, "One of Herod's men comes this way. He will be here in a few minutes."

Hessulah said, "That must be the rider that trailed us on horseback."

Zalman barked a few orders to Michael and his workers. He asked Hessulah and Melchior to wait by his side.

Outside the compound, Jethro stopped and asked a man if a caravan had passed recently. "Yes, some camels, horses, and people arrived recently," was the answer. Jethro walked to the door at the compound and knocked loudly. No one answered. He tried, "Open in the name of King Herod!"

Slowly the doors opened. Jethro walked his mount into the courtyard. Zalman stood in the middle of the yard, flanked by Hessulah, Melchior, and Jacob; otherwise, the yard was empty. Zalman asked. "What can I do for you this time, Jethro?"

Jethro looked around. There were no signs of a caravan or visible exits except the door he entered. Looking around and seeing nothing, Jethro began to sweat, "Where is the caravan?"

Zalman said calmly, "What caravan, Jethro?" Then, with a slight smile, "Have you lost another caravan, Jethro?"

Jethro looked around. "Herod's soldiers are following the caravan. I am sure that they are on their way here."

"They won't find anything," said Zalman.

Jethro looked at Hessulah, "I saw her lead the caravan from Bethlehem. Herod sent troops after them. I fear Herod will do anything to get what he wants. They will slaughter everyone if his soldiers find her or the caravan!"

Pointing to Jacob, "They will recognize your servant who delivered the caravan a message."

Zalman said, "That is my son Jacob; he is not a servant and has always been here."

Hessulah looked at Jacob and understood the resemblance that had caught her attention. Hessulah said, "I am a sailor, a sea trader. I know nothing about leading a caravan. Besides, how could a woman possibly lead a caravan?"

Jethro was confused, but he knew he could not return to Herod. He reiterated Herod's intent, "Herod sent troops to kill the newborn in Bethlehem. I warned people there, but I'm not sure everyone listened. Some of those troops are on their way here. They are following the caravan that I followed here."

Zalman knew Jethro was not a dangerous man. He asked, "What are you going to do, Jethro?"

"I am a dead man if Herod finds that I warned you. Maybe I will go north; I have relatives in Tarsus. I will have to find a place to hide." he said, his voice trembling.

Hessulah, taking pity on poor Jethro, "Jethro, what do you know about sailing? We could use another good man; we also pay a fair wage."

"I am not a sailor, but I can learn!" Jethro seized the chance to escape from Herod once and for all. Jethro asked Zalman, "So where did you put the caravan anyway?"

"It's better that you don't know," answered Zalman.

Hessulah turned toward Jacob. "So, Jacob, you are Zalman's son!" Jacob blushed but remained silent.

Zalman interrupted, "Hessulah, before we get into that, we must figure out how to handle Petrus. He arrived last night, and he is highly suspicious."

"What does Petrus want?" asked Hessulah. Hessulah could not keep the hate from her voice.

"He wants money for more ships. He needs money to finance his venture with Rome. He was with a Roman Centurion named Quintus. Do you know him?"

"I know who Quintus is. I killed his archer in Ephesus. May I ask if you lent Petrus money?" inquired Hessulah.

"No, I don't mind. I told Petrus I would always finance ships for his father's house."

"I understand." said a disappointed Hessulah.

"But I neglected to tell Petrus that his father's house is now in Myra and run by his daughter."

"I see." said Hessulah with a smile forming on her lips, "But why did you send Jacob to spy on us?"

"I needed to be sure that you can handle the investment I intend to make in you. Jacob observed you and Melchior on the caravan. I knew you had never managed a caravan before, and I had to be certain of your leadership abilities. I instructed Jacob to protect my supplies and asked him to report to me if anything went awry."

"Why did you need to know if we could handle your investment?" Hessulah asked.

"It's essential that I trust the person I invest in, especially if I am to finance the largest fleet of merchant ships in the Mediterranean. Jacob's report erased any doubt. Your brother, Petrus, is greedy, ambitious, and very much like Herod. I was forced into business with Herod as he was the king. I don't trust Herod, but we are each other's necessary evil, so we co-exist. I fear Petrus possesses Herod's wickedness, and I choose not to do his bidding.

"My contact at Herod's court confirmed that your brother received that dagger as a gift from Herod. I believe Petrus used it to murder your father. I made inquiries into Petrus's household. Petrus blames you for the death of his mother and your father. You must be very careful. He will do anything to get to you."

Hessulah said, "Thank you, Zalman, for everything. Petrus having a dagger from Herod is confirmation enough for me. I knew in my heart that Petrus had murdered my father. Petrus has always hated me, and I will avenge my father."

"Why did you say that Petrus blames me for killing his mother and my father?"

"I don't have time to explain; that story is for another time, Hessulah," replied Zalman. "Just be careful and keep an extra eye out for Quintus. Back to business, when we built your ship, we bought enough material for two ships. The second ship will be ready in about four months. Shall I hold it for you?"

"Same terms as the first ship?" asked Hessulah.

Zalman exclaimed aloud, "How can I refuse this woman?" he paused, "Yes, same terms. The first ship and the Vixen will be loaded tonight with the goods from the caravan. They will be ready to sail at first light. We must get you out of Caesarea before Herod's men find you or Petrus discovers you are here."

"Zalman, will you be safe?" Melchior asked.

"Yes, I financed most of Herod's construction projects. I am financing the work at the Temple in Jerusalem." declared Zalman. "It is still years away from completion. He will not move against me without a clear motive, nor do I intend to give him one."

Melchior left Zalman and Hessulah and sought out Michael to discuss Melchior's theories on asphalt. Michael saw him and said, "Come, I have something to show you." He brought him to the new boat, still riding high on the water at the dock. "Using your techniques, we reduced the asphalt to a liquid paste. We applied the paste to the joints and covered the front of the bow with it. We applied it while it was still hot. It cooled and dried evenly on the bow. We let it sit for a few days before introducing it to water."

Melchior asked, "How did it work?"

"Fantastic!" said Michael. "Previously, after three months at sea, asphalt had to be repaired; and replaced after a year. The keel of this boat has been on the water for four months, and we have detected no change. We still don't know how long it will last, but we are very encouraged. It's about a third of the thickness of asphalt, so the boat is lighter, and it allows for a better edge at the bow, so the ship glides easily through the water, increasing speed. And as you had hoped, the seal is completely watertight."

Melchior said, "That's wonderful! The boat will be less expensive to operate, and it should require fewer repairs with less time in drydock. We can lower costs and reduce spoilage, especially if we can make faster trips. Hessulah will dominate the competition."

———◦———

Hessulah left Zalman and hurried to the dock, where she met Assab, who asked, "Did anything interesting happen on your trip?"

Hessulah smiled, "I will tell you when we return to Myra. Can you captain the new boat? Melchior and I will sail in the Vixen."

Assab looked at Hessulah; her condition did not escape his scrutiny, and he had a huge grin. "There's something that you are not telling me. Now is not the time for keeping secrets."

Hessulah smiled at Assab, "Yes, I am with child."

Assab controlled his tears, "Hessulah, I am so happy for you."

Meanwhile, Petrus had returned from Herod's palace in Caesarea. There, one of Herod's ministers told him that Herod was concerned about caravans and that a man and woman on trick horses led one caravan. Petrus looked up when he heard voices in the shipyard to see a group of people.

A stableman led two strutting and jumping horses. Then Petrus heard Assab's unique voice with his heavy Egyptian accent. He stared and could not believe his eyes when he spied Hessulah with Assab. He sent his servant to Herod with a message that he'd found his caravan.

Hessulah leaned into Assab to whisper something when suddenly there was a commotion on the docks. Petrus, Quintus, and two bodyguards ran toward them with swords drawn. Michael and Melchior were in the shipyard and heard raised voices. They drew their swords and began sprinting to the dock. Petrus and his bodyguard were the first to reach Hessulah's pier.

Assab fearing for Hessulah, drew his sword and launched himself at the oncoming threat. Assab slew the first guard that approached by sidestepping the cargo on the dock. Then Quintus and another guard bull rushed Assab. Assab fell backward, tripped by a sack of grain. As Assab fell back, Quintus pulled a familiar-looking dagger from his belt and drove its blade into Assab.

Hessulah screamed as the blade went into Assab's stomach. She watched Petrus work his way around the melee, coming for her. He carried a short sword. Hessulah reached for her knife with her right hand and pulled Herod's dagger from her tunic with her left. She crouched with both weapons pointed at Petrus. "Remember this dagger?" she yelled, "You murdered father with it; now I will use it to kill you."

Melchior and Michael jumped on the dock and engaged Quintus and the guard as they scrambled to get untangled from the fallen Assab. Melchior expertly slew the guard, while Michael was slashed on his sword arm by Quintus and bled profusely. Quintus went to finish off Michael when Melchior stepped in and parried an almost certain death blow.

Hessulah instinct to protect her child overrode her desire to attack and slay her brother. She slowly backed up with her weapons in an attack position. Petrus was cautious and assumed Assab trained Hessulah to use a knife. While Michael and Melchior fought Quintus and the bodyguard, she kept Petrus at bay with feints and parries.

Quintus backed up at Melchior's parry and squared off against his new challenger. Quintus tried a power move hoping to engage Melchior and push him into the sea or knock him over. But Melchior reset his feet and efficiently handled Quintus's rush. As the two separated, Melchior charged. His blade sliced into Quintus's thigh. Quintus was expecting a defensive counter by Melchior and quickly discovered he had a capable opponent. Melchior pressed his advantage and drove Quintus back with feints and charges.

Petrus screamed, "Finish him off, Quintus, and come here and help me."

Quintus was under immense pressure, trying to survive. He was in trouble and scanned the area for something to use to his advantage. His eyes caught sight of a cargo net near Melchior's feet. He tried to maneuver Melchior onto the net and trip him up.

Melchior watched Quintus's eyes and knew Quintus would try something desperate. He saw the cargo net and realized Quintus's plan. Melchior purposely moved toward the net, watching for Quintus to make his move. It was over in a second as Melchior moved onto the net; Quintus raised his sword to entice Melchior to parry; Quintus reached with his left hand to grab the net. Melchior ducked under the sword strike and drove his sword into Quintus's stomach. Quintus's eyes bulged; a surprised fatal look consumed his face, killed by someone so unassuming.

Melchior quickly turned his attention to Hessulah and Petrus, facing each other at the end of the dock. If he charged Petrus, he could place Hessulah in more danger. Melchior hesitated and slowly walked toward the brother and sister.

Petrus yelled, "I will kill her if you don't back off."

Zalman ran up the pier, trying to regain control, "There's been enough killing today. Petrus, put down your weapon, and we will let you pass. Melchior, lower your sword." Petrus lowered his weapon, and Melchior did the same. Melchior moved to the left side of the dock as Petrus moved toward Zalman on the right. Hessulah stayed where she was. As soon as Petrus passed, Melchior rushed to Hessulah.

Petrus approached Zalman and said, "This is not the end. I summoned Herod, and he will know of your deceit."

Zalman undaunted, "Get out of here before I kill you myself. Please, tell Herod everything; see what he does to a son that killed his father."

"Whose idea do you think that was?" rebutted Petrus. Petrus retreated from the dock to his ship and waited for Herod.

Melchior and Hessulah rushed to Assab. She checked Assab for a heartbeat, but there was no life, and the ashen color of death transformed his face. Hessulah broke down as she realized Assab was dead. Assab was her teacher, confidant, shipmate, and her friend. He had taught her so much. Hessulah sobbed, "Can we wrap his body in a shroud and gently place it on the deck of the Vixen? He would want his burial at sea."

Melchior examined Michael's wound. It was deep, but with luck, it was repairable. Melchior asked Zalman for some herbs, clean linens, needles, and thread. Hessulah asked, "Is Michael going to be ok."

Melchior replied, "We must clean the wound, tie the flesh together, and keep his arm immobile until it heals."

Zalman told Hessulah, "Hessulah, we must make haste; Herod is surely on his way and could be here by sunrise. Jacob can sail the new ship to Myra, and you can find a new captain there."

Zalman's men finished loading the new ship with the remaining cargo of spices from Babylon. The hold was full as Zalman emptied his warehouse's grain, wine, olive oil, and nuts. They loaded Farrokh and Bulsara into separate pens on the ship. Zalman reviewed all the bills of lading with Hessulah; they agreed on prices and concluded their agreement.

Hessulah exclaimed, "Zalman, I can't thank you enough. I must ask you a question about something you once said. It has been nagging at me ever since. Did you know my mother?"

Zalman said, answering the question and not, "A long time ago, I fell in love with a beautiful girl with bright green eyes. You remind me of her."

Hessulah blinked as small tears formed, "I think this is the beginning of a beautiful friendship!"

Zalman told Hessulah and Melchior, "You should leave before first light before Herod arrives. I do not want to delay the maiden voyage of such a beautiful ship. By the way, have you thought about what to name her?"

Melchior said to Hessulah, "Yes, Hessulah, now that you have the beginnings of your fleet, what will you name both of your new ships?"

Hessulah said, "Would you name them Melchior? You can name a ship after a woman, but they say it's bad luck if a woman names a ship."

Melchior said, "Let's name them after our horses! They carried us to Babylon and back."

Hessulah cried, "Are you serious? You want to name these beautiful ships - Farrokh and Bulsara?"

"No," laughed Melchior, "We will call them Dancer and Prancer."

———◦———

Before sunrise, Petrus stood at his ship's railing, peering through the light morning fog. He watched the new boat set sail. It gracefully cut through the waves. He glanced around the port and spied an old merchant vessel, its artemon filled with wind, its square sail rising. There was something familiar about that boat. He recognized Hessulah standing at the stern; silently, he vowed revenge. He turned as he heard horses trotting in the shipyard.

Herod and his soldiers were making a small commotion. They surrounded Zalman, who stood thirty feet from the dock. Herod said, "I am in search of a caravan Zalman."

Zalman, always truthful, replied, "There are no caravans here, my king."

Herod said, "It's early for ships to sail from the port; something doesn't seem right."

Zalman said, "They wanted to catch an early breeze."

Herod, always suspicious, said, "Zalman, you better have a good reason if you are deceiving me."

With a truthful but evasive answer, Zalman replied, "I would only deceive my king for the love of a beautiful woman."

Knowing Zalman's value, Herod laughed, "Well, I can't blame you for that. God knows how women vex me." Herod paused and gazed again at the ships; his countenance grew stern, "Zalman, I think you are about to reduce my interest charges."

"Gladly, my king."

———◦———

Melchior stood between the rudders on the Vixen, listening to Hessulah teach him how to steer the boat and use the shoreline as a guide. Hessulah relaxed as she felt a tiny foot kick inside, the baby letting her know everyone was safe. The smell of the sea rejuvenated her, with the breeze in her hair and the familiar feel of a boat beneath her feet; Hessulah said, "You surprise me, my dear husband."

"How is that? My dear wife." he replied.

"How is it that a priest is an expert at shipbuilding? I know what you and Michael did with the asphalt. How is it that a priest is an expert at treating the wounded? That was no ordinary wound, and you saved Michael's life. And how is it that a priest is an expert with a sword? You killed Petrus's bodyguard and a Roman Centurion quite skillfully."

"There's a lot you don't know about me, woman."

"I can't wait to find out more," she smiled. "But seriously, where did you learn to use a sword like that?"

Melchior replied, "Zoroaster once said, 'If one would have a friend, then must one also be willing to wage war for him, or her, in your case. To wage war, one must be capable of being an enemy.' It reasons that one should prepare if they must wage war for a friend. Truthfully, I never met anyone that I would wage war for until I met you."

Hessulah smiled and thought, "This man continues to amaze me."

"What did you say?" asked Melchior.

"I did not say anything." "Is he reading my mind now?!?!"

Hessulah bent down and picked up a small box on the deck near Melchior's feet. "What's this box, Melchior?"

"It was there when we boarded. Why don't you open it?"

Hessulah opened the lid to the box and reached inside. She gasped as she pulled out the velvet pouch.

"What is it?" Melchior asked.

Melchior took his eyes away from the horizon, looked at Hessulah, and saw tears stream down her face; in her hands, she held an emerald necklace, emerald earrings, and emerald bracelets.

30

Summer Solstice, Andes Mountains, December

A few days before Christmas 2020 AD, Juan Pablo Coronado, son of Felipe Coronado, walked out of his apartment in the remote mountain village of Chincolco. When translated from Spanish, the Coronado family name means 'Crowned.' In chess, Coronado means 'To Queen.'

Fernanda, Juan Pablo's wife, had just given birth.

Chincolco is a small village, in a high valley, in Valparaiso in central Chile, one hundred and fifty kilometers north of Santiago. Its verdant green pastures are ideal for grazing herds of alpacas and llamas. Several cattle mixed with the alpacas and llamas in the fields. The farmers interspersed donkeys into the herds to protect them from foxes and wolves. Dusty dirt roads around Chincolco fed the two-lane paved road that ran through the mountain valley.

It is a clear, warm summer evening just after sunset. The Milky Way emerged into the evening sky. Buoyant Andean Huayno music, streaming from speakers at the village center less than a half-kilometer away, hung in the air. Spanish Christmas carols played with the distinct sound of the Huayno instruments, interspersed with local folk songs.

That week the Chincolco newspaper published an article that the Star of Bethlehem would appear during the summer solstice. This Christmas is the first time Saturn and Jupiter have aligned since they led the Magi to Bethlehem and the birth of Jesus. The article explained that it appeared once, 2,000 years before the first Christmas. Ancient astrologers considered the five visible planets stars with irregular orbits when compared to the stars' fixed paths in the heavens. The ancients called these five planets, visible to the human eye, 'The Wanderers'.

Tonight, low over the western horizon, Saturn and Jupiter are visible, each planet almost atop the other. Juan Pablo's etched the sight into his memory. These planets' celestial chase culminated in a fantastic display as if a window opened into the cosmos. He watched the planets move close over the last seven evenings, a cosmic dance that began shortly after twilight and lasted an hour or so.

As the cosmic window opened, what appeared to be a tiny dot flickered on and off in front of the closest planet, but Juan Pablo's vision was not quite able to ascertain the import of that dot or determine if he had seen it at all. Saturn, the furthest planet, took on an elliptical shape with rings surrounding its center.

This night, the seventh of the chase, concluded with the 'opening of the window" on the evening of the solstice. Silently, one of the planets slipped below the horizon, and the window closed.

Juan Pablo's attention turned to three strangers who set up a small camp in the open fields across from his dwelling. They arrived shortly before dusk and were watching the stars as the celestial display ended. They traveled in an old Dodge Caravan minivan parked on the shoulder of the road. He heard his baby cry and went inside for the night.

In the morning, the group's male and younger female knocked on their door. The younger woman, Emmanuelle, translated questions that the male, Gregorio, put to her in English. She asked if any baby boys had been born in the village recently.

Juan Pablo said, "Not that I have heard. My wife and I have just welcomed a baby girl. They are asleep upstairs. I think she is the only birth in the village this week. My wife spoke about a few other expectant mothers in nearby villages; perhaps that is who you seek. You can visit the local clinic in the next village and check with the physician tomorrow."

Emmanuelle asked a few more questions and ended with a "Mucho Gracias!" Emmanuelle and Greg walked back to their camp.

Greg asked, "Did you ask anything else?"

"I asked what they named the baby and if La Nena needed anything. La Nena means "the baby." Many Spanish parents call their babies La Nena."

The next evening at dusk Juan Pablo stood outside his door, hoping to see the cosmic chase continue. He also kept an eye on the strangers across the road. The summer evening air was cool as they were high in the mountains. The strangers packed the minivan and prepared to move on. They were staring at or studying the stars in the western sky. The man was pacing up and down as if something was wrong.

The celestial display that settled over the village the previous evenings did not reappear in tonight's sky. Juan walked over with the fresh bread and cheese he had bought earlier. He had a bottle of a local Malbec in his free hand.

As Juan Pablo crossed the road, a loud whine noise came from the village's direction. Speeding towards him was a man on an electric motorcycle. The motorcycle kicked dust as he pulled up to the side by the minivan. A young man dismounted and took off his helmet. He had dark wavy hair and steely grey eyes that shone fervently. The man nodded but mostly ignored Juan Pablo as he walked toward the three strangers. Juan Pablo walked over and checked out the motorcycle. It was the first all-electric motorcycle he had ever seen, manufactured by Mazda. The license plate had four letters on the top row, BLIT, and three in the second row, ZEN. VALPARAISO was in a smaller script at the bottom of the license plate, with the year 2020. Strapped to the electric motorcycle was an antique box with a carved figure of a man with sets of feathers spread from his waist.

The three strangers stared at the motorcyclist as if they saw a ghost. Juan Pablo approached the woman, Emmanuelle, and gave her the wine, bread, and cheese. She briefly took her eyes off the arrival and thanked him, and Juan Pablo returned home.

John stood amongst them, acting as if everything was normal. Mouse, Emmanuelle, and Greg looked agape and tried to comprehend what was happening. "Have you found the baby Boy yet?" the motorcyclist asked.

No one said a word; they just stared at John—young, healthy, and fit. Soon, the realization overcame them; they were witnesses to the extraordinary. Soon their minds accepted the reality. To discuss it would be to question it, and none could do that. The only acknowledgment of the miraculous came from John when he looked at Greg, smiled, and said, "Seems I still don't know."

Emmanuelle spoke first, "John, the Star is gone. No boys were born in this village. We must start our search in the nearby villages tomorrow."

John said, "We must find Him before those that set the fire in the Templar Chapel find Him. They are close."

Greg said, "Well, we can start tomorrow." Lifting the bottle of Malbec that Juan Pablo gave to Emmanuelle, "There's no sense in letting the wine go to waste." He pulled a corkscrew from his pocket and uncorked the bottle. He filled four cups and handed one to each and toasted. "Feliz Navidad, everyone!"

All responded in unison, "Merry Christmas!" They clinked cups and took the first sip.

The four looked at one another but were at a loss of what to do next; their gazes turned to the brilliant Milky Way. Three of them were *slowly* sipping their wine.

"O Little Town of Bethlehem" played over the speakers in the distance.

Greg heard a baby's faint cry across the road, and he turned toward its sound. Juan Pablo and Fernanda stood before their modest home, holding their newborn infant girl. A full moon illuminated the Family with the building as a backdrop, glimmering over the scene.

A smile came to Greg's lips as he stared at The Family. "Emmanuelle, what did they name La Nena?"

Emmanuelle turned slowly toward Greg, "'La Nena?' – the baby's first name is 'Renata' - Renata Coronado, why?"

"What does Renata mean in English, Emmanuelle?"

Deliberately Emmanuelle said, "Renata is a Latin name; it means 'reborn' or 'born again.'" She added, "Loosely translated, Renata Coronado means, "Reborn Majesty."

As Emmanuelle finished her words, John, Mouse, and Emmanuelle all turned and followed Greg's stare. The light of the moon framed their vision of The Family as 'O Little Town of Bethlehem' amplified in the quiet evening air.

John stared at The Family with a stunned expression, almost in a state of shock. Greg glanced at John and saw the look on John's face. He could not help himself and began to laugh his quirky, hehehe, as his sight returned to The Family.

John's mind raced to absorb the enormity of this challenge to his Great Expectations.

Greg took his eyes from The Family and glanced around. Mouse and Emmanuelle beamed with radiant smiles while a look of shock remained on John's face. John, the man with every answer, stood confounded by this revelation.

Greg could not compose himself as he looked at John's expression. Greg's laugh deepened from his quirky hehehe to a robust baritone "HaHaHa." Then the enormity of the moment took hold of Greg; while continuing to look at John, the timber of his voice changed again. The baritone turned to a deep resonating base; the HaHaHa turned into "HO-HO-HO." It would not stop; he could not stop, over and over, "HO! -HO! -HO!"

An old familiar feeling overcame John, one he had not felt for two thousand years; love, truth, and belief welled within every pore of his being. He re-witnessed the extraordinary, and his stunned look slowly turned into a beaming smile. He fully comprehended his role, he understood the challenge facing La Nene and why he would be needed, and the reason his Master had said, "Suppose I want him to stay until I come."

John shouted, "Would you look at that, Papa! The Wonder of our God!"

Mouse and Emmanuelle smiled at each other and said in unison, "A Girl! Finally, it's a Girl."

Hope Renewed.

December ANNO DOMINAE

About the Author

Retired from a 40 plus year career in banking and telecommunications systems and technologies, an ancestry DNA test propelled Greg on an adventure in writing. Greg and his wife Marge, baby boomers born, raised, and wed in Buffalo, NY, eventually settle in Saint Louis, Missouri. Mouse and Papa actively enjoy the adventures provided by four wonderful grandchildren. Reviews, of all kinds, on the Amazons pages are greatly appreciated. Compliments and criticisms encourage more writing and help fuel improvement. Look for the adventures to continue in the second book of the Nicolas Legacy, THE FIRST CAMINO, El Entierro de Santiago.

Made in the USA
Monee, IL
03 September 2023

42020572R00206